Manda Scott is one of the great storytellers of our time. Over the past two decades she has brought iconic historical figures back to life, re-imagined and rebooted for the twenty-first century. Her crime novels have been shortlisted for many awards including *Hen's Teeth* for the Orange Prize and *No Good Deed* for an Edgar Award. Her work has been translated into over twenty languages. Manda's bestselling Boudica series has recently been optioned for television.

'A clever, gripping thriller – a *Da Vinci Code* for those who like their prose to be **elegant as well as page-turning**.'
The Times – Best Historical Fiction of 2015

'*Into the Fire* is a wonderful blend of fast and furious action, bravura storytelling, a palpable sense of place – Orléans past and present – and a whodunnit that will **keep you guessing until the final pages**. Fabulous.' Kate Mosse

'Cleverly plotted . . . salty and vivid . . . **taut and febrile**.'
Toby Clements, *Sunday Telegraph*

'It combines the two things I love most: thrillers and historical fiction. It's well written and offers up **a wonderful puzzle to work out**.' Liza Goddard, *Daily Express*

'*Into the Fire* **is in a word, magnificent.** Page turning. Visceral. Mesmerising. Evocative – it's so evocative. It's filthy-nailed, sweat-stained, blood-drenched, gut-wrenching, tear-inducing, passion-wrenching. It's everything I want a book to be – and as good as the finest historical fiction that's out there.' Ben Kane

'**Riveting** for both the pulse-pounding action and the moral and character complexity . . . What separates *Into the Fire* from many a time-slip novel is that neither narrative seems shoehorned in; Inès and Tomas' fascinating journeys complement rather than compete.'
Tom Tivnan, *The Bookseller*

'This marvellous book presents readers with an over-flowing cornucopia of romance, horror, mounting anguish and two layers of baffling, disturbing mystery enlivened by a crowd of all-too-human people, ancient and modern. It is **exceptionally well-paced**, and altogether a real treat.'
Historical Novels Review

'An **absorbing** thriller that cleverly unites the past and the present.' *BBC History Magazine*

'In *Into the Fire* Manda Scott expertly blends a very plausible solution to a genuine historical mystery with a compulsive contemporary thriller. The result, as the title suggests, is **intoxicatingly fiery reading**.' Robert Goddard

'Manda Scott has crafted a very fine book. I love the prose, I love the history, I love the adventure. Scott's writing is **so grippingly vivid** that once you begin reading, it becomes your reality. Highly recommended.' Elizabeth Chadwick

For more information on Manda Scott and her books,
see her website at www.mandascott.co.uk

Into the Fire

MANDA SCOTT

CORGI BOOKS

TRANSWORLD PUBLISHERS
61–63 Uxbridge Road, London W5 5SA
www.transworldbooks.co.uk

Transworld is part of the Penguin Random House group of companies
whose addresses can be found at global.penguinrandomhouse.com

Penguin
Random House
UK

First published in Great Britain in 2015 by Bantam Press
an imprint of Transworld Publishers
Corgi edition published 2016

A CIP catalogue record for this book
is available from the British Library.

ISBN
9780552169578

Typeset in 11/13pt Minion Pro by Falcon Oast Graphic Art Ltd.
Printed and bound by Clays Ltd, Bungay, Suffolk.

Penguin Random House is committed to a sustainable
future for our business, our readers and our planet. This book is made from
Forest Stewardship Council® certified paper.

MIX
Paper from
responsible sources
FSC® C018179

1 3 5 7 9 10 8 6 4 2

For Millie, Laura and Sarah,
warrior women of the future,
with love

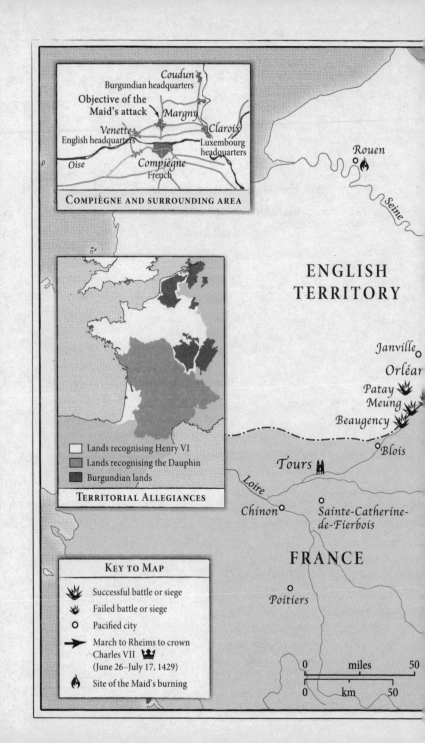

COMPIÈGNE AND SURROUNDING AREA

Coudun
Burgundian headquarters
Objective of the
Maid's attack
Margny
Claroix
Venette
English headquarters
Luxembourg
headquarters
Oise
Compiègne
French

TERRITORIAL ALLEGIANCES

Lands recognising Henry VI
Lands recognising the Dauphin
Burgundian lands

ENGLISH
TERRITORY

Rouen

Janville
Orléans
Patay
Meung
Beaugency
Blois
Tours
Chinon
Sainte-Catherine-
de-Fierbois

FRANCE

Poitiers

Loire
Seine

KEY TO MAP

Successful battle or siege
Failed battle or siege
Pacified city
March to Rheims to crown
Charles VII
(June 26–July 17, 1429)
Site of the Maid's burning

miles 50
km 50

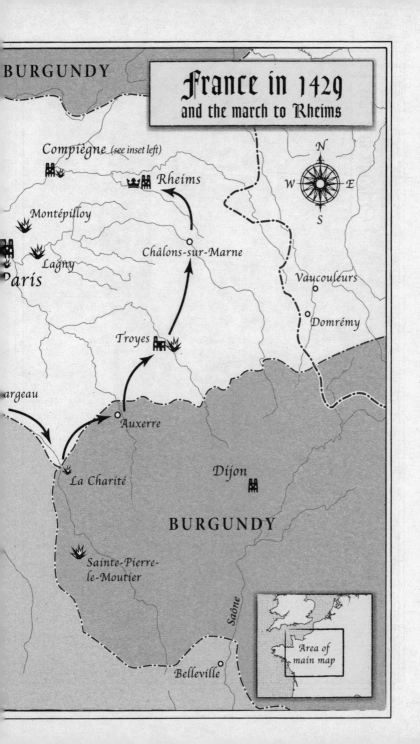

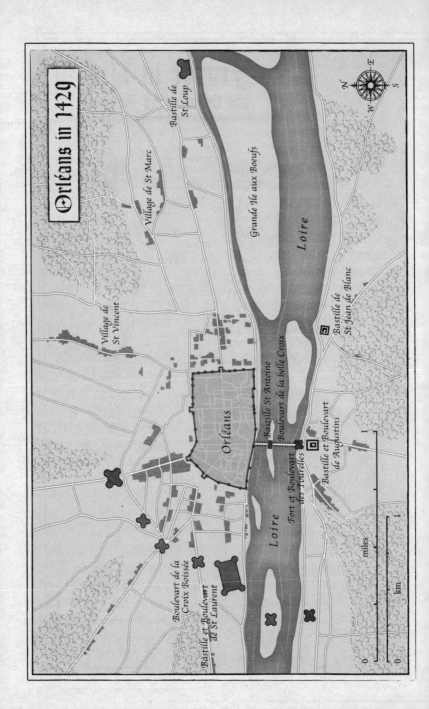

Orléans in 1429

Bastille de St Loup

Village de St Marc

Village de St Vincent

Grande Île aux Boeufs

Loire

Orléans

Bastille St Antoine

Boulevart de la belle Croix

Bastille de St Jean de Blanc

Bastille et Boulevart de Augustins

Fort et Boulevart des Tourelles

Boulevart de la Croix Boissée

Bastille et Boulevart de St Laurent

Loire

miles

km

'How often have I said to you that when you have eliminated the impossible, whatever remains, however improbable, must be the truth?'

Sherlock Holmes to Watson
The Sign of the Four
Sir Arthur Conan Doyle

CHAPTER ONE

ORLÉANS,
Monday, 24 February 2014
02.00

E^{NCORE UN FEU} ... Again, another fire, and this one a vast, leaping beacon, fit to melt the rooftops of slumbering Orléans.

Picaut can see the glare from the window as she throws on jeans and jacket. Outside, she navigates by its light, following the scorched sky through winding streets in her car and then on foot.

A paved courtyard ten metres deep acts as a break between the fire and the road. This close, a savage heat sucks the breath from her lungs, dries the film of tears from her eyes. The flames are many times higher than the building on which they feed and brighter than any man-made light.

The roar is deafening, loud enough to swamp the traffic and mute the many sirens. This fire is bigger than any of the three that have come before it and this, unlike its predecessors, has been lit in the old town, in the pattern of narrow, cobbled streets between the cathedral and the river.

Nothing is isolated here. Tonight, Orléans could lose its ancient, beating heart.

Worse, the air is dense with the taste of evaporating iron, of molten plastic, glass and mortar, but under these, threading through them, rising, is the stench of burning hair and blood and bone, and this is new. Before, the fires ate buildings, not people. This one is feasting on flesh and, by the look of the municipal police and state police and random hangers-on, all standing at a safe distance, no one can get close enough even to begin to find out who the victims are. Were.

'Capitaine!'

The call comes from behind her. Turning, Picaut takes a moment to see who it is, and then wishes she hadn't.

She nods a kind of greeting. 'Lieutenant Garonne.'

When they were lieutenants together, he was Guillaume and she was Inès and they were as close as any professional relationship could be that stood just on the safe side of intimacy. They were matched in temperament and style, and had forged in the furnace of detection and risk a friendship that was greater than the job, or so they told themselves.

But that was then and this is now, and now he speaks to her only when he has to, which is more often than either of them would like.

Garonne is a soft man in a hard man's frame which has begun to revert to type. He is of an age where the last round of promotions was his final chance to make captain. Nine months later, he carries his disappointment in bags beneath his eyes.

Tonight, though, he arrived at the crime scene several minutes before Picaut and he wishes her to know this. His notepad is thick with new writing and he flourishes it as evidence that he is the better officer, she in dereliction of her duty.

'Hôtel Carcassonne. Owned and run by Madame Foy, who was present when the fire began. She had seven patrons; six are there—' He gestures over his shoulder to the refugees clustered at the margins of the firelight. 'The seventh remains unaccounted for.'

Even by the standards of the last few months, Garonne is angry with her, which is saying something. His eyes search her for hidden clues. He called her home number and she wasn't there and she didn't answer her mobile until the seventh ring, or maybe the eighth, and so he knows that she knows that he knows that she didn't spend the night at her apartment, and, because this is the way of things, he suspects that, wherever she slept, she wasn't alone. And she knows, and he knows that she knows, that he's Luc's friend now, not hers, and will report in detail anything and everything that he suspects.

A pair of wraparound shades rests on his brow, a ridiculous affectation in the middle of the night. Looking into the lenses, Picaut sees herself reproduced twice over; small, slim, slight of build, with short-ish, ragged-ish, unruly hair that is never quite blonde. She thinks her face is too freckled for grace, her grey eyes set too wide apart for beauty. Luc, at his most romantic, called her 'fascinating'.

She is not fascinating now. She is tired and fed up and wants to go back to bed, and where that is, and with whom, if anyone, is her own fucking business.

She doesn't smell of sex, she isn't wearing lace underwear and because she's wearing what she always wears, which is yesterday's jeans and a sleeveless white T-shirt that wouldn't hide anything, under an oversized buckskin jacket, Garonne, and so Luc, should know that she has nothing to hide.

She presses her fingers to her face, crimps her eyes, shuts out the past. 'Who's the seventh patron? The one left inside?'

'Madame Foy can't remember his name. He booked in this afternoon, but she was talking on the phone to her daughter, who has just been told that she's carrying twins. In her excitement, Madame Foy failed to commit her new guest's name to memory. He was tall, moderately good-looking, but not excessively so. He was Caucasian, dark-haired. She thinks he was English, or maybe American. Which is to say his French was perfunctory and he spoke English with an accent.'

Which narrows it down not at all. 'Fucking wonderful.'

'The German' – Garonne jerks his thumb over his shoulder – 'thinks he was American.'

'Why?'

'He overheard a phone call at dinner at which our missing man referred to colleagues at Cornell University and said he had asked them to "expedite the results".'

'How good's his English?'

'Better than mine.'

That sets the bar fairly low, but not impossibly so. Picaut turns to look. In the sorry huddle of the former hotel's patrons, any one of the men could be German.

The women, though . . . There's one who catches the eye, set apart from the rest. 'What about her?'

'Who, the black?'

Oh, dear God. To Guillaume Garonne, anyone is black who can't trace a dozen generations of pure white French ancestry to before the First Republic, but just this once, he's right: this woman is not the Arab black that is really olive brown, but ebony black, West African black, tall, lean savannah black with brilliant black hair that falls to her shoulders in an avalanche of polished treacle.

She is interesting, that's the point. Anyone who stands out from the crowd is interesting and tonight, in this company, this woman is the shining jewel in the coal pile, the bird of paradise amongst sparrows.

The rest are no different from anyone else who has been dragged out of bed in the pit of night at the time when plasma cortisol runs well below coping levels, saggily uncomfortable in hotel dressing gowns and bare feet. This woman, by contrast, sports an effortless Paris chic: agnès b. meets Jean Paul Gaultier with just the right hint of nostalgia for Galliano's bad-boy Dior. She could grace the front cover of *Vogue*. She probably has.

'Who is she?'

Garonne consults his notes as if she hasn't burned herself on to his memory. 'Monique Susong. She's from Paris. She—' His eyes grow tight at the corners. 'Why is that funny?'

'Never mind.' It's late. Picaut is tired. A year ago, less, he would have seen the humour in this. A year ago, he wouldn't have thought it necessary to state the obvious in the first place. She hasn't the energy to cosset him. She substitutes briskness for what once would have been humanity. 'What's she doing here?'

'What do you mean?'

'It doesn't look to me as if the Hôtel Carcassonne is – was – a five-star venue. What's someone like Monique Susong doing in a place like this?'

'I haven't—'

'Find out. And get any CCTV from the area and have it ready viewed by tomorrow morning with notes of anyone or anything that might give us answers.' Picaut spins back to the hotel. 'Is he definitely inside, our missing man?'

'Nobody knows. They all followed the fire drill – there are cards prominently displayed in every room, we are not to suggest otherwise – and came out when the alarm rang. By the time Madame Foy had counted them and realized he was missing, the fire was too fierce for anyone to go back in. She swears she didn't see him leave at any point, but that's no guarantee when—'

'When her family's fecundity is quite so mind-numbingly astonishing. So we need to start taking statements from anyone and everyone, particularly from the German who sort-of speaks English and our Parisian peacock. Find their home addresses, why they're here, how long they were planning to stay, what they ate, thought, said. Get their mobile records, everything. Then we can—' Thank Christ. At last.

With flashing lights and screaming brakes: the Fire Department. In truth, it hasn't been long since the proprietor first rang with the news; just that time becomes more flexible when there's a fire at hand.

The small square in front of the burning building knows a brief, frenzied chaos, but they have had three nights of practice within the past three weeks and the disorder resolves itself with remarkable speed into the kind of order that kills fires, even this one.

The river runs less than three blocks away and the winter has been a wet one. They have enough water to drown the town; all they need do is get it to where it needs to be, and they are good at this.

A dozen jets of water arc into the fire's heart, wearing it down. In the morning, Picaut and her team will be permitted to don hard hats and sift through wet soot and falling masonry in an effort to work out who did this and why.

Actually, if this fire is remotely like its predecessors, a coded call will come in to the central office in west Orléans any time now from a man with a strong (and therefore possibly fake) Malian accent, claiming to represent 'Jaish al Islam'.

He will tell them that his group lit the fire as 'a statement against the infidel' which represents a part of the ongoing retaliation for France's role in the internal affairs of that small African country. An hour later, he will email a .wav file of his statement to the national and international news agencies and by dawn, therefore, it will be playing in every household in France.

To date, these 'statements' have detailed the destruction of the homes and/or businesses of: a professor of literature; the owner of a small boutique wine grower who sells well into London and New York; and the leader of the Orléans branch of the Young Socialists.

All three are women. All three have written a post at some point in the last year on a blog called 'La Femme du Jour', which claims to be dedicated to 'celebrating all that is best of French women'.

All three are also Caucasian, middle class and attractive and, while they have not died, they have been rendered homeless, their livelihoods assaulted, their very Frenchness sullied. Their portrait photographs have graced a series of front pages whose editors have wept tears of unrestrained joy with every new addition.

Everyone else has wept over the front pages, too, though not with joy. It is an election year – in France, when is it not? – but this year more than most, the popular fury is a palpable thing. Last year's gay marriage demo-riots have segued into running battles with the police sparked by anything from the rising price of bread to youth un-employment to a shipload of illegal immigrants found at a southern ferry terminal.

Orléans was a bastion of relative calm until the fires began. Now, even here, small clots of disaffected youths prowl the streets seeking reasons to turn feral. In the living rooms of their elders, with the ballots due to be cast in just short of a week's time, the polls are shifting increment by increment away from the parties of liberal ideals and towards those who favour an all-white France, populated by real men who will defend their women, to the death if necessary, from coloured incomers who choose to tell them what they can and cannot do.

Lieutenant Guillaume Garonne is thrilled by this. In his lifetime, his dream of white supremacy may come true.

That time has not yet come and, in the meantime, as Picaut points out, Garonne is obviously aching to return to his taking of statements from the hotel's owner and her six surviving clients.

Glowering, he leaves her. Picaut is about to join him, to interview the alarmingly chic Monique Susong, when her Nokia rings.

'Picaut.'

'It's Patrice,' says Patrice cheerfully. Patrice Lacroix is the team's technological wunderkind. A skateboarding, kite-surfing computer gamer, who lives on a diet of Red Bull and coffee and seems never to sleep.

'Your call's come,' he says. 'Same voice, same signal. See if you can hold him on the line.'

'I won't be able to. He never says anything beyond his prepared statement.'

'Still, try. I need just shy of thirty seconds more. Ask him out on a date; tell him how hot you are for him. Anything to keep him on the line.'

'Fuck you, too.'

'Any time.'

They are recording this call. In the old days, you could tell by the hollowness when a line was being recorded. Now it sounds the same as all the rest. Picaut waits to hear it connect.

'Ici L'armée du Prophète Jaish al Islam . . .'

The call lasts twelve seconds. Patrice does not get a trace.

* * *

20

Picaut watches the fire fight against the water, spitting steam and ash and smoke. The roar becomes a wail, undercut by a tympanic stutter of things warped and stretched beyond the laws of physics.

Garonne marshals all the hotel's residents and stakes out his territory right across the courtyard. He may be angry with her, but he is good at this. The traumatized men and women will feel safe in his hands, even Monique Susong of the black skin and wild hair.

Leaving him to it, Picaut steps round a corner, and then, because she can still smell smoke, can still feel the falling cinders, and truly she thinks better in the quiet dark, she steps round another, and another, until the flames are barely a sulphured rent in the sky, showing through to a hell of others' devising.

Four fires in under three weeks and only this one with a body inside. Why change the pattern now? Did he die by accident, caught in the fire? Or was the fire lit to kill him?

And before all of that, why here? Of all the places in France and the world, why light four fires in Orléans?

Ideas come best to a free mind. Picaut tilts her head back, looks up at the obsidian sky, at the orange tint along the western edge, at the pinhole pricks of stars. Clouds streak across that at any other time would be whispers of wind, bearing the promise of rain, but here, tonight, are too much like smoke.

Her gaze comes to rest on a plaque on the opposite wall.

SIÈGE D'ORLÉANS
OCTOBRE 1428 – MAI 1429
LA VILLE D'ORLÉANS RECONNAISSANTE DÉDIE CETTE
PLAQUE EN HONNEUR DES SOLDATS ECOSSAIS DE L'AULD
ALLIANCE VENUS COMBATTRE POUR LEVER LE SIÈGE
D'ORLÉANAIS . . .

The Auld Alliance: Scots brogue carved into immortality. If she is not careful, she will start to see her father here, which is impossible. By chance – it does feel like chance – Picaut has come to his place of pilgrimage, the stopping-place where he rested when his breathing was bad but he could still walk down to the river. Long before that, it was the place he brought her to when she was too young to walk, but old enough to listen to the stories that fired his passion.

'It was here, *chérie*, in the heart of France, that the tide of English ambition broke and broke and broke and was turned back. See? Their names . . .'

JOHN STUART OF DARNLEY, PATRICK OGILVY,
HUGH KENNEDY, THOMAS BLAIR . . .

She knows those names by heart. As a child, she stood in her father's study and recited them as a way to lift a smile. For a while, say until she was ten, this strategy worked. They were the good years, when he was free of the world's scorn. She remembers them as she remembers old films, as an interesting narrative of someone else's life.

THOMAS HOUSTON, EDWARD OF LENNOX,
MICHAEL NORWILL . . .

'Papa, why did they come?' She is six years old, perhaps, or seven. Old enough to know that dying is not good; young enough not yet to know that sometimes it is better than living.

'Because the enemy of my enemy is my friend.' Her father's laughter is dry. In retrospect, it perhaps harbours layers of inference she does not understand at the time. 'The Scots hated the English with a passion and when a whole succession of English kings tried to claim France as their

22

own, generations of Scots came here to fight them off. They were more loyal to our king than was his own cousin, the Duke of Burgundy. The Burgundians fought on the English side then, to their eternal shame.

'But it was the Maid who broke the siege. She led the army out against the English.' This she has known from her earliest years.

'She did indeed. The Scots may have helped to hold the walls, but it was the Maid who turned the tide. Close your eyes. Can you see her? There she is, astride the king's great, white war horse, clad in unmarked plate, lance in one hand, small-axe in the other, riding out of the gate at the head of the army.

'Think of that! In a world where women were chattels, she was passion incarnate. France had lost so many battles then, many they should have won when they had superior numbers, superior arms; still, they lost. Our knights were demoralized, our armies shrunk to nothing: who wants to fight when they're guaranteed to lose?

'Then the Maid arrived. She took the war-weary, war-feart, war-lazy men of France, and she shamed them all into action, until even those who didn't want to fight found themselves winning, and once they were winning, they found that they liked it.'

He scoops her up, her father, whirls her round, sends the stars spinning. 'But the old goats who surround me, even now, in the twenty-first century, are so afraid of the idea of a girl who can fight that they clothe her in magical myth . . .'

And he is off again, staring out into the place only he can see, where past and future come together and a wrong is put right and the frayed fabric of history is made whole again.

Except, of course, that it is not. He is ruined, his reputation shredded by the old goats who had no qualms about assaulting anyone with the temerity to question the sanctity of their beliefs.

And he is dead.

He is dead and his obsession is dead with him, and if there is grief there is also an overwhelming relief, and one day she will come to terms with the uneven balance of these.

In the meantime, she has a fire to contend with, and a whole new set of enemies, far less evident than the English, who would make of her city a battleground in a war for which she does not yet understand the reason.

She salutes the plaque in the way she has done for most of her life and retraces her steps round one corner and another and then round a third and back to the smouldering wreck of the hotel, which is now the site of a murder.

CHAPTER TWO

IN THE LATE AFTERNOON, a lance of naked sunlight spears the gunsmoke and strikes Tod Rustbeard square on the chest. Looking down from the stone and timber rampart on which he stands, he thinks a shot must strike after it, or a bodkin, or a French axe hurled up from below. He will die filthy, his beard a clot of spittle, his mail a mess of crusted gore, brown as cow dung, rough as a ploughed field, textured with other men's deaths.

But not his own. From somewhere behind his left shoulder, an English gun vomits another round into the ranks of the enemy. Smoke lurches skyward to kill the sunlight and he is still alive, unshot, unstruck, undead. He peers through the haze to the waves of Gallic fury heaving at the foot of the ramparts.

Fuck them and fuck their mothers. They don't know when to give up. They, too, are filthy now, who were crimson and nettle-green and white this morning; Frenchmen who have found their fighting spirit.

It wasn't supposed to be like this. They should have

surrendered a week ago. Rustbeard knows: he spent five stinking winter months masquerading as a Frenchman in the heart of Orléans, speaking in dusty corners with men whose ears were open to gold and promises.

Listen to me. Your weak and mewling king does not love Orléans; he languishes in Chinon and will not send aid. Send word to the English that you'll open the gates after Easter and we shall all be safe, our fortunes made. William Glasdale commands them and he's a decent man. He will not sack a city that has opened its gates. Let it only get to Easter and you will have done your duty . . .

Gold makes men nod. Promises extract oaths and the gates would have swung smoothly back on Ascension Day, except that a letter came near the end of Lent, *To the citizens of Orléans, in God's name, from the Maid* . . . and all his work undone.

And now this.

The smoke drifts and sways, a traitor-curtain hiding attackers and attacked alike. But in the mess below is order, and— Ladders? *Fuck!*

'Arms! God damn you! Arms to the south side!'

His sword is not sufficiently long, but there are arms here enough for the end of days: hammers, archers' mauls, falchions, big two-handed bastard swords, daggers, pikes, all manner of polearms; dead men's weapons.

A hammer lies to his left, three feet of ash haft, leaden head. Tod Rustbeard is not the tallest man in the English army, but his chest is broad and he can lift gun stones one in each hand and run with them; he has the power of a smith if not the skill.

The big two-handed hammer floats to his grip. He braces his feet, sweeps and sweeps and makes the sweep a swing, a full circle-spin, a whirl that lifts an ox-head's worth of weight in a cartwheel of death, and when he has it up to speed he aims himself at the ladder that has come up over the stone lip and the face that is appearing there and he lurches one step, two, and the wheeling lead barely falters as he makes contact and the face dissolves in a bright, bright plash of blood.

More spit in his beard. More gore on his mail. And fragments of bone and tooth and eye.

He kills two more, still spinning, but there are more and ever more. He sets the head of the hammer on the ladder's top rung, braces one foot on the wall and shoves. The ladder falls back, taking men screaming to their deaths.

Men with pike staffs come running at last to fend off this and other ladders, for there are more now, sprouting left and right, bringing Frenchmen into the fastness of their stone and wood rampart. Here to help are Walter Golder and Jack Kentishorn, John of Gayleford and Alfred Rake. And then Sir William Glasdale, commander of the heights, himself in full Italian plate which has not yet lost its lustre.

'Push them back! Send them crashing! Will you be beaten by Frenchmen? Are you children? You! Rustbeard! Swing that hammer harder!'

Here is the best of English soldiery. Here is the reason England will prevail and France is doomed. Glasdale's voice is the bellow of a bull, of a bear, of thunder, of God Himself. Men find strength who were losing it, and apply themselves anew to the job of sending ladders back to the earth.

The enemy have pikes, too. On a ladder? Are they insane? Mad or not, they are certainly ardent. A point skewers past his face and he ducks only by chance and instinct and slashes back and here's a long sword, swinging, and an axe, striking overhand, seeking faces, bare hands, anything.

Jack Kentishorn goes down, gargling on his own blood. A new man takes his place. Oliver? Or maybe a Harry; there are many of those about these days. The hammer head is wedged now in the top of the ladder. A blade screams down by his elbow. Oliver-or-Harry thrusts a sword forward, and misses.

'For God's sake, man! Can you not strike a Frenchman at two paces? We'll have to—' But what they'll have to do is lost, because he has seen what nobody else has seen and his stolen-borrowed hammer won't do for this. He drops it and spins round, unarmed, frantic, looking for whatever he can find that—

A bow!

He leaps on it, fiercely. He is not an archer, to send a dozen arrows a minute with such accuracy that he can hit a wren's head in a summer-leafed oak at three hundred paces, but it isn't summer and there are no leaves and his target isn't a wren's head, or even an eagle's.

He's aiming for a slight figure in unadorned plate, standing in the press at the foot of a ladder. He knows this shape, has been trying to find it in the havoc all day.

And here, now . . . left hand to bow-belly, fingers to string, arrow to nock. A fine arrow, with a savage, bodkin blade to the head that will pierce plate, even good plate. Even plate commissioned by the weak-chinned, jug-eared idiot who calls himself King of France but never stirs himself to fight. What kind of king doesn't fight?

Rustbeard draws with the best smoothness he can muster, feels his shoulders bunch and sigh. He is a mess of contrary levers, and yet the bow is drawn, his lips kiss the string, his better eye sights along the arrow head and she is there, the demon in white plate, or the witch, or the heretic, or the boy, pretending womanhood because that kind of thing boils French blood and makes them go back on their winter promises of surrender.

Eye. Bodkin. Armour. All in line. Others might send a prayer with the loose, but he's not that kind of

man. He sends hatred instead. Die, God damn you. Die.
And . . . loose.

A hit! He hears a curse in French, sees the white armour topple, hears a name shouted, feels horror ripple through the mess of men below.

'She's hit. The Maid, she's hit. The Maid! The Maid! The Maid!'

'Nicely done!' Glasdale's plated fist fetches him such a blow between the shoulders that he thinks he's been shot. He staggers forward. Glasdale catches him in his other hand, lifts his bow arm and the bow in it so everyone must stop and turn and see him.

Glasdale's bull-voice bellows out across the barbican. 'See? Rustbeard is more a man than the rest of you put together. It's not a demon if it bleeds. It's not a demon if an arrow can send it back off a ladder. We'll beat the fuckers now. Get to the walls and build up the breaches and we'll have the bastards and their shitty little town by sundown. Tomorrow, we'll have their bastard king's head on a dish.'

A sword cut to his head slices open the red-gold light and nearly blinds him. Rustbeard ducks sideways, stabs forward clumsily, puts his shoulder behind the thrust and a Frenchman falls. He is too tired to feel the surge of satisfaction that fired him through the day, but at least there is space around him, here on top of the boulevard, and he can take another step back and chop with his axe to the left and slash-skitter his sword off someone else's mail and another step back and Glasdale is off to his left somewhere, in the gloaming, and the sun is leaching the life from the sky and all he can hear is the surf of his own blood in his ears in the echo of his helm, and the ring of iron, as it has rung all afternoon, for the French saw the swing of the witch's standard and found their courage again.

French. Courage. Tod Rustbeard never thought to stitch those two words together in the same hour, never mind the same breath. He squeezes his eyes tight, takes another step back. There is stone in front of him now, which is something. He is nearly free of the rampart and back on to the Tower proper: les Tourelles. Only a temporary wooden bridge to cross and he'll have real stone walls between him and the oncoming French.

Someone passes him water. He drinks and tips back his face and splashes it on and feels it trickle back behind his ears, over his jugular, and the hot, hard pulse. He is not going to die here. He has orders, and they require that he remain alive. He has a plan, except that he has not yet worked out how to make it happen.

'Watch out!' A shout from his right. He snaps upright. The French are coming again, damn their black souls, armed with hammers and pikestaffs, culverins and petit culverins and someone with too good an eye for a shot has already hit Stephen of Dulwich and Gereint the Sheep who came from Powys and should have been on the French side, hating the English, but for the small matter of an ewe smuggled to the wrong side of a ditch, or maybe a whole flock, and a warrant out to stretch his neck on the border marches, so he must come to France and fight for England. And die.

'Back!' Glasdale is close now, standing on what's left of the wall, dull in dented plate. 'Back into the Tower!'

His commander's voice is gone; he can't shout over the guns any more, but word passes man to man: get back into the Tower. Back to stone walls too high for a ladder, and arrow slits, and maybe a fire and food and wine . . . Safety. Nobody will look anyone else in the eye now. This is the way of men facing defeat, who have known nothing but victory for years.

Tod Rustbeard takes a breath, strikes out again. Again. Again. He is an automaton, made for fighting. The sun has abandoned them, the evening is a tepid grey, until suddenly it isn't. Brilliant gold light spumes off a helm to his left, slices wide on a blade to his right, lights his feet. He looks down. The sun is below him and it is not a sun, but a fire. The fucking French have lit a fire on a barge, floated it down the river and moored it directly beneath the bridge. *Damn* them.

'They're firing the bridge! Back!'

He moves back. Flames dance and dart at his feet. The planks linking rampart to Tower are new, still full of resin and the French have laced their fire boat with pitch; the smoke is treacle-thick and strong. The French stop coming. They're happy to stand at the edge and watch Englishmen burn.

On the far side, Rustbeard stands in shadow; a habit that has kept him alive this far. If he had a bow . . . but he doesn't, not any more. He has an axe and a sword and neither can reach the men who have gathered to watch the bridge burn, and any English foolish enough to stand on it.

In time, the fire-sun beneath him begins to set. Down in the river, the barge is moving, towed by an iron hawser; it has done its job. Opposite, the French call back to summon up planks, ready to throw them across. They didn't want to destroy the bridge, just drive the English back into the Tower. Someone on their side has a brain and is using it. This in itself is a wonder. Nobody on the French side has had a brain to speak of since they lost all their decent fighting men at Agincourt in '15.

Half of their army now is made up of Scotsmen: small, swarthy lowlanders with cudgels or big red-haired Strathclyde men wielding bastard swords and small, wicked spikes in the off hand. Did not the pope in Rome say that the

Scots are a sure and certain antidote to the English? Maybe one of these is doing the thinking.

'Rustbeard?' Glasdale appears at his left hand. Inside his armour, the English commander is a shrunken man. He is not used to defeat. Red-eyed, he stares out across the charred bridge to the mass of French beyond. 'Is she there?'

'The witch?' He peers into the dusk. In all the fighting, he'd forgotten she existed. 'I can't see her. She might be dead.'

'No, she's alive. I heard them shout it halfway through the afternoon. She had them pull out the arrow and pack the wound and she's back leading the assault.'

The distress in Glasdale's voice, the shame . . . They have lost to a woman. Or a boy dressed as a woman. It doesn't really matter which; the dishonour is visceral and deadly. Glasdale has traded insults with her these past few days. She sent them a young herald with a letter telling them to surrender. When the lad was arrested and chained to a post and threatened with burning, she shot arrows at them with messages attached. And the French allowed it.

Tod Rustbeard spits. His mouth tastes of bile and filth; the taste of defeat. The Tower is holding, but it won't for long. He has his own plan, growing by the moment.

He says, 'My lord, you'll be ransomed.'

Lords don't die, except by accident or at Agincourt, when things got out of hand. Things often did when Henry was leading, but he's dead and William Glasdale is a gentleman. The French will know him from the quality of his armour and they'll have him inside the walls drinking wine by moonrise; knights always cleave together when the mess of killing is done.

'No.' Glasdale, too, is looking down at the river. 'Tell the king . . .' He shakes his head, starts again; the king is six years old. Woe to thee, O land . . . Everything bad can be charted back to the king's death, the late king, Henry, fifth of the name, victor of every battle he fought, more or less. He may have been a hard bastard, but he was *their* hard bastard and he won for them. Oh, my king. Why did you have to die when we were winning?

Glasdale fixes his mournful gaze on Tod Rustbeard. 'You are Bedford's man?'

'My lord?' That's like saying 'You are English?' Which of course he is, or at least half English, and that's the half that counts. John of Lancaster, first Duke of Bedford, was brother to the late King Henry. He is now, therefore, uncle to the infant King Henry, sixth of the name, and now regent of England, which post he will hold until his nephew comes of age. Or dies. True-born kings have reigned for less time and transformed the fortunes of their nations. Sickly princelings have died in fewer years. 'I serve my lord of Bedford with all my heart.'

'Of course you do.' A scowl creases Glasdale's much-creased face. 'I mean, you are his *man*. His . . .' A wave of his fist says what words cannot. Bedford's agent, his spy, his knife in the dark, his hammer in sunlight, his to order, his to command, his in heart and soul. His to send into the dark places where decent men do not venture, to do the things that decent men cannot do.

Glasdale is not supposed to know this, but Glasdale is a lord and the workings of almost-royalty are not the same as those of other men.

Tod Rustbeard bows. 'I am, my lord, and at your service.'

'You have to go back to the French side.'

'Lord?'

'Stop playing with me, Rustbeard. I have my own spies. You were in there through the winter.'

Ah. Now, that is interesting.

'Lord.' A nod. A tacit agreement. Nothing said aloud, not even here.

'So now you have to go back.'

'To kill the witch. Yes.'

'*No!*' A hard fist catches his arm. Glasdale's face is an inch from his; less. Nose to nose, eyes to mad-red, desperate eyes. 'Not just to kill her. You have to *destroy* her. You have to find out who she is. The men say she's a demon, but I know she's—'

'A girl from Lorraine sent by God to aid the French.' Really, everyone knows this, they just don't want to admit it.

'Ha!' Glasdale's laugh is raw and ugly. 'I will not believe that God changes sides. I shall meet Him before sundown, and if I am wrong it may be that I shall burn in everlasting hell for saying this, but He was with us at Agincourt, at Verneuil, at all the battles between and I tell you that God does *not* change sides.'

'There's a prophecy . . .' Even the English have heard it. A seer-woman has written that France will be redeemed by a maid from Lorraine. Aided by God, of course, that goes without saying. The French want God to change sides, just as much as the English want Him not to.

Scorn sweeps Glasdale's countenance. 'Is Bedford so desperate that he takes on fools? Truly, I had thought better of you.'

'My lord?'

'Think, man. Had you heard this prophecy nonsense before Advent? Had anyone? And yet by the New Year it is old news and everyone has known it all their lives. Ha! This girl came out of nowhere, and nobody does that. Nobody. She is not what she says.'

'What, then?'

'How would I know? But you listen to me, Tod Rustbeard. It is not enough that you kill her; you have to expose her for the liar she is, and then use that lie to destroy every part of her memory. You must shatter the myth, choke it stillborn before it has a chance to grow. Do you understand?'

'I do, my lord.' He does not necessarily agree, but then he doesn't have to. Bedford's orders have priority and they are to kill her, however he can. When she's dead, the stories will wither without his help.

For now, though, his nod is enough. Glasdale relaxes his grip, forces a smile, of sorts, looks over his shoulder to where the French are striving to lay their temporary bridge. In the set of his shoulders is a new certainty. He begins to move towards the breach in the wall that lets out on to the river below.

It's not far: four paces, maybe less. Halfway, he turns back, meets Tod Rustbeard square in the eye. 'Tell my lord of Bedford that I died with honour.'

Oh, sweet Christ.

'Lord . . . No . . . !' He lurches to grab at a cuff, a belt, anything. But Glasdale is already filling the breach. One raked look east to west, to the evening star, to the red line of the sun's last edge, and he steps off into nowhere.

A swift drop. A sound like a horse, drinking, just once. Sixty pounds of plate armour and a man, into the mud-silt waters of the Loire. Nothing shows where he hits, and there are no bubbles to show he has breathed. Death may be swift this way, but Tod Rustbeard doesn't want to think how the last few moments will feel.

He backs deeper into shadow. He is surrounded by death; it is nothing new. But here, now, he can feel its cold breath on the nape of his neck, the suck and sigh of it, the temptation to follow Glasdale. He looks across at the French, at the smug torch-lit faces, the smirks, the pumped hands, the cheers as a good man, a decent, honourable man of courage, drowns in that fucking French river.

He knows these men, French and the Scots alike; he has

spent a winter clasping their craven hands, buying wine for their pig's bladder bellies. He notes one without hair, another with a nose hooked as a hawk's beak, a third with blazing red hair and beard that are brighter, fierier twins to his own, so that they could be brothers. It's not impossible; who knows when else and where else his father sowed his bastard seed?

Patrick Ogilvy of Gairloch, I know you. And Ricard the crossbowman. And Hugh Kennedy and Georges and Raoul d'Autet. I know every man of you. Celebrate all you like now, you bastards, for soon I will kill you with my bare hands, half-kin or not. I will tie anvils to your necks and watch you drown in horse piss. I will . . .

He backs away before the heat of his fury touches them. They still don't know he's there; too busy staring at the place where Glasdale fell in case iron turns to cork and he bobs back up. They have a woman who fights; all the laws of God and man have been overturned. Today, anything might happen.

He slips away. He is thinking now, fast, clear-headed, certain. There are more ways to skin a bear . . .

In the tower are long shadows and the approach of night. He knows how it is: on the ground floor is an armoury, with the main door opposite, barred with oak, and a postern on the other side. He runs down on memory and hope and yes, it is as he remembers.

Nobody is near the stairs. The eighty or so English men at arms still living are all at the front, barricading the main door. These are his brothers-in-arms. He knows them and they know him. He calls out as he runs down the last steps.

'Cyril! Stephen! Here to me. We have to block the postern gate or they'll come in at us from the back!'

They trust him; he is ever the one with a good idea. Cyril

arrives first. Sword and shield, no helm. Stephen is heavier, and slower. Mail shirt, a borrowed helm tied on with leather, mail gloves, a bastard sword, held two-handed. Stephen first, then.

The armoury is on his left, the racks emptied of weapons but for a pike with a shattered haft left leaning on the wall.

'Damnation, I thought there'd be more shafts here.' He spins on his heel, a man with fortitude, in the midst of a defence. He flashes a bright smile. 'Cyril, find us a pike or two. Anything long with something on the end sharp enough to kill a few Frenchmen. Stephen, help me break up the racks. We can jam them across the door.'

Cyril runs back for the pikes; he's young and ardent and doesn't want to die. Stephen . . . Stephen is already dying, his throat sliced raggedly open, scalding blood a fountain in the air – step sideways, now, don't get caught by the spume – his last breath frothing out as he tries to shout a warning – Tod Rustbeard! Traitor! – and finds his voice doesn't work and he can't think why, and already the light is fading from his eyes and he falls back into Rustbeard's waiting arms, to be lowered to the floor; just in time.

'I got the best I could, but there isn't mu— *Oof!*' And thus Cyril is poleaxed, the hilt of a sword smashed into the bridge of his nose so hard that the bones pop and his eyes are split open and he is crumpling before he can bring up the shield or the sword or the three pikes he has balanced across his forearms.

They clatter as they fall, but none of his fellows is listening; they're all at the front gate, placing barricades on barricades, getting ready to hold it for the night, for the next day, for as long as it takes for reinforcements to come. It's not a bad plan, it just needs to fail.

Cyril is still alive. Rustbeard rams his sword into his unarmoured gut. It's blunted with a day's use and won't bite properly, so the first strike is a mess of mangled jerkin and barely a cut.

He gives up and uses the back edge of his axe in a short, savage chop to the temple. He's a hammer man out of choice, and the dent it leaves is satisfyingly deep, ramming hair and skin into bone and brain. He lets the lad's body fall back so he can drive his sword home properly, up through the belly into the air-filled mess of the chest. He feels the sudden release of pressure, the pad-pad of a just-beating heart, stilled.

There's blood everywhere, but that is rather the point; blood and heroism are welded one to the other in French minds and he needs to be enough of a hero not to die as soon as they see him. He strips off his English colours, the red and the white, and wrestles them on to Cyril, who has lost his somewhere in the fight.

At the front gate, French rams are pounding, but he knows this gate; it will not break easily; that's why his offer of a back route in will be so very welcome. He straightens, runs his hands through his hair so it sticks up, stiff with blood, red as a cock's comb, and as rigid. He thinks of childhood, and summer rivers, and his mother calling across the orchards. *Chéri! Viens ici.*

The postern gate is the height of a man, wide enough only to let through two at a time. It is held shut by three iron bolts, all well-oiled. The hinges sigh on goose grease; other men than he have planned secret entry or exit from here. Outside, the evening air is mellow. In Orléans, they are lighting fires of celebration, and on the south bank of the Loire. Bastards. Fifty yards away, two hundred Frenchmen are assaulting the front gate with rams and torches, pitch and hammers, blades, fists and feet.

No going back now. He steps outside, where he can more readily be seen, brings to mind the names of those he saw

38

from the tower top, cups his hands to his mouth and shouts, *'Patrick! Georges! Ricard! Venez ici! Ici, au nom de Dieu! Ici! Aidez-moi!'*

A dozen men peel away from the mass and run towards him, blades out. He doesn't raise his sword. In fact, he slams it hard and clearly into the sheath at his belt, and continues to shout. 'Guillaume de Monterey! Laurent de Saval! I know you're out there. Come to me here! In God's name, come!'

They come as a pack, and he knows none of those at the front, nor they him, and his hand is heading down towards his blade, because if he's going to die it won't be empty-handed, when he sees—

'Patrick Ogilvy! You red-haired bastard! It's me! Tomas! Here! Gairloch, to me! Patrick, in the name of God, come to me here! Tell them I'm the king's man! Tell them I'm for France!'

They are running flat out, but Ogilvy is a Strathclyde man, half Norse, with the fire-hair of the Vikings and a big, broad-shouldered body to match – truly, they could be brothers – and he breasts through the crowd, slamming men left and right, taking liberties that on other days would see him stabbed between the ribs by his own side, but this time he's a captain, friend of the Maid, and he's shouting, 'Leave him! Leave him! It's Tomas Rustbeard. He's one of us! Leave him!'

And they are together, clasping arm to arm, beard to beard, chest to chest, and Patrick Ogilvy is gabbling in a mix of French and lowland Scots, 'Tomas? We thought we'd lost you. We thought you'd gone over to join the bastard English.'

Well that's reasonable, because he had done exactly that, and it would have been fantastically unlikely if nobody at all on the French side had seen him these past few days. Which is why he is ready with an answer that makes sense of it all.

'I did. And now I've come back. I did say that I would.'
Stepping aside, he gestures back to the broken remnants of
Stephen and Cyril and all their blood.

'My God . . .' Ogilvy is a fighting man of many years'
experience, but he grows white now, and cannot find words.
A crowd gathers and, gratifyingly, more men than just the
Scot are crossing themselves.

Tod Rustbeard, also known as Tomas, whose mother
came from Normandy and who claims his Frenchness more
firmly with each passing word, claps the big Scot about the
shoulder. 'You can kiss me later, but for now get your men in
here fast, or the English will hear us and more will die who
don't have to.'

Ogilvy can move swiftly, when things are explained to
him. One meaty arm sweeps back at his fellows. 'Swords up,
mes enfants. Let's take these Godless bastards from behind.
Tomas, you coming?'

'Aye.' He has not forgotten Glasdale, not his death, nor the
promises made above the water in which he died. Later, he
will honour them. Today, here, now, he is Tomas Rustbeard
who smiles to the French and to the Scots and nods forward
to the ram-pounded gate. 'Quietly now. Shields up, swords
out, and don't miss when you're close enough.'

He helps them with the killing and if some amongst the
English side recognize him, it is only with their dying
breaths and they are not in a position to do anything about
it. The battle of the gate is short and fast and ugly, and of the
garrison of five hundred English men at arms the last fifty
surrender.

Tomas doesn't stop to herd them into the city, but seeks
out Patrick Ogilvy. If anyone can get close to the Maid, it's
him: with his red hair and his Scots air of casual brutality,
he's always close to the leadership in any fight. Tomas clasps

him, arm to elbow, draws him close, brother-in-arms, at the end of a victorious battle. 'We won! By God and all the saints, we won!'

'By the Maid.' Ogilvy can't stop grinning. He has no idea the effort of will it takes not to cut his throat. 'By the Maid we won, and will keep on winning. You're in good hands now, Tomas. The bastard English are learning what it's like to be on the losing side at last. We'll push them all the way back to Normandy and beyond. We'll be in London drinking wine from gold cups by the year's end, just see if we're not.'

He will not be. Here, now, Tomas swears one more binding oath to the memory of William Glasdale that, whatever else the fucking French may be doing, Patrick Ogilvy will be dead by the year's end, and the Maid with him.

CHAPTER THREE

ORLÉANS,
Monday, 24 February 2014
06.38

AT 6.38 AM – THE PRECISE time is recorded in Picaut's log book – Martin Evard, chief of the Fire Department, deems it safe to enter the saturated mess that was the Hôtel Carcassonne on the rue de la Tournée, three blocks south of the cathedral in Orléans town centre.

It is one of the few new-builds in an area of ancient, wood-framed terraces. Here bombs fell – Hitler's or the RAF's – with a surprising degree of precision and only this one single block was destroyed. Its replacement was not built until the early twenty-first century, by which time it was required to conform to more modern building regulations and leave a substantial gap on each of its four sides.

This foresight has prevented the entire north bank of Orléans from joining in the conflagration, although nearby dwellings have suffered smoke damage and a few have been scorched badly enough to peel paint from the shutters. In the usual course of events, insurance teams would follow soon after the police to assess the damage and define the costs of repair. Now, though, the investigation has progressed beyond simple arson. Not long after dawn, the Fire Department confirmed the presence of a burned corpse in a bedroom on the ground floor of the hotel.

As a result, the square is now crowded with three photographers and five specialist forensic investigators, plus the one person who needs to be here and nobody really wants: Maître Yves Ducat, the prosecutor.

Ducat is the man from whom Picaut requires permission to investigate and to whom she must present her case, should she ever get that far.

If Garonne is a soft man in a hard man's body, Prosecutor Ducat is his opposite: a man of granite, encased in pudgy flesh and a peg-toothed smile. Clean-shaven, with a bull's nose and a low brow, he flashes his Neanderthal grin at everyone who passes through his office without favour or discrimination. Perpetrator and victim, prosecutor and defence; all and each are treated to a bear hug, a crushing press of his chubby cheek to theirs, a booming welcome.

Picaut fell for the false bonhomie once, and watched an almost-certain child abuser walk free on a point of law. Since then, she has treated him with extreme care and has never made any allegation she couldn't back up with at least one piece of indisputable evidence.

He is there now, standing four square in front of the sodden remains of the Hôtel Carcassonne, picking his nose with assiduous attention. He shoves his hands in his pockets as Picaut walks up.

'Body inside?' he says.

'According to the Fire Department, yes.'

He shakes his head, as if this is news. 'So this is like but not like the others, yes?'

'Yes. And no.' Picaut phrases her report carefully. She is good at this, the summary of incidents, and she has had plenty of time to prepare. 'There are differences to the previous fires, but there are also similarities. The body is the most obvious difference. We need first to establish if he died because he was caught in a fire that was lit for other reasons, or whether killing him was the point of the fire.

'Beyond that, this fire is less contained than its three predecessors. It may have been less carefully lit; perhaps there was more accelerant, or it was spread more widely. This may be accidental, or it may point to a different perpetrator, but equally it may indicate that the increased damage is a deliberate escalation of the war currently being waged on Orléans.'

'You have had the phone call?'

'An hour after the fire was first reported. The same voice, heavily accented. He spoke for no more than twelve seconds. There was no chance of a trace.'

'What did he say?'

Picaut opens her phone, thumbs across a screen or two, reads out the transcript Patrice sent her after it was over. "*Ici L'armée du Prophète, Jaish al Islam.* This fire, too, is ours. The occupant, Madame Rivette, trades in sex. This is not allowed under the laws of Islam. She will do so no longer."'

'And Madame Rivette; she is mourning the loss of her brothel?'

'She doesn't exist.'

'What?'

'Exactly. This is the other major change in the pattern: we not only have a body in a bigger fire, we have less than perfect intelligence on the part of our arsonists. The Hôtel Carcassonne is owned by a Madame Foy and has been since the unfortunate death of her father-in-law last August. It is to be regretted that the hotel website has not been updated, but there is no doubt that she has been the owner for over half a year.'

'Was it ever a brothel?'

'If it was, it specialized in middle-aged, overweight foreigners who had sex only with each other and heard of it by word of mouth. If you suggest this in any way, Madame Foy will require that you do so in the presence of her brother who is also her lawyer and will take appropriate action in defence of his client's reputation. Madame Foy is already aggrieved that she wasn't mentioned by name in the Jaish al Islam phone call. She would sue them for that if she knew who they were.'

'*Merde.*' Ducat pinches his upper lip between thumb and forefinger. 'They haven't made mistakes before. Tell me it's not a copycat.'

'It's not. Patrice checked the voice print: it's identical. They may have their intelligence wrong, or they may be covering up a murder with a fire, but it's the same group.'

'We shall be grateful for small mercies. So who's dead? A fat German?'

'All we have so far is a white male in his forties, possibly American. We'll know more when the duty pathologist has examined—' And here he is: Éric Masson, the pathologist, with his customarily impeccable timing. He waves at Picaut then sees who she's with and drops his smile and, after it, his hand.

Masson is one of the few people who don't have to be nice to Ducat. He uses his privilege with a diffidence that does him credit. Walking over, he gives a small bow to Picaut, nods to the Prosecutor. 'Maître, it seems my services may be required.'

This is a politeness. He has already been inside; the smell of smoke on his clothes is a dead giveaway.

Ducat grunts by way of greeting. 'Only one body?'

'Only one that has been found so far.'

45

Ducat gives his peg-broad smile. 'Collateral damage or deliberate target, either way he's dead on our precinct. In view of which, this is now a murder inquiry under the investigation of Capitaine Picaut. I shall require the results of a full autopsy at your earliest convenience. You don't have to be here, you know . . .'

They dance this duet at every single crime scene for which Masson is on call. Since 2010, no forensic pathologist in France has been required to visit the scene of the crime; the investigating officer should, in theory, be able to provide all the necessary detail.

Not being required to attend, of course, is different from not being permitted to do so and Éric Masson, who thinks the new legislation is bullshit – pardon the captain's presence and no reflection on her competence, of course – wants to see the body in situ for himself. Picaut considers this wise and, this once, Ducat is in full agreement.

Still, it is their custom that the prosecutor points out the law and the pathologist acknowledges it. Masson repeats his bow. 'With your permission, maître?' And then to Picaut, 'Shall we go?'

'Lead on.'

Éric Masson, twice divorced by the age of thirty-five, is tall and thin and acidly crabby and Picaut likes him a lot. His marital catastrophes have etched fault-lines across his brow, but not yet stripped him of his humanity, his humour or, indeed, his hair, which grows thickly dark with a widow's peak that flops over his right eye. Immaculate in a white paper suit, yellow hard hat and latex gloves, he leads the way to the burned-out building.

'Is he making trouble?' He nods back at Ducat.

'No more than usual. What have you got?'

'Male, Caucasian, good height, middle-aged. Exactly what the Fire Department said. The fire cooked him fairly comprehensively.' He sends her a warning glance. 'He's not pretty.'

'They never are. I'll be fine. Really.'

'Take this, then.' He hands her a spare safety hat. The weight settles cold on her brow. She follows him, ducking under a fallen lintel held up by a jack, into the sodden, aching building.

Inside, the fire has rendered everything in shades of black and white; coloured only by flashes of blue sky that let in the morning in places where the roof has fallen away. They enter a hallway, walk past remnants of picture frames slewed on smoke-blackened walls. In one corner is a mess of melted plastic that was once the telephone. The air hangs thick and damp, scented with an unholy hybrid of wet dog and sodden wood with the first taste of burning flesh.

There was a time within living memory when the Fire Department moved dead bodies from their location to somewhere 'safer' in a fire-wrought building. Now they know better, and so Picaut follows the pathologist along a smaller hallway and left into a good-sized double bedroom with en-suite shower and views that are notionally north towards the cathedral, but in fact are of the street opposite, a landscape of pale stone and buff-painted wood.

With one long, sweeping look, she takes in what might be the blackened remnants of a woollen carpet, a broad bed, furniture with classic, cool French lines. The fire has destroyed everything in this room, but the withered, blackened skeletons left behind still speak of taste and discrimination on a limited budget. The Hôtel Carcassonne was not as cheap as its situation and exterior might suggest, but nor was it ostentatiously expensive.

A photographer steps back as they approach, leaving a space around the body. The smell of overcooked meat is strongest here. Breathing through her mouth, Picaut tastes it on her tongue.

The victim lies on the floor to the left of the bed. He is curled in a foetal position, knees and elbows tucked in, face behind fists. His body is a black hulk, impossible to see where his burned clothes end and his burned skin begins. His hair has vanished, leaving no clue as to its colour. His eyes have broken apart and all that was liquid is gone. Vacant sockets stare at the wall.

Never in human history has this been a good death. Six hundred years ago, the Maid of Orléans was fixed to a stake and burned. When she was dead, the executioner stripped her naked to prove to the crowd that she was a woman, then built up the fire and burned her to ashes, and then took those ashes and burned them again, to be sure nothing was left. On English orders, Frenchmen destroyed her. Turning her into a saint has done nothing to wash away the horror.

Picaut closes her eyes. 'Tell me he died of smoke inhalation . . .'

'Possibly.' Masson is kneeling, careful to keep his white suit white. Already, Picaut's is smudged and smeared. He has second thoughts; truth is his touchstone. 'Actually, no, but for what it's worth, I don't think he was conscious.' He takes a step back, leaving her to study the body.

He has given her a clue but she likes to think she didn't need it; after nearly two years of tuition, she can see almost all that he sees.

She points just above the dead man's left eye. 'Fractured skull?'

'Good.' He lectured once to students at Harvard, and the habit has never left him. Now, he pulls a Bic from an inside pocket and uses it as an extension of his finger, sweeping it in an arc from the eye socket up and out towards the temple. Viewed from a particular angle, it is possible that the blackened skin in this area might be slightly depressed. 'I'd put good money that there's a fracture under here. If he was hit hard enough to break the bone, he'll have been dazed, at the very least.'

Not an accident, then, but still possible that he is, as Ducat said, collateral damage; an unfortunate who disturbed the fire setters in their act of arson, the wrong man in the wrong place at the wrong time.

Picaut stands up and a photographer steps in and leans over the body. Three bright-white flashes light the room. In their wake, both Picaut and Masson take their own images with their phones. They're not for use in court, but they'll be uploaded on to a computer back at the lab and case notes will be built around them.

'So who was he?' she asks.

'No idea.' Masson sweeps his pen in a wider arc that takes in the fried mess of the bed, the burned remnants of the dressing table, the wardrobe that has fallen in on itself . . . and the absolute absence of anything to mark the man on the floor: no clothes hanging over chairs, no suitcase lying open. 'No passport, no credit card, no mobile phone; nothing. The room's been cleared out.'

So, not collateral damage. 'Fuck.' Picaut stares down at the charred remains of her maybe-American visitor and counts the ways in which her life has just become more complex.

Éric Masson's quiet smile greets her as she looks up again. 'I think this is what they pay you for.'

'And they pay you to get me DNA and a dental imprint in record time.' They are friends; the words lack any sting. 'I can't find out why he was murdered until I know who he was.'

'Give me two hours.'

Picaut sinks down to her hands and knees, peers under

the bed. 'He had a mobile phone. He was seen speaking on it at dinner. It must be here somewhere.'

It isn't. Later in the day, a fingertip search by the forensic team finds fragments of plastic and some parts of a battery ground into the carpet as if the whole thing has been crushed underfoot, but of the phone there is no sign. Nor is there any particular sign of who has been here, or why, although Martin Evard of the Fire Department tells her that, as in the previous fires, all the surfaces in the room were soaked with gasoline before it was set alight.

Picaut follows the stretcher bearing the charred remains out into the small square in front of the building. Her car is covered in a fine layer of soot and ash. She is the same. Every time she runs her hands through her hair, they come away grimier.

It is four minutes past seven. She weighs risk and counter-risk and decides that being (and looking and feeling) clean matters more than being at her desk ten minutes ahead of time. Pocketing her car keys, she sets out to walk three blocks west towards the apartment she once shared with Luc; the place she still notionally calls home.

On the way, she prepares in her head the report she will email to Ducat, the prosecutor, and the broader-ranging, more speculative one she will present to her team when they gather in her office later.

She has had less than three hours' sleep.

CHAPTER FOUR

JARGEAU,
12 June 1429

TOMAS RUSTBEARD'S FIRST CHANCE to kill the Maid comes on the second day of the assault on Jargeau, just over a month after the disaster at Orléans.

The army is camped in the suburbs, preparing for another day of fighting. The king has been prevaricating or they would have been here a month ago. His advisers are divided. The Maid, to whom all now look for advice, has spent the past month persuading him to let her march his army against the English garrisons of the Loire valley.

The king, not surprisingly, is somewhat reluctant to let a woman lead his troops; it's not a good precedent. Also, his religious advisers are divided between those who think she is a gift from God and can do anything, and those, most notably the Archbishop of Rheims, the king's spiritual adviser, who think she is a charlatan at best, the devil incarnate at worst, and should be sewn in a leather sack and thrown in the river forthwith.

The army wants her, but the army's view is not the one that counts. The campaign to free France of the English, therefore, stalled temporarily, while the French, yet again, squabbled amongst themselves.

As far as Tomas is concerned, any delay is good. He spent this time in the taverns and back rooms of a celebratory Orléans, seeking out all the possible variations of the warrior-Maid's story. There are not many; it has a remarkable uniformity, which is in itself suspicious, but he has listened to the telling and the retelling, and he has found that Glasdale was right: there is the legend, and there is the truth, and in the gap between these two lie the seeds of her destruction.

Thus does he find himself part of the Maid's waiting army, roving to and fro along the banks of the Loire, identifying the good men, and undermining their strengths, finding the weaklings and bolstering a false bravado.

He also speaks with the women who cluster round the camp. The ever-pious Maid has driven out the whores, but these are mothers, sisters, wives. They cook and bind wounds, sing psalms and wash linens, spin and weave and sew.

And they talk. Tomas has become known for his ready ear and so they talk to him: Jeannette, Marie, Violette of the sad, red eyes, who is friends with Claudine, whose brother, Matthieu, it seems, met a violent death on the night the Maid first met the king at Chinon.

'Claudine says Matthieu greeted the Maid on the bridge as she was walking into the chateau. He was not respectful as he should have been.'

Violette stands near a fire, beyond the tent lines, stirring a boiling pot of small clothes with a stick. Tomas takes over and stirs for her. He feels like a hound that has caught a ten-day-old scent. Claudine is the one, he can feel it in his marrow: his key to destroying the Maid. 'Did she know what her brother said that gave offence?'

'That the Maid should come and meet him later and he'd see she wasn't a maid by morning. Can you imagine it?' Violette is young and skinny, with straggling black hair and eye teeth that grow out like the tushes on a small boar. 'He was dead by the morning. Claudine found him floating face down in the river. Marie-Paul said he'd been struck by God, but Claudine said he had a big mashed place on the back of his head. Somebody hit him and pushed him into the river to drown.'

'You think the Maid did it?'

'No!' Violette recoils, covers her face with chapped pink hands, peers at him between her fingers. 'Why would she do that?'

Because he knew who she really was and had threatened to tell the king?

Tomas shakes his head, gently says, 'You're right, of course. A footpad, a thief, an unfortunate accident. But if we could find Claudine, it may be that the Maid would want to help her. With Matthieu gone, she must be . . .' Prostituting herself? Sewing winding sheets? Stirring laundry in a barely boiling pot? Whatever girls do who are unmarried and destitute in the Loire valley.

He waits, but Violette doesn't help him out, only stares into the rolling water. 'She's gone and I don't know where. I haven't seen her since the army gathered.'

Claudine may be dead, but Tomas's instinct tells him not. With practised care, he finds out what she looks like: straw-blond hair, a fine nose, freckles, a scar on her left hand from a spill of hot oil in her youth. It's not much, but it's better than nothing. He gives Violette back her stirring-stick.

He may not have been as delicate as he thought, because she gives him a sideways glance. 'Jean-Pierre might know more. They were . . . friendly . . .'

Friendly? In an army where the Maid has banned the

whores? I'm sure they were. 'How might I find Jean-Pierre?'

'He's the gunner. The one the Maid says is blessed by God.'

Oh, yes. Today is a good day. Newly cheered, he heads back to the army, to the men preparing for battle, and to the guns, which are already firing.

The French love their guns the way the English love their longbows. The Rifflard may be able to hurl shot the weight of half a horse, but it's the smaller, more manoeuvrable, culverins that are wearing Jargeau down. The French gunners are good, and Jean-Pierre is the best. He can fire one single ranging shot and the one after will hit whatever he chooses: a wall, a tower, a man on that tower.

The little gunner is constantly moving, shifting gun placements, the better to harass the ramparts of Jargeau. Once in a while he'll pretend he's been hit, clutch at his chest or his side and fall back and lie like a broken puppet and a great cheer will go up from the English side – until he bounces to his feet and leaps on to his gun and makes the pumping motion with his fist that drives the English wild. Wild men are reckless and reckless men die. And die.

At noon, those inside grow tired of dying and send out a herald to sue for surrender.

Seeing the gates open, and the single rider squeeze through with a feather in his cap for parley, Tomas seeks out Patrick Ogilvy and tugs at his sleeve. 'Look.' And when he turns: 'Come on, we can't miss this.'

Alone, he might be noticed. With the big Strathclyde man at his side, it's easier to weave through the pack of French men at arms, until they are close enough to the Maid and her small entourage to hear most of whatever transpires.

The herald is a white-haired Frenchman who eases off his horse stiffly, as if his hips are carved in poor stone.

Three French knights ride up to stand their horses before

him: d'Alençon on the right, then the Maid, then La Hire; each has a squire and a page just behind. None of the three dismounts. The herald should, perhaps, take notice of this, but he's too busy following what he thinks is protocol. He bows to the right to La Hire, left to d'Alençon, ignores the Maid.

'Jesu. The man's a fool.' Patrick Ogilvy says what everyone is thinking, but he says it quietly.

In the shocked silence, the herald raises his head. 'The garrison offers the keys to the gates if they can march out with their weapons and their horses.'

'No.'

'We will cease firing and march out in good order, and . . . What do you mean, no?'

Body of Christ, how stupid can you be? And how stupid the men inside who picked this numbskull and sent him out to negotiate?

Patrick Ogilvy and his companions cannot conceal their mirth. Oh, Holy Mother. Did you see her face? She'll have him skinned alive.

Tomas Rustbeard grins along with them, but he is not laughing inside. His attention is all on the Maid. She is not laughing either.

It's not that she doesn't ever laugh. Over the past month he has watched her with all the intensity of a new lover. He knows the swings of her mood and they are many and swift and only rarely concealed. She is impetuous, forthright. Without care for the opinions of others, by turns she laughs, rages, grieves.

This is the first time he has seen her school herself to still-ness. She is, he thinks, very, very angry, but she's keeping it under cover; a hot vat, sealed.

She moves her horse two paces ahead of the others and halts it, which does not sound much, but you have to understand that her horse is not one for whom stillness comes naturally.

This is her courser, the one Duc Jean d'Alençon, the king's cousin, is supposed to have given her back in February, when she was newly come to Chinon.

As the story goes, d'Alençon saw her running up and down in a meadow with a lance, the way the squires do, and was so impressed with her knightly conduct that he offered her a full-trained war horse, the worth of a prince's ransom. That evening, watching her riding, the king was so impressed with her skill that he ordered a suit of armour made for her.

It's not clear whether this is true, but certainly somebody has given her two thousand marks' worth of hot-blooded, thoroughly nasty grey-white horse and she rides it the way Bedford rides his coursers, one hand on the reins, bending it round her leg into a fluid traverse, holding it steady or stepping it two paces forward when it so very clearly wants nothing more than to run and kill, kill and run, until its legs are bloody and its flanks run black with sweat.

Tomas Rustbeard has met horses like this. Once, he has tried to ride one. He is not in a hurry to repeat the experience.

Here and now, though, the French herald is either too stupid or too distracted by the destruction being visited on his town, to understand what he is up against. Luckily, he doesn't have to. The Maid spells it out for him.

'You will leave your horses, your weapons and your armour behind, or you will not leave.'

The herald gapes. His eyes flit left and right, to La Hire, to d'Alençon, men whose colours he knows. He pleads with them, silently: you are men, you are knights; you know the rules of warfare. This is not how it is done.

Except it is, of course. This is exactly how the late King

Henry did it, and you can blame him for destroying the laws of chivalry if you like, but he's dead. Do you want to be dead too?

She says, 'You have an hour. March out in linen, or stay and die.' She spins her horse on its quarters and lifts it into a half rear.

The herald evidently doesn't know this move. Tomas himself has only seen it once, when a Portuguese riding master with far too great a sense of his own importance was invited to put on a display for the late king.

He had a horse not unlike this one, come to think of it: milky white, half a hand taller than the average courser, with quarters like a bull and a head like a snake. Halfway through a performance of traverse and capriole and canter-on-the-spot it lifted in a half rear just like this and then the double kick with both hind feet straight back.

By perhaps the width of a hand, the herald is not killed. There is a moment when he looks as if he might vomit or void his bladder or otherwise disgrace himself, but presently he turns, mounts his own horse, and rides back in through the gates, with the jeers of the French army hurrying him forward.

Tomas stays in the middle of the mob, where it is safest.

Patrick Ogilvy keeps to his side, grinning like an imbecile. 'What will they do?'

'If they have any sense, they'll march out in their small clothes as she ordered.'

'When did the English ever have sense?'

Oh, I don't know . . . At Agincourt? Verneuil? Crécy, even? Any of the dozen similar battlefields where a small force of massively outnumbered Englishmen trounced their French assailants?

Tomas grins mindlessly back and makes another mark in the mental tally against Ogilvy.

The defenders of Jargeau, it seems, have abandoned all sense. The hour's grace passes and nobody marches out. At a given signal the gunners recommence their firing.

A flash of silver moves to his left. Tomas tugs at Ogilvy's sleeve again. 'Look, the Maid's heading for the battery. She'll be telling the gunners how to fire next.'

'That should be interesting. Let's go up and watch.'

That's the great thing about Ogilvy, he's pliant. Give him a lead, and he'll think it was his own idea. They hike up over towards the guns, after the Maid, Tomas and Ogilvy and a mass of knights and squires and pages and anyone else who has nothing better to do.

There, a man in his element, is Jean-Pierre, Claudine's friend, with a row of smoking guns. The Maid asks, 'Can you bring down the south tower by the gate?'

He grins. He has not many teeth left, and those powder black. Claudine kissed this? Really? He bows. 'Ask and it shall be given.'

This might be blasphemy but the Maid does not shout him down, only nods a salute. 'Do it.' She backs her horse a safe distance.

Jean d'Alençon is with her; he can't keep away.

The priests say she's a maid, that no man has touched her, which they cite as their proof that she can't be consorting with the devil. Tomas thinks that if she's consorting with anyone, it's d'Alençon, whose pretty wife beggared herself – and him – for his ransom only two months ago.

The Maid's attention appears to be entirely on the damage being done to Jargeau, but she says, 'Good my lord, don't stand there. You will be hit by the enemy's next shot. Move back.'

He looks at her queerly, but grasps his horse and does as she says.

And the next shot kills the gunner's boy, who might

be a little deaf, or just doesn't listen to the conversations of his betters and, accordingly, has taken three steps sideways and is moving through the spot d'Alençon just vacated.

The guns pause in their havoc. All around, men are crossing themselves. Tomas finds his own hands moving in sympathy, brow to heart, shoulder to shoulder. Of course, it was a lucky guess. Or she knows more about artillery than anyone except Jean-Pierre. Possibly more than Jean-Pierre. He does not believe it to have been magic.

D'Alençon is grey-green from chin to his receding brow line. 'My lady . . .'

She looks unmoved, but Tomas is coming to think that there is little of which she is not aware.

She nods. 'The English are not coming out. We can attack. Call the men into order. Three columns. One to each gate on my signal.'

Here is his chance. Tomas feels it in the pit of his stomach, in the sweat soaking the back of his tunic. With Ogilvy as his shadow, he follows her into the thick fighting at the walls, pressing for the gates.

Here are ladders, men with pikes, others with crossbows trying to pick defenders off the top of the walls. Truly, this is just like Orléans. The Maid and her vicious horse are in the midst of it, her knights in a ring around her. Tomas is one step further away, just beyond kicking range, watching her, close as any guardian.

He sees the moment when she decides to go forward on foot and calls for help to dismount and he's there ahead of anyone else, holding her reins, keeping his fingers out of the way of the grey's snapping teeth, offering his knee for her to step down on to, handing her to the ground.

He did this once for Bedford and he thought he'd never walk again after the crush of an armoured man on his leg.

The plate alone weighs sixty pounds, and what does Bedford weigh? It doesn't bear thinking.

The Maid is more lightly made, or she takes more care. She grasps his outstretched hand and swings down.

Now! But his good, one-handed hammer that he brought from Orléans is in his belt and he has one hand on the horse and the other . . . she grips it, squeezes, just a little.

Their flesh does not touch. Her gauntlets and his gloves separate them, but, truly, it might as well be that her naked palm burns into his. His bones become as candle wax, soft of an evening. His blood surfs in his ears. His world halts.

He kneels on the summer-hard dirt, offers no speech, no thoughts, no offence against her person, and she steps on him so lightly he barely knows she's been there. There's a shared glance, full of humour – is she laughing at him? Or with him? Neither? Both? And she is past, looking to the walls, and his hammer is still in his belt and La Hire is there and d'Alençon, God rot his sycophantic soul, and she lifts off her helm and runs a mailed hand through her scandalously short hair and something mellow and meaty twists in the nether portions of his belly.

He is nothing to her. She no longer even knows he's there. Looking right, looking left, she says, 'We need to get to the south tower. Bring the ladders,' and his chance is missed and gone.

Men run to her order. Tomas Rustbeard rises from his knees, reeling. In time, his hands close again on the haft of his hammer. The wood is planed to his grip, smooth, cool. He gathers himself, takes a breath. Another. Presently, he follows her to the foot of the wall. Here they walk on wood.

There was a ditch, which is now full of faggots. This is how she got close to the Tower at Orléans: wood in the ditch to walk on. Here, near the wall, is chaos. He thrives on chaos. It is his milieu. He flexes his fingers.

A ladder is flung up beside her. Nobody hurls it down. He says, 'Lady, let me go first.'

Him up, her behind, there's his chance, but, 'No. I'll go first. The men need to see me go up.'

She can climb in full plate. You'd think she was born in it, raised in it. She swarms up to the place where Jean-Pierre's guns have taken down the top third of the wall. Tomas follows her up.

Nobody on the walls makes any effort to stop her. The defenders are all at the gate where another ram is breaking down those parts that Jean-Pierre's guns have not destroyed.

She's within three rungs of the top, sword out, climbing half-handed when he hears a shout. 'She's there! Get her!' and – *finally!* – stones start to fall. The fools inside don't have oil or water or sand in a vat on a fire (how long have they had to prepare? Over a month? They deserve to lose), but they have pieces of their broken town in abundance.

Thus, the sky rains rocks; small ones that a child could lift in one hand and great boulders the size of half a sheep that must have taken three men to lift.

Tomas grasps the sides of the ladder and slides straight down, fast. And then the Maid falls after him, uncontrolled.

She has been hit by something big, and falls without caution. He is her cushion, her straw-filled mattress, a beetle, crushed flat by the weight of her armour. She's not light as thistledown now, and he is smashed beneath her, the breath stunned from him, his whole chest bruised.

'My lady!' D'Alençon, of course, bends over, all solicitude. And then La Hire, d'Aulon, her squire; little Louis de Coutes, her golden-haired page. They're all gathered round, patting at her, stricken. Nobody attends to Tomas Rustbeard.

He squirms out from under her and pushes up, fighting for breath. Croaking, he asks, 'Is she dead?'

His question sparks a wildfire; men hear the one word they fear and spread it.

'She's dead . . .'

'The Maid is dead . . .'

News flashes outward as oil across a millpond and the entire French army stops in its tracks for one heartbroken breath; a gap, with a world of grief pressing around it.

What follows when that breath ends is a thunderstorm, an earthquake, a bull erupting in a catastrophe of rage. The noise! Sword hilts pound on shields, axes clash on blades, men scream their hearts out in a fury such as Tomas has never heard, not at Agincourt, not in the siege of Orléans, not anywhere.

Just with the power of their anger, the French could smash the walls of Jargeau. Those inside are buffeted to silence. No rocks fall. No man will dare to stand against them now. Here, in this moment, five thousand men and boys swear a lifetime's vengeance and know that they can win. This is not a bluff. This is the certain promise of victory.

And this is new. It didn't happen when Tomas's arrow hit her at Orléans, but she hadn't won a battle then, not a big one. She hadn't led a charge from the front. She was admired, she was different; she was a novelty and a source of hope. Now she is adored, and will be avenged.

It's a long time since Tomas Rustbeard has been afraid of the power of an army, not one he's notionally part of at any rate.

The shade of William Glasdale appears to him, solid under the afternoon sun; plated, wry, dry of eye and leaking weed and river water from the hinges of his harness. *Did I not tell you? Killing her is not enough. You must destroy her. And for that, you have to find out who she is.*

Matthieu knew and Matthieu is dead.

There are others who know. What about the men who brought her to France? Find them! Question them!

Tomas eases his hammer from his belt, swallows on a throat gone dry, looks to where he can insert himself into the action in a way that won't lose the respect he's creating for himself among these people.

'She's not dead.' He's at the wall when word passes from Raoul to Ricard to Patrick Ogilvy, to him. 'She's not dead. Praise be to God, the Maid is not dead. She's coming back to the fight. We shall take Jargeau in her name. Pass the news. The Maid is not dead.'

'Thank God.'

'Thank God.'

'Thank God.'

Tomas is not a godly man; he has killed too often in far too venal circumstances for that, but he thanks God aloud with the rest, and continues to make a fine acquittal of himself.

The army breaks into Jargeau in the evening. The Maid has recovered from her fall and been back in the fray again. She comes into the main square at dusk, to supervise the securing of the town. Tomas, naturally, is nearby and so is witness yet again to the moment when she sweeps off her helm and runs ungloved fingers through her boy-short hair.

She is not a boy, whatever the English say. He has never thought she was. Her eyes meet his. Her black eyes, sharp, hot, prideful. He can sustain this. He can. He is not a man to hide from his enemies.

Her gaze passes on. He is one amongst thousands, no different from the rest. His loins ache and it doesn't help to know he is not alone. A thousand men, five thousand, are with him. They have all turned to face her, waiting.

'France!' She raises her fist.

The army echoes, five thousand throats as one. 'France!'

And then she lets them loose. This is war. If you resist a siege, you will suffer. Over the next forty-eight hours, the Maid's army lays waste to Jargeau, to its wine, its women, its velvets and linens, its goldware and silverware and pewter. Nobody cares that the defenders were French, that the women they rape may be the cousins of their wives, that the men they rob were once their friends. They were allied with the enemy, and now every man in every town between here and Paris knows that if you resist, your women will suffer the fate worse than death, and you will be ruined.

What Tomas Rustbeard knows is that he has missed his chance, and he is not – even now, lying in another man's goosedown bed – sure quite why he did so.

CHAPTER FIVE

Orléans,
Monday, 24 February 2014
07.35

HER APARTMENT IS EMPTY. Picaut knows this as she puts the key in the lock. Relief slips down her spine as she mounts the steep stone stairs from the door.

The restaurant below is closed and quiet, although by the first turn of the first flight she would be unable to hear anything even if the occupants were in full party mode. Luc's mother, who bought this place and furnished it for herself in the last year of the last millennium, had it soundproofed to industrial standards. A bomb could explode outside, and provided it was less than six kilograms of plastic explosive no sound would penetrate the living space above.

It gives a strange, dead feel. When she lived here, Picaut made a habit of throwing the windows open to let life back in again. Now, standing at the top of the third and last flight of perfect grey-pink marble, the soundlessness is her guarantor of solitude, and she is grateful.

She keys an eight-digit number into the pad on the right-hand side of the door and waits for two further hot-cold seconds to find out if Luc has been up here and changed the code.

He hasn't. On the third count, the door swings wide on buffered hinges.

She steps inside. This is her home, and at each return she feels more alien. This is why she sleeps elsewhere. Whatever Garonne thinks, it's not about sex or the comfort of intimacy, it's about avoiding the pale marble Louis XIV floors, the eau-de-Nil walls, the kitchen that looks like the flight deck of a 747, the dustless, soulless, silent judgement that weighs her as she walks through the door and finds her wanting.

The apartment is a shrine to a France that does not exist: a post-revolutionary monarchy, where the rich rule and the peasants know their place. Picaut has been the blot on its landscape from the moment Luc's mother gave her the deeds as a wedding present.

The wedding itself was a fiasco. Hélène Bressard had so carefully underdressed, not to outdo the bride, that she could have walked naked into church and made less of a sensation. To give her due credit, she kept away from the crowds, but the paparazzi still caught on camera the moment when she cornered Picaut and kissed her on the cheek, pressing the envelope into her hands.

The images didn't record the conversation, but they caught the look on Picaut's face as Luc's mother said, 'You're one of the Family now.'

She wasn't. She wasn't ever likely to be, but she understands now, as she didn't then, that this was their way of buying her in. They didn't know her, nor she them. Her doubt was obvious enough for Hélène to tuck an arm beneath her elbow and press her head close. 'Landis drew up the deeds. They're watertight.'

Picaut didn't know Uncle Landis then, either, but she knew his reputation. The cameras caught her blistering smile and that was the image that graced the magazines and made her a celebrity for the whole of the next week so that her friends walked on eggshells in her presence, thinking her lost to them for ever.

She, of course, thought she was bringing Luc to the light, that he was a wild and radical maverick who had dared to step out of his family's reactionary straitjacket for the love of ideals based on worth, not on gold, for equality, for grace, for understanding: for her.

Here, now, five years on, this apartment is the morgue in which lies her self-delusion. In the kitchen, where the smell of fresh coffee sharpens the air, is the early row over the morning papers that broke open the sham of Luc's politics. It took her longer than it should have done to realize that he had never walked free of the Family, never could, never would, never wanted to. He is, was and will always be a dyed in the wool conservative, more dangerous, more insidious than any member of Le Pen's *Front National*, because he knows how to cloak his extremism in the language of reason.

She carries her coffee to the bedroom, where lies the over-sized bed in which it became painfully clear that her role was to bear the next generation of Bressard men – and that conceiving a girl would be as much of a failure as failing to conceive at all.

She had her pills, and never stopped taking them. No children, ever; she had said that from the start. Luc had not believed her. She wasn't the only one who had grown to regret their early self-delusion.

Leaning into the walk-in wardrobe which still contains her clean clothes, she selects a winter shirt, clean jeans, socks, underwear, trainers. Her leather jacket remains; it always remains. She hasn't taken it off yet. She closes the bedroom door behind her. She couldn't sleep here if she tried.

There's a pile of post in the hallway. She lifts it on to a side table, sorting the bills from the circulars and leaving both for later.

She does not – will not – go into the living room, but she pauses in passing, much as she did just after midnight on New Year's Eve when she overheard the mellow, man-to-man conversation in which Luc and Uncle Landis rehearsed the detail of her husband's proposed ascent to power: election to Mayor of Orléans in 2014 and from there to the presidency in 2016.

Hollande, however much they loathe him, proved this route was possible, and the Family is ready to stretch its wings. For generations beyond counting, it has spread its influence across the south of France, into Germany, Switzerland, trans-Alpine Italy. In every conflict, it has posted people on either side: for the English, against the English; for the Spanish, against the Spanish; for Napoleon, against him; for the revolution, for the king . . . actually, rather more for the king than against him, but that has been massaged out of memory.

More recently, they had collaborators in the Vichy government and the Milice even while others slipped into the forest to join the Maquis, or hid English agents for the Resistance. In '44, they sent younger members to infiltrate the Communists when it seemed as if they might conquer the whole of France after the war, and they had others already working hand-in-glove with the Americans to make sure such a catastrophe couldn't happen.

But until now, they have been contained in the south. If you were to draw a line from Lyon to Bordeaux and look down, everything below it is theirs and has been for ever. This is where the money resides, where the sea laps at Marseilles, Monaco, Montpellier. Stretch a little east and you can touch the contacts in Turin, the banks in Zurich, the big families of Barcelona. Now, though, they have a new goal. In two years, the Family plans to sweep Luc along a route that took the current president nearly a decade. Lack of ambition has never been one of their failings.

This, then, is what they were planning, the detail of it, as Picaut passed the door.

'And what about your wife?' Uncle Landis asked. All the weight in that one word.

'Inès will be at my side.' Luc spoke with the precision of one who has drunk to the point of absolute honesty. 'She may be difficult in some things, but in this she knows her place.'

Picaut was gone by the morning. Since then, she has communicated with her husband only through her lawyer and has made sure she is never alone in his presence.

She owns this apartment; Landis was true to his word. If the divorce gives her nothing else, this is her pension, and a good one. Luc left within a week, but it still doesn't feel secure and her own lawyer has told her not to change the combination on the number pad that locks the door, not to do anything that might give Landis ammunition to suggest her a less-than-perfect wife. She has not been back often in the past eight weeks.

She reaches the wet-room at the far end of the hallway and stands on the heated marble floor, discarding her ash-strewn clothes.

This, oddly, is her favourite place. In here she is safe. She can lock the door if she needs to, and because she can, she doesn't. The window faces east, to the rising sun, the shutters are open, the glass opaque. She stands in front of it naked, feeling the grit of the night rough against the soft skin under her arms, in the fold beneath her breasts, in her ears, her hair, her eyes, her nose.

She turns on the shower. The steam builds to the high

ceiling. She steps underneath and hot water seeks out the places where falling cinders burned her.

She burns again, and there is a part of her that revels in the pain and draws it inside, as if by this she might come to know what burning is, might reduce it, might make it manageable. The sight of a man's incinerated corpse will not leave her, nor the manner of his death. She could be sneezing out charred parts of the body, washing him out of her hair . . .

She turns round and lets the power wash her shoulders, the curve of her back. She leans into the pressure, is held by it, could sleep in it . . . Is sleeping in it—

'Inès? Is that you?'

She rockets forward into dryness and cold. Her eyes snap open.

'*Luc?*'

He is standing in the doorway to the shower room, his eyes wide, his hair awry. He is a dark god, a sculpture of pure beauty, and the shock of his presence punches through her belly, a raw, ripe thing, snatching at animal instincts that have lain dormant these past four months. She draws a halting breath.

'Inès . . .' With one hand, he reaches for her. Lust lights his eyes, carves new lines around his mouth.

She hasn't seen him since January, and he is here, and he wants her, and every plane of his face, of his being, is stronger than memory, more glorious. She remembers his touch, his breath on her cheek, his hands on her breasts, on the flat of her abdomen, the downward drift of his lips. Her nipples should be rosily soft from the heat. They are not; they are brown and solid as chalk stubs and they ache for—

Inès knows her place.

She grabs a towel and scrubs herself with it. 'Get out.'

70

Her eyes are windows to her soul. His reaching hand drops. He takes a breath to speak, thinks better of it and backs away, shaking his head. '*Pardon. J'suis désolé. Pardon.*'

Luc never apologizes. Not ever.

She asks, 'Why are you here?'

'They said . . . The fire.' He looks haggard, as if he, too, has had no sleep. He pulls himself together, gives a brief, apologetic shrug. 'I thought you wouldn't be here.'

'That's why *now*, not why *here*.'

'I needed some clothes.' He glances down at the heaps on the floor, one filthy, one ironed by the day-woman. 'Like you.' He has backed right to the door. He makes another conciliatory gesture with his hands, palms up, submissive. 'I'll come back later. If that's all right?'

She shrugs; she cannot trust her voice. He eases himself out. His head is the last to go, his eyes feasting on her, his voice a caress. 'You are so very beautiful.'

Now, he says it: *now*, and her father not alive to tell. Listening to him leave, she stands dry-eyed in the folds of her towel, and wonders what it will take to make her weep.

CHAPTER SIX

THE CAR RADIO SPEAKS to her endlessly of the fire, and of the possible identity of the body.

A woman from the US State Department says the National Security Agency is focusing its considerable resources on Jaish al Islam. The implication is that America will succeed where France has failed.

Picaut hits the column switch. The hush that fills the car could all too easily be filled by Luc. He hovers half a thought away, and his closeness threatens to melt her marrow.

She stares ahead, but he smiles back at her from every second billboard: Votez Bressard!

The trams are no better. She turns on to the bridge across the Loire, looks down at the heavy, chocolaty water. Here is the bridge to the tower of les Tourelles. Here is the site of the battle that launched the Maid as the city's hero. Here are the crowding memories of her father, which are not useful. Two deep breaths and she's safely across and on into the new development south of the river, that didn't exist in the Maid's time.

She considers the water. Yesterday it rained and today, here, now, the Loire is gorged to fullness. But it was not raining last night, when the fire was lit. The arsonists have one eye on the weather forecast, which, if nothing else, is part of a pattern and it is in patterns that answers are found.

The traffic is easing. Just before nine, she pulls into the car park of the pathology suite adjacent to the Hôpital de la Source in southern Orléans. The receptionist nods as she passes, heading for the second floor.

'Have you a name for me yet?'

Black on silver, cased in white, the roasted body of the unknown maybe-American lies curled on a stainless-steel table in the shining new white-tiled autopsy room.

Free of Luc, dressed and clean, Picaut feels sharper than she has any right to do after a night of so little sleep. She docks her phone in the slot on the wall and hitches up to sit on a stainless-steel table.

'Not yet.' Éric Masson does not raise his head. 'One eighty-six, Caucasian, fitter than average, a runner, or more probably a climber; his upper body has muscling here – here – here.' His pointer circles shoulders, pectorals, biceps. 'No ID so far.' He looks up. 'X-rays. Get clear.'

Picaut hitches off the table, slides behind a screen of leaded glass and watches him work with a professional appreciation for his clinical precision.

The facility is a little over two years old, a relic of Sarkozy's pre-election largesse. Beneath the scents of antiseptic and death, it's still possible to smell the faint new-build aura of paint and plaster.

Lured here from the Hammersmith in London, which

73

had lured him from Harvard, which had lured him from Montpellier, Dr Éric Masson has been in place since the day the lab doors opened.

He had considered and rejected offers of post-doctoral funding from Groningen and Heidelberg. When asked why he eschewed honour and fame in favour of a relative backwater, he says that his second wife was from Orléans, but, if he's honest, it was the chance to mould the department in his own image that persuaded him to come.

Picaut has never asked. She watches him, crisply green in theatre scrubs and latex gloves, his widow's peak trapped beneath a neat green cap. He is silent, immersed in that technology and its pleasures.

Three days a week, Rosa, his technician, turns her hand to radiography, but she has four children under the age of ten and he is kind enough not to drag her into work when he doesn't need her. There is an office rumour that Rosa – dark, petite, with ravishing eyes – is the reason for his latest divorce, but Picaut has seen them work together and thinks they are too comfortable in each other's company ever to have been lovers.

Fifteen minutes pass, in which time Picaut checks her phone and reviews the report sent in by Garonne, bracketed top and bottom by a rant about Jaish al Islam and the damage they are doing to the fabric of France.

He has statements now from all the witnesses. The only one remotely of interest is Monique Susong, the tall black woman who works for *Vogue Paris* and has come south from the capital, so she says, on the strength of a fashion rumour concerning some minor celebrity who was said to have been spotted in an Orléans bar wearing something off-trend.

Garonne thinks this is so laughably implausible that it's clearly a cover story and even Picaut, who could not be less interested in the vagaries of fashion, could have told anyone who'd asked that the chances of a Celebrity Event's taking place in Orléans were vanishingly small.

She is not, however, inclined to let Monique Susong get on the next train to Paris, however loudly and frequently she offers the view that Orléans is a tedious little dump and she would be eternally happy if she could return to the metropolis at their earliest convenience. Picaut sends a text to this effect to Garonne, then docks the phone and allows herself the luxury of Éric Masson's latest coffee.

Along with his acknowledged expertise in forensic pathology, Éric nurses a passion for single-estate beans, freshly ground and brewed with spring water. This month's sample is from Tarrazu in Costa Rica. A map showing the exact location and a review from Fortnum & Mason grace the data card pinned up behind the grinder. *Creamy and full-bodied, yet with a citrusy flavour . . .*

Picaut doesn't often get to grind the beans and she loses herself in their earthy sensuality, the roll of them in her hand, the spin and jive in the grinder as they leap and leap away from the blades. She catches the tang of citrus but it's the caffeine that sweeps away the fog and lets her think again.

A man of unknown identity has died in a fire.

Luc was at the apartment.

A man of unknown identity has been murdered in the latest of four fires, each of which has fallen within the confines of the city of Orléans and is therefore under the jurisdiction of her department.

Luc was at the apartment and he looked more unsettled than she has ever seen him. He said she looked beautiful.

A man of unknown identity has been murdered in the latest of four fires, each of which has been claimed by Jaish al Islam, an organization about which she knows nothing, and nor does anyone else.

They have not managed to infiltrate it, or tapped its phones, or listened to its email traffic, or met any of its members. As far as the world is concerned, Jaish al Islam did not exist before the first fire, but now the global anti-terrorism fraternity wants to know everything she knows, which is painfully little. Luc is a minor problem when set beside the scale of this. She can ignore him. She will.

Her Nokia, parked in its dock, lets loose the medley of Inuit throat singers that is Patrice's ring tone. Touch-sensitive areas on all four walls allow her to pick up the call.

'Picaut.' The water is boiling again. She pours it on to the filter and watches black gold drip into her cup.

'Did the Hôtel Carcassonne keep a backup in the Cloud?'

'Slower, Patrice. That sound you can hear is only the second coffee of the day.'

His laugh is muted, for the sake of her fragility. She can imagine him, hunched over the phone, his platinum-blond pony-tail gathered back in a magenta scrunch, his nose a little too big to be classical but matched by strong features, a black T-shirt adorned with the latest design, crowd-sourced from a cultural milieu Picaut has never explored.

He lives in a parallel world, which runs a little bit faster, a little bit younger than her own. Now he is trying to reach over to her side of the line. Slowly, he says, 'I had a thought: did the owner of the burned-out hotel—?'

'Madame Foy.'

'That's the one. Did Madame Foy keep a backup of the hotel's hard drive on a remote site, or in the Cloud some-where? If she did, we could access it and find the name of your corpse.'

'To access anything, we'd need the permission of Madame Foy which she is hardly going to hand over, given her current state of high umbrage. And we won't get a war-rant for a fishing trip.'

76

There is a delicate silence. Patrice's father was something big in military cyber-security, which means the young Patrice was playing Diablo pretty much as soon as he could speak and graduated on to World of Warcraft in its vanilla incarnation at launch.

From there it was a short step to darker waters. He was a black-hat hacker, and founder member of S1NK, otherwise known as the S1lverFish Ninja Kolektiv, until a plea bargain with someone a great deal higher up the food chain brought him across the legal side of the line. Mostly. The silence has weight.

Picaut closes her eyes. 'Whatever you do, I don't want to know.'

'What if I get a name?'

'Match it to the dentals from Éric. Or the DNA. Or something.'

'Done.'

Patrice hangs up. Picaut hits the touch-square with the point of her elbow. On the inner surface of her closed lids is an image of Prosecutor Ducat and what he will do if he finds out.

'*Capitaine?*'

She opens her eyes and finds Éric Masson standing in front of her, his head cocked towards the darkened viewing suite to one side of the pm room. His radiographs are ready.

'Want to see?'

'You tell me.'

He gives his quiet half smile. 'You'll want to.'

Packed with the highest of high technology that only Masson and Patrice understand, the suite is nonetheless a place for calm reflection. Picaut has seen him in here with Patrice, and knows that whatever he says about his ex-wife, it was this meeting of minds which lured Éric Masson away from what he called his H^3 post-doctoral pop-idol posting.

The place is snug without being claustrophobic. It has no windows and the lights are adjusted to dusk or dawn temperatures; the décor is quietly minimal. One wall is made up of a video screen, on which swirling pastel screensavers further pacify the mind until Masson begins to call up the images.

There are no keyboards here; everything is done by touch or voice.

When she first came here, if she looked at a radiograph at all she saw a haphazard array of white blurs on a black background, repeating patterns that made no sense, however hard her brain tried to fit them to something she knew.

Now, after two years of Éric Masson's tuition, she can start at the top, with the outline of the cranium, and immediately pick out the irregular spider's web of fractures above the black space of the left eye socket and the greyed mess of haemorrhage behind it.

'Big cranial bleed? Was he hit on the crown of the head as well as over his eye?'

'Good. Go on.'

She runs her gaze on down from there to the mandible. She takes another sip of coffee, rolls it round her mouth. Her tongue curls against the bitterness. Her body craves more.

'Did you send the dental images?'

'Patrice is working on them now.'

Picaut eases out a breath. The threat of Prosecutor Ducat takes one pace back.

She checks her watch: 09.27. She places a small bet with herself as to how long Patrice will take to ID their man. And then, because there's clearly something else she is supposed to be seeing, she scans on down from head to clavicle to sternum, to ribs, spine, arms, hands, pelvic girdle, legs, feet.

And back to the thorax, the cage of white, splayed ribs overlaid on the grey shadows of the heart and lungs. And in that cage, a foreign object, bright-white, with square, manu-factured corners.

'What's that?' She taps the screen with a pointer.

'Good question. I'd say it's what our American cousins call a thumb drive and the rest of us in the civilized world call a USB drive.'

'What's it doing in the middle of his chest? Is it even possible to stab someone with a USB drive? Was there an entry wound? I didn't see one.'

'Look again.' Masson is in teaching mode. Picaut is not in the mood to be a student, but then she rarely is, and he's taught her anyway.

She reviews her understanding of basic anatomy. In the chest are the heart, the lungs, the trachea . . . and the route from the mouth to the stomach. 'Is it in his oesophagus? Has he *swallowed* it?'

A broad smile transforms Éric Masson's lean face; he is young again, animated. 'Swallowed shortly before death. It got this far and no further.' He leans back, the better to watch her. 'He knew he was going to die. He left you the answers to your questions.'

'Fuck . . .' She whistles. 'Patrice will think it's Christmas.'

'If the fire hasn't cooked the data to illegibility.' Masson sees the look on her face. '*Courage, mon brave.* Shall we find out?'

He works swiftly, neatly, cleanly. Charred skin peels back from roasted flesh and the brown bone of the cooked sternum. The bandsaw whines and the smell of burning bone is the same as it was in the night.

Picaut's phone rings again. She checks her watch. 09.40. Patrice is two minutes inside her estimated time. Grinning, she hits the elbow switch, putting the call on to speaker. 'You win. Who is he?'

'Luc,' he says, and the echo of his voice in the hollow room sounds as if he's taken a mouthful of dog shit. 'He's here. He says he needs to see you. Actually, he says he needs you. On a different note, the dead man is a Dr Iain Holloway from Glasgow. That's Glasgow, Scotland, not Glasgow, Kentucky.'

'He's not American?'

'Doesn't look that way. I'll have more on him by the time you get here. Just don't let Luc drag you down into whatever hole he's digging for himself.'

CHAPTER SEVEN

TOMAS RUSTBEARD'S SECOND CHANCE to kill the Maid comes three days after the first, at night, during the attack on the gatehouse protecting Meung-sur-Loire.

It is the middle of June and the nights are as short as they're going to get. Dusk bleeds into dawn with scarcely enough dark between to blink, although in that scarcity is enough to do what they must, or so the Maid has said and nobody contradicts her now. Since Jargeau, she is the army's favourite: men will die for her and think themselves blessed.

From the wave of fury that followed her injury, Tomas has learned that he dare not kill her in the open field. He may, however, assault her in the dark, with few around. Beyond that, he has long recognized that night loosens tongues which the sun holds fast, and, tonight, he is seeking answers as much as action, for on this expedition are some of the men who brought the Maid to Chinon and began this whole misadventure.

Thus does he find himself part of the Maid's assaulting troop, which at this moment requires him to crawl across a hundred yards of open ground and flop belly down in a ditch, less than a hundred paces from a gatehouse that stands on a bridge which in turn guards the route across the Loire to the town of Meung.

Summer has been kind. The ditch is dry. It smells of good, clean earth and crushed grass. He leans out, watching, waiting for the right man to pass by, and when he does . . .

'Hey!' As if by chance, a hoarse whisper. 'Here!'

'Where?' A bulky figure, good boots, an axe in his belt, slowing.

'Here, by your feet.'

A slide, a shiver of mail, a crunch, and he has company: Bertrand de Poulangy, man at arms, former equerry to Yolande of Aragon, Queen of Sicily and Naples and the King of France's redoubtable mother-in-law.

Yolande is a woman of notorious fortitude. When the present king's two older brothers each died in 'accidents' at the hands of their mother, it was Yolande who rescued the young Charles, brought him south to her lands of Aragon and then dared anyone to come and get him. Without her, nobody is in any doubt that Charles VII would be dead and the young Henry VI would be king of a united France.

Tomas, of course, loathes her. Bertrand de Poulangy, by all accounts, worships the very air she breathes. A handful of years into his fifth decade, de Poulangy is an old man to be running round the countryside at night. Old, and acting very much beneath his station. His mistress, it is said, trusts him beyond anyone else. Which is rather the point.

He rolls over now, peers out into the inky night. 'Where's the Maid?'

'Over there, by the oak.' Tomas points right and forward. 'Body of Christ, but it's dark.'

'Ha!' De Poulangy's fist bounces softly off his arm. 'You shouldn't swear. She can hear you at a thousand paces.'

'What's she going to do? Make me confess again?'

When he was on the English side, Tod Rustbeard confessed once a year at Easter, if he remembered at all. In the weeks since he came to the French side, he has knelt in penitence more often than the sum total of the rest of his life. He has not, of course, confessed the nature of his business here. His father was a bishop. He lost his fear of the church a long time ago.

De Poulangy settles deeper into the ditch. 'Think yourself lucky you're not taking Mass with her. She made us stop at dusk and dawn when we brought her up to Chinon in February.'

'You were one of . . .' Tomas feigns awe. '*You* brought the Maid to the king at the year's start?'

He hears a humble, self-denying laugh. It has had a lot of practice these past few months, that laugh.

Careless, Tomas says, 'I heard it took you thirteen days each way, riding only at night.'

'Eleven,' Bertrand says, which, actually, is exactly what the gossip said, but it never hurts to underestimate a man's accomplishments to his face if you want to oil his tongue. 'Eleven nights in the first days of February, through enemy lands; me and Jean de Metz and the Maid, riding flat to the ground in the pitch black and filthy rain and mud up to the girth and frost making ice on the tracks when it wasn't raining. By day we slept under the trees in the forest, and even so, I lost count of the times we had to hide in a ditch while Burgundy's men went by.'

To think Burgundy could have caught her at the outset. And he'd have killed her, too, no question. The English might bear no love for the French that stand against them, but there's nothing like a falling-out among family to foster a genuinely vicious hatred. The Duke of Burgundy may be the King of France's cousin, but the Duke of Burgundy prefers to swear his allegiance to England. Burgundy's loathing of all things French is mutual and mortal.

That's not the point tonight, though. Here, now, Tomas Rustbeard has other toads to skin. Carefully, carefully, keeping it as a joke between men: 'So did you teach her to ride on the way?'

Because this is one of the biggest gaps in the whole improbable story: he is supposed to believe that a peasant girl brought up in a land reduced to penury by eighty years of warfare could make the kind of ride that leaves his joints sweating just to think about it.

She rode from Vaucouleurs to Chinon in eleven days? At night? In *February*? Are you insane? When would she even have seen a riding horse, still less learned to ride one well enough to stay on for that distance?

'Ha! No, no. That one's been riding from the time she could walk. Her father taught her and he was the best in France. I heard her tell Jean d'Alençon that she spent five years posing as a horse b—'

De Poulangy's teeth click tight shut. Oiled, but not loose. Incautious, maybe, but not stupid. And infinitely loyal to Yolande, and now to the Maid. He grunts, rolls his shoulders, eases his blade from his belt, peers out over the edge of the ditch. Gruffly: 'God, but I hate waiting. Come on, you English bastards, come out and get us.'

So close. So very close. This is better, even, than getting near to Claudine. The effort it takes to match the other man's tone is as great as any Tomas can remember. He says, 'They won't. Nobody leaves a fortified emplacement at night.'

'So we'll have to go to them.'

'That's the plan.' Take the gatehouse and block the bridge and lock three thousand English men at arms across the river in Meung where they can't do any harm to the French cause. It's a decent plan, more humane than the assault on

Jargeau, and it'll work as long as the English don't realize what is happening.

They haven't done yet, and when the call of an owl sounds three times, Bertrand de Poulangy, queen's man and now Maid's man, looks left and right and slips over the edge. Tomas's hammer weighs in his hand. It's tempting to take de Poulangy down with a swift tap to the back of the head, but this is not the time to give way to passing fancies. Follow, then, and swiftly.

From right and left, men crouch-crawl-slither over meadow grass, past scrubby thorns, sliding in from their ditches and hedges, gathering on the Maid, where she waits behind a fallen oak.

What were you? A horse boy? A horse breaker? Horse buyer? Did you take to doublet and hose before you ever set out for Chinon? Half a sentence more from de Poulangy and he'd know.

Even without that, she's barely a hammer's throw away. He might just try his luck and be done with it, but d'Alençon is crowding close and with him are Jean d'Aulon, her squire, and Étienne de Vignolles, called La Hire for his hedgehog hair, or his ire, nobody seems to know which.

If there are any men left in France who can fight, it's these three. Any one of them could crush Tomas without a thought and he's not ready for that. He wants to witness the chaos when she's gone. He has an axe now, to go with his hammer. He hefts one in each hand and slides in closer to the oak tree and the gathering men.

The Maid sits on her heels and counts them all in: fifty men at arms, all with their harness bound up with rags for the quiet, all eager as hound whelps, kneeling in the summer grass, filled with love and holy ardour.

She rises, a shining beacon in her unmarked armour. She wears it as Henry did, the late king, as a second skin. She sleeps in it, which is as good a defence against nocturnal assassination as any; only her face shows, heart-shaped in the bassinet, strong black brows, curved mouth, sharp, black eyes.

She says, 'Fifty English men at arms hold the gatehouse. We need to take it before anyone comes across the bridge from the town.'

She points a mailed fist. 'La Hire, take a dozen to the left. D'Alençon, a dozen to the right. You know what to do. Those who remain are with me for a frontal assault.'

Jesu, but she speaks like a general. Glasdale himself didn't give orders less precise than this. And men snap to her bidding: La Hire is a knight; Jean d'Alençon is a cousin of the king. He's married to the Duke of Orléans's daughter, for God's sake. Has he no shame? It isn't *right*.

Men edge close to her, not wanting to leave. La Hire and d'Alençon have to prise their groups away. Tomas has not been sent off; he knows how to make himself small and readily missed. With La Hire and d'Alençon gone, he manoeuvres himself to the front of the main body as they stride up the last fifty paces to the gatehouse.

No hiding now. If the watch isn't asleep . . . no, they're not.

'French! Goddamned French! Sound the—'

'Ricard.' The Maid's voice is a bell in the chaos.

She doesn't have longbowmen, but she has Ricard de Saran, who is handy with a crossbow and has three men loading spares for him. His second bolt takes the watch in the throat, which is what you get for standing in plain sight while you yell your warnings.

And then everyone is in plain sight. Fifty English men at arms, who have slept with their harness on their backs and their blades in their hands since Jargeau was lost, are up and at the walls and a bailey is calling orders and a horn sounds, and if they're not fast now the enemy garrison in the main defences a quarter of a mile across the river will sweep down and slaughter them and . . . damnation, but it's hard to remember which side he's on.

Tomas is running with the French, but the English will kill him if he doesn't kill them first. He's wearing mail and his beard is hidden; nobody will know him. So just for now, he's French. *French*. Scream at the English. Hit them if you have to. Run.

The Maid has brought a ram: an oak trunk with lead set behind an iron tip. Eight big Orléanais carry it at a swift trot. Eight others hold shields above their heads to ward off arrows. Or oil. If they have any sense, the defenders will have had oil on the fire. Or sand. Or water.

It seems not.

Fools.

Ten men are left around the Maid, of whom Tomas is one. He presses closer. Hammer in the right hand, axe in the left; swap them over. Swap them back. One day soon, he'll fight with two hammers. Or two axes, maybe?

The Maid's an axe-holder too; you don't need a shield when you're in full plate. Shields are for children and peasants: she bears an axe always in her left hand, her Crusader sword in her right. It was owned once by Charlemagne, dug up from some distant church at her command. One day, Tomas will find out how she did that. It flashes now in the light of new torches lit by the English. Where are the English archers? They must have—

The ram is through. God damn, but that was fast. Half a dozen thundering blows and they're in! Run! Run! Through the broken gate and duck under the lintel and into the dark courtyard with the flashing torches and already the place smells of latrines and blood. It's too dark to tell whom he's fighting, only that someone is trying to kill him and he has good reason to stay alive.

From his left, he hears, 'On me! Men of France! Gather on the Maid!' Her voice is deep for her sex, but still flexed with the timbre of womanhood, not the coarse burr of a man. She's gone ahead. Tomas pushes up towards her.

Iron flashes front and back. The entire defending force is here at the gate. Are they insane? There are two groups coming in from the sides and they haven't left anyone on watch. This is what fear does, and losing, and thinking you have a demon sent against you.

'Die, God damn you! Die!' In English. From the side.

His hammer is up, swinging hard to the right. Someone dies, his side or theirs, he honestly doesn't care. The Maid's ahead and he has to get to her. He sweeps his axe in a vicious back-handed cut at a looming face, fends off a thrust with his mailed elbow, traps the sword under his armpit, bears down.

Teeth shatter. A head snaps back. If not dead, then down, and she's three paces in front, her blade a whipcrack in the leering orange torchlight, her voice pure as a choirboy's, pealing over the fray.

'France! France!'

I'll give you France, you little bitch. A leap, a twist, past two men locked fist to face and back again. A spin of his hammer – God, he loves this hammer – and a helmet dented deep enough to thrust your fist halfway in, and an Englishman screaming, trying to pull it off. Stamp on him as he goes down and – *yes!* – he's beside her. This is it. Her back is to his back, plate to mail; he can feel the press of it. He could howl for sheer satisfaction. Nobody will know whose blow killed her. Already he is cradling her ruined body, carrying it back through the broken gate, weeping bitter tears as the French gather round him and retreat. There aren't enough of them here to cause the cataclysm of Jargeau.

Or maybe he rips off his helm and declares himself English: 'Tod Rustbeard has just killed the demon!' Talbot and Scales, the English commanders, will honour him; Knights of the Garter, both. He'll be knighted, at the very least. Bedford will give him a manor; he has enough to spare. They'll forgive him the men he's killed; these things happen in war. One day, when the infant King Henry is grown, he'll call him in to listen to the story and . . .

He feels her shift towards him, turns, lifts his hammer high. His shoulders are hot, burning with the need to strike. One blow. Between the eyes. She is not a demon. God does not watch over her. Do it!

'Look out!' The press of her plate springs clean away. She's spinning. Her axe is a blur of molten metal, scything down to his left. A sword shatters; not hers. 'Tomas, look right!'

No!

Three of them, bearing York's colours out of Ludlow. Big men of the Marches with polearms fit to skewer him. He ducks down under the first as it jabs at his face, drops his axe, grabs the haft, pulls hard, sharp, angles the wood down and stamps on it and throws his hammer – gone! His hammer! – into the oncoming face.

'With me!' She's making space for him, sweeping sword and axe in two killing arcs. Men slew back out of her way. She is a knight and in truth only other knights can hope to match against her and there are none here: Talbot and Scales are across the river.

The pikemen are doing their best, but she uses her body, cased in plate, to block the next strike, rides the blow, lets it spin her in towards the third of the three. 'Ricard! Here!'

They are mailed, not plated, and Ricard the crossbowman pitches his quarrel from less than twenty paces. He might as well stand right up against them. The bolt punches straight through. The third of the men drops like a stunned heifer even as his pike scores along Tomas's chest.

He feels the sting of it, and the rush of relief, and the last man is his to take, stooping for his fallen hammer, left and right, hammer and axe in a blizzard of battle heat. They tried to kill him. Him! Fuck them all. It doesn't matter which side they're on, he will kill anyone who tries to kill him. He is not ready to die. Not here. Not now.

And the Maid is away, calling La Hire at one side and d'Alençon at the other as both come in over the walls and these three meet in the middle, the king's three knights, and she is one of them, shining.

Alive.

He watches her go, and curses her shade and her shining face. You did not come out of nowhere. Somebody made you. Whoever you really are, wherever you came from, I will kill you, and then I will destroy the legend you have made for yourself. I, Tomas Rustbeard, swear this.

The next day, rising early, Tomas hears a rumour that Bedford has sent reinforcements from Paris, commanded by no less than Fastolf himself, Knight of the Garter and one of England's best.

Nobody cares. No man among the French army stirs himself. They don't believe it, and even if it's true the English did not arrive in time to save Jargeau or Meung. Nor, as the days pass, do they arrive in time for Beaugency, the next town along the Loire, which surrenders without terms.

The Maid's victorious army grows in numbers. It's not true, evidently, that the French have no knights at all; simply that they choose not to fight for a weakling king.

Being on the winning side, though, that's a different matter. Men appear who have not dusted off their plate in over a decade, and they ride with a new sense of purpose.

They head north, aiming for Rheims, where generations

of Gallic kings have been anointed with holy oil and thereby acknowledged monarch of all France in the eyes of God. The English have not yet brought the young king Henry VI for any kind of anointing. To get there first will go a long way to silencing those who say that Charles VII of France is not his father's son and has no legitimate claim to the throne.

Tomas Rustbeard rides north in the wake of the Maid. He is not in her inner circle, but he is close enough for there to be other chances to kill did he try to take them.

He does not. Jargeau and Meung together have combined to teach him that Glasdale was right and he, Tomas, was wrong: it is not enough to kill this woman, he must destroy her, and to do that, he must expose every part of her fabrications.

Accordingly, he lays plans, or rather a single plan with many threads to its weft, first of which is that he needs to get to Paris to see Bedford, because if he is going to change his mission he has to speak to the regent, a lord who does not take readily to his servants having their own ideas.

CHAPTER EIGHT

LUC IS IN THE FOYER.

Picaut feels him before she sees him. She feels him in the stares of the men and women coming down the steps, in the tilted heads, in the questions that are given no voice. It's astonishing how many people work in this building, and every single one of them has come down to take a look.

Luc shines. He is their hero, so French you could press wine from his bone marrow and olive oil from his tear ducts; so well bred, he is the closest they have to royalty.

He is only one seventy-eight, not Sarkozy-small, but not so tall as to be intimidating. He has perfect teeth and southern skin and he wears just few enough clothes to let everyone know that it's all muscle under there, no fat. His hair is lushly black and flops across his face in a way that is at once shy and full of courage. His cheekbones are Bogart, his eyes pure Clooney. He is the young Alain Delon, c. 1964, straight out of *The Unvanquished*, and even men grow silent in his presence.

He is standing now in the seedy foyer of the police station that is Picaut's place of work and half the women will be having orgasms at the mere sight of him and the other half will stare at Picaut as she walks in, wondering how, and why – for fuck's sake, *why?* – she ever left him.

Nobody has yet asked if he beat her, but the question hangs over their heads, just waiting for someone to pick up the courage to speak it aloud.

Patrice remains unmoved. He pushes through the crowd and takes the steps in one leap to land before Picaut as she stands at the bottom.

'Sauron,' he says, as they press kiss to cheek, which is distracting enough to draw Picaut's attention away from Luc.

His T-shirt says, VICTOR IS DEAD. GET OVER IT. with a particularly angelic image of the wide-eyed revenant child beneath.

More importantly, her memory of him is badly askew. Sometime since she last saw him – yesterday? Maybe the day before? – he has found the time to dye his platinum-blond hair in a shade of sparkling, metallic, kingfisher blue. The trailing tip of his pony tail reaches down to his waist, which she thinks is also new. It is possible that he may be wearing hair extensions.

She is not sure of the implications of this. Is it more or less a sign of metrosexuality than eye shadow? She hasn't actually seen him wearing that, but she thinks he has turned up in mascara more than once. She realizes that he has spoken and she has no idea what he has said.

'What?'

'Sauron. From LOTR. In Warcraft, he'd be the Orc Warlock standing in a corner of the flag room spamming chaos bolts while—' He sees her face, the incomprehension spreading across it, flashes a grin that is all mischief. 'Never mind. Power turns him on the way gold turns on some men, or drugs, or money. That's so not you. Why did you marry him?'

'I was young,' says Picaut, which just about covers it. 'And the sex was out of this world.' She can say this safely to Patrice, in ways she couldn't to Ducat or Garonne, even in the good times. The rise of his brow is wry, not lewd. Unwilling, she asks, 'Did he say what he wanted?'

'No. But if he's trying for mayor, he's going to need arm candy.'

'Fuck that. He can find someone else.'

'No, he can't. His type doesn't like to be seen to be cheating on their wives. It hurts their core vote.'

'Give me a couple of weeks and I won't be his wife.'

Patrice shrugs. 'Elections wait for no man. Or woman. He hasn't got a couple of weeks.'

'Jesus, *fuck*.'

'No.'

Patrice was right. Luc is in her office, which has glass walls and stands in the south-western corner of an open-plan set-up with desks for thirty officers. It's about as private as a fish tank, but at least the doors are closed and they can speak without every word's being tweeted to the world.

'I'm not being any man's arm candy.'

'I did *not* ask you to be my—'

'Yes, you did. Don't spin words at me. You want to be seen with a wife as a political accoutrement. You can call it what you want, but I think Patrice pretty much nailed it. You want me to know my place and you can fuck right off. I have no wish any longer to be your wife, trophy, anything. Find someone else. Walk out there and take your pick; you must know you can.'

'I can't.' He has vast, dark, liquid eyes. Picaut could drown

94

in them. This morning she nearly did. The skin behind her knees sweats at the memory and something bucks deep in her gut with a brutal, unforgiving urgency. She presses it down out of his sight and hers. She can outstare him if she has to.

He looks away. 'It has to be you,' he says. 'You're my wife.' And then, 'I love you.'

'*What?*'

She could count on the fingers of one hand – actually, just one finger – the number of times he has said this. It was six o'clock on the evening of 14 September 2009, the day he asked her to marry him. Not before, not since.

'I love you. I can't bear this separation. It's eating me alive. It's what I wanted to say this morning, but didn't have the courage. I know you don't want to be with me, and I'll accept that – but for now, please, I beg you, will you stand on a platform with me and smile as if you at least don't loathe me?'

'The papers, the news . . .' The gossip magazines trumpeted their break-up as the hot story of the winter. What they will do with this doesn't bear thinking about. Monique Susong will be glad she didn't leave Orléans. Her magazine will pay for her to stay.

Luc says, 'Let the Family deal with the media. The PR department has it in hand.' He gives the small smile he used when the Family was their in-joke; the two of them against the rest. 'Just don't deny any of their spin.' He leans over to kiss her cheek.

'Luc, I haven't—'

'I know. Let me say this.' His breath is feather-light on her cheek. 'The morning after I am elected as mayor, my lawyer will sign whatever your lawyer asks him to. Anything.'

'Don't be ridiculous. He'll never let you.' Uncle Landis is Luc's lawyer, a legal mind so expensive that not even Luc could afford him if he wasn't Family.

'He thought you'd say that. Here—' He produces a folded note from his pocket. The paper is faux parchment. Or perhaps it's real. One of the many reasons Inès Picaut could never truly have been Family is that she can't tell the difference. The seal is red wax, and breaks easily. Inside, the writing is in fountain pen, in a hand she knows.

Luc is telling you the truth. For your co-operation in his endeavour, we offer you freedom from your marital vows, on the terms of your choosing. This is our promise. Whatever you know of the Family, you know we never break our oath. Keep this paper. It will stand in court.

Landis Bressard, Monday, 24 February 2014

She stares at it a long time. Her lawyer is afraid of Landis Bressard. Nothing has been said, but Picaut knows the smell of terror. She knows, too, that he will lose any confrontation that comes to court.

She says, 'Say you get to be mayor, on a ticket of Bressard-flavoured rationality. At what point do the people of Orléans realize they are led by a family that makes the mafia look like a boy band and who thinks that the only problem with Hitler's vision of the Third Reich was that he just didn't have quite enough *conviction* to carry it off? Or do we wait until you're in the Elysée Palace and then all of France discovers it?'

'Inès . . .' He pinches the bridge of his nose. 'I know we have our differences, but I'm not . . . that. Do you honestly think Christelle Vivier's vision is better? Or that of the men behind her? Troy Cordier makes me look like a bleeding liberal, I promise you.'

Christelle Vivier of the *Front National* is Luc's main opponent in the mayoral race and Troy Cordier is her campaign manager. In truth, it's hard to imagine anyone being further to the right. The difference is that everyone knows what Troy is and Picaut is not sure even she knows what Luc really is, only that it's not what she wants him to be.

Luc drops his hands. He shrinks before her. 'Please, Inès. I won't win without you. And I honestly believe we are better than the Front.'

She holds up Landis's note, a barrier between them. 'I'll take this to Ducat. If he tells me it has no legal standing, I'll call a press conference and read it aloud. Your campaign will die on its feet.'

Ducat is no friend to the Family. In the past, this has been one more bone of contention. These last months, it has been his one saving grace.

'Even Ducat won't find holes in this, I promise you.' Luc's gaze is warm, friendly, conciliatory. 'Just stand by me and smile. Be my kingmaker. We ask nothing more.'

She shakes his proffered hand.

CHAPTER NINE

PATAY,
18 June 1429

IT IS ALMOST THE SOLSTICE. A week has passed since the assault on Jargeau which saw the Maid fall from the walls and rise again, victorious. Tomas and Patrick Ogilvy break fast together by a small, hot fire in the heart of the Maid's army.

Patrick Ogilvy says, 'Claudine was a ward of the king. And her brother, too.'

'Which king?' This may be a foolish question, but Tomas is newly woken, and the greater part of his mind is on the landscape around him, on the lowering thorns on every side, on the dips and valleys that might hide scouts, on the reported presence of five thousand English men at arms in the land they're about to ride through, and the likelihood of ambush sometime in the day.

In any case, even now, when someone says 'king' his mind goes to the English, warrior king, victor of Agincourt; Henry, fifth of the name, who may be dead, but was the king a man could fight for and not feel ashamed. That king would not have taken a whore as a ward, even if she wasn't yet a whore.

Because Claudine, it transpires, is not only friendly with Jean-Pierre, the master gunner, she has spread her favours through the French army, at least before the Maid made such freedoms fewer. By happy chance, Patrick Ogilvy was one of her winter friends. It has taken many days of quiet, casual questions to get this far, but, this morning, on waking, he remembers her fondly. 'She knew what a man liked. Cheerful, she was. Always grateful.'

Tomas rolls his eyes. 'The French king took wards?' It doesn't sound likely. What king takes in other men's children if he doesn't have to? Most of them have enough of their own, by the time you take in the broods of legal off-spring and the byblows.

'Her father died on the field of Agincourt. Her mother . . .' He frowns. 'I forget what happened to her mother, but anyway, she was dead. Claudine and her brother had nobody. And so the king took them in. He was called Best Beloved as well as the Mad. Charles le Bien Aimé. Maybe he just liked children.'

This is not a path Tomas wishes to explore. He begins to pack away the remnants of the morning's meal: oat bannocks, crisped black at the edges, and a duck egg, brought from Jargeau, that might not have been entirely fresh. His guts gripe mildly in its aftermath. 'So, why did she end up servicing the men? Did she not have a place in the king's household?'

'Not for long. She was thrown out after the old king died. Her and Matthieu – that's her brother—'

'The one who was murdered.'

'The one who spoke ill to the Maid and was struck down by God. Don't roll your eyes at me, Tomas Rustbeard, even the priests name it a miracle. Anyway, Claudine and Matthieu were turned out on the street with no money, though the king had left them silver in his will. As she tells it, Matthieu spent the last five years growing more bitter. He swore he'd find a way to get the money they were owed.'

Ah.

So we have a child who was once a ward of the king; a boy who might have become confused about his station. A youth, coming to adulthood, consumed by the need for vengeance, and an escape from penury. And then one evening he encounters the Maid as she enters Chinon. He says something – we know not what – and in the morning, he is found floating face down in the river with a hole in the back of his skull.

Why did you die, Matthieu? Did you recognize her, this girl who pretends to come from Lorraine? Was she a ward too, another whose father had died at Agincourt, as yours did?

Did you threaten to undo her?

And if Matthieu recognized the Maid on a footbridge in the dark of a February evening, then his sister should be able to do so in the full daylight of high summer.

It's a good morning, bright and sharp and clear, and the world is full of possibility. What Tomas Rustbeard needs now is to get to Bedford, the late king's brother and now, by God's grace, regent of France and England, and tell him what he knows.

His problem: Bedford is in Paris, which is to the north. The Maid is heading north and her army with her, which is all to the good, but five thousand Englishmen stand some-where between here and there, bent on murder. The scouts have been out all night, searching. Tomas has counted three back in since he awoke. The fourth, who went north, is returning now.

He finishes packing his kit, not looking at where the man slides off his sweating horse and kneels for the Maid.

'Hello . . .' Ogilvy looks back across his right shoulder. 'Is that a scout?'

'Is it? You might be right, at that.' Grimacing, Tomas pushes himself to his feet. 'Get your boots on, Ogilvy. Ten to one says we're going north to meet the English.'

'I don't have new boots. Not like some of us.'

'That's because you didn't earn them.'

'Earn them? For half a heartbeat spent kneeling in the dirt!' And they descend to squabbling, because Tomas Rustbeard has new boots and a new mount and today, of all glorious days, is feeling decidedly happy with both.

The horse is a gift from the Maid; a bay gelding with exceptional paces taken from the stables of Jargeau and given to him for his services in helping her to dismount. She did notice him.

The boots are an essential component of his unfolding strategy. He ordered them himself from Ricard's younger brother, Arnaud, who cut them to measure from dark, much-oiled bull's hide, and tooled them around the top with a running imprint that is both the Fleur de Lys of France and the Cross of Lorraine, which the Maid has on the blade of her Crusader sword. Thus Tomas marks himself her man in a way that everyone will recognize. In six thousand men, nobody else has boots like this.

Six thousand is about the right number for the Maid's army, because if the early scouts are right, then the English commanders, Talbot and Scales, fleeing north from Meung-sur-Loire with their defeated force of three thousand, at least one third of them bowmen, have at last met up with the unbeaten, Fastolf, who has been ordered south from Paris with a force of two thousand (one third likewise armed with bows), and the resulting five thousand thoroughly aggrieved English men at arms are disporting themselves somewhere across the route the Maid must take if she wants to get the French king – she calls him dauphin still, having not yet seen him crowned – to Rheims.

Tomas Rustbeard still needs to speak to Bedford, though, and needs to find a way to do it that will not destroy his standing with the French. The threads of his plan are elastic; he revises them on the hoof and on foot and sitting on wet, lichen-covered logs at dusk, watching the fires burn to white ash.

He is still revising them when a horn sounds, long and looping, and the shout after it, 'Ready to ride!'

'Did I not tell you? Ten to one?' Tomas holds out his hand.

Patrick Ogilvy spits on it, laughing. 'Fuck yourself, man. I didn't take the bet. It was obvious.' They laugh together, as they do a lot now, and everyone thinks they are cousins at the very least.

Tomas himself asked, once, 'Was your father a bishop, by any chance?' Ogilvy was drunk, but not that drunk, and it took several more jars to heal the affront, and a night spent listening to the tales of Ogilvy *père et fils* and their undying devotion, one for the other. Not a shared father, then. But close enough, and growing closer by the day.

The newly returned scout rides past, seeking food. Ogilvy shouts to him in passing. 'How many?'

'Half of the total. Over two thousand men. Fastolf has them marching.'

Fastolf, Knight of the Garter, a name to strike fear into the heart of all France. The mere whisper of his presence near a battlefield is supposed to make his enemies weep. The men of the Maid's company do not seem to be weeping to Tomas; quite the reverse.

To the scout, Tomas shouts, 'Do they know we're here?'

'They do now. We killed one of their scouts, but the other got away.'

'Good. Good. Good.' Patrick Ogilvy punches his palm with each word. 'We'll get a real fight. None of this standing back and letting the gunners have their day. Let's go!'

The word rings round the camp and soon they are heading fast along the northern trail, faster and faster because if the English dig in across the way, and set their archers behind stakes as they did at Agincourt, then it's over and the king – sorry, the *dauphin* – can crawl off to Spain or Scotland in penury, and everyone else can learn English and kneel for Bedford.

Except the Maid, of course, who will have to hide in a nunnery or die. Tomas has tried to imagine her in a nunnery, but his mind explodes every time. She would destroy them, given time, except that somebody, somewhere would betray her to Bedford and he is not a man given to mercy.

'Halt!'

A messy, disordered halt, but necessary; if the scouts are right, the English are up ahead. The air is drenched in horse sweat and nerves. Men cross themselves and fidget with their blades. The priests at the front grow silent. Just as Henry did, the Maid brings a mass of priests with her on campaign. At first they were on foot. Now they are fewer, but those who are here are riding; this is a horseback army, designed for speed.

The Maid is in a knot of knights. Tomas Rustbeard and Patrick Ogilvy are close because . . . well, they're always close. Tomas might earn another horse for handing her down from her mount, after all.

An argument rages. The Maid doesn't have command of this army; for propriety's sake, leadership has been granted to d'Alençon, the king's cousin, and the good duke is doing his best to issue orders. For her own sake, the Maid must not ride in the van, it's too dangerous. Remember Agincourt. Remember the carnage and the risk. The English longbow can punch arrows through plate the way a farrier drives nails through a hoof. It's just not *safe*.

Even her squire is arguing this; he has been ordered by the Duke of Orléans himself not to let his mistress ride at the front. She frowns, bites her lip, signals to him, Tomas Rustbeard, the man to whom she gave a horse. 'Can you squire?'

There's a challenge in her look, an invitation that makes his throat run dry. In his time as Bedford's spy, he's tried his hand at many things and found himself able. He makes a decent archer and a competent enough water engineer. He's been a priest on occasion, and found facility as an apothecary, but he has never trained as a squire. He couldn't hold a lance to save his life; at least, not in the tilting position. But it is possible that he could probably ride with one in his hand and pass it across to her at the right moment. He nods.

The Maid gestures to d'Aulon, who looks relieved and passes Tomas the lance. 'We're in the second row, behind La Hire and Poton de Xaintrailles.'

Jesu. Poton de Xaintrailles is one of the foremost knights of the tournament circuit. He makes his living riding the breadth of Europe, challenging men to fight. They say he lives to kill. Certainly, he's not safe to be near.

'My lady—'

She is already gone.

Thus does Tomas Rustbeard find himself in the midst of fifteen hundred mounted knights and their squires.

Somebody told him once that you could fit a hundred mounted knights to the acre. He doesn't know if this is true, but he can believe there are fifteen acres of knights here, if not more, in all the colours and patterns of heraldry: or azure, sable and argent, bend and quarter and boars and goats and lions rampant and lions couchant – and lilies: everywhere the lilies of France.

They are a forest of brilliance, and him a russet smudge among them, his red hair and near-black boots his only distinguishing features.

The Maid is riding d'Alençon's black-hearted grey-white courser. Xenophon. She has named it Xenophon. If that isn't hubris, Tomas doesn't know what is, but a fancy Greek name doesn't keep it from being thoroughly dangerous. Out of choice, he wouldn't go within spitting distance of its hind feet, but a squire must perforce ride at the quarters of his knight, close enough to pass the lance, and, in any case, he is curious to see how she handles herself.

She may have been a horse breaker (or buyer, or boy), but that doesn't make her a knight. If Bertrand de Poulangy was right that her father taught her to ride – and who was her father? Is he another that died at Agincourt? Does Claudine know? – what else did he teach her?

They ride on down the sward. Fifteen hundred men in full plate. A squadron of heavy cavalry as great as any Tomas has seen. The earth quakes at their passing. His heart soars; he can't help it. He is a functional rider, but in this company he rises, his horse lifts. It may be that he is flying. And he can hold a lance vertical while doing so, for which he is uncomfortably proud.

'Ahead!' La Hire roars like a mastiff. 'Knights, arm yourselves!'

The Maid reaches out her right hand. He must pass the lance at the canter. He has heard stories of this from childhood, but he has actually seen it done only twice.

He presses his horse with his knees and moves it up close to the snake-headed grey. It occurs to him that if he unbalances and falls, his head will be a smear of bone and blood. He reaches out his left hand, braced against the weight of fourteen feet of solid wood with an iron tip.

Ahead and all around, a forest of painted lances moves

and shifts. They are masts at sea, a giant flotilla, as the pass is made.

He makes it! He makes the pass, smooth as you like. He wants to punch the air, but all his attention is on managing his horse, because the squires must slow their mounts and let the knights behind come on and those knights fit themselves into lines with the practice of decades, and somewhere ahead La Hire calls, 'Couch lances!' and the forest falls flat.

Flat. So she can couch a lance. It takes two decades of training to do this, and she can do it: he has just seen it happen. Flat and rigid and aimed ready to kill whomsoever she chooses.

Fifteen hundred lances and one of them hers and the greensward ahead, and Fastolf's men just visible down a slight incline, desperately trying to hammer in the stakes that will murder the French horses, and to the left a hawthorn thicket, quite large and very still, and he has a thought that if he were Fastolf, with a knowledge of the land, this is where he would set his bowmen to—

'Halloooooooo!' In English, the soar and call of a huntsman.

And bounding out of the wood, a hart, twelve-pointed, white tail a-flashing, and another call, 'Halloooo, boys, a stag for the taking!'

Are they completely mad?

He thinks they are not mad, because Bedford would not set madmen against a victorious French army, but they will be hungry and perhaps they are deaf and cannot hear the thunder of the incoming French, or the wind is blowing in the wrong direction, or they just can't resist the sight of a stag even if it means betraying their position to their enemies . . . any or all of these, and it doesn't matter which.

All that matters is that the French now know there are

Englishmen hidden in the thicket and if they are hidden they are bowmen, and the thing about bowmen is that if they can't let loose their arrows they're dead meat because what can you do with a bow against an iron-tipped lance and an iron-shod horse and an iron-clad man – or girl – with an iron sword who can stick you and pound you and slice you and ride you into the mud?

Which is exactly what happens.

Tomas cannot see the Maid; she is hidden by a screen of horseflesh and arms, but she is there at the fore when France meets England. He feels the moment of impact as a suck on the air, a rebound that presses his eyes into his head and his tongue to the roof of his mouth.

The screaming comes later, delayed, a barbed rack of sound that twists his toes in his new boots. You'd think he was used to this now, but there is something desperate about men on foot ridden down by knights, the inequality of it, and these are knights who know how the bowmen destroyed their fathers, uncles, brothers – even sons – at Agincourt; they are not inclined to mercy.

Down in the open ground Fastolf hasn't got longbows, he's got his men using their heavy-headed mauls two-handed, trying to ram in their stakes, but they're losing concentration somewhat at the sound of their fellows being slaughtered and Fastolf is losing discipline. Even from this far back, you can see that the men are beginning to run.

And so, his plan. Now.

He spins his horse, searching the mass of men behind him. 'Ogilvy? Patrick Ogilvy? Are you there, man?'

'Aye?' By his face, the Scot is not liking the tortured sounds from the thicket any more than anyone else, and he a Scot who loathes the English with a passion that makes French hatred seem like a thin cloud drawn past the moon.

Tomas Rustbeard spreads a wide grin across his face,

raises his hammers. 'We're not knights. We'll give them something more equal. Shall we hunt us some English?'

'Aye!'

Dusk finds them still hunting. They have killed twice. Good, solid kills, setting hammer and blade against men who could, at least in theory, have killed them first.

As the light fails, they are in a wood, north of the battlefield. Far south, early fires clip the darkness, and the skirl of Scottish pipes wrings out the dusk. Here, shadows draw traps on the loam, fit to break a horse's leg. There is really very little light.

Tomas circles his horse beneath the trees. 'We should dismount,' he says, and does. Ogilvy, as always, follows. They draw along the forest's edge. Oak and beech and thorn hang to their left, enough to trap a horse. Or a man.

'Did you hear that?' Tomas cocks his head, his whisper barely voiced.

Ogilvy stops, looks around, puts one hand to his ear. 'What?'

Tomas points left, behind the oaks, mimes an archer with a pick-maul. He lets go of his reins. His horse drops its head, begins to nip the turf. 'Hush now, let me try something . . .'

It's a while since he spoke English. He has to think of his father, and the men who surrounded him. Clearing his throat, he shouts out, 'Ho there, we are friends. We come with our hands raised . . .'

Nobody responds, which is not surprising, but Tomas hefts his hammers, rolls his eyes at Ogilvy, and jerks his chin to the left, round the bole of the grandfather tree.

'Aye.' Ogilvy nods, crisply, begins to walk round to the left, as instructed.

Tomas heads to the right in an obvious pincer movement; sometimes the easy things work.

Three steps on, he turns and doubles back. He walks quietly, on the edges of his feet. His new boots are supple: he can feel the footing, roll over fallen wood, slip silently on the leaf mould, the cracked acorn husks that are the leavings of rodents.

Ahead, Patrick Ogilvy of Gairloch has stopped, sensing danger, not seeing it, not hearing it. His red hair is the only colour in the gloaming. A perfect target.

A single hammer blow to the head kills him. After all that's happened since May, it would be good to make this death last longer, but Tomas has his priorities and a long, leisurely murder is not one of them. Still, killing alone is not enough.

He grabs Ogilvy's Norse-red hair, smashes his head on the oak trunk, a smash, a smash, a smash; all the tension of the day, of the past months, goes into this. Crack. Eyes snap wide and shut. Crack. A nose pulped. Crack. Bones fragment under his hand. He smashes on until what's left is barely human.

He slips off his boots with some regret, but this is why he bought them; no chance to stop now. He slips off his colours, argent and gules, barred. Both fit on to the mess that is Patrick Ogilvy, with his bloody hair and matted remnants of a rust-coloured beard.

Ogilvy's boots are a nightmare. Ogilvy's colours are sable and argent, so utterly unimaginative that Tomas is ashamed to take them on. He rolls them in a pack and slides them on to Ogilvy's horse and mounts it, leaving his bulky bay gelding for the French to find in due course; abandoning the best horse he has ever ridden.

Alone, with blood in profusion on his hands and hose, he rides north, towards Paris.

CHAPTER TEN

'. . . OUR SINCERE CONDOLENCES TO his family and friends. We will release the body as soon as we have cleared up some of the outstanding questions relating to his death. Thank you.'

Picaut always feels self-conscious speaking English and it isn't helped by the fact that Éric Masson is listening, who lived and worked in London for three years, and Patrice, who laces his emails with lols and omgs and wtfs as if they were his mother tongue.

She hangs up the phone, staring at her reflection in the glass wall that surrounds her office. She looks exhausted. She is exhausted. Éric Masson's coffee has long since filtered out of her brain and there is nothing that can give quite the same kick. It's eleven o'clock on Monday morning and already she's running on empty.

She faces the room. Garonne, too, is sour from lack of sleep and square-eyed from staring at the CCTV footage from around the hotel. If there were anything useful he'd have told her. Another lead burned before they start.

Rollo, the team's resident thug, is rough-shaven and looks as if he spent the weekend lifting car engines and hasn't changed his T-shirt since. He leans against the farther wall, filling and refilling the magazine of his SIG-Sauer. He has a pathological gun fetish, which makes him the one you want beside you when the shooting starts.

The other fully slept team member is Sylvie Ostheimer of the spiked white-blond hair. Sylvie thinks laterally into realms nobody else would dream of entering, which is useful about one per cent of the time. The rest of the time, she's as computer literate as any normal IT graduate; far less than Patrice but more than the rest of the team put together, which, in today's world, makes her indispensable.

Picaut looks down at her notes.

'So it goes like this: according to the Glasgow CID, Dr Iain Holloway is – was – thirty-nine years old, divorced, a consultant orthopaedic surgeon at the Western Infirmary in Glasgow, Scotland. His ex-wife lives in Norway with an oil company executive. The divorce was amicable; he pays her no alimony, there are no children. He specialized in the forensic analysis of massed war graves, in the numbering and identification of the victims. He spent a year on sabbatical with the UN in Iraq and then another year seconded to Médecins sans Frontières in Bosnia. They didn't know he was coming to France, but he had booked three weeks' holiday, which is what he usually does when he's working on a war grave.'

She looks around the room. 'Do we have any war graves in Blois or Orléans? Is there a Gestapo mass burial we don't know about?'

'We might have to go back further than that.' Patrice is sitting on the floor with his laptop balanced on his crossed legs. His kingfisher hair, now that Picaut can see it from above, is apricot pink at the roots. He is wearing a copper bangle on one wrist and a rainbow threaded bracelet on the opposite ankle. He looks like a long-haired, post-modern, techno-grunge Buddha and he is her best hope of an early break.

His fingers flit across the keyboard, drawing secrets from the web. 'Your man's got an obsession with the fifteenth century. In the last month, he posted a handful of comments on two Yahoo forums referring to the Battle of Patay, which was the big French victory in the weeks after the relief of Orléans. We captured English commanders and the English knight, Fastolf, was stripped of his Order of the Golden Fleece for letting it happen. It was one of the greatest victories of the Hundred Years War.'

'What's that got to do with a Scottish surgeon?'

'He's an expert in battlefield forensics. Someone found part of a skull of the right era some way from the battle site, and he was consulting on whether the wounds were right for a war injury and what that said about the accepted location of the battle.'

'Are you sure it's our man?' Picaut says. 'Just because he can read a battlefield, doesn't mean he's— Oh—'

Patrice has swung the laptop round so she can see the man's face filling the screen; he has long, lean features, somewhat like Éric Masson's, but with the cheekbones less pronounced.

His hair is dark, greying a little at the temples, allowed to grow to his collar. His eyes are steel grey, and sharp, but with a hint of a smile. It's not easy to transpose this face on to the charred husk in the path lab, but it's not impossible.

She says, 'We need everything you can get on him.'

'On it.'

Picaut drifts to the place where thinking stops and instinct begins, and soon her mind is empty but for the disparate, shifting pieces of the latest pattern. In the patterns lie the answers, always. Four fires in three weeks. All at night. All claimed by Jaish al Islam. All the property owned by white, French women. But then a death. A man, not French, killed before the fire, and his room emptied. Why him? Why here? Why now?

She is staring at the spinning fragments when Patrice announces that he has tracked down a home address in Glasgow's West End for a Dr Iain Holloway, who may or may not be the one who has a presence on various Internet forums, who booked a return by train from Glasgow Central to London and then the Eurostar to Paris and an overland train to Blois. There is no record of his having bought a train ticket to Orléans, nor any sign of a hired car.

'When did he get to Blois?' Picaut asks.

'Thursday.'

'He didn't book in to the Hôtel Carcassonne until yesterday afternoon. That leaves us three nights unaccounted for. See if you can find his credit card details. A plastic trail is as good as a paper one.'

'On it.' Patrice doesn't even look up.

'Find out about Monique Susong, too. She's not telling the truth, but I can't hold her much longer without a way to prove it. If we can place her and Iain Holloway in the same locations, it would be a start.'

Picaut can feel exhaustion roll in, squeezing her into ever smaller corners of clear thought. She makes herself think from the bottom up; from the hotel to— 'Garonne, nothing on the CCTV?'

'Nothing. There are only two cameras, both on five-minute interval stops. Whoever did this knew enough to miss the tracking points.'

'Great.' Picaut presses her fingertips to her eyes. 'First

forty-eight hours matter most. We need more than this or the trail goes cold. Éric, have you brought—?'

'Here.' Masson produces the USB chip with a conjuror's flourish. It's a small thing to have so much power, shorter than the end joint of his thumb and that's including the loop at one end that will have held it on a key ring. It's red and looks as if it has recently been softened. It is otherwise utterly unremarkable.

Patrice holds out his hand. 'Mine, I think?'

'You want to be careful where you put that,' Masson says. 'It could be crawling with viruses.'

'Trust me. I eat viruses for breakfast.' Patrice is the master when it comes to sleight of hand. He has the chip out of Masson's palm and into his machine before he's finished speaking. His hard drive makes barely a whisper. The keys sing their comfort songs. And then don't.

'Shit.' He frowns, hits some more discordant keys, frowns again. 'What temperature did this get to?'

'Our man was cooked through and his bones are brittle as brick. So eighty or ninety for over an hour with peaks up to one fifty or thereabouts.' Masson pulls a face. 'I did warn you.'

Picaut leans back. Her head bounces softly off the glass wall behind. 'Tell me you can get something from it, Patrice. Anything.'

No answer. A new dance across the keyboard, the longer murmur of a hard drive called to serious action. Patrice bites his lip.

'Well?' If he's worried, she will be worried. She's never seen him look remotely serious before.

He shrugs. 'The NSA have ways of getting data off a disk that's been wiped clean and written over seven times. They can rebuild entire drives from fires a lot hotter than this.'

'But can *you* do it? Even Ducat hasn't got what it takes to commandeer the US.'

Patrice rolls his eyes at her. His grin burns as bright as she remembers. 'If the Americans can do it, I can do it. Just give me time.'

'We don't have time.'

'I know.' He jumps off the table. 'I have better kit at home. If you can live without me ... ?'

'Whatever it takes. Call me when you've got an answer.' Picaut turns to the rest of the team. 'Sylvie, if Patrice is on the chip, you're on the credit cards. I want to know every electronic payment Iain Holloway made while he was in France. See if we can create a time line that goes from Thursday to Sunday night.'

'On it.'

'Rollo, follow up the witness statements and see if daylight has helped jog anyone's memory. I want background details on all the residents, staff and owners of the Hôtel Carcassonne. Include the recently departed residents. Go back a month and see if anyone stands out.'

'On it.'

'Garonne, call in at the Fire Department and see if they know more about the accelerant. See if it's the same as the first three fires. Text me if you find anything. If not, go home. Don't shake your head at me. This is the fourth fire in three weeks and the intervals are decreasing. If they're following any kind of pattern, there'll be another one soon. I need you sharp.'

'And you?' Éric asks. 'Don't you need to be sharp too?'

'I'm going to see Ducat. We might need some phone taps and I don't want him pulling the rug from under us for the fun of it.'

Prosecutor Ducat's oak-lined office is in the shadow of the cathedral, so close that in the old days, when he left his windows open, the clatter of tourist cameras was a constant counterpoint to the typewriter of his clerk.

Now the tourists take their pictures silently on their mobile phones and his clerk uses a soft-touch keyboard on her iMac and Ducat has one less thing to complain about. Which leaves him free to pick other, more personal, targets.

'What's your husband doing interrupting your work?'

'Bringing me this.'

It wasn't how she meant to start, but it's as good a place as any and the maybe-parchment has been burning a hole in the pocket of her leather jacket since Luc gave it to her. 'He suggested I show it to you. For verification.'

She drops it into the anal neatness of Ducat's desk and waits for him to snatch it off, or at the very least lay it straight.

He does neither. Seeing the signature, he doesn't touch it.

'Why is Landis Bressard writing to you?' The flatness in his tone is testament to his loathing of the Family. Orléans was his demesne until the Family came north and spread their largesse and their threats. He is diminished now, in his own eyes, if nobody else's.

'To make me an offer I can't refuse. Read it.'

He does, and when he looks up he makes full eye contact with her for the first time in their joint history. 'What's your former husband asking you to do that is worth so fulsome an undertaking? Or is that too intimate to reveal?'

'I have to agree to be his arm candy.' Her smile does not withstand his stare. 'He wants to have a wife he can show to the press. Specifically, he wants me to be at his side for a press conference at eight o'clock tonight.' The text containing this particular request – is it a demand? – came through as she was parking the car. 'If I do what they want, then the moment he is elected I am free. If that letter is worth anything at all.'

116

Ducat nods and goes on nodding to the rhythm of some inner dialogue. At the end, he opens a drawer in his desk and slides out some paper of a weight only slightly less than the one used by Landis Bressard. He thrusts a fountain pen into Picaut's hand.

'Write what you just said to me, without the crack about arm candy. Write it all, sign it, date it, time it.'

She writes, signs, dates, times. He signs beneath it, then calls the grey-haired woman who has organized his office for the past thirty years.

'Mademoiselle Templan?'

He is not supposed to use the diminutive any more. She should be Madame, regardless of her marital status. As a lawyer, Ducat knows this. As a man of a certain age, he will not consider it. As a lawyer's clerk, Stéphanie Templan knows it, too. As Ducat's clerk, she knows it will never happen.

She is neatly conservative, in her late fifties, heading to retirement. If she was ever going to suggest to Maître Ducat that he had made a mistake, she would have done it thirty years ago, and would be employed elsewhere, in an office that might, perhaps, close over a weekend.

She reads what Picaut has written, and then she too, appends her signature, the date and the time. With no further urging from Ducat, she makes a copy, which she gives to Picaut, and locks the original into the safe in the wall behind his desk. With a nod to them both, she returns to the outer office.

Ducat sits back behind his desk and regards Picaut over the steeples of his fingers. The peg-toothed proto-simian smile has gone. There is no bonhomie now, false or otherwise.

'Is it worth this price to you, to be free of him?' he asks.

'Yes.'

'Then I wish you good luck in front of the cameras.' He bites the edge of his thumbnail. 'They don't flatter me. You, they will like. Particularly if you can tell them that you know who is lighting the fires that are consuming Orléans. Can you?'

'Not yet. I can tell you the burned man was a consultant orthopaedic surgeon from Scotland, who had an interest in forensic archaeology and a passing fascination with the Battle of Patay. We don't know what he was doing in Orléans, or why he died. We have a USB chip that he swallowed before he died. Dr Masson has sent you the details. Patrice is on it now.'

'Was it murder?'

'I can't prove it yet. I can't put a name to whoever is lighting the fires, either.'

'Other than Jaish al Islam.'

'If they're for real, I'll buy you dinner.'

Another man might grin or wink or comment on her recklessness, might endeavour to take her up early on her offer. In the past, Ducat might have done any or all of these.

Today's new, serious Ducat raises a single brow. 'So then find me who is doing this. One death is one too many.'

As if she had not thought of it before, Picaut says, 'We have some computer data. I may need a tap.'

'Call me. Anytime, night or day. Just make sure it's worth it.'

CHAPTER ELEVEN

THE STABLES OF THE HÔTEL DE VILLE, PARIS,
June 1429

GREAT GOD IN HEAVEN, it's Tod Rustbeard without his beard! I wouldn't have known you, man! Fuck, your own mother wouldn't know you like that. What's happened? Are you ill?'

Tomas – now once again Tod – Rustbeard bows to his master. Actually, there are at least two occasions when Bedford has seen him without his beard, he just didn't recognize him either time.

He says, 'There wasn't a house or a hovel between Patay and Paris would offer food to an English voice. The whole of France has gone French again.'

'Fuck them. They won't stay that way long. No nation loves a weak king.' Bedford can ignore the fact that the King of England is six years old and showing no signs of martial vigour. In his head, he is all the strong king any two nations need, and Tod Rustbeard agrees with him, heart and soul.

John of Lancaster, first Duke of Bedford, is a bull of a man, straining through his doublet, greasily sweaty, his breath a swamp of wine and garlic and a discomfited liver. He is a soldier's lord, thick-fingered, his rings set about with garnets big as knucklebones, fit to break open French skulls.

Just now, one hand grips the stall. The other soothes his sword in its sheath, out . . . in . . . out . . . in . . . a finger's length at a time, a fornication in metal. One can pity his wife, or perhaps rather his mistresses, his wife being safe in great wealth in London. But even the mistresses have it relatively easy, for Bedford is a man given to warfare, happiest in the gore and drench of battle.

Above all else, Bedford lives to kill Frenchmen. He will have France made English within the year and Tod Rustbeard, his agent, will do whatever is necessary to facilitate his lord's desire.

And so to his plan. 'You received my message, my lord?'

In. Out. In. Out. The hiss of metal on metal. Bedford nods. 'You want us to put out word that we've captured Patrick Ogilvy of Gairloch, and are ready to swap him for Talbot, Suffolk or Scales. A fine plan, but what do we do if they agree?'

'They won't. Ogilvy had no kin in France and the Maid wants to swap those three for Charles of Orléans, the dauphin's uncle.'

Bedford, sharply: 'We can't do that. My brother ordered Orléans kept until the king is of age and can decide for himself if it's safe to let him go.' In one sentence, the power in England and France: dead king to living regent until the boy is old enough.

'I know. So there's no risk. Leave it a few months and you can let it out that he's had an unfortunate attack of gaol fever and you are grieved to say you cannot even return his body.'

My lord of Bedford is not his late brother, to kill a man out of hand for insolence, but he is not known for his patience either. He flogs men for such behaviour and few of them live long after. Tod Rustbeard leans back against the nearest stall. He takes a breath, takes a risk. 'Sir William Glasdale died bravely. He wanted me to tell you that.'

'I heard he threw himself in the river rather than surrender to the witch. Self-murder is a sin. He'll rot in purgatory at the very least.' Bedford makes it sound mildly inconvenient; like being in Paris when your enemy is heading for Rheims with an army that grows by the day. He draws his sword half out, slams it home again. 'You haven't killed the woman.'

Obviously. The whole world would know if the Maid were dead.

'I came close, twice. The first time, when the men thought she had died, I saw what they would do if she were martyred. Lately, I have come to think that Glasdale was right.'

A space. A chance for my lord of Bedford to think. He is not a stupid man, far from it. In the stall to their right, a liver chestnut mare with a white off hind lifts her tail and heaves out a succession of small, hard pellets.

The sword slams home. Bedford says, 'Go on.'

'He saw her fight; Glasdale, that is. He saw the Maid fight, and before he died he told me that it wasn't enough just to kill her. We need to find out who she is, and use it to destroy her.'

'What do you mean, he saw her fight? Women don't fight.'

'My lord . . .'

How can he say this without causing offence? She fights as you do? Actually, she fights as did your late brother, the king, and that is not a thing I thought to see ever again in this lifetime.

Carefully. Carefully. He is not altogether tired of living.

'My lord, five days ago I saw her couch her lance and ride down Talbot's archers. She is not natural, but nor is she a demon. She has been trained, and well. I think . . . I have heard things that lead me to believe that she may have been a ward of the king of France. The late king.'

'Daft Charles?' Bedford laughs. 'Did you ever meet him? No? Mad as a snake. He sometimes thought he was a footman called Georges, made of glass, and he'd break if he bumped into the walls. In the bad years, he kept that up for months at a time. His brother of Burgundy had the devil's own job to keep control of him. You can't run a country like that for long, not when even sane men get a taste for power.'

Rustbeard says, 'They say he lived for the tilt. He fought in the tunnels beneath Melun. He went incognito to the match at the bridge at Saint-Denis.' A famous tourney: three knights took an oath to hold the bridge for three weeks. And the King of France dressed in black, pretending to have no name, came to test them on it. They say that nobody knew it was him until after. Mad he may have been, but he was also king; nobody was going to talk against him. If he'd ordered a girl to be trained, he could have taken her anywhere as his squire. Nobody would have known.'

'Jesu.' Bedford is frowning. 'Is this possible?'

'Lord, I believe it is. She understands artillery and battlefield tactics, and she can think strategically. She took the gatehouse at Meung and neutered Talbot and Scales without ever meeting them in battle. By the time we'd taken Jargeau and Beaugency, they'd run. We took the town with ease.'

'We?'

Tod Rustbeard holds his lord's gaze. 'I was in the French army then—'

'And killing Englishmen to boot, I'm sure. If I ever grow tired of you, I'll have you hanged for treason.'

Bedford takes a turn around the mare, tests her tendons, her hooves, pats her arse. He is kinder to his horses than he is to his men; the horses cost more to raise and train. 'I still find it hard to believe that the drivelling fool who calls himself king has raised an army. He can't even lie in a bed without its falling through the floor. Did you hear about that?'

Did he hear that the French excuse for a king took a room one night in an inn and woke halfway to midnight with his bed falling through the floor? Yes, he heard it. In fact, he saw it. He may even have caused it, although he will kill any man who suggests so.

He says, 'She has sworn in God's name to see Charles anointed king at Rheims. That's where they're heading.'

'*What?*' Bedford's blade comes clear of its sheath. He, Tod Rustbeard, loyal servant, could die here, now, the bearer of bad news. But then, 'Ha!' and 'Ha!' and '*Ho!*' and Bedford is doubled over, both hands to his weapon, weeping tears of mirth. The chestnut mare stands quite still, ears flagging back and forth over the noise.

'Rheims . . . ? *Rheims?* A month's march through our territory. Can she fly?'

'There will be those who claim she can. Once they invoke God, they can say anything, and there will always be someone to believe them.'

This is a sobering thought. Bedford's brother invoked God on every step of his military journeys, and look where it got him.

Henry the fifth of England was a man to make his brothers look genteel, humorous, kind; even this one. God took him early and as many men sighed relief as wept in mourning, but he was the victor of Agincourt, of Sens, of

Melun, of countless other bloody battles, and he married Catherine de Valois, the mad king of France's unmad and beautiful daughter. Nobody questioned *his* right to rule; not twice, at any rate.

Bedford pulls himself upright and fits his sword back into its sheath. He is not laughing now. Perhaps he is remembering his brother. Perhaps he is seeing Henry's ghost, hearing promises of the future and what he must do to make it happen. With this family, you can rule nothing out.

He turns and leans over the mare, finds the sweet spot on her withers and scratches it. His face, when he raises it, is heavy with dark thoughts. 'So what now?'

'She must die, but it must not be in battle. As William Glasdale said with his dying breath, she must be defeated wholly, fully, publicly, and then captured and tried. The church must arraign her. Her lies must be shown for what they are. If she pretends God's aid, then that is a heresy. One lie is enough to unravel the rest.'

'And for heresy, she can burn. Good.' Bedford does not flinch from this, the crisping of human flesh, of a woman. His war is total, his need to reign paramount. 'But it must be done by France, not England.'

Thus do they ease on to safer ground. Breath by breath, the sense of close and pressing danger diminishes until Tod Rustbeard can say, 'It will help in our destruction of her if we know who she really is.'

'You have a plan?'

Of course. Why else has he shaved off his beard? Why else refrained from meat and mead that might otherwise have let him regain the bulk he lost on the hell-ride from Patay?

'I will get close to her, but not as a man at arms; she has too many of those. What she lacks is a priest she can trust: a confessor.'

'She does not confess?' The heavy brows spring upwards. Bedford's brother was the one who instigated the idea of confess-on-the-march. He thinks, now, that this is what all armies do.

Tod Rustbeard shakes his head. 'She confesses daily, sometimes hourly, but it is to a priest the king pressed on her, and who has made it abundantly clear that he disapproves of a woman who fights. She needs a confidant, a friend, an ally.' At some point, he must reveal his hand. This is his second point of danger. He licks his lips. 'You have a . . . correspondent . . . I believe, who is high in the French king's regard? A man of the cloth, one might say? One who might facilitate the entry of a new priest into her circle?'

'How do you—?' Bedford scowls. 'You have told no one this?'

'My lord, I would never tell anyone.' He is not supposed to know the name, not even to know the existence of an English agent in the French king's innermost circle. He would have to be stupid not to have worked it out, but still . . .

Bedford nods, slowly and then with more force. 'I will not endanger him. He has been ours for too many years now to risk it. Yourself notwithstanding, he is our greatest hope for the saving of France. Besides, the French know you as a man at arms, not a priest. How will you conceal yourself from them?'

'It's what I do: change who I am.'

You'd be amazed how a man changes without beard and hair. Lose a bushel of weight and put on the cloth, dye the skin a little, stoop, round the shoulders, look at the edges of men's faces, not into their eyes. Truly, nobody will know. He's done it before, in more straitened circumstances than these, and his own lover didn't know him.

'Only get me close and I will do it. We may not be able to stop her crowning the chinless bastard king, but by the year's end I shall have found truth enough to burn her. You, meanwhile, must see to the defences of Paris. They are sadly lax.'

'You think the bitch will go for *Paris*?'

'In her place, I would.'

CHAPTER TWELVE

O RLÉANS IS AFIRE WITH election fever, and its name is Christelle Vivier.

Walking from her apartment to the hotel where Luc's family is holding its press conference, Picaut passes three separate posters. Each one is larger than life, vital with Christelle's scorching red hair, her emerald-green Lanvin suit, her polished smile.

In the first of the three, she stands alone before a perfect sky with a flagpole starkly white behind her. This is Orléans and the inference is obvious, but for infants or foreigners, or the hard of thinking who might not immediately grasp that the flagpole is a metaphor for a stake and Christelle's hair for fire, and that she is therefore the new Maid of Orléans, the *Front National*'s emblem of a flame wrought in the red, white and blue of the French flag is stamped at her side. There is no text; none is needed.

In the remaining two posters, she is standing with her

arm looped touchingly through the elbow of her Resistance-hero grandfather.

Old René is in his nineties. He stoops with the beginnings of scoliosis, and what's left of his hair is white, tinged to yellow with tobacco smoke – but that's not where you look. You look at his left hand, which is resting on the handle of his carved hickory walking stick. You look at his thumb and first two fingers, or rather, you look at where they should be but are not, because they were hammered to bloody pulp, slowly, one joint per day, by the Gestapo, down somewhere near Lyon.

As everyone knows (because he has said it himself and his story has become a national legend) he is lucky they didn't gouge his eyeballs out with a fork. He thinks he might have talked if they had done that. As it was, an Allied air raid destroyed the prison where he was being held and Old René escaped.

You might expect him to have run to London, to the shelter of de Gaulle's ex-patriot government-in-exile, but no, he stayed in France, hunting the enemy, his kill total by the war's end in the dozens. He was awarded a Croix de Guerre and palm before the war ended. In 1947, he was made a Knight of the Légion d'Honneur, among the youngest ever. He has been a hero ever since.

Now, in his dotage, still proud, still a fighter, Old René's poster-sized gaze is a challenge, set in delicate counterpoint to Christelle's glowing youth, her vitality, her absolute conviction that her cause is right, and she will prevail.

Beneath them stands the slogan 'No More Fires!' and, because Christelle is on every news bulletin, radio channel and talk show, making her fluent, media-tutored case, it is easy to remember that this means 'Vote for the *Front National*, because only we have the heritage, the courage, the conviction of belief that will rid France of the unFrench and so keep you safe.'

The proto-feral youth gangs are listening to this. They have taken to wearing the tricolour flame on their sleeves. Some are now tattooed with it, proof that their convictions will never waver.

Picaut doesn't quite spit as she passes the third poster, but she comes close and her own vehemence surprises her. She thought she was too caught up in the arson that is eating the city, or too awed by Old René and his wartime valour. She thought she was too impressed by his legendary loathing of the Bressards. Rumour has it that a scion of the Family betrayed him to the Nazis, and even Ducat cannot hate them more than does Old René.

Most of all, she thought she didn't care about politics. Evidently, now that her future depends on Luc's success, or at least on his not failing abysmally on her account, she has a new and personal interest.

Propelled by this thought, Picaut leaps up the stone steps to the Maison de la Pucelle, the small, chic-beyond-stars hotel that Luc has hired in its entirety to use as his venue for tonight's press conference. It stands a mere three doors west of the Maison Jeanne d'Arc, the house-turned-museum where the Maid of Orléans is reputed to have stayed when she came to break the English siege. If Luc wants to wrest her mantle from Christelle Vivier, this is the place to do it.

Whatever his intent, Luc has booked Picaut into a single suite on the third floor, into which he will not intrude. He has provided a Chanel dress for her, in a deep bronze silk that cost many times her monthly salary and hugs her figure in a way that would normally repel her but this evening, unaccountably, does not.

It requires, of course, that she wear high heels, which goes against her determination at all times to be able to run at least as fast as anyone she might be trying to bring down. It also requires a ridiculously small clutch purse into which she can barely fit her keys, but since Luc has asked that she leave her mobile phone in her room, it is sufficient.

She has had plenty of time to consider the implications of what he is doing, and so when she emerges, showered again, changed, with her hair blown dry by Luc's hairdresser and her face oddly tight beneath a fine natural-look make-up that took an hour to apply, and he is standing there waiting for her, it is his unspoken contest against Christelle Vivier that drives her forward, the unnecessary, impossible futility of it; and the irony.

'You should have married her. She has the right pedigree, the right height, the right accent, very nearly the right politics. Give her some training and she could turn her cartoon rhetoric into pure Family prose. She's a Bressard in all but name.'

She slows to a halt. Striding in high heels is beyond her. Luc presses a flute of fine white wine into her hand and chastely kisses her cheek. 'You look stunning. I knew you would.'

He is standing in the anteroom to her suite, which is as close as his new, self-imposed boundaries will allow him. His suit is pale, almost white, and it shows his unblemished tan to best effect. His shirt is bright as packed ice, his tie black, in honour of the body found in the latest fire. He shimmers, alive with that essence of barely suppressed wildness that snared the deep ancestral parts of her brain long before the rest of her caught up.

She doesn't know how to be with him now. She says, 'Christelle Vivier would look better.'

He smiles his old smile. 'Only if she wore that ghastly green jacket and then I'd look as if I had flu standing beside her. It wouldn't work.'

'But she's stolen the fires. They are hers, and she is the new Maid, rising to save Orléans. Have you heard the talk in the bars? On the trams?'

'So she is unconquerable.' He is laughing at her, but only with his eyes. His face is serious.

'You don't think so?'

'I think the people are fickle and their love is fickle. At least they're beginning to care about politics, which has to be good for all of us in the end. And I think you're wrong about her prospects. No amount of training would get her beyond the cartoon rhetoric. As our American allies say, she hasn't got the bandwidth. You, on the other hand . . .' His expression is pure regret, gone before she has truly taken note of it. 'I take it you haven't eaten? No, me neither. In which case—' He holds out his elbow, and looks like Old René, but six decades younger. 'Shall we go down?'

The main dining room of the hotel is perhaps four times the size of the living room in Picaut's apartment; not huge, but big enough to provide intimate, five-cover tables for the thirty or so representatives of the local, national and international media who have received Landis Bressard's invitation.

Christelle Vivier may be flavour of the moment, but everyone knows that Luc is a serious player. And a free dinner at the Maison is not something one is offered every day.

Wide double doors at one side open into the small and private lobby, from which Picaut can see into the main room. At one end a small stage has been erected, with a speaking podium set slightly off centre. The back wall and the podium's skirt are both draped in spectacular crimson velvet. It looks like a waterfall of blood. Two shades brighter and it would be the colour of last night's fire.

She stops on the threshold. 'Is this setting the tone for the evening? Bad taste in primary colours?'

'I thought you'd hate it, but we had to find something

that would show us both up well without us becoming lost against it. And it'll be gone by halfway through.'

Luc is being wired for sound. A technician is fiddling with his collar, while another runs a connection down the inside of his jacket. He is nervous, but Picaut can only see it because she knows him exceptionally well. A fall from a horse in the Argentine left him with an injury to his left hip. He can usually disguise the slight drag to his left heel, but she's noticed it today.

To the manager, hovering close, to the black-tied waiters, the maître d' whose attention is almost all on the diners and their nearly finished meal, he will, she is sure, seem perfectly at ease.

'What's behind the curtain?' she asks. 'If it's going, it must reveal something.'

'To be honest, I'm not sure. I'm told it will do what we need it to and I trust— Ah, we're on. Enter the beautiful couple, stage left. There will be TV cameras, but they're not live. Face the front if you can, stand firm, smile as much as you feel able to, and answer honestly if they fire questions at you. They shouldn't, though. Cousin Lise is on guard and she'll deflect most of them.'

Television cameras. Plural. Someone, somewhere, will pay a lot for this when it's over. If it goes right. Picaut has given too many press conferences to count. She should be used to them by now. But this is different. The thought sucks the saliva from her mouth, sets her heart crashing into her lungs. She holds her head high and walks up the steps at Luc's side.

They reach the stage and the clatter of dessert, the hum of conversation, fade to silence. On her own, Picaut has never commanded this kind of natural deference. Her palms prickle and the back of her neck is damply cold and all of her attention is focused on maintaining balance and poise. This is the price of her freedom.

Uncle Landis is at a table towards the right, and she gives him the full benefit of her calm. He raises one index finger in salute. She lets her gaze drift on past and counts, but does not look directly at, three cameras. There will probably be more, but she dare not look for them overtly.

Moving to the audience, she counts the heads, notes the names: the political columnists of the national press who have travelled down from Paris and will stay overnight at the Family's expense; the editors of the local and national and international news channels; the editors of *Time*, the London *Telegraph*, *Der Spiegel*; the bloggers from the *Huffington Post* and *Daily Kos*. Everyone is here who needs to be.

Luc halts at the podium. Picaut moves on past him to stand fractionally behind his right shoulder. In some things he is perfectly correct: she does know her place. If Landis were to catch her eye now . . . but he doesn't. He's looking down at his table, careful not to throw either of them off their game.

Cousin Lise – more properly Annelise – sits three tables away, from where she can command the left half of the room. Tall, dark, dangerously intelligent, her authority is as effortless as Landis's, only differently applied.

'Ladies and gentlemen . . .'

There is no autocue, no written speech, no prompt cards. Christelle Vivier uses none of these and so Luc, too, must dispense with them. This election will be fought from the heart.

From the heart, then, Luc is funny, he is friendly, he is eminently reasonable. He mentions by name several of those in the room, always with a warmly amusing anecdote and a political point.

At its heart, his message is clear: Orléans is no longer an impoverished outpost of Paris that has to look back to the fifteenth century to find anything or anyone worth talking about. We who live here might honour our most famous saint, we are proud of her peasant origins and her meteoric rise to fame, but we have moved on. Our city has become a cultural and industrial heartland. We are growing. We are good. We are proud. The only flies in our ointment are the recent arson attacks.

'About which all of you know the sorry and distressing facts. I don't need to go into detail, but I can say that my wife' – they turn a little, each of them, and again they are intimate, richly alone in the gaze of the world's press – 'is working insane hours to find who has done this, and to bring them to book. She was up last night at a time the rest of us were safely in bed, and I have to say I think she looks better than anyone I know on less than three hours' sleep.'

Picaut feels the slither of silk as the curtain is swept aside, and the whole room can see what's on the wall behind them, except for her.

All she can see is the widening eyes, the round 'O' mouths, the nods, the thoughtful smiles, and the smattering of applause that is not started by cousin Lise and uncle Landis but is fostered by them and still she cannot, must not, turn round to see what they have seen.

'There are those who will tell you that we must root out the foreigners, those who would destroy our land, our livelihoods, our very lives. The fires are their battle cry, the dead are their martyrs.

'And yet those who weep the loudest, our opponents in the coming election, are not the ones who have suffered. Have they died? No. Have they spent their nights and their days working to rid our city of those who would assault it? No. And have they plans to build and rebuild, to move beyond the horror of the fires to a city that teems with life and productivity? I think not.

'The fires, in so many ways, are their friends. Without

them, who are they but the same old tired reactionaries we have rightly dismissed so often before?

'So when my wife has found the perpetrators – which she will – and our prosecutors have convicted them – which they will – those siren voices will be silenced. I hope at least the first of these will be in sight before the polls open on Sunday. But if not, I will continue to offer the voice of reason against the extremes of those who would paint us as children. We are heading towards an election, ladies and gentlemen, and for everybody's sake I intend to win it.'

Some of the most media-aware men and women on the planet are in this room. They know when they are being played, but Luc has offered them a lever they can use to undermine Christelle Vivier's hard-core platform.

He has all but written their copy for them. If they didn't love him before – and most of them did – they love him now.

The applause is long and rich and deep and they stand as Luc gathers Picaut into a deep embrace, kisses her brow, and then escorts her down the three steps from the platform. The spring in his step has returned.

Released, she can at last glance back.

'My God . . .'

The screen behind them is a solid wall of fire. Vast flames rendered in high-res clarity lick from floor to ceiling in a way that is so familiar that she is in danger of falling into them. And the focal point of the shot is a small figure in an oversized leather jacket, walking beside a stretcher on which lies a man's charred corpse.

She might be weeping; it's hard to tell (was she? She can't remember), but it's clear someone has just spoken to her (Ducat? Garonne?), and the look on her face as she lifts her head to answer, the determination, the sheer, undiluted fury, is so raw that it catches at her throat.

'Why the *fuck* didn't you warn—?'

'Inès, won't you take some wine? And perhaps a canapé? The maître d' will faint clean away with horror if you refuse. The roulades are smoked salmon and avocado; we told him you'd adore them. The macaroons are chilli, lime and raspberry. Honestly, they're to die for . . .'

Luc has gone to meet and greet. Here, in his place, is his cousin Lise.

Like Luc, Annelise Bressard is the product of a hundred generations of blue-blooded breeding. Taller than her cousin, her hair a shade darker, her eyes deeper pools, she was born with perfect skin, perfect features, perfect etiquette.

The only thing that sets her apart from her many cousins is that she has not yet married. Being a woman, she is being held in reserve until the Family needs to make some kind of strategic alliance; certainly there is no other obvious reason why she hasn't already swept some Rothschild or Murdoch off his feet and into the boardroom.

Now, she is sweeping Picaut off her feet. Arm in elbow, she steers her away from the steps, away from the end-wall mural, away from the crowd, but not too far. They come to rest in the anteroom just through the big double doors, neither part of the party nor yet divorced from it.

A waiter presses a silvered tray between them and yes, the chilli, lime and raspberry macaroons are outstanding and the smoked salmon, of course, is a delight. Another waiter appears with water.

Picaut drinks deeply. Back in the dining room, Luc, the flame, is meandering through the media moths.

From her side, cousin Lise says, 'Do you want to go back in?'

'Do you want me to?'

'I think it would cement certain ideas in their minds if you were to talk to them, but you are under no obligation to do so . . .'

God, but this is the kid-glove treatment. Picaut wants to change into her own clothes. She wants time to work out what Luc is up to. She believes none of the evening's rhetoric, but cannot yet read the undercurrents.

'How did Luc know I'd had so little sleep last night?'

'Lucky guess?'

'Taking that picture wasn't a guess.'

'No. But we'd had half a night's warning from the fire's start to the moment you walked out of the hotel with the stretcher bearers. We had someone in place long before then. She took a great many more images. That was simply the best.'

'What would you have done if none of them had been usable?'

Lise's gaze is frank. 'Made one up, of course.'

Of course.

Of course, of course, of course. This is the Family; what isn't real, they will fabricate. Picaut starts to laugh, leans back against a wall, slides down it, and sits on the floor, where it seems as if the laughter could last for ever.

A circle of waiters surrounds her; she is invisible to the press pack inside. Lise waits until she runs to a halt and then says, 'Home? Sleep? In that order?'

'No.' Picaut hauls herself upright. 'If you think my talking to the sharks can help to sink Christelle's campaign, then I'll do it. For Orléans. And for Luc.'

She finds a smile and offers it up. 'Trust me. I'm tired, I'm not incompetent.'

CHAPTER THIRTEEN

B ROTHER TOMAS?'
'Aye?'

Two months have passed since the miracle of the relief of Orléans and the Maid's army has grown beyond all dreams. They are big enough now that the King of France has graced them with his presence. The road to Rheims is open, and even were it not, with this many men, no army of England would dare come to drag him away.

Of lesser note, Brother Tomas, white friar, lately come to join it, is standing knee deep in water when the two boys slouch their mounts to a halt at the stream's edge.

Like most of their comrades, they are poor youths recently given good cloth. Their doublets have the shine of new wool, their hose are unpatched, their boots are almost as good as the ones he put on a dead man when he counterfeited his own death in the forest north of Patay. They ride like sacks of corn thrown on to horses, but then that's half the army, too.

They are brothers, by the look of them, the one on the left

half a handful of years older than the one on the right. And they are shy.

Tomas pushes himself upright, squeezing his bare toes in the cooling mud. The day is catastrophically hot. Twelve thousand fighting men want water, food, latrines. He, who was once Tomas Rustbeard, is now shaved of crown, shaved of face, with brows so dark they might have been dyed with walnut juice, and a gauntness of cheek that suggests much fasting.

So far, nobody has recognized him. They see his cloth, his head, his cross, his stoop. More importantly, they learn in conversation that he was once a water engineer (not a hammer man, never that) and they put him to work.

Today, he is busy organizing the distribution of water from a clean stream. The army must not go down with the flux, which is what happens if the drinking water and the latrines are set too close together.

He shades his eyes with his palm, lets his gaze slide from one boy to the other. 'Best decide if you want confession or clean water, because you cannot have both and if this siphon does not run you'll likely have neither.'

The younger one grins, the comedian. 'Neither. We want you to write. That is, our sister sends to ask if you can write.'

Really? What kind of woman in the middle of the army sends for a—

Their faces give them away, the unaccustomed pride. There is only one woman in the middle of this army who has the authority to send for anything.

'The Maid is your sister?' She is not. He would lay his life that she is not. He has studied her at length and while these two boys are evidently leaves from the same tree, their 'sister' is of different stock altogether. She is slimmer, taller, her nose more prominent, her cheekbones higher, her chin more angular. That she dares this lie says a great deal about her confidence.

Still, the boys are pleased at his question, not insulted. They nod, more or less together. One day they'll perfect that, and do it in unison, but this is raw for them, the sense of almost-royalty; they can't have been with the army more than half a month, and they have not grown into the role. The Maid is their sister. The Maid, who all of France, all of Christendom, knows has come from God to save France from the English. God moulds her to His hand, obviously. If God arranges it, anything is possible.

Brother Tomas eases himself out of the river. He washes his hands clean, takes a while over it.

It matters that he not appear too keen. He has been with the army five days now, and is making a name for himself as a useful man to have around. Brother Tomas, so say the whispers, was a soldier before he found God. He has lately been in Germany, and before that Poland, or perhaps it was Spain, and all manner of other places, always with the small mercenary bands who make their money on the fringes of battle, who kill and come away, but need spiritual support as much as any man. If you need help with clean water, he is your man. It is a useful thing to be.

The boys are waiting. He spreads his hands. 'I can write, but have neither pen nor ink.' He is a mendicant, and perhaps quite godly, for nothing hangs on his belt and the scapular that crosses his shoulders is thin and threadbare and was never smart to begin with.

They nod at him, ever cheerful. 'The Maid has ink.'

'Then I am at your service.'

'Follow us.' They are not trained to ride; they pull their horses round the way men pull gun carts. It would make their not-sister crack her teeth in pain did she see it. Brother Tomas follows across the field to the royal tents. The king is here, and his councillors. Some way to their left stands a smaller pavilion, flung open at the front, with a desk inside, a chair, a dented helm, abandoned in the process of being hammered out, and an armoured figure.

'In there.' The elder boy points.

The younger says, 'We will see to your siphon,' and they are gone, and Tomas is alone before her tent.

He brushes his hands dry on his tunic, careful not to sully the wool. So this is the test. If she knows him, he will be dead by nightfall if he's lucky and by tomorrow's dawn if he is not. He wears a white cassock with a black cincture and no shoes. He has clipped his own tonsure, shaved off his beard, darkened the skin of his face where it was pale. Even the hairs of his arms and legs are dark; he knows that it is the failure to attend to every detail that betrays men to him, and he does not intend to betray himself to anyone.

'My lady.' He is humble, genial; everything Rustbeard was not.

Her gaze unstitches him, sews him back together. The skin of her face, too, is darker than when he last saw her, but with sun, not dye.

Her eyes are still so dark as to be almost black, but they have a new depth. She is learning that coming with God behind her is not enough; men of the king's court who have pandered to his favour for years are not ready to give it up. She is coming up against opposition and not all of it martial. Her hands are bruised, her nails bluntly short.

This is all he can see of her; she is still in her plate. It is dented, worn at the elbows and knees. She spends a great deal of time praying in public. From a distance, he has seen her kneeling, face turned to heaven. He is not sure it is God she is asking for help, but that, perhaps, is Bedford's fault; those last days before Tomas left Paris, Bedford spent a lot

141

of time saying she was in thrall to the devil. Either way, if she is going to kill him, it will be now.

She nods a greeting. 'Brother friar, be welcome.'

He breathes out, smiles, enters. The shade is like a pail of water emptied over his head. He stands a moment, revelling in the cool. At another nod, he sits on the camp chair with its unstable legs dug into the mortar-hard ground.

The table is similarly unlevel and almost unusably small, but the parchment is medium grade; pigskin, he thinks, finely scraped and powdered. The ink smells of wine vinegar but looks thick as batter. The quill stands upright in a beaker of sand, heated but not cut, and a knife with it. He tests the blade's edge on his thumb and finds it could kill. If he still wanted to, he could slice her throat open now.

He sits on the stool and trims the pen to an angle that suits his hand. It's a long time since he has done this, the cross cuts and the vertical, the small shavings at the side, like snicking hairs off a chin, the long strip that denudes the quill so his hand holds a smooth, beautiful artwork.

He is pleased that his body remembers how. As with firing a longbow, it is something the hands recall when the mind has long forgotten.

He smiles for her. 'At your word, my lady.'

'Jhesu Maria. Start with that, as it says on the ring on my finger, and on my standard. *Jhesu Maria*. And then a new line. *Very good and dear friends, loyal townsmen and residents of the town of Troyes . . .*'

He writes as she speaks. His script is good, well formed, sharp on the upstroke, with strong curves and even spacing. The letters are sound made into form; a kind of magic. They whisper into ears that do not yet know they exist.

He makes small amendments here and there. Where she says 'the king in heaven' he says 'the king of heaven', and when she says 'my father in heaven' he writes 'God'.

It is faster, and means the same and he thinks his script is better than her dictations, and the end result is a powerful command to surrender.

Loyal Frenchmen, come before King Charles, do not fail to do so, and since there is no fault, have no concern about the safety of your lives or your property if you do so; and if you do not do so, I swear upon your lives that with the help of God, we shall enter into all the cities which should be part of this holy kingdom, and make there a good and forthright peace, regardless of whomever may come against us. I commend you to God; may God protect you, if it please Him. Reply soon.

'Write also on behalf of the dauphin, this:'

We, your king, Charles, seventh of the name, do guarantee and indemnify all those who surrender to our cause; that they shall suffer no harm to their lives or weal, nor to their gold, nor to their dwellings, unless they fail to surrender to us, in which case, we shall seize their town and much unhappiness shall fall on them.

There. Even he would open gates to this kind of pressure. Mind you, he might have opened them already. Against the French force of twelve thousand men and knights, there are perhaps five hundred men at arms inside Troyes for the whole of its defence.

They – the brave five hundred – sallied out earlier in the day, all bristling swords and proud shields and fancy hats with peacock feathers, but when they saw the size of the army they couldn't get back inside fast enough. The drawbridge is up, the moat is full of water. Either the magistrates inside are impossibly stupid or they haven't yet heard of the sacking of Jargeau.

He sands the letter, and holds the pen for her to sign. He

makes himself look away; he has much practice in schooling his face, but perhaps not this much. His thoughts lie flat across the inside of his mind.

You know how to write, don't you? But you have to seem not to, because illiterate peasant girls can't write any more than they can ride.

'Have you a herald, lady? If not, I can deliver it.'

'No, there are heralds aplenty and you are better here. We have few engineers and they are mostly with the guns. I am told you have an interest in water.'

'Every army needs fresh water, lady.'

'And so we need you. You will stay close.'

Of course he will.

She takes off her helm and shakes out her hair. It is longer than it was, but not greatly. It shines, like silk rope, with her sweat. To herself, thoughtfully, she says, 'Troyes was the shame of the king. We will not pass it by.'

The king? Amongst all his other shame, Troyes is somehow unique? And then it comes to him that she means the old king, the mad king who had Matthieu and Claudine as wards, and perhaps one other, who would care that at Troyes was signed the treaty that gave France to Henry V of England, and made of the giver a laughing stock throughout Europe.

He, Tomas, takes breath to ask, but the Maid is still staring at the blank, stone walls. 'If they don't surrender we will have to go in, or else every other town will know it can hold against us.'

'You are thinking of Rheims?' Rheims, where Charles must go for his anointing, is still loyal to England and is watching carefully what happens at Troyes.

She glances across at him, black eyes, black brows, dancing. She inclines her head. 'And Paris.'

Ah, yes. Paris. 'It will take a great deal of money to

pay twelve thousand men to march all the way to Paris.'

'When the dauphin is king, he will pay what it takes to rule all of France.'

Not if Brother Tomas can stop him, he won't. And the thing is, it may be that he can.

Troyes holds out for three more days.

In those three days, the Archbishop of Rheims, Regnault de Chartres, argues hotly in the king's council that they should leave Troyes; that they should, perhaps, go back to the Loire. Or send the army to take Normandy, why not? It's there and ripe for the picking.

On the third day, the archbishop suggests that Brother Tomas, by now the encampment's foremost water engineer and an assiduous confessor – though he has not yet had the honour of ministering to the Maid – should attend the council as a scribe. Thus he sees for himself how effective is the archbishop's persuasive technique, how plausible, how immensely charming, practicable, obvious.

Yes, Normandy is by far the better target. Bypass Paris; it's not that important. Forget about crowning the king, or maybe do it quickly, with not much pomp; it's not as if you want anyone really to take any notice, and you certainly don't want to stir up the English: that would be a disaster when you have twelve thousand men behind you and the enemy has just lost its three best commanders.

Then string your army out over a hundred miles, why not? And try to keep the supply lines going while you waste men and guns on a place nobody cares about; would that not be clever?

It's a miracle of smooth talking. Mildly astonishing that nobody has dragged the man out of the tent and struck his head from his shoulders for arrant treason, but he's the king's closest spiritual adviser and there's a miasma that comes over men when they hear a powerful man speak nonsense. They nod, and think it must be sanity, and wonder at their own judgement.

Tomas wonders exactly what Bedford is paying the archbishop, and whether it is all gold, or part of it is some kind of promise for later, when English rule is complete. Whichever it is, payment is happening because, unquestionably, Regnault de Chartres is Bedford's agent in the French king's court. He and Tomas have not spoken yet, but messages have been sent in a complex cipher. Each knows the other's intent.

The king's council meetings are held in the king's pavilion: a vast panoply of red silk that casts bloody shadows across the assembled body politic.

De Chartres is in ripe flow. '. . . the whole ride north was folly, and who cares if all the towns on the way opened their gates to us? England will soon take them back, and then we'll be sorry we ever—'

'Stop this! We should listen to the girl. Do these men speak from God as she does?'

Thus does an old voice float out from somewhere across the far side of the tent. It is Robert de Macon, who has fought too many battles to be afraid of anyone, and has recently dragged himself from retirement to join this new army.

Robert is not interested in the politics of court, who is in favour and who not, who wields power. He does not care that no less a man than Regnault de Chartres himself has let it be known that he thinks the Maid is a fraud. He has seen at first-hand what she has achieved, which is more than the archbishop has done.

He stands, quavering. 'The Maid gave us Orléans, Jargeau, Meung, Beaugency, Patay. She it is who says the king must be anointed by God's command. Let her speak here instead of these wastrel men. Ask what she thinks of Troyes.'

The king, when backed into such a corner, assents. He may not be a master strategist, but he can count and he knows that twelve thousand soldiers who think the Maid is divine outweigh one archbishop who does not.

'Find her. Bring her here.'

Of course, it is Brother Tomas who heads out in search; this is too interesting to miss. He finds her with Jean-Pierre, the gunner, talking about the size and weight of shot they should use on Troyes and where the walls are weakest; how much powder they have and where best to store it.

Tomas stands to one side until he is noticed. 'The king would have you speak in council, lady.'

'Why?' She's busy. She doesn't like to be interrupted.

He bows a little, self-effacing. 'To say what must be done here, at Troyes.'

'We have to take it, of course. I said so. Does the king not know this?'

'His councillors might benefit by hearing it from yourself.'

'You mean the archbishop?'

'My lady.' He bows again. They share a moment's exasperation. She rolls her eyes, tucks her helm under her arm, shifts her sword belt, and follows Brother Tomas to the blood-red tent to tell the king what the king should already know.

This is the first time Tomas has seen them both together close up.

The Maid.

The king.

One is regal, and it is not the boy. The Maid's growing legend says that when she first came to Chinon, the king hid amongst his courtiers; two hundred men in a room and every single one of them dressed in the nettle-on-white livery of Orléans. Still, she walked straight to him, and fell on her knees at his feet, then rose up, and took him aside, and told him things that made him smile for the first time in years.

They say it is proof that God speaks to her. Tomas thinks it is evidence that she knew the king by sight, one more nail in the scaffold he is building that will prove her a liar and a heretic.

He looks at Regnault de Chartres, and finds that the archbishop is staring at him, flatly, with a kind of question in his eyes. Tomas brings his palms together in piety. The archbishop pulls an acid smile and looks away. He does not look at the Maid. It may be that he cannot bring himself to do so.

She is repeating what she said earlier. 'We must take Troyes, or others will know they can close their gates to us.'

There is a murmured upswell of support from men who want to fight and know what it takes. Hearing it, Regnault de Chartres, all emollience, changes tack. 'My king, she is so sure. She should be given charge of the proceedings.'

The bastard king, Charles, swivels his narrow neck right and left again. His knees poke outwards, and his elbows. It is not a prepossessing sight.

Today, the king believes that Regnault de Chartres with his oiled language will keep him safe. He sees the trap that has been laid to catch the Maid, and approves of it. He turns to her his widest smile.

'Go then, and see what you can make of Troyes. I give you command.'

The Maid kneels in thanks, but not before Tomas catches sight of the look on her face. She has had some practice in masking her thinking, but not yet quite enough. The king has not seen her in action before. Now is her chance to show him what she is, that he is not. She is not shy of the opportunity.

Before they leave the tent, the army gets word, as armies do. They believe God has set the weather for the Maid, with the crystalline sky and lambswool clouds.

Her enemies are buzzards, circling. Regnault de Chartres is foremost among them, and his ally, Georges de la Trémoïlle, the chancellor.

Together, these two pace through the camp as the men come alive, as the guns are set ready, as the powder is poured, as the wood is gathered and bundled. They peer and prod and poke and ask rhetorical questions, one of the other and back again.

'What for does she need so much wood, my dear chancellor?'

'I have no idea, my dear archbishop. What for do you need so much wood, girl?'

'Watch.'

They were not at Jargeau; they genuinely do not know. As she did there, the Maid has the men set the bundles on the edge of the moat, ready to fill it. In half a day, they have enough to build a pathway to the walls.

Jean-Pierre brings up the great bombard, Rifflard, and lines its stones to left and right: twenty smooth grey granite boulders, big as bullocks, ready to render into pulp stone and wood and flesh and bone.

Tomorrow, the gunner will fire them at Troyes. Later, he moves the smaller cannon into lines, until there is not room for another.

The army is confessed and pure, but the men contemplate the delights to come.

The Maid can forbid swearing – and has. She can throw out the whores from the army – and has. But if this city does not yield to her, then when she takes it – and not even Regnault de Chartres doubts now that this will happen – she cannot stop the men from making free with its women, its gold and its wine, its damask and candlesticks, pearl earrings and haunches of ham.

The jeering begins after Mass, and by vespers the ranks are making pantomime of what they will do. The Maid talks to the provisioners about the supply of wheat for the men and corn for the horses, to Tomas about new latrines and where they must be dug. She does not interfere.

The men of Troyes stand impotent upon their walls. Their women begin to weep. Twelve thousand Frenchmen; the women of Troyes will be serving three or four each at the very least when the army breaks in. In the morning, the magistrates send a herald to the king to sue for surrender.

Before noon, to the muted cheers of the citizens, the King of France enters the gates of the city that shamed his father. The men and women of Troyes, who had been so wholeheartedly for England that King Henry promised to make it his capital when he took all of France, must learn to love their Frenchness again, to take pride in it.

For now, it is enough that they wave with empty hands and do not throw eggs or ordure or old food.

The Maid rides at the king's right hand. He looks better on horseback; armour hides his bone-button knees, his squab neck. His gull's-egg eyes are shaded behind his helm. Above them *Jhesu Maria*, black on white, aloft, fluttering. Her banner: her dauphin to make into her king.

Brother Tomas rides a dozen ranks back. He looks. He learns. He plans. In his head he sends messages to Bedford. Not yet, my lord. Not yet. But your servant will defeat her so completely that her ashes will be ashes, strewn upon the sea.

CHAPTER FOURTEEN

Orléans,
Monday, 24 February 2014
21.15

THE JOURNEY HOME TAKES Picaut somewhat less than ten minutes. Her Nokia is switched off. Her landline is ringing as she walks in the door.

'Picaut.'

'Are you on Twitter?' It's Patrice, sounding alive and vital and electric. Just to listen to him makes her smile.

'Not at this precise moment. Should I be?' She thumbs open her Nokia, fires it up. 'What am I looking for?'

'What you are definitely not looking for at all is hashtag Orléans Take Back the Night.'

So, of course, she looks.

—@whiteisright We are power! Join us!! #Orléans #TakeBackTheNight
—@Coolman #flashmob #Orléans C. says bring a bottle. Full. Not with wine. <G> #OrléansTakeBackTheNight
—@Stephanie6787 Four hundred? Five? Count for yourself!!!11! lol #OTBTN #flashmobsofinstagram

This last links to an image of Orléans youth doing its best

to imitate the feral youth gangs of Paris. Thus far, it looks distinctly middle class and well behaved; clots of teenagers grinning self-consciously into each other's phones, but all are white, and there are placards on the fringes that have the ring of Christelle Vivier's more routine pronouncements: Foreigners Out! Keep France for the French! And one, just in view: Our Maid Died For This? The date stamp is 21:04, which means they're still on the streets.

'*Merde!*' Picaut reaches for her keys. Patrice calls through her phone.

'Don't! Don't go out. You'll be a YouTube sensation in half a minute. Ducat will skin you alive in the morning.'

'You want me to hide behind the shutters while Orléans is overrun by teenage anarchists?' She opens a window, letting in the sounds of distant discord.

'I would. Stay in, listen to music. Play Grand Theft Auto. Sleep, even. It may be old-fashioned, but some people still do it. Do whatever you do to unwind. Just don't go and look. If someone's hurt, you can go in an official capacity. Until then, it's not your problem.'

'And when the press wants to know why I'm not there?'

'Tell them your team is monitoring the situation. Which we are. I've got fifteen hashtag streams open on TweetDeck. You, meanwhile, are busy solving a murder. With that in mind, Rollo, Sylvie and I have Iain Holloway's itinerary sorted out and I'll have something for you from the chip by the morning. I've got into the files: it was locks, not heat. The stuff inside is scrambled; I'm just trying to decipher it now.'

'You are a magician, you know that?'

'Always.' He is laughing, and then he isn't. 'Something else you might want to know.'

'What?'

'You remember the Internet firestorm last September when your dad was sacked?'

'He resigned.' Six weeks before his death. She is not laughing now, either.

'Sorry. Yes. Well, there was a petition supporting him and his point of view and Iain Holloway was part of the group that set it up. They called themselves Coalition of Truth. Holloway was the tenth signatory.'

There was a time when that would have mattered. Against her better judgement, she asks, 'How many signed altogether?'

A pause. A flicker of keys. 'Four thousand nine hundred and sixty-two. That's not bad, given the numbers on the other side.'

It's pitiful, but it's better than nothing and she is grateful for his care. 'Thanks.' She pushes her head into her hands. 'If that's it, I'm going to bed. It's been a long day.'

In Patrice's universe, sleep is for old people and losers; she knows this, waits for him to say it and instead hears the slip of a shrug. Tonight, he is being kind. 'Sure. I'll pull all the data together and we can work out what he was doing in the morni . . .' He drifts to silence, in a way that makes her throat run dry.

'Patrice?'

'Just go to bed.'

'No. What? Tell me.'

'Have you seen the news?'

There's a plasma screen in the corner. One-handed, she hits the remote. 'What channel?'

'Doesn't matter.'

Christ.

She heads for the rolling news and it's there, or rather she, Picaut, is there; the video of this evening's performance.

She had wondered what the Family would charge for the

rights. She had imagined that a minor bidding war might take place through the night with the victor screening the results on the morning news.

But there has been no bidding war, and if there is a price, it is low enough for every terrestrial, cable and satellite channel to gain unrestricted access. She surfs across the news and comment channels and cannot escape herself. Where Christelle Vivier was once ubiquitous, now Picaut is there twice over; in a shimmering bronze Chanel dress, and in a leather jacket with soot and ash on her face and the nightmare of the fire behind her.

Neither of these is the truth of herself as she knows it, but that doesn't stop her admiring what they have done.

In the brief, edited clip, she walks on to the platform and smiles at Luc. Because she is watching for it, she sees the smile first, but knows that the outside world will see instead the bronze silk dress and they will not think about how long it must have taken to set up the lighting, so that the reflections from the crimson curtains create the illusion of flame rippling over her as she moves across the stage. They will only see the flames, rippling, seeming to consume a woman. Even for those not brought up with the legend of the Maid as their daily bread, it has had enough of an airing to trigger something deep and primal.

And then, bracketed by Luc at his most reasonable, his most liberal, they will see the curtain sweep soundlessly sideways, more flame leaping up Picaut's silk-clad form, and the illusion will merge with the real flame on the vast, pixel-perfect image behind, in stark contrast with Christelle Vivier's brash attempts to steal the mantle of the sainted Jeanne, Saviour of Orléans.

'Have you seen Orléans! 24/7?' Patrice is still being careful with his words.

'On it.' Orléans! 24/7 is one of the new, edgy cable

channels. It is spooling the same footage, but the floating footer is newly theirs: LA NOUVELLE PUCELLE?

It is too much. Picaut stabs at the remote, closes the screen to black, sets the alarm on her phone to wake her at six. 'I'm going to bed. I'll see you in the morning. Sleep well.'

'Night . . .'

Her bed is more welcoming now; the ghost of Luc lingers in the newsreels, but nowhere else, and she can sleep.

She is deeply unconscious when her phone rings.

She reaches for it, groggily. 'Picaut.'

'Inès? Inès Picaut?' The voice is hesitant, rising halfway through her name. 'This is Henri Aubel. From your political science class at the university? You might not remember . . . ?'

He is afraid she won't, and hopes she will, and she does, more or less, in a woolly-headed, dream-laden kind of way: a skinny boy, with lank hair and glasses. Verging on Asperger's, and chronically shy. His grades in exams were inversely proportional to his success with women. She borrowed study notes from him once.

Thickly, she says, 'Your father was an engineer on Concorde.'

It is perhaps not entirely kind to remember a man by his father's occupation, but Henri is thrilled. 'That's it! Thank you!'

She is so very nearly asleep. 'What can I do for you?'

'You could make my career, actually. Or break it.'

He has a career. Somehow, she had imagined him as a clerk, adding up columns of figures in a dusty attic. Her images are of a forgotten century; more than likely, he is another Patrice.

'I'd hate to break anyone's career. Will it endanger mine if I help you?'

155

'I hope not.'

'You're supposed to sound more sure than that. What is it you need me to do?'

'Come to the studio in time for the early slot at six a.m.'

Six? Oh, God . . . 'What studio?'

'Orléans! 24/7. Actually Orléans! Six–Huit.' He leaves a polite gap, for her to fill with the right kind of impressed noises.

She hasn't the energy, and truly, if Patrice hadn't just pointed it out, she'd barely remember its existence. It's been on air for less than a month and is trying to make a name for itself with a mix of edgy, investigative journalism and gossip. She struggles to remember something useful about it.

Henri breaks the silence. 'You don't watch it, do you?'

'Sorry.' She shrugs an invisible apology. 'Why do they want me?'

There is a blank, discomfited pause. Then Henri's rising, quizzical note, 'You're a celebrity?'

Oh, dear God. 'But I'm not . . .' Not a celebrity. Not television material, however hard the Bressards might try to change that.

'I know.' He sounds crushed. Alarmingly, he might weep. 'I did tell the producer you wouldn't do it.'

'And if I don't, you'll be looking for another job?'

'It's not your problem, Inès. Don't worry. I had to ask, but it's fine.'

'Don't hang up . . . Oh, fuck.' She grinds her knuckles into her hairline, tries not to think of Uncle Landis and what this could do to his carefully sculpted campaign. She has not closed her windows and sounds still carry to the bedroom. Somewhere outside, a siren wails. She can hear glass break, to the north and west, beyond the cathedral; too close, too urgent, too angry.

Distracted, she says, 'I can't discuss details of the murder investigation. Or in fact anything about any current case. Your producer does know that?'

'Of course! Totally! Absolutely! Does that mean you'll do it?' He is weeping now, tears of pure joy, from the sound of things. 'Inès, you've saved my life! I promise you! Thank you so much!'

She checks her Nokia, resets the alarm to five o'clock. Fuck it all. 'Will you be there?'

'Oh, Inès! I wouldn't miss this for worlds!'

She falls asleep with her phone still in her hand.

CHAPTER FIFTEEN

ORLÉANS,
Tuesday, 25 February 2014
05.50

FOR THE SECOND TIME in twelve hours, a make-up technician brushes a fine sheen of powder across Picaut's brow, her cheekbones, the bridge of her nose.

Orléans! 24/7 is housed in a newly refurbished single-storey building in the north-eastern section of the city. The entire place is a testament to the Internet age, Wi-Fi ready, Bluetooth-compatible, bustling with ardent, enthusiastic interns of Patrice's age, if not his sartorial style, all of whom look as if they have been up all night and enjoyed it. They wear barcoded, laminated tags round their necks which give only their first names.

An intern was waiting at the door to welcome Picaut. 'I'm Marianne.' Marianne had dark hair, darker eyes, and black and white fingernails with small silver skulls on the tips. She was wide awake, friendly, efficient. 'This way.' They processed past whispering doors that slid aside before they were touched, through a white-tiled corridor that smelled of new paint, into a small, tidy green room with fewer mirrors than Picaut had feared and more than she would have liked.

Once there, Trudi (blonde with pink highlights; green eyes of a hue that can only be coloured contacts; sky-blue nails) brought her coffee. Albrette (straw blonde, blue, acid green) brought her gossip magazines and then, when she asked for it, *Le Monde*. Suzanne (blonde curls with a black forelock, grey, scarlet zigzags) fetched the make-up tech who is called Esteban (a goth). Each of them has been endearingly helpful.

Picaut herself has done nothing to prepare for this beyond the fact that her T-shirt is clean and her jeans are relatively new. Her leather jacket still smells of fire smoke and she will not change it. She has done enough interviews not to care what they say, even when fed suggestive images by the Bressard spin machine.

The door behind her slides open on a huff of techno-air. In the mirror, she watches the interns stand straighter.

'Done?' Colin Graves, the producer, is English and speaks French with a broad London accent. White-haired, bluff, jut-jawed, it is easy to imagine him as a knight in the army that tried to take Orléans by force.

Today, in the tamer twenty-first century, he looks very much the type of man who might sack an AP who failed to produce the latest hot topic for the morning's show. Or someone more senior than a producer. In the ten minutes before she was asked to switch her phone off, Picaut used the search engine to good effect. She knows, she thinks, what they plan. Her only hope is that they are not as good as Patrice; that they don't know every detail of Iain Holloway's past activities.

Esteban steps back, lifting the tissue clear of her collar. Graves gives her a bland smile, his gaze already sliding out to the screen mounted in the wall to her right, where the channel's overnight news anchor is beginning to wrap up on a résumé of the night's demonstrations. Picaut has not yet been to look at the scenes of broken glass and discarded litter. The world's media are there in force, and she probably has a better view of it on screen than if she walked along the streets.

She makes herself look away from the chaos, searches instead for Henri Aubel among the studio engineers, the assistant producers, the lighting people. She hasn't seen him yet, and doesn't, as she is ushered through three more whispering doors into the hot-white goldfish bowl of the studio.

The Bressards kept their cameras small and inconspicuous. Here they are big beasts, prowling. The sofa of her imagination is not a sofa but three swivelling office chairs – padded, leather, expensive – set in an intimate circle around a smoked-glass coffee table on which lies a selection of the morning papers and a steaming cafetière (standard blend, boring; Éric would spit it out) and three mugs, already poured, with milk and sugar added, or, in Picaut's case, not.

Three chairs. Three mugs of coffee. So she was right. The sofa of her imaginings was built for two, but only because she prefers optimism to its opposite. It doesn't take much deduction to work out that she is most likely to be sharing her morning interview with . . .

Christelle Vivier, shining in emerald green, her hair a banner of flame laid full about her shoulders. She has been brought in by another door and she, unlike Picaut, was not remotely expecting this. Across her face flows surmise, fury, the promise of revenge.

'Capitaine Picaut! I didn't know—'

'Neither of you did. Don't blame each other. You wouldn't have come if we'd told you.' Behind her, Henri Aubel sounds altogether more vibrant than he did on the phone last night.

He is taller than she remembers, no longer bespectacled, newly possessed of American-white teeth, and if he was ever truly shy, you wouldn't know it now.

'Ladies—' A long stride, a flourish of the arms. Is he wearing a bow tie? He is! How very . . . English. Is that Colin Graves's idea? She wouldn't have thought Henri up to this, but then there is no part of him that is as she remembers. His shirt is silk, the colour of white gold. His suit is pale blue Italian linen and Landis Bressard would look twice at the cut and enquire as to the name of his tailor. Henri manages to look at once louche and raffish, edgy and thoroughly radical.

He sweeps in, long-legged, to take his seat in the centre. 'Christelle, if you'll come on my right, Inès on my left.'

She catches his eye, flatly. He gives a single truncated shrug, no smile to go with it, no apology, and then he is facing the camera, asking a question of the producer, pressing his finger to his ear for the answer, and then the signature tune is caterwauling in the background and the light on top of the leading camera is blinking red and red and red and . . . green.

Henri, radiant, to the camera. 'Ladies and gentlemen, welcome to Orléans! Six–Huit this Tuesday morning. We are less than a week away from an election that will decide the fate of us, the ordinary people of Orléans, in ways perhaps we cannot yet imagine, for this campaign has always been electric, but recent events have made it – dare I say – incendiary? Another fire on Sunday night, and then last night further demonstrations in favour of the *Front National*. For now, the streets seem to be calm again, but for how long? Will we even get to the polls in safety? We are caught up in a time of unprecedented social and political unrest and here in the studio to discuss it with me we have two of our leading lights.

'On my right, Christelle Vivier of the *Front National* whose members have been conspicuous by their absence from last night's . . . what shall we call them? Gatherings? Although many in the crowd have been retweeting their slogans in defence of a France kept wholly French.

'On my left, we have Capitaine Inès Picaut, the police officer responsible for bringing to justice those who have lit the fires which, I dare say, are at least part of the cause of the recent events. Both have recently been likened to our city's heroine, our national saint, and their resemblance to her is obvious in each case.

'Christelle Vivier, let's start with you.'

He turns to his right. The cameras track across. 'As we all know, Jeanne d'Arc, also known as the Maid of Orléans, was a figurehead, the poster-child of the French fight back against the English. She rallied the troops. She rode her white charger into the besieged city of Orléans and brought hope to the people, but legend says that she didn't actually *fight*. So given that your campaign team have gone to extraordinary lengths to frame you as the new Maid, are you likewise a powerless puppet?'

Whatever Christelle is expecting, it isn't this. Her interviews to date have been with pliable news anchors solidly briefed by her team on topics previously agreed by both sides.

She opens her mouth, shuts it, makes up her mind and changes it, all in the time it takes to turn towards the giant Cyclops lenses, three of them, homing in on her face. She's had sufficient media training to know that three seconds of silence is quite enough to stop the early breakfast audience in its tracks.

'You flatter me,' she says. 'But I think the Maid did everything she could possibly have been expected to do, given the time in which she lived. As a woman – a girl, really

162

– it was extraordinary that she even rode to war. Nobody expected more of her. As to any similarity between me and her, that very flattering comparison grew on its own.' Her voice is soft, unthreatening, early-morning parlour. She sips at her coffee, not a strident strand in her entire DNA.

'So you're saying that it was there before the posters? You were not picked as candidate, then, because of the colour of your hair?'

He is good at this, the sudden, unexpected thrust. Christelle tilts her head. Her bones are strong, the way they catch the light; she knows how to control the cameras. 'I don't think anyone has ever suggested that the Maid's hair was red.'

Luc says she hasn't the bandwidth to be a Bressard and he may be right, but she's no Sarah Palin, to be reduced to dithering word-salad by a single unscripted question. Christelle can think on her feet, and is doing so.

She says, 'The Maid clearly saw the injustice of a France occupied by invaders who were not and never would be French. In trying to correct this injustice, she came up against opposition as much from the different factions within the French court as from the English occupying armies. With the benefit of hindsight, we know she was right. Our hope – our prayer – for this election is that it doesn't take us six hundred years to realize the danger we're in today.'

'Indeed. So, seventy years after the end of Nazi occupation, are we once more on the brink of an occupied France, with foreigners endeavouring to take over our institutions?'

Henri's eyes shine. He swivels his chair left to face Picaut. 'Capitaine Inès Picaut, good morning. Leaving aside the demonstrations for the moment, because these are not your affair – not yet, anyway – are you, too, seeing an injustice of epic proportions in Orléans today and if so, are you endeavouring to rectify it?'

163

She shakes her head, plays it straight back. 'I am a police captain, doing my job. I am seeking patterns, and where we find them we will find the details that will lead us to the perpetrators of the arson, who will now also be charged with murder.'

'You're looking for patterns in the fires?'

'Naturally.'

'Which are lit by a group calling themselves Jaish al Islam, which means, I understand, army of Islam?'

No insinuation, no slandering of the Islamic community, only a question left to hang in the air.

Picaut spreads her hands. 'Just because someone makes a claim doesn't mean that claim is true. When you have worked in the police for longer than about two days, you realize that there are dozens of people who will claim to have committed a high-profile crime. Often those who keep the quietest are the most culpable.'

'So you think the Islamists are not responsible?'

'As my job requires, I'm keeping an open mind. If I did otherwise, you would be first to complain.'

'Do you think the rioters – sorry, demonstrators – are right to seek a whiter France, a France free of incomers, just as the Maid did?'

'I think you can turn any demonstration into a riot if you keep naming it as such often enough, particularly on television.'

'You credit us with more power than we deserve.' There's a particular double blink Henri does when he's thinking; she's seen it twice already and again now. 'What of the Maid? Are *you* the new incarnation?'

'Certainly not. I couldn't be less like her if I tried.'

'Really? Editors across the nation will be sorry to hear it.' One by one, he flips over the newspapers that lie on the coffee table in front of them. LA NOUVELLE PUCELLE? is all or part of the main headline on each. Somewhere else, a camera takes them in and hoists them on to the screens of the watching public.

'Your father, of course, was Charles Picaut, the famous – some might say infamous – historian and anthropologist. Was he not dismissed from the faculty of the university here in Orléans for his radical views on the Maid?'

You have to admire the skill. He has dug the hole. It would be so easy for Picaut to walk into it. A single step, and she'll be up to her neck in the old, familiar shit. She can smell it, taste it, drown in it.

She is not her father. His obsession is not hers.

She says, 'If we're going to stick to facts, he published one paper in 2013 in which he analysed the historical record of the Maid's actions and known statements and drew certain inferences from them.'

'For which he was dismissed?'

'After which he retired.'

'Because three million, two hundred and eighty-seven thousand, three hundred and fifteen people signed an Internet petition asking for him to go.'

The number spins out into the ether. Picaut can see it out of the corner of her eye. She looks away. 'We live in the age of Internet petitions, Henri. Given the coalition ranged against him, it's surprising it wasn't thirty million.'

'Coalition?'

Thank you, Patrice. 'What would you call it? The Catholic Church denounced him from the pulpit because they need their saint to be a weeping virgin who had visions of angels, in spite of the fact that she never once spoke of them when she was a free woman. The historians who were his colleagues hung him out to dry because their careers are built on the fantasy of magical thinking that has a mythical God who can bypass twenty years of training and teach a peasant girl how to ride as a knight in full plate. The political parties made mincemeat of him because they have harnessed her myth in defence of their own rampant xenophobia, and when he questioned its veracity, they were prepared to do whatever it took to destroy him. He had death threats near the end from members of the *Front National*, which, for a man dying of laryngeal chondrosarcoma is hardly an intelligent manoeuvre.'

'Indeed.' Blink-blink. Henri is staring at her, one finger tapping his jaw. She can't tell if he's shocked or smug or simply listening to instructions in his ear. He nods, pensively, and turns to his right.

'So Christelle, you are a member of a political party which has hijacked a false legend to justify your rampant xenophobia. And you or those around you sent death threats to a dying man. How do you respond to that?'

Christelle's smile is drenched in acid. 'I have never in my life sent a death threat, nor been party to such a thing. If Capitaine Picaut wishes to suggest—'

'They're a matter of record.' Capitaine Picaut can dip her smiles in poison too. 'I can send your campaign the IP addresses from which they came. They all traced back to Troy Cordier, your campaign manager.' For which, once again, thank you, Patrice.

'What about the Maid?' Henri is like a bloodhound chasing down a trail, and Christelle is his quarry. 'What do you say about her? Are you clinging to a dying myth to support your own views about the purity of French descent?'

If Christelle could spit . . . But her training has been extensive, and she knows how the polls will react if she loses her temper.

She spreads her hands, tilts her head, becomes the very model of reason and sanity. 'My church tells me who she was and I would never disagree. I will say this much: whoever she was, the Maid understood that we need a France that is French, governed by French citizens for French citizens, by those of us who have lived here for generations beyond counting, who know the suffering of this land, and its greatness. In that, I am hers, one hundred per cent.'

The Family would love this. Truly, Luc should have married this woman. She's just produced a perfect on-message answer, blown every single dog whistle that Christelle's campaign wants her to sound. Henri's smile never slips, but he's lost his chance to break her open and he doesn't push again.

The remainder of the interview offers neither spark nor danger. They discuss the size and fervour of the demonstrations, and nothing new or surprising emerges. Henri wraps to a close in time for the next news round-up.

Released, the same energetic interns who ushered them in escort Picaut and Christelle Vivier back out again with no diminution of vigour or enthusiasm; except this time they are not kept apart.

The door behind them sighs shut. An electronic lock snicks into place. Picaut feels the afterburn of the interview sing through her veins. A glance to her left shows Christelle Vivier standing loose-fisted, staring into nowhere.

Picaut says, 'I think they call it an ambush.'

'What? Who?'

'Television executives. This. What happened. It's the aim of every current affairs producer to have one ambush per week and we were it. Don't worry, Troy will be ecstatic. You said all he could have asked for.'

Troy Cordier, the *Front National*'s Aryan-blond attack-dog of a campaign manager, is an enigma. His record is entirely clean: not once has he been in any extremist party, but there are whispers upon whispers and they all say that he has channelled money to the Golden Dawn movement in Greece, and to the EDL in England, and that he is the kind who will cleanse Orléans by force if he is ever given the chance. If Christelle is not afraid of him, she is stupid, and she has just shown herself far from that.

There could be a moment's connection; the edge of it is there, in spite of everything, a whisper of empathy, of adversity shared. Picaut has no idea how old Christelle is. She hovers somewhere in that ageless space between twenty-five and forty-five when women change only their wardrobe. Hers is chosen for her, and is no indicator of anything. Just now, with her mask down, she looks at the very low end of that range, a vulnerable young woman, out of her depth in an increasingly vicious political war.

Then the door opens and Troy Cordier is there, with his blond hair a halo around his head and his teeth perfect. When he smiles, sharks cower.

Christelle spins to face him. Her hair spins with her, a weapon and a cloak. Her face closes over; her mouth sets back in its line. Age settles on her, and a loathing that relishes the fight ahead.

'Five days.' She makes a half turn back and points her finger at Picaut. Her voice is shrill. She *is* afraid of Troy Cordier. 'We have five days until the polls open. Tell Landis Bressard that this is a beginning, not an end. Tell him we shall have Orléans, and when we do, there will be no place here for him. Or his family.'

I am not his family. Picaut thinks but doesn't say this. She watches Christelle Vivier stalk out on to the street to be absorbed into the heart of Troy's team, the perfectly sharp young men and women in their perfectly tailored suits and wraparound shades. These are her Praetorian Guard, ready to whisk her off to the next appearance. Picaut has nobody to greet her. She was afraid the Bressards might have sent a limousine, but they have had the sense not to. She walks back to the car park and takes the long route in to work.

Orléans is slowly waking to another Tuesday morning. No demonstrators wreck the streets. But one of the three posters of Christelle Vivier by the cathedral has been replaced with a shot of Picaut in the shimmering bronze dress. There are no words; none are necessary. The heavy lifting has been done; people are free to draw their own conclusions.

Driving through town, she sees the same poster at least eight times, always overlaying one that previously showed Christelle, and when she stops to pick up *Le Monde* on the way into the station, she sees that the early editions have been replaced and that LA NOUVELLE PUCELLE has lost its question mark.

A scrum of press photographers has gathered outside the front door of the police station and there's very little hope they're waiting for anyone else.

Fuck.

Fuck and fuck and fuck them all. Fuck their mothers and their grandmothers. Fuck their ancestors back twenty-three generations.

In a foul temper, she dumps her car in the marked slot and sprints up the steps with her head down, dodging the flashing cameras.

CHAPTER SIXTEEN

Rheims,
17 July 1429

Rheims is in celebratory mood. Until yesterday loyal to the English crown, the city is now resolutely, overwhelmingly, ecstatically French, rolling out all manner of pageantry to mark the consecration of his august majesty, King Charles VII.

If the fountains do not yet flow with hippocras as they did at Troyes on the occasion of the king's sister's marriage to Henry of England, it is only because those who might have made it happen did not have sufficient warning.

A month ago, nobody believed the king would safely come this far north. Even a week ago, there was every chance that Bedford might raise an army to match the Maid's and march to meet her.

But he didn't and he hasn't and now the Maid is in a hurry, so the mould is being sponged from the banners that celebrated the last coronation nearly fifty years ago, and the velvets are shaken out and steamed and young women with bony fingers stitch pearls on to stiffened collars and mount scarlet and lemon silk on high, conical bonnets and the sun is out, blessing it all, which proves that God is on their side.

Regnault de Chartres, Archbishop of Rheims, returns to his see, which is a sight to behold in itself. In theory, he is ecstatic to be reunited with his flock; certainly, he must appear so.

He is not good, though, at dissimulation. The smile he has fixed on his face bears the look of one who has strained many hours to pass a stool and been interrupted partway through its completion. His cheeks are ruddy, his face sweats. When, in the robing room of the cathedral, he finds himself happily alone with Brother Tomas, he lets drop the pretence and smashes his fist off the oak panelling in sheer frustration.

'This was not supposed to happen.'

'But it has.'

'What do I do?' This is the first time they have dared to meet alone, but the ciphered letters have been fulsome in their detail of the archbishop's distress.

Today, it is evident that Regnault de Chartres has not been sleeping. His skin has the translucency of age; the folds beneath his eyes could nest a dormouse. He winds his hands one round the other.

'Bedford will sew me in a leather sack and throw me in the Seine if I anoint the snivelling little bastard with the oil of Clovis. It's sacred, do you understand? The kings of France have been marked with this oil since before there was a France. You can't undo it. Nobody can.'

'My lord of Bedford understands. Just do what you must. It matters more that the king trusts you and listens to you. We have to destroy the Maid before we can destroy the king and that won't happen overnight.'

Tomas pats the archbishop's arm. He is the kindly uncle, the priest with the penitent, finding words that will work to the right end. 'It'll all be over in a year, you'll see. Just don't let them march on Paris after.'

'How might I stop them, pray? The little whore doesn't listen to me. She doesn't listen to anyone except her "father in heaven".' The archbishop rolls his eyes skywards. One might almost think him angry with his god, were he not one of those who helped make the latest pope. He knows that God's will is what he says it is.

Tomas shrugs, a man of the world. 'But the king listens to you, and he holds the purse strings. He gives the orders. He will listen to her less once he is consecrated. He doesn't want Paris. And he doesn't need it. He must be made to see that it is not in his interests to take it by force. Begin peace negotiations with Philip of Burgundy.'

'Burgundy? Are you mad? He thinks Charles ordered the assassination of his father. He's sworn to see the entire house of Valois ground to dust and blood.'

'Even so.' Tomas ticks off the reasons, finger by finger. 'He is the king's cousin. Notionally, he holds Paris for the English. Send word that the Maid won't be allowed to attack Paris if Burgundy agrees not to harass the king.'

'Harass the king? That girl has twelve thousand armed men at her back and all of them begging God to let them kill an Englishman. Only a fool would go near them!'

'But the king doesn't know that. Burgundy's a knight. He's proved he can fight. The king isn't and hasn't. Make sure the boy knows that you're all that stands between him and a big man with a mace.'

'And the Maid?'

'We shall destroy the Maid, you and I. But we need time to find out who she is . . .'

'I know only that she is not what she claims. She is a liar and a heretic.'

'Then we shall prove it, and in proving it, destroy her. You do your part; I'll do mine.'

* * *

172

He leaves carefully and is accordingly late for his next meeting, in the stables behind his lodgings. The location may be unoriginal, but he has learned the value of setting his meetings in stables; high born or low, horses will always tell you if someone is to be trusted.

He has a new horse now, a wall-eyed chestnut mare, on loan from the Maid so that he might not overturn his vows of poverty by ownership. She flicks her ears at him, and rests her off hind, wary, but not restless; here are new, unknown men, but not yet danger.

The butcher and his son who sit on the upturned barrels rubbing oil into a headpiece are not overly concerned with his punctuality or lack of it; there is enough silver involved in their current transaction for time to matter exactly as much as he says it does.

They set aside the harness as he enters. Their flat, hard gazes follow him from door to stall to the wall-eyed mare. They are big men, easy with their knives, dressed alike in unremarkable wool and a soft leather jerkin. You wouldn't look twice at them in the street, but they stand in balance, and the son has a knife in his boot.

They could kill Tomas, probably, or at least make his life briefly difficult. He comforts himself with the thought that Bedford's men are picked for their level heads and they wouldn't attack him in here even if they were sure he needed to die. He leans into the mare, speaks from the far side of her neck.

'The Maid. Watch her. Follow her. I want to know where she goes when she's not with the king; who she speaks to, who her friends are, her enemies; everything and everyone. Bring it to me here, daily, at this time.'

They nod, get ready to go. They haven't spoken a word. He doesn't know if they're French or English. Or anything else. They could be German, Italian, Genoese, Venetian;

173

there's a market for foreign mercenaries now. They make no sound as they walk to the door. They could be ghosts. He says, 'It may be that I bump into her in the street. It may be that I require your help. Be ready.'

His next meeting is less salubrious, in an alley behind a tannery, where the vats of hide soak in urine and faeces and the air furs his tongue and pricks tears to his eyes.

The small man he meets there looks as if he feeds off the scent, cuts it up and chews it, and nothing else.

'Stefan.' A hand raised in greeting. He suspects that Stefan is not his name, but he doesn't want to know the truth. Bedford has sent him to ferret out the Maid's past and he is here to report what he has found to the man who most needs to know.

'How went Domrémy?' Tomas asks. Domrémy is the Maid's home village, so she says.

A shrug. 'You're not going to like it.'

'Why? You found a maid who is the Maid?'

'I found a village full of people who think themselves blessed by God to have harboured a prodigy. They all remember Jeannette growing from her childhood through her youth, and not one of them has anything to say about her you wouldn't want to hear about your sister.'

'They may be lying. Yolande of Aragon's men brought her to Chinon. There may be southern silver behind their stories.'

Stefan spreads his hands, sits on the edge of a foul vat. 'If it is, there's enough of it to stand up to gold, wine and . . . affection.'

Affection? Jesu. It's better not to ask with whom. In any case, it hardly matters because this one thing takes Tomas's careful theories and destroys them. He falls back against a wall and doesn't care that it will stain his cassock.

'She is real? The Maid is from Lorraine? It's all true?'

That shrug again. 'In Domrémy there was a maid. And now there is a Maid in Rheims who leads the army. Her father, her brothers all agree they are one and the same. Who is going to say they are wrong?'

Bertrand de Poulangy, Yolande's man, might do so, if he were pressed in the right way. But it would take blood and pain and possibly many days, which Tomas does not have. Yolande herself, the king's mentor, saviour and mother-in-law, might be manoeuvred into speaking, but she has kept away from the consecration, perhaps to avoid anyone asking exactly this. He has only one real hope.

He holds out a coin. Silver glimmers. He says, 'There is a girl called Claudine; straw-coloured hair, a burn on her hand. She used to service the soldiers. Her brother, Matthieu, died on the day the Maid first came to Chinon. These two were wards of the old king. Find me Claudine. She's an army whore and the army is celebrating. She won't be far.'

The coin is gone and 'Stefan' with it, and Tomas is out, and striding in clean air, trying to shed the stench that clings like a suit.

The anointing of King Charles VII of France takes place on the seventeenth of the month, a spectacle of gold and glitter, a pageant of furs and feathers, of silk and damask and velvet, of calf's hide and kid's hide and gold and silver, turquoise and diamond, emerald, ruby and sapphire.

Lacking only Yolande of Aragon, who claims a head cold, the lords and ladies of France gather in the cathedral of Rheims from early morning. Tomas slides in at the back and worms his way forward until he has a view to the front, where stand the lords and the archbishop, the king, and the Maid.

Her armour shines. Today, it could be cast of solid silver, set off with a surcoat of cloth of gold, boots of tooled calf hide and a coat braided with gold thread. Above all of that shines her smile. If she has been on occasion taciturn, moody, angry, vengeful, wrathful, today she is exultant, prideful, blazing with an arrogance nothing and no one can dull.

He cannot blame her. She is, what, twenty-three? Maybe twenty-four at a push. She has fought with blade and axe and lance, but she has also fought the detractions of Regnault de Chartres and his allies. She has submitted more than once to the intimate intrusions of those who would ascertain that she is truly a maid, known by no man. She has been called a whore and a heretic, has been questioned for ten days without break by dusty old men whose sole qualification was gained in Paris in their youth and who concluded at the end, not that she came to the king with God's blessing, but that they couldn't prove she didn't.

They asked her for a sign from God. She told them the relief of Orléans was her sign, and to let her go there. They found themselves unable to stop her. She went. She conquered. She rendered them silent. And now she marches at the king's right hand up the aisle of the cathedral of Rheims, and the archbishop, who openly hates her, must smile and bow and lift the crown.

And he does.

You could hear the cheers in Paris, did you find yourself minded to try.

He is only a man, Charles de Valois.

He is a young man lying face flat on the dressed stone steps of the altar with naked legs sallow between the stone and the white linen of his shirt. The cathedral of Rheims swells bare above him, a heaven of old, pale stone granted the grace of God's gold sun in the heights, while below is ruin and poverty, for England has taken the plate and chalice, the vestments and the altar cloths . . . everything that could be carried has gone to Paris for the coronation of their boy king who claims rule of France.

Some things they did not find: the crown; the two sceptres, one of gold, one of ivory. Most important of all, they have not the sacred oil that the angels brought for the true consecration of Clovis a thousand years ago, which has anointed every true King of France since. Everyone knows that Gilles de Rais hid that when Regnault of Chartres, archbishop of this place, would have handed it gladly to Burgundy, and so to England.

It is as archbishop that de Chartres must use it now to anoint a king, in the presence of his god. He trembles, the archbishop, under the greatness of this; it was not of his making. He holds the flask with unstable fingers, scrapes with a gold pin the smallest clot of the air-shrivelled wax from its base, dissolves it in myrrh, the Holy Chrism that anointed the Child in the crib, and blesses now the new-made king on his head, on his breast, on his bony elbows, shoulders, wrists.

'Arise now.'

The trumpets! A silver clarion of France to make the walls shake and lift the flutter of the Maid's standard. On such a sea of sound rises a gauche young man in his night-gown, his knees red from the scrape of the steps.

Charles d'Albret, the comte de Dreux passes to the king a tunic of shimmering red damask that reaches to his knees, and he becomes in the moment a man. A coat over it, of deep sea-blue brocade with gold fleurs-de-lis scattered over, each as big as a palm print. He is almost a king.

Pale gloves of kidskin, supple as a spring leaf, and a ring; the sceptre of ivory and the other of gold and, last, caught in a strand of high sun, mistletoe-pearls shimmering, bleeding with rubies, the crown of France passes from hand to hand to hand of the gathered peers of the realm – except Burgundy, obviously, who would not come – and the gauche youth *is* a king, ascending his throne. The Maid is beside him, she and her banner, in the place of majesty.

When she descended on Chinon, she said her father in heaven had set her three tasks: to relieve the siege of Orléans, to bring the dauphin to his consecration at Rheims, and to free the Duke of Orléans, the rightful duke, who languished in an English prison.

She has achieved two out of these three and has set her mind on Paris in lieu of the third. She is a miracle made living: Maid of Orléans, Victor of France.

CHAPTER SEVENTEEN

'SHE'S NOT THE FUCKING MAID. She never has been, she never will be, and if I see you with this trash anywhere near here again, I'll rip your head from your shoulders.'

Picaut hears Garonne before she turns the corner, and stops out of sight, that she might not interrupt what is clearly not meant for her ears. She was at boiling point long before she parked the car and ran the paparazzi-gauntlet into the Police Department. Each additional stare has pushed her further down the line towards some kind of physical explosion.

It hasn't occurred to her that this would be obvious to her team, nor that they'd take action to protect her from the fallout, but as she turns the corner she sees Rémi Meuret from the drug squad bent backwards over a desk on the end of Garonne's fist and Garonne's other hand crushing an A4 sheet with her image on it.

Garonne catches sight of her and flushes an ugly purple. He opens his fist and lets Rémi fold to the floor. The look he gives Picaut is complicated; she's his to diminish, not anyone else's. There's an odd kind of comfort in this thought.

The remainder of her team are waiting in her office. Patrice is sitting cross-legged on the floor with a laptop balanced across his knees. His hair is one long titanium-oxide braid that hangs straight down his back.

His T-shirt tells the world that he has taken back the night. Above the text, a stick figure sleeps on the curve of a new moon. Beyond him, Rollo is leaning on the door, hands in pockets. Spiky-blonde Sylvie sits on the only spare chair. Éric is at the back. He'll have driven through the epicentre of the demonstrations; that he could get here at all bodes well for the day.

They all rise as Picaut comes in. She waves them down and takes her usual place, sitting with her legs hanging over the edge of her desk.

It's just another day at work. If she can believe this, perhaps the building will cease to hum with gossip; perhaps she will be left alone to do her job.

As on any other day, therefore, she takes the coffee Patrice hands her and launches into the results of the phone calls she made in the short hop between the television studio and the station.

'The Fire Department has nothing for us on Sunday night's fire beyond what they said at the time: that the accelerant was ordinary gasoline. Forensics say it's the cleanest site they've ever met. Every room in the house had the prints of the occupants and signs of their presence – except Iain Holloway's. In there, they have found not a single print, no DNA, nothing.'

'So it was cleaned,' says Éric.

'Exactly. But if one line of inquiry is closed, we can put our resources into whatever's left. We have Iain Holloway's basic itinerary from when he stepped off the Eurostar in Paris a week ago, to when he ended up in the Hôtel Carcassonne late on Sunday afternoon. Most of it has come from his credit card trail; we need to fill in the gaps.

'Sylvie has made a list of the addresses where it was used. We'll each take a day. Garonne, you have Wednesday in Paris, moving to Blois on Thursday morning. Sylvie and Rollo, take over Thursday evening, Friday and the first part of Saturday in Blois. I'll take Saturday and Sunday, when he moved from Blois to Orléans. Take a picture and see if you can get any sightings.'

Patrice has printed out copies of Iain Holloway's image from the various Internet forums. Picaut passes them round. 'Someone should recognize him from these. Look for any connections. He was Scottish, he worked on war graves, he had contacts in Glasgow and maybe Cornell. He had an interest in medieval battlefields and he took my father's side in the debate last year, so he's not completely clueless. If we can work out what he was doing and why he was doing it, we might find out why he was killed. Any questions?'

'What's Patrice doing?'

That's Garonne, who has just worked out he's about to drive to Paris and of course thinks this is a slight. A year ago, he'd have taken it as a perk: two hours in a car each way and nothing to do but shuffle tracks on his iPod. A year ago, someone else would have given the order.

'Patrice is code-breaking.' With a nod, Picaut cedes him the floor, or rather the desk. He is definitely wearing eye shadow. And lip gloss. He still looks ruggedly male. She hasn't worked out how.

He hops up on to her desk and sits cross-legged with his iPad balanced across his ankles. He has no fear of public presentations, of talking to those twice his age with a kill count he can match only in online fantasy games. He blesses Rollo and Garonne with his easy grin.

'So: Iain Holloway's USB chip has been swallowed and then cooked. Short of smashing it with a sledgehammer and feeding the bits to an alligator, there's not much more you could do to destroy the data that was stored on it.'

'But you got something.' Rollo is not known for his patience.

'I did. It took a stunning amount of time and some software I've never seen before, but yes, we got to the data. Or at least to some encrypted files. Opened, they look like this—' Patrice holds up his iPad.

Rollo ignores it and carries on picking dirt from under his fingernails. Sylvie frowns at the screen, mouthing words to herself, but it's Garonne who grabs it in his meaty fists, stabbing it with his forefinger in a way that makes Patrice wince.

'This is garbage.'

'No, it's hexadecimal code.' Patrice prises the Pad from Garonne's hands before he can do real damage. 'Which is to say it's alphanumeric, written in base sixteen instead of base two so we can read it more easily. Some of us can read it more easily. You, obviously, are an exception.'

Sylvie says, 'But there are no letters here. It's all numbers, except maybe an exclamation point, and a colon?'

Sylvie can read hex code. Her stock amongst the team rises appreciably. Patrice, delighted, offers her a salute, fist across chest.

'Right,' he says. 'Yes. Exactly. There are two colons, an exclamation point, an ampersand, an apostrophe and a few other minor dots and dashes. Beyond that, we have a string of numbers of ever-increasing length, which is a fairly standard cipher technique. We need the key to this, and to the other two files on the chip. Just getting this open took all night. I haven't broken into any of them yet.'

'You will,' Picaut says. She has faith. She needs to have faith.

'I'm doing my best, but if it's PGP, we're screwed.' Patrice glances over at Garonne. 'That's Pretty Good Privacy.'

'And Pretty Good Privacy is . . . ?'

'Unbreakable. You don't want the detail of how, but the important bit is that if every particle in the universe was a computer and they had each tried one iteration per second of all the possible options that might break it since the dawn of time, they still wouldn't have worked it out.'

There is a moment's silence as they grapple with the enormity of this, then Picaut says, 'Iain Holloway swallowed this chip. He wanted us to have it. He wouldn't have left it in an unbreakable code.'

'That's what I thought.' Patrice loops his fingers together, turns his hands over and cracks all the knuckles at once. 'So there'll be a key. If it's short, like a name, we stand a chance. If it's long, like a book, we don't. I can tell you now it isn't his mother's maiden name, his address, the name of his cat, his ex-wife's cat, the street address of his childhood home or any variant thereof.'

'How do you know that?' asks Éric Masson.

'I tried them.' Patrice is serious now, and Picaut can see how his night has been spent. 'I've tried every iteration of all his close relatives, his colleagues, his home address, his work address, his alma mater, his pets, and the names of the people he talked to on the various historical forums he was on or the messages he left. None of them fits. He was intelligent enough to encode this, so he's not going to use something that every hacker and his parrot could find. It will be obvious, but only to someone who knows him well.'

'Or someone who has his laptop,' Picaut says. 'Which his killer may well do.'

Patrice chews his lip. 'If he's as bright as we think he is, he won't have left the key on the same machine as the cipher text, but the bad guys may still be one step ahead. Depends how good the hackers are.'

'Is there anyone else in Orléans better than you? In the whole of France, even? Europe?'

'I'd like to say not, but I don't want to lie to you.' Patrice ticks the names off on his fingers as he thinks of them. 'Geraldine in Cork has been busy recently and won't say what she's doing. Tahar went off the radar in Sintra this weekend when he was supposed to be in a Guild Wars tournament. Wolf Nijenhus in Utrecht has been in lockdown for the past fortnight and isn't answering emails. Any one of these could have a serious go at cracking any cipher in the world. The best we can hope for is that now we've got the hex code, we're faster than they are at finding the key. He was an intelligent guy. It'll be something we can find out as we get to know him.'

'Right.' Picaut rounds on the rest of the team. 'Our priority is breaking this code and for that we need to know what Iain Holloway was doing, who he spoke to, what he said, and why. Which means everyone needs to do some actual, boots-on-the-ground police work. Go carefully, keep your eyes open and for God's sake call for backup sooner rather than later. I'd rather drive halfway across France on a false alarm than lose one of you to a broken skull and a fire.'

She stands, snapping her fingers. 'Let's go, people. First one with something concrete that takes us forward gets free drinks for a week. Pray for me as you go. I'll be stuck between Ducat on one side and the press on the other.' She pats Garonne on the shoulder as he leaves. 'I promise you, driving to Paris is better.'

CHAPTER EIGHTEEN

'Course I knew her. Grew up with her, didn't I? Do you want me to . . ?'

'Not yet. Today is a special day. Will you sit with me awhile?'

Claudine, army whore and former ward of King Charles VI, is not sober.

She is hardly alone in this. The entire population of Rheims is unsober, with the possible exception of Brother Tomas, white friar, who has paid a whore for her services for an hour in the late afternoon of the day of the new king's anointing.

He has not taken Claudine indoors; today of all days, there is not a room to be rented anywhere in the city. He is forced, therefore, to sit in front of a smithy on a bench made of sawn planks laid on barrels, with a girl who will get on her knees and wrap her lips around him if he gives her half a chance.

And then she will leave, and seek more coin elsewhere, which is not what he wants. He folds his hands together and leans forward and slides another coin under the leather beaker. 'For your memories. I would know more of God's creation that walks among us.'

'God's . . . ? Ha!' The snigger is stifled for care of his faith, not the Maid's, he thinks. 'If she's of God, He works through the King of France. The old king, the one whose wife got her sons from his brother. This one' – she nods up the hill to the cathedral – 'is no more king than I am. And she's no more a maid from Lorraine.'

The king's bastardy is yesterday's news. The Maid, though . . . Tomas leans forward, a man enthralled. 'And yet there was a maid. Her brothers are here. And her father.'

'I don't know who they are. But I fought with the one who calls herself Maid when I was ten years old and she was seven. It was the day of Agincourt. The day my father died. I won't forget it.'

'You fought with a seven-year-old girl on the field of battle?' Truly, he knew the French were insane, but . . .

'Don't be daft! We were at Rouen, waiting with the ladies and the king for news of a great victory.'

She laughs again, more throatily. She is not a bad-looking girl. Her hair is the colour of good straw, and it shines in the sun. Her features are thin, with a knife's edge to her cheek-bones and blued thumbprints beneath her eyes. Her mouth is generously wide; easy to imagine it working. Her breasts are small, wasted for lack of food, but still they are more than he has seen since . . .

He looks away. A dazzle of gold catches his eye, from the porch of the great house at the head of the street. The Maid, who else? She has a surcoat of cloth of gold, set off with silver buckles, shining armour, and the helm that bares only her face, and not all of that. Even today, she wears armour. She has a lot to prove, or to hide.

What do you not want us to see? Are you deformed under

there? Do you carry marks that would give you away? Or is your face just too well known?

He drags his attention back to Claudine, to the grubby shift and third-hand gown, to the clogs worn through at the heels.

'In what way, then, did you fight with her?'

'In the courtyard. Matthieu and I had been sent out to bring in firewood. We were carrying bundles past the stable yard and she was there, fighting with de Belleville.'

'Who?'

'Jean of Harpedene, whose father was sieur de Belleville-en-Poitou. We were . . . my father was a man at arms with the sieur d'Orléans. He fell when Duc Charles was taken.'

Tod Rustbeard fought at Agincourt. He was in the company who took the king's cousin, deemed the most dangerous man in France. He may have killed her father. It is entirely possible. 'I'm sorry.' He lays his hand on hers. 'That must have been hard.'

She thinks about this, as if newly. 'The old king was kind to us, after.'

And the father, perhaps, had not been? He can imagine that. 'So the heir of Belleville was fighting with the Maid. What kind of fighting? Were they wrestling? Hitting each other? What?'

'They had sticks like swords.' She slashes the air. 'They were pretending to be knights. Like the men on the field. De Belleville was twelve. I remember, because he thought himself almost a knight.'

'And what about the girl who became the Maid? Did she think of herself as a knight?'

Claudine sneers. 'Always. She carried a stick that was supposed to be a sword, and charged at the tilt as if she was riding a horse. She was strong for her age, and she fought hard. Sometimes they duelled, one against the other, but this time, because of the day, and the battle, it was a mêlée. We went to de Belleville's side – he was almost a lord – and the Maid called for help and young Jean d'Alençon came, who was only—'

'Four years old. His father died on the field of Agincourt. He became sieur before nightfall.'

'Exactly. So he was too young really to fight, and she hated that. She always wanted a fair fight. Like a knight. So she called again, and Huguet came, who was de Belleville's friend and later became a priest, and so we were even, three against three, and we pushed them back so the Maid was behind a water trough and then she jumped out and was going to take me hostage, I think, or maybe . . .'

Claudine drifts to silence, lost in memory. He waits. There is nothing to be gained by pushing now, and everything to lose. He wants to take this girl and make her sober. He wants to pay her enough gold to buy a new shift: think! Clean linen next to your skin! And a new gown. You could have red wool. The ladies of Rheims love red wool. And a hood for the winter, and good leather boots that will keep your feet warm. And . . .

'Claudine?'

'She came and spoiled it.'

'Who did?'

'We called her the Princess. The king's daughter. The king's . . .' a long, slow leer '. . . bastard daughter.'

That word. It strikes him like a knife to the chest. He is grown now, it shouldn't hit him thus, but there's no denying it does.

Something must show on his face. Claudine grabs at his arm. 'Sorry, but it's what she was.'

'Nevertheless, you called her the Princess.'

A shrug. 'She behaved like one. We saw her hardly at all; months passed at a time when she didn't appear, and then,

188

when she did she was with la Petite Reine, or my lady of Aragon, or someone else who dressed her in silks and tied ribands in her hair. She looked like a statue. Marble. Perfect. If anyone came from God, it was her. His daughter. She was ... an angel.'

He has heard a lot, these past days, about the old king's bastard daughter. He has caught a glimpse of her from a distance once or twice, although not close enough to say if she is truly an angel.

He knows her name, though, everyone does, and her story. She is Marguerite de Valois, daughter of Odette de Champdivers, the king's mistress, known universally as la Petite Reine for the obvious reason that the real queen was vast as a toad, and in any case, didn't live anywhere near the king. When he was in Paris, the Queen was in Chinon. When he went south to the Loire, his wife travelled north. They kept well apart from each other and the King's sun rose and set in the eyes of Odette, the girl from Burgundy. They say her name was the last word he spoke, but still, she was left destitute when he died, and her bastard daughter with her.

A lot of people, it seems, were left destitute after the old king's death. Claudine, Matthieu, and now la Petite Reine and her child. Six years on and Odette de Champdivers is dead. Her daughter, though, is the protégée of Yolande of Aragon, brought back to the court from her exile and legitimized by the new king's decree, the stigma of bastardy wiped away as if it had never been.

It's useful, evidently, to have a pope in your pocket. A holy father who, for sufficient gold, can make everything right. Your father was not married to your mother? No matter; God may hate bastards, but now you are no longer hated, you are the king's beloved sister, fit to betroth a man who has an income higher than the king's, if the wagging tongues are right.

Thus did Marguerite the bastard become Marguerite de Valois. And then in May, soon after the relief of Orléans, she was betrothed to Jean, her childhood friend who had lately inherited his title of Belleville-en-Poitou, making him one of the richest men in France. Not a bad lot for a girl got out of wedlock.

In a different world, she would be queen. After all, nobody questions that she is the old king's true daughter, while everybody, even the king himself – both kings, actually, old and new – believes her brother is not the old king's son.

Claudine's head sinks on to her folded arms, cheek to elbow, ear to wood. She wets her finger in a puddle of wine and draws a sword on the rough bench. Tomas brings his own head down, chin balanced on his interlocked fingers. He is eye to eye with her, as with a child. 'She broke up your play fight, the angel?'

'She . . . No. The Maid went to her. They were . . .' A scowl. Two fingers crossed, one atop the other, inseparable. Claudine is not part of their closeness. A wound from the past, an exclusion, even then. 'But it was the king who broke it up.'

'The old king.'

She nods and nods again, and keeps on nodding, as if her head has forgotten how to stop. 'He was nice. He was good to us.'

'But he broke up the play?' Don't stop now. Please God, don't stop now. How often do men say that to her? If she was only wrapping her lips around him, he might say it aloud. He catches her eye, smiles, does his best to be friendly, interested, unthreatening.

'It was the day of the battle. Agincourt. The king took her to ride on his own horse, Poseidon. His battle mount.'

'His daughter?' The old king was a bad ruler, but he was the best horseman in the land. Tomas tries to imagine the

190

fragile angel that is Marguerite de Valois being taught to ride on one of the king's war mounts. The royal horses were notoriously savage. He fails.

Claudine gives a sly smile, brings one finger up to tap the side of her nose. 'Not the angel. She was never a rider. He took the Maid.'

The Maid, who, at the age of seven, could ride. The Maid, whose father had taught her.

Who was she? Who was her father? Did he die with yours at Agincourt?

So many questions, and no chance, now, of any answer. Claudine's eyes may be open, but the spark is snuffed out. She is gone to him. He might rouse her with slaps and cold water, but he can't do that here.

And perhaps this is enough. He imagines Bedford's face when he tells him that he has a witness who will testify that the Maid was a ward of the old king, who treated her as well as he treated his bastard daughter, because the angelic princess didn't want to ride, and in her stead the mad king found a girl who absorbed everything he could teach her of chivalry and horsemanship.

With his prize secure, Tomas settles back against the sun-warmed walls of the smithy and watches as the citizens of Rheims abandon themselves to revelry.

The fountains may not flow with hippocras, but it is as great a spectacle as any he has seen. Even the dullards have realized by now that this is a thing that will never be repeated, that they will want to remember, to rehash, to tell in all the gold and glory into their ageing years.

Men kiss women and women kiss men and three quarters of a year from now Rheims will sigh sleepless through the nights to a rash of new-born infants, the boys all called Charles for a change, and the girls Jehanne or Jeanne or Jeannette. Already, you can see how they will look.

* * *

An hour or so later, Brother Tomas departs the smithy and the gently snoring Claudine and wanders through the town. His cassock picks him out for a man of God and men and women come to kneel at his feet for a blessing. He has no shame; he gives what they ask and if the God who oversees all this cares that he is not a real priest, there has never been any sign. His father was a bishop, after all; maybe he is close enough.

Up on the high table, the king's six-year-old son, heir to the newly confirmed throne, is being shown to the crowd. If he lives to inherit the crown – if there is a crown for him to inherit – he will be Louis XI of France.

Just now, he is no more obviously regal than Henry VI of England who is a few months his senior. Stiff in cloth of gold, he waves where he is told and when he is told at whom he is told, which is everyone. Tomas waves back, one amongst thousands. He walks on.

Through the crowds, from time to time, he sees Bertrand de Poulangy, and Jean de Metz, Jean d'Aulon, Louis de Coutes. All the Maid's men are out today and they look every inch as sober as he is. He avoids their gaze, slouches, pulls his hood over his face, keeps walking.

In the mellow evening, the crowds begin to disperse. Tomas finds a bench outside a tailor's shop and leans back against the wall with his hood flopped over his brow, to shield his face from the sly evening sun.

He is within reach of the flat-faced butcher and his son; the father round the corner, lounging outside a weaver's shop, and the son further away, sitting on the dirt, weaving willow twigs into baskets. That's where they were when last he stepped away to relieve himself.

He is within sight of Jacques of Domrémy, the peasant farmer who claims to be the Maid's father. A fat, fleshy individual, with a drinker's broken veins webbed across his cheeks, he has spent all day punching his fists in the air, screaming her name with the rest, raising toast after toast in other men's wine, and nobody telling him to stop. Not today.

Tomas thinks it might be an interesting thing to seek this man when he is sober, and talk to him. Tell me about your daughter. Do you really expect us to believe it was you who taught her to ride, to manage a war horse better than most men in the kingdom? To wield a lance with such accuracy? They say she killed twelve and captured twice that many on the field outside Orléans on Ascension Day. Once, I did not believe it. Now, I rather think I do.

She has read Homer, I'd swear, and Caesar. Can you write? Can you even read? Because I think she can do both of these things, although someone with a quick mind has impressed upon her the need to appear unlettered. And if that wasn't you, then who? Who has the wit, the understanding, the knowledge, to take the ward trained by a king and turn her into God's miracle for the French? It certainly wasn't you, but it was someone who understands what she is, and who knows that France needs her.

And then another conundrum. If the Maid is the king's ward, who in the name of all that is holy is the maid from Domrémy, of whom an entire village speaks only good things?

Perhaps the bench was not the best place to sit, for Jacques lurches closer, making yet more noise in his daughter's name. Nobody has had the bad grace to point out that he is said to have beaten her the first time she tried to come to Chinon.

He shouts her name again, and men around him cheer, somewhat flatly. He is a bore to the marrow, but it is growing dark, and he lives by the sun. The time comes when even he must take leave of all his hundreds of new friends and head off to his lodgings, swaggering, unsober, dressed in new clothes that his daughter has clearly bought for him, or the king on her behalf: fine wool topcoat, good boots, a hat topped by three feathers, dyed crimson. Useful, that; a man can follow it. Three men, in fact.

Tomas rises slowly, adjusts his own tunic and sandals, turns the corner and nods to the butcher out there in the fading light, who nods to his son. He lifts his hand to his head and makes a mime of three feathers, touches a piece of red linen that drapes loosely from the eaves. They nod, father and son, and ease into the dusk.

He is following, has gone three dozen steps, when he sees her: the Maid.

She is not in cloth of gold now; no gilt or silver, precious little shine, except it's still there about her temples and the cut of her collarbones, a fine eldritch glow that lifts her as she walks, makes her seem as if she is floating.

She's done her best to hide herself: dressed in dark hose and a doublet, a belt with one knife and that old, a cap that hides most of her shining black hair. If you only looked at her clothes, you'd think she looked like a stable boy; even her boots are scuffed and worn through at the heels. So you *were* a horse boy. I believed it before. Now, I know it. Perhaps a horse breaker, too. These two are not in- compatible.

Tomas, who knows what it takes to change his looks, admits to a small flicker of . . . something. He calls it interest. He will not admit to admiration of her, who is the destruction of all he holds dear. Nobody else seems to notice her, which is good.

She, too, is following this man who claims to be her father. Tomas has not time to call back the butcher and his son. He has to hope she doesn't see them, but that hope is dashed.

She doesn't stop and turn, or run after them, or shout; nothing so obvious. She sidesteps into an alley where the grey dusk light is dimmed to night darkness, and from there she watches, and does not follow.

Which means he must watch her, and not follow. And not be seen.

She is good. He is better. He is not seen, but he loses sight of the red feathers in the jaunty little cap and the two flat-faced butchers who follow it.

The problem with his guise as an Augustinian friar is that he has to wear white. It may be a trifle dusty now, with mud at the hem and the occasional spot of blood from some broken nose or other from men overwrought with heat and lack of English to fight, but the stains are not what you'd call concealing and so he has to keep well to the shadows. He sees the Maid vacate her alleyway and they drift north-east, back towards the cathedral, a dark-clad horse boy and his off-white shadow.

The butcher and his son have made themselves scarce. He can feel them, but can't see them; they are a malevolence in the night and the Maid can feel them too. She leads him a circular route that jinks in and out of alleys, and by the end of it the sense of a knife-thrust heading for his kidneys has faded away.

The night is nearly dark when she comes to a particular door, old, with peeling paint, no other distinguishing marks, and raps on it a particular rhythm with her knuckle.

Inside, a man is snoring. It could be her father, or it could be almost any man in Rheims. Whoever he is, he jerks awake at her knock, cursing foully. If the Maid heard him, she'd have him on his knees with a priest in a heartbeat confessing his sin, but this is not the Maid, not outwardly. To anyone watching, this is a youth in dark hose and a cap with a knife at his belt. The door opens.

'Oh, it's you.'

Tomas watches them meet: the man who has spent all day celebrating the good fortune of his daughter, and . . . his daughter. They stare at one another. This is not their first meeting, but nor is it a heartfelt reuniting. He does not invite her in.

She goes anyway, a foot in the door and then a shoulder. She *is* taller than him, and leaner, and while she does not look like him any more than she looks like her 'brothers', she has the same air as the butcher and his son: she could kill this man and not feel the need to confess it after.

The man backs away. She kicks the door shut with her heel. Damnation. Still, it is an old hovel and they are not known for the solidity of their walls. This one is made of thin brick held by sour old mortar easily picked at, a door that has warped in the summer's heat, shutters that she closes. But they don't shut tight.

The cottage stands at the end of the line, so Tomas can slide round the side, out of sight. Inside, the Maid lights a candle, which is just perfect, because the thing about standing in almost-darkness is that slivers of light snick through the gaps, little gifts to eye and ear, so that he can press his eye here and cup his hand there, and if he is not quite in the room with the two of them, he is not so far off.

The Maid's candle sits within a lantern, its light cut by the frame. Blades of black and silver slice across the wall. Tomas sees straw strewn on the floor, an unlit fire by the door, cobwebs everywhere. A wooden bench, a table, a fat candle, wilting, and Jacques d'Arc propped at an angle, his arms folded, legs crossed at the ankle, leering at the girl.

He looks her up and down and when he speaks, it has the air of something he has planned for many months; the words come out folded over themselves, kneaded into shapelessness from the times he has practised them in his head. Tomas hears them with perfect clarity.

'I could tell the king who you are.'

The Maid leans against the door, holding it tight shut. Something moves on the room's far side, becomes a scarlet and gold cockerel, and three shabby hens scratching for grit in the dirt. Her attention is all on them; this man is not worthy of even a look. She laughs.

Jacques bristles. 'I can!'

'Do you really think he doesn't know?'

Outside Tomas holds his breath. Say it. Say your name. It's all I need to know and then I have everything. *Say it!*

She doesn't. Even here, she is careful.

The man who is not her father says, 'Regnault de Chartres doesn't know. Men say he is your enemy.'

'Certainly he thinks I'm a fraud. He has said so repeatedly and in all kinds of company. He questioned me for ten days, trying to prove it.'

'He'll pay, then, for that proof.'

'He might do. But he has just held the crown for the king, has just had the chance to dip his needle in the oil of Clovis; the first archbishop so to do for forty-nine years. He may prefer that the whole of Christendom not laugh at him for a fool.'

'He would see you burn.'

'And you, possibly, for having waited so long to tell anyone.'

The Maid turns away from the window. Jacques d'Arc takes a step away from her, lifts his hands as if she has just unsheathed her blade. Sweat leaks down his brow. His mouth moves but no more words fall out. The spiders have caught them all, hung them out in dried husks on the lace-works that droop in the corners of the room.

She says, 'The king will honour you and your family: a stipend, and a family name.'

Jacques' eyes flare. He is avarice made mortal. A knife in the gut would do the world a service. 'How much? What name?'

'In amount, twice what the old king gave when you took Hanne in. As to the name, that is up to the new king, but you will be noble, and your sons after you.'

Hanne. There's a warmth in the name, the first time Tomas has heard the Maid speak of someone as if she cares. So the mad king paid this oaf to take in . . . Who? A waif? Another of the many orphans of Agincourt? Were there so many he had not room under his own roof?

Whatever the reason, the payment must have been good, because Jacques likes what he hears. His eyes bulge.

'When will this happen?'

'Before the year's end.'

It is July. The year's end is six months away. Jacques grunts, calculating days and dates and how much else he can ask.

Tomas is increasingly inclined to use his knives to good effect on this man. He is not surprised, therefore, when the Maid slides her hand under her cloak and pulls out what hides there, only disappointed that it is not cold iron. The old man flinches, even when he sees it is a copy of the testaments.

She sets it on the table, a challenge. 'You will lay your hand on this now and speak an oath to hold secret all that you know. If that oath is broken, I swear by all that is holy that you will die, and not swiftly.'

Oh, nicely done!

Jacques' tongue smears across his lips. 'You are more likely to die before me. You insist on riding into battle like a man, against God's will. What then?'

The Maid laughs again, a sound that scorns every breath he takes. 'If it were not God's will, I could not do it. And if I die, that shall be His will also. But trust me when I tell you that there will be those left alive whose pleasure in life will be to kill you and all you hold dear. You won't know their names, and you will not know when they will come, but no amount of gold in the world will bring you to life again, I promise you this.'

Outside, Tomas thinks he will remember that line, and use it. He also thinks that what she says is true. Bertrand de Poulangy would kill for her, and Jean d'Alençon, and Jean d'Aulon, her squire, or indeed any one of twelve thousand men at arms who would kill any man they thought was a threat to her without needing to know the detail.

Inside, Jacques too knows the truth when he hears it. His tongue lies trapped between his lips. His eyes disappear with the effort of his thinking.

She says, 'You understand? Your immortal soul will suffer if you break this oath.'

Jacques doesn't care. He is about to be free of her. He discovers his courage. 'Twice what I was paid before, or I go to the archbishop.'

It's extortion, but he gets what he wants. She nods. He lays his hand on the bible and swears to keep his truth and it would be a very brave man who would risk his soul's chance of heaven after that.

The Maid leaves as quietly as she came. Tomas lets her go ahead and follows at a good distance. At a certain point, he feels the tingle at his kidneys which tells him the butcher and his son are back again, ghosting along some distance back. Sometime later, they cut in ahead of him, and he can fall back and let them take over.

She's heading back to the king's lodgings, anyway, which

is of limited value. Half the court is lodged there, or close to it. If there's a Hanne amongst the wives and daughters, Tomas hasn't heard of her. But he will.

This is his new project: to find the girl who was raised in Domrémy. He runs her name in his mind, repeating it in the way he heard it said. So subtle a thing that if he had breathed out at the wrong moment, slid the wool of his tunic against the shutter, he wouldn't have caught the change in the tenor of the Maid's voice, the deep, rough edge of care. Hanne matters.

Hanne matters and so he, Tomas, will find her and he will chain her, with gold if he can, with iron if necessary, and then the Maid herself will give up her name.

CHAPTER NINETEEN

ORLÉANS,
Tuesday, 25 February 2014
08.15

'. . . CAN REST ASSURED THAT we are doing everything we can to find the killers of Dr Iain Holloway and bring them to justice. I have every faith in Capitaine Picaut. She is one of our foremost investigators and it is to her credit that we already know the identity of the man who was left faceless and nameless in a burned-out hotel. We shall honour his memory in the best way we know how: by finding those who left him to die.'

Ducat does this well. The big-windowed press room in his office has the cathedral as its backdrop and he has positioned the podium so that every photograph will show him set against the towering spires of *his* city.

More important from Picaut's point of view, his sheer bulk is armour against the press pack clustered below the small stage. Half of them are British, relishing the horror of a Scotsman murdered in a French fire. They think in monosyllables and have fastened on to the latest new-Maid meme with the tenacity of leeches.

The French press, tutored carefully by Luc, are not notice-ably more sane. There are only so many columns you can devote to asking who Jaish al Islam might be and dissecting its possible motives; only so many times you can admire Christelle Vivier and her *Front National* opportunism while asking guarded questions as to their long-term aims.

Picaut is their gift from heaven, and if they treat her with more respect than the British press, it is out of awe for the woman whose mantle they have thrown on her back.

Ducat steps off the podium. His defensive line collapses, and lets them at her. Neon lights glint on their cameras, as on helmets in battle. She steps up on to the boards and into a wall of sound.

'Capitaine?'

'Capitaine Picaut!'

'Inès!' An English reporter from the *Mail* thinks he'll catch her off guard like this. Already she hates him and she doesn't even know what he looks like, only the sound of his voice.

'Capitaine Picaut, how does it feel to be the new Maid of Orléans?'

She doesn't smile. Ducat advised against it when they met in his office. *The Bressards have cast you in a light of their devising, but you don't have to feed the frenzy they have started. Be yourself. They will all have seen your display this morning, but most of their audience won't, so bear that in mind as you answer.*

As herself, then, or as close as she can be, she says what she said this morning, only in a different order. 'It feels the same as it did when you pinned the same title on Christelle Vivier. It wasn't true then; it isn't true now. I am a police officer and it's my job to find who's lighting these fires; and since the weekend I have also to find the killers of Iain Holloway. I will accomplish both tasks better if I'm left to get on with them.'

She speaks through a cloudburst of camera flashes. If she were prone to epilepsy, this is when she would be on the floor, foaming. Because of the bouncing light, and the flashes, she doesn't see Luc until he's standing beside her, his arm draped loosely on the podium next to hers, not quite touching.

He smiles, nods to a couple of men, and a woman, and like that, effortlessly, he has them holding their breath to see which amongst them will receive his next blessing. They fall silent. The flashes continue, but fewer and further between.

The quality of their attention means that his words have a peculiar intimacy, as if he were speaking to each of them in private; each hears, therefore, as if alone.

'There comes a point when you have to accept that this is the twenty-first century, not the fifteenth. The Maid was a remarkable woman. So is my wife. But they are different, and as she says, she has a job to do. If, like me, you want her to succeed, you will give her the space – and the respect – to do it without any need to bring up the past. So now, if you've taken all the pictures you need, I think you might find it's time to leave.'

He steps back, indicates the door. The pack, chastened, press out into the street.

Ducat could have got them to leave, but he would have had to bully them and they would have gone resentfully. He seethes; the raw heat of it scorches Picaut's back. For it is Luc and Inès Picaut who will share tomorrow's headlines.

She turns towards him. 'Maître, if we could discuss—'

Luc is at her elbow. 'I'm sorry. We were trying to draw them off Christelle Vivier and her whole *Front National* insanity. I swear we had no warning about Henri Aubel's act of sabotage this morning. We'll do what we can to deflect the damage.'

'I'm sure you will.' She takes a step away from him. 'I

have, as we both pointed out, a job to do. For which I need to speak with the prosecutor . . .'

'Of course. My apologies.' He lifts her hand, kisses it. They have stepped into the lobby of Ducat's office. The pack is outside, standing on the steps, between Picaut and her car. She turns a full circle, looking for a way out. There is the fire escape, and a back door. And between them Lise Bressard, wearing a platinum grey Saint Laurent suit and a Chanel scarf that sets off her night-dark hair.

Here, now, she is the closest thing to a friend Picaut has got.

She says, 'Lise, I have to go somewhere without the pack on my heels. How would you feel about leading them astray?'

It's probably the first time she's ever addressed this woman by name. She might well be rebuffed; just now, she doesn't care.

Perhaps because of that, Lise looks interested. 'What have you in mind?'

'Take this.' Picaut shrugs out of her buckskin jacket. 'And these.' Her sunglasses are Police, not police, but still far inferior to anything Lise Bressard might choose to wear. On the other hand, every shot the pack took this morning had her wearing them. 'If you tuck your hair in at the back, it'll look shorter.'

'And if I'm wearing your jacket, you must have mine . . .' Luc's cousin slips out of her slubbed silk creation, grey with maroon points, and hands it over. Her scarf is a matching shade of quiet red, the silk smooth as sunlight. 'Luc will have to drive you away from here,' she says. 'It'll look strange otherwise. He needs to go to the office. After that, you can take the car and do with it what you will. I'll drop yours back here at the station when I'm done. Where should I go, and for how long?'

Lise looks cheerful, buoyant, even; a side of her Picaut hasn't seen before.

'North towards Paris. An hour should be enough.'

'Consider it done.'

They watch her go. She has modified her walk, Picaut realizes; her stride is longer, lower to the ground, somehow.

'Do I walk like that?'

'You do.' It is Ducat who answers. His face is unreadable. 'If you have a minute?'

She leaves Luc by the window. Ducat lets her lead the way into his now-empty office. Truly, today is a day of firsts.

Inside, he says, 'Where are you going?'

'Meung-sur-Loire. Iain Holloway used his credit card at the station there on Saturday morning, before he came to Orléans. I'll pick up the trail there.'

'And what if our friends in the press aren't fooled by Annelise's little stunt? Are you seriously going to start looking for witnesses with a TV crew on your tail?'

Picaut presses her fingers to the closed lids of her eyes. 'Is there any kind of injunction . . . ?'

'Not that I could enforce.'

'Great.' She slides into Lise's jacket, brings her shoulders back, tries to think how Lise might walk. 'Let's hope it works, then.'

At the door she stops. 'Patrice is trying to break the code in the USB file. He may need to . . .' Her hands move in a vague circle. Ducat scowls in a way that is hearteningly familiar.

'I don't want to know. Nor, I think, do you. Tell him to obey the eleventh commandment. And that he's on his own if he fails so to do.'

CHAPTER TWENTY

Meung-sur-Loire and Cléry-Saint-André,
Tuesday, 25 February 2014

LISE BRESSARD DOES DRAW off the media hounds. Driving fourteen kilometres west along the line of the river, Picaut sees not one single press photographer behind her. There is a small pale yellow Peugeot that seems to remain a steady distance behind her, but it continues on the main route when she turns into the town.

It is nearly noon when she arrives in Meung-sur-Loire, barely more than a village, at whose minuscule railway station Iain Holloway bought a cup of coffee and a bar of chocolate and paid for it by credit card on Saturday afternoon, just over twenty-four hours before he died.

If he knew his life was under threat, did he know this far ahead? And why was he here in the first place?

After much thought, the Asian woman at the kiosk in the corner regrets that she does not recall the gentleman from any of the images Patrice has provided. Her daughter, however, who comes to take over at midday, may do so. In the meantime, if Madame would like a coffee and perhaps a cake?

She offers this with no sideways looks, no sense of awe, and it may be that she genuinely doesn't recognize Picaut in her current guise. What this says about her reliability as a witness is a moot point, and entirely overshadowed by the relief of anonymity.

Picaut sits on one of the high stools and drinks the cat's-piss coffee and eats a croque-monsieur and when the kiosk-owner's daughter still has not appeared, she walks out on to the platform and shows the picture of Iain Holloway to the two women with the four children, the man reading *Die Welt* who doesn't understand French and has only the barest smattering of English, and the stationmaster, a broad, well-fed, grey-haired Parisian, who comes to see if she's causing trouble.

'Capitaine? I have seen you, no? Pardon – my apologies. The newspapers, they make things up. Here, we do not believe their fantasies. This man? Yes, he was here on Saturday. Twice. He arrived in the morning, around nine o'clock, on the train from Blois, and he left in the afternoon, perhaps around one o'clock, going to Orléans. I was leaving my shift then. I saw him standing on the platform with his coffee. In the morning, he took a taxi. I know not to where, but you could ask in the rank? I'm sure they'd be happy to help someone of your stand— Yes. They will help.'

The men of the taxi rank are positively effusive. One owns to having taken Dr Iain Holloway – or at least a man very like him, if you'll excuse the uncertainty, one would hate to bear false witness – on a tourist trip through the town, not just once, but three days in a row last week, Thursday, Friday, Saturday.

—A tourist trip? In Meung-sur-Loire? What is there to see?

—Ah! The *capitaine* makes a joke. He could have visited the chateau, of course.

—Did he?

—No.

—The taxi took the gentleman from the train station to Cléry-Saint-André and thence to the basilica where the gentleman, doubtless very devout, spent the morning. Yes, four hours. He called for the same taxi to return him to the station. He had done the same, more or less, on Friday and Saturday.

—He used you each day?

—He did.

—Why?

A shy shrug. I speak good English. I used to work for Apple in their foreign sales department. And the gentleman, he had hardly any French at all. That's why he wanted me. The *capitaine* has her own car. Does she know the way?

Picaut knows the way.

Cléry-Saint-André is a fleck on the map in which the only building of any note at all is the basilica.

Picaut was brought here by her school when she was nine. She remembers being awed by the size of the church; it was nowhere near the size or complexity of the cathedral at Orléans, but it was still *big*.

Tall-spired, with the angular Gothic architecture beloved of the fifteenth century, it dominates the surrounding cottages. A king lies here: Louis XI, son of the man the Maid of Orléans put on the throne.

He it was who took the village church and ordered it rebuilt into a resting place fit for a monarch and his wife. A vague memory from her school visit says that both the original tomb and its successor were destroyed in the various wars and revolutions that convulsed the region; not everyone reveres royalty.

Entering quietly by the small door in the long side, nearest the road, Picaut leaves the sun and the startling blue sky for the cold, shaded interior, the hard wooden pews, the smell of damp and age and bone-dry dust.

The tomb of Louis XI is the first thing she sees: an unfortunate Gothic monstrosity of pillared marble set just inside the entrance. A low fence of iron railings protects the tomb proper from prying fingers, while four marble pillars hold aloft a marble roof, on which the statue of the king kneels in eternal prayer. Four of the near-naked cherubs the Church loves to spread around its places of worship attend him, one at each corner.

Walking around it, Picaut imagines Iain Holloway doing the same. She learns nothing. Whatever he was doing here, it didn't take him four hours to look at one tomb and it's hard to see what else he might have done with his time.

There are rows of wooden pews, and an altar to her left, and all the usual trappings of a church, but they are not especially interesting. Picaut checks them out, just to be sure, and then heads up to the opposite end and the west door. A small side room is set off to the left, empty, softly echoing, as if the ghosts of the past wait for her there. She backs out. To her right is the main entrance.

She is standing there in shadow, when the side door by Louis's tomb opens and, as quietly, closes. A figure appears, dressed in black.

There is a moment when Picaut thinks it may be the priest, and feels a flash of guilt for desecrating his church with her presence.

Then the figure steps into the light and is not a man but a woman, and she is not dressed in black, she *is* black. She is dressed, in fact, in autumnal shades of browns and faint greens that must be entirely on trend in Paris but, here, look urban and slickly professional.

Monique Susong stands with her head bowed and her

fingers looped before the tomb of Louis XI, and Capitaine Inès Picaut praises all the listening powers that her trip has not been in vain.

CHAPTER TWENTY-ONE

Rheims,
19–20 July 1429

Tomas has not found the Maid's friend, Hanne. Two days of quiet questions and he has not found a Hannah or a Hanni, or any woman whose name is remotely similar.

He is in a foul temper, but in that, at least, he is not alone. In the days immediately following the king's anointing, Rheims is a hushed and sluggish place. Men and women, if they walk at all, step heel to toe, silently, as if their heads are blown eggshells, and their feet stabbed with glass. Fresh vomit curdles the air.

Tomas, sober, clear-headed, coldly furious, meets Stefan, his small, dark agent, in the same back alley as before. This time, the stench of old urine and rotting faeces is an improvement on the air he has been breathing.

'I need you to find me Claudine.' At least he knows who she is and what she looks like. 'Bedford will want to question her. If you can get her to—'

'Gone.' Stefan leers.

'Gone where?'

Stefan points between his feet, then reconsiders and

points to the sky. She is in hell, or maybe in heaven.

Tomas's knife is in his hand. His palm itches. 'She was the witness who would have testified that the Maid—'

'Bertrand de Poulangy was looking for her. She'd have betrayed you.'

Tomas is not Bedford. He has never yet slain a man without good reason. And Bertrand de Poulangy is not a man to bed a whore as low as Claudine. He slides the knife away. 'You saw this, or you heard it?'

'The one and then the other. I heard it. I followed him. He led me to her. I made a disturbance. He went to look. When he came back, she was gone. He won't find her.' Stefan's small, black eyes search his face. 'If she had remained alive, and had talked . . . you would have been in a stone cellar by now, making close acquaintance with knives and hot irons. De Poulangy is the arm of his lady's law.'

'You did right.' This is what Tomas pays for: intelligence and forethought. 'What else have you for me?'

'News of the Maid. She is lodging in the house of Jean de Belleville, and his betrothed. They treat her like an old friend. The future lady of Belleville is Marguerite de Valois, the old king's bastard daughter. The new king's sister.' Stefan casts a sideways glance. 'I have heard that the lady Marguerite is very godly. In her piety, she may wish to welcome a new priest.'

'Ah.' This is worth silver. Possibly, it is worth gold. Tomas throws a coin. If he cannot find Hanne, who grew up in Domrémy, the angel-princess who stopped the battle amongst the king's wards on the day of Agincourt will have to suffice.

Tomas steeples his fingers, taps them together. He needs to be closer. With Bertrand de Poulangy sniffing around, he cannot simply walk up to the door and introduce himself. He will need to be invited in, and then to stay.

So. A plan . . . a plan. One shapes in his mind, even as he speaks. 'When is she alone? The Maid?'

'Not often. In the mornings, she schools her horse down by the river. The vicious one d'Alençon gave her that was the old king's breeding.'

'Alone?'

'She was this morning.'

And that, for certain, is worth silver. Tomas pays what is owed and goes in search of the butcher and his son; his idea grows with each stride in the new direction.

Thus it is that, on the third day after the king's coronation, Brother Tomas rises early and heads down to the meadows by the river, south and west of the cathedral, where, if Stefan is right, there will be . . . and yes, there is: a solitary figure, showing no signs of drink or pain, riding her snake-headed grey across the flat ground.

She loves this horse. She enjoys its company. On the water meadows of Rheims, on the third day after the king's coronation, she rides it as if the gift were still new, as if they were still learning each other, the horse and the Maid, preparing for some display to assembled knights that might show each to the best advantage.

Brother Tomas settles on a fallen trunk to watch. The morning's mist rises from the river in great, flat plates. At this distance, she could be sailing on top of them, horse and mist are woven so tightly together.

As the sun dries out all it glances on, she becomes more distinct, a lean whip of a girl, riding a lean greyhound of a horse, both of them so intent on their work that Tomas thinks they have not seen him, and today's implementation of his plan will fall apart because of it.

He waits. He is good at waiting.

The sun warms his back. Blackbirds thrill the steady

213

air. Doves roll and burble. Dew blooms fat on the grass at his feet, hangs in great pregnant pearls from a thousand morning cobwebs. He watches her reflection in one, the sway of white and black, the rhythm of hoofbeats, falling to stillness, and looks up, and she is there, a lance-length away. She has no lance.

'Brother Tomas.' She blesses him with recognition. He does not have to counterfeit the flush of pleasure.

He says, 'My lady . . . you ride well.' This does not do justice to her skill. There should be another word for it. He considers perform, or display or fly. None of them fits.

She makes a small bow. The horse, he fancies, drops its head. It is that kind of morning. She frowns a little, as if coming back from some far dream. 'Did you need me for something?'

'No. I just . . . needed some quiet, and you were not disturbing it.'

'So then we are alike.' She smiles a little, awkwardly stiff.

He nods but does not rise, jerks his elbow back at the path. 'I'll follow you in.'

She hesitates, and he sees for the first time that not only does she behave like a knight, she thinks she *is* a knight. She cannot go ahead of him; a knight would not take the path ahead of a priest. She is nailed to the meadow as surely as Christ to the cross.

The old king taught you this. He believed in chivalry. It was the undoing of the French, because Henry really didn't. Not at war, anyway.

The moment threatens to slip through his fingers. The words come out unthought, so fast that he must trust to their trajectory.

'Please, my lady. I would have some time alone with God's silence and my own. I beg of you, please, to go ahead.'

She cannot argue with that. Released from obligation, she

nods, brighter, and sets the horse at a long rein on to the hard, flaking mud path.

There's half a mile before the town. He makes a slow count to fifty, does not let himself hurry the last few, and sets off after her. He can stride, when he has to, almost as fast as an ambling, cooling horse.

The path widens. Cottages grow out of the grass, with turf roofs and walls in need of whitewash that grow green mould, so that they are part of the landscape. Their inhabitants are already gone into town, to scrub or brush or tan or weave or whatever they do to keep body and soul from parting.

Ahead, the Maid's horse is a white blur set against the backdrop of brick and whitewash and small, red tiles.

The cottages become more frequent; they lean inward, shading the path against the sun. He feels the threat of violence now. The effort it takes to walk on, not to reach for his knife, to run, to call out.

Not yet. Not yet . . .

Now!

Two shadows. Two men. A butcher and his son. They are armed only with clubs, because it matters that Tomas not die. How much have they been paid? Is it enough? Is it ever?

They converge on him from both sides, hauling him into the gap between two cottages. He screams, and it's as well this is part of the planning, because he couldn't avoid screaming if he wanted to.

'Help! Heeeeelp! *Hel—aaa—oof!*'

He takes a club to the gut, right up high, at his diaphragm, that leaves him crumpled and fighting to breathe. He wants to know if it was père or fils, and can't see. He kicks out, feebly, rolls over, protects his head with his arms as the clubs bounce down on to his ribs, his legs, his protective, shielding arms, his *elbow*, dear God in heaven, his elbow. Not that hard, you bastards! A snap like a cracked whip

215

breaks near his ear. He feels the sting up his left arm and thinks they have brought blades after all, then a shattering numbness, which leaves his arm limp as a landed fish.

He finds he can howl in a breath, and give it out again, in a harsh, crippled whisper that barely reaches past his ears. Still, he tries.

'Stop! God damn you, stop! It isn't worki—'

'Back! Back or you're dead! Back, both of you.' A woman's voice. At last! What took you so long? He hasn't heard the horse, has no idea how she got here, but he knows the tone of her command.

The blows diminish, and then, of a sudden, stop. Relief leaves him weakly panting, staring up through closing eyes at a heaven gone red and black and purple, tear-blurred. He can hear the clash of arms, though, which isn't right; the butcher and his son were supposed to run when she came back.

'Run, God damn you. Run or she'll—'

He hears a breath that is not human, and the sickening strike of plundered tissue, a dissolution of bone and flesh, sinew and rushing blood. Rolling over, he forces his right eye wide enough to look through and sees her, a dark strip against the light, her Crusader sword a dart in shadow.

She is one against two; they have not run. In fact they can't run. The devil-horse is snaking its head left and right, ducking, weaving, snapping to either side of the path like a hound before a bull. The Maid has dropped the reins and is leaning over, blade in one hand, axe in the other, vengeance made manifest.

He thinks he ought to rise and help . . . help someone. He cannot just now think whom he would help and in any case it's academic. He cannot rise.

He is experimenting with which arm works, and whether he can even lever himself up to sitting, when something

216

falls on him, hard and hot, spraying scalding water across his face.

His mouth is blocked. He can't scream. He flails and rolls and struggles free and squirms back to find that he is lying beside butcher père, and the hot water is blood from a throat laid open to the glistening backbone. Blank eyes stare whitely, round pebbles punched into the dead man's face.

The Maid is still fighting the son, who is by far the more dangerous. Using the father as a counterweight, Tomas drags himself to kneeling. His eyes are swelling closed again, and his hearing isn't right; a river-flood-thunder rushes through his head, but if he concentrates, he thinks the Maid is calling for help.

Sensible girl. Whom is she calling to? Whom does she trust? Bertrand? D'Alençon? De Belleville? He should listen to the rest of this, but he can't. He can barely stand upright. And when the butcher's son falls beside him with a cratered axe wound splitting his skull from crown to left eye, he stops trying.

The earth rises to receive him, briskly, and is still. Her voice reaches into him. 'Brother Tomas, do not die. God does not need your company yet, and we do.' He wants to answer her, but the distance is too far, and the pain too great and the blackness too inviting.

CHAPTER TWENTY-TWO

RHEIMS,
July–August 1429

TOMAS WAS NOT AWARE, until now, of the sweep of the Maid's lashes, their length, their contrast with the white of her skin. He had thought her sun-washed, brown as any man of war, and he was wrong. She is alabaster and ebony, except, tantalizingly, at the curve of her neck, below her ear on the right, where is a small red strawberry-shaped mark. He thinks for a while that it might be a mark of desire, a transient imprint of a night's passion, but it remains unchanging over the days of his convalescence until he comes to know it for a God-mark, set at birth.

He feels privileged to have seen it. Until now, it has been covered by her armour. Here, in this place of comfort and care, she wears velvet gowns in crimson and marine blue, with the fleur-de-lis of France in gold damask, with her hair swept up into just-visible confections of silk and wire that add to her height and reveal a neck he could hold in the curve of one hand, if he were well enough. If she let him.

Her hands are fine-fingered and tender. She ministers to

him, takes away the pain, washes him clean, changes the linen beneath him when he vomits, applies compresses and creams to his contusions, a sling to his arm. She prays aloud a great deal, with a fervour he has not heard from her before; not real, not like this. There is a clarity to her, a lucidity of soul that he has never before encountered. He feels blessed in her presence.

His mind is not clear, he knows this. He thinks himself indoors and yet she ministers to him beneath an infinite blue sky. Beneath it, sand spreads from left to right, and on this fight many men. Charlemagne is there, and Roland, of whom the song was written. The Maid fights with them against the Saracen, but she fights also in France. He knows this because from time to time he hears voices, not far away, that say so; two men talking together.

—Guerite says he will live. She cares for him, I know not why.

—She sees things we don't see.

—Always has done.

A reflective pause, a silence, measured by the tread of feet on sand; a steady tread, men assured of their own worth. And then:

—Paris next?

—Compiègne, I think. The king is with the army. He must give permission for the assault on Paris.

Tomas cannot remember why this matters. Or what he is supposed to be doing about it. He knows only that it does, and there is something.

The Maid's cool voice tugs him back. 'Does your arm hurt?'

How could it not when the elbow is broken? He pulls a wry face and is rewarded with a smile that opens some gateway of his mind so that memory crashes over him, a small deluge of isolated episodes: the raining of clubs, a blade, sharp as lightning in shadow, a girl putting a horse through its paces. Bedford. His promise. His Englishness.

He seeks refuge in darkness, and leaves her.

Sometime later he asks, 'Where are we?'

She looks pleased that he can speak. 'Rheims.'

He frowns. 'You have come back from Soissons to care for me?' It's a day's ride, even on her devil-horse.

She tilts her head, purses her lips. He does not remember them curved like this. 'I am not the Maid.'

'My lady . . .' He struggles to rise. Pain defeats him; his left arm is a lance of fire, of acid, of lye, poured on living flesh.

'Be still.' Her hands press him back. He screws up his eyes, tries to focus. Black hair, black eyes, black brows. A mouth like a bow. Skin fine as alabaster.

'Who are you?'

Her gaze flickers a moment upwards, to heaven. He thinks she is seeking permission to answer him. If so, it is granted. She says, 'By God's grace, they call me Marguerite de Valois.'

Ah. The king's sister. The angel. The godly one who loves priests. His plan, after all, has worked better than he intended. He is here, in her care, and Claudine – poor Claudine – was right. She *is* beautiful.

The voices wash over him, in memory.

—*Guerite says he will live. She cares for him, I know not why.*

'You are Guerite?'

She frowns at him. The bow of her lips flattens. He wants to reach for her, to kiss her to bruising, make her his own. At length, she says, 'It was my father's idea. It means—'

'Little war . . .'

Her father being the late, mad King of France, nobody

cared to tell him that naming your angel-princess 'little war' is not conducive to maidenly comportment. She has not, for fortune, grown up manly; quite its opposite. She is a Marguerite, lovely as a flower; impossible to think of her otherwise. And she cares for him. They said so, the voices beneath the window.

He lies back, grinning foolishly. She lifts him with an arm about his shoulder, tilts his head, gives him dwale to drink, the bitter drench made of boar's bile and henbane, juice of lettuce, poppy milk and bryony root. He knows the taste, learned of it from his father's priests, part of his two-colour childhood: a French life of sun and blue sky and archery and watercourses; an English one of drear and monasteries and his only escape the herb garden and, later, war.

She departs, leaving him marooned beneath the Saracen sky. He hears the Song of Roland sung in different keys by nightingales and crows. A hundred times, Roland blows his oliphant and dies on the blood-blackened sand.

Wet. Drizzling past his ears to chill the nape of his neck.

He opens his eyes. The angel is leaning over him, close enough to kiss. Guerite, whose father was mad. Looking at her alabaster profile, he decides that the royalty of France manifests better in its women than its men.

She is watching him. She says, 'You speak English when you are in fever.'

He laughs, rolls his eyes. 'Scots. Same words, different accent. Some words the same, anyway.' He remembers something that makes him smile. 'The Scots who are a certain antidote to the English.'

'As the pope said.' She touches her rosary and mouths an Ave Maria. Her skin has the translucence of frequent fasting. He has forgotten what it is like to be in the presence of the truly holy. It is possible he has never known.

221

He sleeps. It comes on him suddenly, discomfitingly, and when he wakes a new day has dawned and she is spinning, so that he lies listening to the whick and whirl of the drop bobbin and drawing in the light scent of new wool. Shearing has not long since passed. He can't remember how the sheep looked when last he rode past them.

He stares up at the ceiling. The painting has grown flat of a sudden. He can see the brush marks if he tries. Amazing that it ever seemed to him alive.

'Where are we?'

'You asked that already.' Whick. Whick. Whick. 'We are at Rheims.'

'You told me that already, lady. Where in Rheims?'

'At the lodgings of my betrothed, the lord of Belleville.'

How had he forgotten she was promised to de Belleville? He fastens on something else, looks around the room. It is big, with wide windows and carved shutters. The ceiling is high. The fire roars. Tapestries stripe the walls, of kings and saints and knights in bright, new colours: madder and saffron, onion-juice yellow, gold and silver. Lodgings? Really? Who owns this place?

'You did well,' he says, 'when a single room in Rheims was going for three marks on the night of the coronation.'

'We made the arrangement in April,' she says. 'Rheims was cheap then.'

In April, he was in Orléans on the English side, still sure of victory.

He says, 'The Maid told you even then that she would come to Rheims?'

'She told us in February, when she first came to Chinon.'

And you believed her. You had that much faith. But then you knew her as a child, you were close as two fingers intertwined; you knew what she could do. Do you know who Hanne is? I'm sure you do.

222

He is spending too much time drinking in the loveliness of Marguerite de Valois, thinking of ways to open her, body and soul. He needs to be gone. He pushes on the bed, trying to rise.

Marguerite moves to help, but he shakes his head and, left alone, he works his good hand underneath him and pushes, slowly. He is standing, if dishevelled and sweat-stained, when a tall, grave man sweeps in, clad in dark, sober velvets and small hat. Marguerite spins to him, bestows on him a smile of such delight as to blind all those caught in its blaze. Tomas is not blind, but then the smile is not for him.

So this is the man you will marry; one of the wealthiest in France.

At first glance, were you a dullard, Jean de Belleville might seem to you a man of limited means. You have to know velvets to see the quality of these, the depth and evenness of the dye, the fine fall of the fabric. His boots are doeskin, lined with swan's down. His belt is set with silver and small, subtle gems. Marguerite's future husband is not ostentatious, therefore, but also not unvain.

'I am told you are fit to see visitors.' His face is long and lean, his eyes clear and grey. He bows, neatly, nicely, gives a swift, sharp smile, that manages with great economy to convey sympathy and good humour at once. 'Sieur of Belleville at your service. And this—' he indicates the serious young man who has entered behind him, 'is Father Huguet Robèrge, our family priest. He has been helping to care for you these past nine days.'

His hosts are impeccable. Their eyes meet past his shoulder, man and woman, and they share whatever secret is passed by those who plan to share a conjugal bed. Tomas feels like a bystander, and faintly soiled.

And then he watches as both turn back, and his gaze follows theirs, and here is the priest, Huguet Robèrge, sandy-haired, wide-faced, possessed of that evident innocence of soul to which few men aspire and fewer still attain.

There is something here he does not understand, a question asked, an answer, all in silence; a pulse of something raw and powerful and—

Are you lying with the priest, my lady? Your childhood friend? Surely not. He will believe such infidelity of a priest readily enough, but he cannot – will not – believe it of Marguerite de Valois.

Tomas does not say this aloud. Rather, he assays a small bow and doesn't fall over, which is more cheering than he wishes to acknowledge. He says, 'At your service, my lord.' Mindful of the priest, he remembers his own role. 'May God bless your care of me.'

De Belleville smiles his grave, grey-eyed smile. 'Thank the Maid. She gave you into our care with orders not to let you die.'

'And she is at Paris now? Assaulting it?' Please God, let that be not so or Bedford will find ways to kill his servant that will make a flogging seem like a stubbed toe.

'Not yet.' A cloud temporarily obscures the sun that is the lord of Belleville's visage. He shakes his head. 'My lord d'Alençon endeavours to persuade the king that Paris must be taken swiftly. There are those who feel . . . otherwise . . .'

Regnault de Chartres. Good man.

Guerite says, 'And Bedford has taken to the field. He brings five thousand against her.'

'Bedford has . . .' Bedford? *Bedford* has taken to the field and he, Tomas, did not know of it. His world sways.

De Belleville steps forward, catches him. 'Tomas! It is not so bad. He hasn't engaged yet. He is afraid. Our army is the bigger.'

224

They are watching him. He presses his palms to his face and finds calm in the dark.

He says, 'I should be there. With the Maid. I may be one man, but surely God will more likely heed my prayers if I am with the army than not. Messengers must be riding back and forth from here to there. Would it be possible to travel with them, do you think?'

They have considered this, de Belleville, his priest and his betrothed. A glanced confirmation draws all three together, no language needed.

Marguerite is delighted, enchantingly so. 'The Maid would be very happy to have you back. She believes you are favoured by our father in heaven, and that with your presence on the field, the king will let her fight.'

De Belleville says, 'Soissons is for France now, and is only a day's ride east. Then another day on to Compiègne. Can you manage that, do you think? If we started in the morning?'

'We?'

'Father Huguet and I also have reason to be with the Maid. We waited only until you were fit. We can provide a carriage for you—'

'I can ride.' Tomas pulls a grimace. 'If you have a quiet horse?'

'I'm sure one can be found.' De Belleville bows once more. He is the perfect foil to Marguerite; manly enough to complement her, but graceful, cultured, the soul of tact. He says, 'We would be honoured if you would share dinner with us tonight, so that you are fortified for your journey.'

Dinner is in the classic order, well presented, but not overly fancy: oxtail soup flavoured with anise and ginger; carp baked in saffron with verjuice, violently orange, but the flavour bursts like small miracles across his tongue; a

225

blancmange of chicken ground into milk and almonds, and then suckling rabbit, roasted with wild garlic and pepper: uncoloured, unfancy and unforgettable. The wine is good, the music subtle and inoffensive. He has stood guard at meals like this, but never eaten one.

The de Bellevilles – he includes Huguet Robèrge, the priest is so evidently a part of the family – treat him as a friend. He responds in kind with smiles and laughter and clever compliments in Scots, English, French and Latin so they think him at least a graduate of some university – Paris, most likely – only too modest to mention it. He is happy in their company, and they with his. This is his strategy, and if he takes some pleasure from it, who will say he is wrong? He drinks in the night as a gift.

In the morning, they give him a pacing palfrey with a long, smooth, mile-eating gait that does not jolt his elbow. He rides right-handed, with the left strapped across his chest under his friar's robes. The sun shines. He has the company of Jean de Belleville, Huguet Robèrge and eight men at arms who have sworn to defend his life with their own. He has rarely felt safer.

On reaching Compiègne, Tomas and his companions learn that the Maid is with the army at Montépilloy, half a day's ride away. They set an easy pace and arrive in time for evening prayers.

Her army is smaller than it was; only eight thousand strong.

Bedford's army, by contrast – *Bedford* is here! Tomas has to get him a message, but cannot think how – is five thousand, and has drawn up in a field not far away.

The travellers have arrived, it seems, just in time for battle. It is the fourteenth of August, four weeks to the day since the king was anointed in Rheims. The month has been lost thanks to Regnault de Chartres, without whom the Maid's army would have been in Paris by now.

The Maid is in her tent with her entourage: d'Alençon and La Hire, Jean d'Aulon and Louis de Coutes. Tomas pauses at the door, kneels on one knee. These four have been with her since the beginning. Any one of them could recognize him. He has almost forgotten that danger. He is thinner now than he has ever been, and his slung arm changes his shape. He slouches his shoulders, endeavours to look godly. Nobody rises to kill him.

'Brother Tomas!' The Maid makes the three strides to reach him, raises him to standing.

The jolt of her touch is as it was at Jargeau, a stunning of his thoughts, a silencing of his speech. She presses a kiss to each cheek, swift, sure, dry, affectionate. He has to think of war and water or he will disgrace himself; his tunic is not such as will disguise a man's leaping member.

'My lady.' He looks down, away from her. 'I owe you my life.'

She shakes her head cheerfully. 'If you must thank anyone, thank my horse; without him they would have got away. But we are glad to see you. You brought us luck at Troyes and will do so here, too. With you at our side, and the help of our father in heaven, we shall face Bedford and show him what French heart can do.'

'You will prevail, lady, I am sure of it.' What else can he say? And actually, he has walked through the army. He has tasted its heart, and its certainty. Self-belief is nine points of any battle. He cannot imagine this one defeated. Not just now.

She is delighted with him. A hand claps his shoulder, his good one. 'Tomas, sleep now. Tomorrow we shall take on the might of England, and win.'

They give him a tent with half a dozen other priests;

newcomers, most of them, men who have joined her army since the coronation at Rheims. They do not speak to him, but pray by turns through the watches of the night. If he had any idea of sneaking out in the dark to Bedford, he forgets it. One day he will do so. For now, all he can do is watch and wait and pray. He is closer to her inner circle. He is not in it. Getting there is his priority. He prays through compline and then sleeps, ready for the morning.

CHAPTER TWENTY-THREE

Lise Bressard says, 'That was fun.'

It is evening. The trolls of the press pack have returned to their burrows to write up tomorrow's copy. Lise has returned to the police station unharmed, unassailed. Her eyes shine with the adrenalin of the day.

'Those few who failed to succumb to cousin Luc's charm I have terrified into submission. I let them catch me, and then let them see that it was me, and not you. The effect, I have to say, was gratifying. I have rarely heard apologies so profoundly expressed. Even the most dimwitted of them has realized that you're under the Family's protection. I'll be surprised if they hinder you again.'

Picaut hears something sour under all the enthusiasm. Curious, she says, 'You don't like being the Family's enforcer?'

A shrug. 'It's not a role I would have chosen. But the cross-dressing was quite enchanting.' Lise slips out of Picaut's

229

jacket. Her smile is brief and alive and all Luc. 'We should do it more often.'

'I'm not sure your jacket is built for it. I walked into a church and out again and I think even that may have destroyed it.'

'Yours, on the other hand, could survive an earthquake. It probably has. I return it in exactly the condition in which I received it. I am thinking I should have one.'

'Your family would fall into fits.'

'Precisely so.'

They embrace fully, heartily, as if they were not caught on either side of a knife blade with the cutting edge between. Lise leaves.

At five thirty, the team assembles in Picaut's glass-walled office to share the spoils – all but Rollo, who came in early and was sent out again straightaway.

Picaut has collated the individual reports on her laptop, printed the resulting timetable and pinned it to the cork board that is the hub of any investigation.

Iain Holloway: Known Movements

WEDNESDAY 19 FEBRUARY (Garonne):

10:24 Eurostar, LONDON ST PANCRAS -> PARIS GARE DU NORD AT 13:47.

CCTV footage clearly shows him at the station.

14:15 -> MAISON FAVART (*4* luxury boutique hotel booked on the Internet from London 3 days prior to arrival – data from Patrice Lacroix (PL)*).

21:00 dines at the TERMINUS NORD. Returns to hotel at 23:27.

Time unaccounted: 2 hours.

THURSDAY 20 FEBRUARY (Sylvie & Rollo):

Departs 08:15 -> metro -> PARIS GARE D'AUSTERLITZ -> Blois, arriving at 13:41 [check].

Taxi -> Hôtel de l'Abeille (*4* boutique hotel, booked London, PL confirms*). Pays for 3 nights.

Departs hotel approx. 14:00. Returns 23:50.

Time unaccounted: nearly 10 hours.

FRIDAY 21 FEBRUARY (Sylvie & Rollo):

Departs 11:03 (hotel staff assessment: late riser, late breakfast, tips well).

18:00 returns, dines, works in his room till late. Maid reports light on and computer working at 02:00.

Hotel server logs activity until 03:18.

Time unaccounted: nearly 7 hours.

SATURDAY 22 FEBRUARY (Sylvie & Rollo):

08:30 breakfast, departs.

The hotel never saw him again. They have his overnight wash bag, a pair of very English striped pyjamas and a case for an iPhone. They were not expecting him to leave.

09:00 Meung-sur-Loire station by train.

Taxi to Cléry St André – the same taxi he had taken for the past two days.

13:00 approx – returns to Meung-sur-Loire. Agitated. Train to Orléans.

18:00 ORLÉANS – checks in at the MAISON LOIRETTE (*1*, off-grid. Where does he find these places if they're not on the net? PL*). Pays cash.

Staff assessment: a man in grief. Claims his wife has died and he needs some peace away from the world. Tips handsomely, in euros.

20:00 eats at next-door restaurant, returns at 21:00, works on his computer all night. (*PL – without wifi? What is he doing?*)

Time unaccounted: 4 hours then 3 hours.

They all study the page. Sylvie says, 'He went from four star
to one star in a hurry, didn't he?'

'And no Wi-Fi, which, as Patrice will tell you, is almost
impossible. In Orléans, everyone is on the net. So we can
assume some of the lost time on Friday was spent finding
one of the few off-grid hotels in the city.' Picaut is sitting
on the table with her laptop balanced across her knees. Her
gaze sweeps them.

'So we have a break in a pattern: Iain Holloway, a man
who lives on his broadband connection, shifts for no obvious
reason from four star, full Wi-Fi, to one star, off-grid. Added
to which, he tells the hotel staff that his wife has died and he
wants solitude – and at least the first part of that is untrue.
So he was lying and people don't generally lie unless they're
running from something.'

'He had good reason,' Sylvie says. 'He burned to death
twenty-four hours later.'

'Only if we assume that whatever he was afraid of is the
same thing that killed him,' Picaut says. 'We'll hold an open
mind on that one and keep looking.'

Leaning to her left, she picks up a yellow highlighter and
runs it across the unaccounted hours on each day. 'The gaps
are too long. Somebody must have seen him. I've sent his
image to the press pack. It'll be on the next news bulletins.
Expect a flood of phone calls with a less than one per cent
hit rate.'

Sylvie says, 'We've already got some sightings. There are two witnesses who think they saw him getting into a car driven by a woman in Blois on Thursday evening.'

'Was she black, the woman?'

'They didn't say. They didn't say much at all. They weren't what you'd call credible witnesses; that's why I didn't mention it before. Why?'

'Because according to a moderately credible taxi driver in Meung-sur-Loire, Iain Holloway arrived by train from Blois three days in a row and then went to the basilica at Cléry-Saint-André. There's no credit card trail on this, so he must have paid cash, which is interesting in itself. And if it's true, most of the missing hours on Thursday, Friday and Saturday seem to have been spent there. Monique Susong spent nine minutes in the same basilica today, at around one forty-eight p.m. She left a note taped to the bars that surround the tomb of Louis XI. This is it.'

Picaut tabs across and opens the image on the big screen on the back wall. They can all see the note reproduced as it was when she took the photograph with her phone.

Iain Holloway sent me to speak to you. 06 89 61 98 71

Sylvie asks, 'Is that Monique Susong's mobile number?'

'It is.' Picaut doesn't say, 'I told you she wasn't all she seemed,' but Garonne nods as if she has, feels in his pocket for a ten-euro note and slides it across the floor towards her.

Coupled with his taking down of Rémi from Drugs this morning, she would like to read into the gesture a thawing of their nuclear winter, but can't bank on it without more evidence. Still, she is unusually pleased.

He says, 'Have you brought her in?'

She shakes her head. 'Rollo is at the basilica with a camera. We need to know who picks up that note before we move.'

'Has Patrice tapped her phone?'

Patrice affects an air of injured innocence. 'That would be illegal without a directive from Prosecutor Ducat, who—'

'Who will look the other way until the moment you're caught. At which point he'll publicly guillotine you on the steps to his office.' Garonne makes a swift, decisive gesture with the edge of his hand to demonstrate Patrice's probable fate. 'But in the meantime, we will hear every word she says. Has she said anything useful?'

'Not yet,' Picaut says. 'If she does, a transcript will go up on the board. Until then, all she gets is a picture.' She has already pinned an image of Monique Susong on to the board to the right of Iain Holloway. 'We know she's lying to us. I'd like to find out as much as we can about why before we lift her. In the meantime, Patrice has made a breakthrough on the USB chip. Patrice?'

Patrice has had some sleep and is recharged. He hops up on to the desk, leaving Picaut to sit on the floor by the door. She thinks better, sitting on the floor. She can rest her forearms on her knees and stare at her feet and see whatever she needs to see in the blur of not-looking.

Just now, she sees Iain Holloway as if still alive. He is an organized man, who plans his weeks ahead of time. He sets an itinerary, but has the flexibility to break it if he has to. He has obsessions and follows them wherever they lead. He has the resources to find off-grid hotels in a country where his grasp of the language is not great. Last, but far from least, he is a man who has knowledge, and swallows it to keep it safe. A man who, when he knows death is imminent, leaves behind a code. It therefore follows that he must also have left the key.

Patrice is speaking. She hears him through a mesh of clashing patterns.

'Holloway was a good orthopaedic surgeon. We have

his CV from Glasgow and he was a busy man. When not working, he was an obsessive who spent all his free time examining war graves, trying to put names to the dead, often from minimal information. His wife says this is why she left him; he spent all his time digging up the dead and none of it with her. Even his holidays were spent at war graves. In 2006, he worked in Bosnia under the auspices of the UN. There was a grave with five hundred and eighty-three bodies in it, all men and boys down to the age of ten; he identified all but nine.'

'He's good, then,' Rollo says from the door. 'Most of the war graves are lucky if they identify fifty per cent.'

Picaut feels him come in and find his usual place, leaning against the side wall by the window. She doesn't look up.

'He's good,' agrees Patrice. 'And the list of names of those men and boys, in alphabetic order, is the key to the first of the ciphered files on the USB chip.'

'*What?*' Picaut's head snaps up. 'How?'

'It's a standard document number code.' Patrice is a man in his element, a fish flashing through a sea of figures. 'You number each letter in the source text, then use them in sequence. Easy to make, there are programs that will do it, but completely impossible to break if you don't have the source.'

Sylvie says, 'You're going to have to give them more than that, Patrice.'

'OK, so suppose you wanted to use my name as the key, you'd write out Patrice Lacroix over and over and then number the letters, so P=1, A=2, T=3 and on. Then if you wanted to write the word capoeira – which is a Brazilian martial art and happens to be a partial anagram of my name – you'd write 6, 9, 15, 26, 35, 41, 46, 51. You never go back in the list; you always look along for the next number in the sequence.'

'What happens if I want to write "Happy Birthday Patrice" and your name doesn't have the right letters?' Picaut asks. 'No H, no B, no Y.'

'That's why you need a long document for this kind of code: a book or a play or a scientific paper – or a list of names from a war grave – that's going to have the entire alphabet multiple times over. The result is utterly unbreakable unless you've got the key.'

Sylvie says, 'There's a three-part code in the US, where the middle section is based on the Declaration of Independence. It's been broken, and what it says is that the other two parts give the exact location of where a pile of gold bullion is buried that was worth twenty million dollars at the time of burying it in the mid-nineteenth century, which means it's worth about as much as Facebook and Google put together by now. But nobody can work out the keys to the other two parts, and they've been at it for nearly two centuries.'

Patrice is visibly impressed. Picaut rolls her eyes. If these two end up in each other's beds . . . it's not her business. But still.

She says, 'So if all the codes are number codes, you need the keys.'

'Yep. We'll be collecting our pensions before we ever break them otherwise.'

'We'll deal with that when we get there,' Picaut says. 'What have you got from this one?'

'This.' Patrice opens his laptop and connects it to the screen. His hands blur across the keys and a single white page snaps into view.

Jon – Too much to say, too little time. Know that I love you, and wherever we go after death, I will wait there for you. Don't hurry.

As my gift to you from beyond the grave – and with

236

apologies that it's not more exciting – I've sent you two samples. A is from Iii [*note from P: I'm not sure this is right, but
have checked it*], B is from the subject. I would bet rather a
lot that they're related. If it transpires that I am right, I would
appreciate your telling as many people as possible: tell the
whole world. Call it my legacy, or hers, either way, you will
be safe when it's fully public. Until then . . . there are those,
clearly, who will kill to keep this secret. Stay somewhere
very safe. Don't trust anyone.

Keep well, beloved. Don't mourn me; just be yourself in
all your wonder.

I love you. IH

There is a hush as Picaut's team reads to the end.

Sylvie speaks first, thoughtfully. 'Divorced. No children.
And he writes love letters to Jon. Was he on any gay dating
sites?'

Patrice shakes his head. 'Not that I can find and, yes, I
have looked.'

Picaut says, 'Forget that, it's not our problem. We just
need to find out who Jon is, where he is, what he does, and
what kinds of samples he's just received. If nothing else, we
don't want to see him added to the body count.'

Garonne: 'It'll be whoever Holloway was calling on
Saturday night in the hotel. The one the German overheard,
at Cornell.'

Picaut: 'Possibly. So we need a list of possible contacts
at Cornell, and another of people who worked with him
in Scotland, or on his foreign forensic expeditions, or the
various historical forums he hung out on. After that we can
spread the net, and— Yes, Patrice?'

Patrice has his hand up, like the kid at the back of the
class who knows the answers without having to work at it.
His attention never leaves the laptop.

'There's a Jonathan Stephenson, ophthalmic surgeon on the clinical staff at Cornell University medical school. He's English, but he did his degree at Edinburgh at the same time Holloway did his in Glasgow, so it's possible they could have met. He's married with three school-aged kids, but that doesn't mean he isn't having an affair with his old friend from college. The best option is to get into his email and find out if he had any contact with Iain Holloway, but I'll need an hour or two. He's behind the university firewall, and getting through that isn't as trivial as it sounds.'

It doesn't sound trivial to anyone except Patrice. Picaut pushes herself to standing. To Rollo, she says, 'We're all waiting to hear who took the note Monique Susong left in the basilica.'

He rolls his eyes in a way that says she's not going to like the answer. 'Father Raymond,' he says. 'He's the priest of the basilica. But he called for backup straight away. Enter Father Cinq-Mars, personal assistant to the bishop. Here—'

He passes her the chip from his camera. She slots it into her laptop and brings up the contents on to the screen.

A series of images shows a portly, balding priest, with nothing to distinguish him from a world of portly, balding priests; black shirt, white collar, black cassock, black trousers, black shoes.

Father Raymond checks that he is alone, takes the note, reads it, scowls, walks a tight circle, and makes a phone call. Later – the time stamps are on each frame – a second priest arrives. This one is thinner and younger, but with markedly less hair: Father Cinq-Mars.

With some animation, they discuss the note, then both take pictures of it on their phones, much as Picaut did, although they spread it out flat on a pew where she spread it out on the top of her thigh, with her jeans as a backdrop.

She put it back where she found it. Cinq-Mars produces a disposable lighter and destroys it.

All eyes are on Picaut. 'Sylvie and Rollo, I want everything you can get on these two: find where they live, their phone numbers, their past history. Anything and everything. I want a watch put on their homes. Patrice, can you get me a list of the numbers Monique Susong has called or texted since the fire?'

He nods.

'Good. We'll want to—'

The phone rings. *The* phone; the line they have set aside for the fires. Even as she lifts the handset, Picaut is checking her watch and writing the time on the diary that lies open on her desk.

17.58. If it's a fire, this is a major break with tradition: all the others have been lit in the small hours of the night, when police, firemen and press were all asleep.

'Inès?'

Martin Evard of the Fire Department is on the line. She can hear sirens behind him. Her mouth runs dry. She doesn't need to ask what, only where?

'The newly refurbished warehouses in the South Orléans Project area west of the hospital. The exact location is being texted to you now.'

The warehouses are Luc's pet project; once, she sat up with him, helping him design the layouts. Every other fire has targeted women. Now they are targeting him. Unless they're targeting Picaut through him.

The ramifications are too complex. She doesn't have time to work them through. She grabs her jacket and heads for the door. Her team is already moving out.

The last thing she hears as she leaves the room is Evard, in despair, saying, 'Be careful. The press are on their way.'

CHAPTER TWENTY-FOUR

PICAUT DOESN'T OFTEN RESORT to the siren, but it sits aslant on the roof of her car now, clearing a path through the early evening traffic, south over the river and then a right turn towards the industrial park west of the hospital.

Once a faceless sea of rotting concrete and corrugated iron, it is being reclaimed one unit at a time with the kind of edgy twenty-first-century architecture that manages to make a single-storey box look interesting.

Luc has personally overseen most of the restoration. The South Orléans Regeneration Project is part of his legacy to the city, his belief in the power of Orléans to rebuild itself. He wants to invest in the highest of high technology. He wants to create a Silicon Loire, and he is starting here, on this site. If not the centrepiece of his election plan, it is one of the keystones.

Was one of the keystones. Now, it's in flames. The horizon has acquired a smeared saffron tint long before Picaut crosses the river.

With Patrice as her navigator, she weaves through the maze of service roads with their executive signage and hints of a technological future.

'When we get there, check out the CCTV. If there's any that might have picked anything up, get hold of the feed.'

'On it.'

The fire is deep within the complex, at the very latest conversion, right on the boundary where new meets old. Picaut parks at a safe distance, and Patrice heads off to find the CCTV footage, while she walks in towards a towering banner of flame. The heat is appalling, the air full of soot and cinders. The stench is of burning plastic. She inhales in short, sharp bursts, like a hound on a spoor, but finds no taint of flesh or blood or bone.

Martin Evard is ahead of her, grimly silent.

'Anybody inside?' Picaut asks.

'Not that we know of.'

'What's the risk to other buildings?'

'Depends on the wind.'

Just now, there is no wind; not so much as a feather of a breath on her cheek. This is the saving grace; even the slightest breeze would torch half the industrial park and it would be down to fate as to whether it was the new half or the old that was destroyed.

It may yet come to that. Picaut studies the gap between this warehouse and its neighbours on all four sides. Paint is blistering in the heat, but the units are not yet burning. Martin Evard's men are playing water across them, working inwards to the fire's heart.

She turns back to discover that the press pack has arrived. Cameras begin to flash. She wants to run and has nowhere to go. She is considering whether she can face calling Lise Bressard for help when she sees Patrice in a hooded sweatshirt that covers his hair, standing on the bonnet of her car, signalling joyously. Her phone pings on a text from him.

CCTV Gold. COME!

'There – Honda Civic, coming from the main road.'

They are in the tiny not-quite-a-cupboard surveillance office of the tech company building that is one unit away from the fire; an empty unlet lot separates them from the blaze.

Inside, Patrice is running a bank of monitors, watching eight screens at once. This is the latest technology; nothing fuzzy or uncertain here. In perfect clarity, Picaut watches an old-model Honda that has seen better years, perhaps better decades, take a corner too hard and speed down the service road heading right to left across the screen.

Programmed to follow motion, the camera pans round after it. At the very margin of its viewing arc, the car stands on its nose and two lean, fit men – thirties rather than twenties; maybe Asian? She can't see enough of their faces to be sure – fling the doors open and tumble out as if they are under machine-gun fire. They delve into the trunk and come out with two oil drums of such size and weight that each can only just be lifted. They carry-roll-kick them out of sight of the camera.

A breath-held pause follows, in which neither Picaut nor any of her team says a word. They are all here now, packing into a room that was crowded even when Patrice and she were in it alone.

Picaut wishes for sound to match the non-action on the screen. She watches the time stamp tick over, trying to work out how far they have got, how long it will take to spread the fuel around, how far away they'll be when they light the rag or the bundle of paper and hurl it into the wall of vapour they have created. She wants to hear the explosion, to know when the worst has happened.

Without warning, the screen blasts to white so they all flinch away, and when they look back, it has refocused on the two men sprinting back to the Civic.

Their handbrake turn would put a Hollywood stunt team to shame. They speed back the way they have come, towards the main road and the city. The camera watches the space where they were, then tracks back to the new source of motion, the flames that lick at the edge of its vision.

'Four forty-nine,' Picaut says.

'What?'

'Four minutes and forty-nine seconds from leaving their car to getting back in again.' Sylvie, too, has been watching the date stamp; she can answer Rollo's question. 'They knew where to go and what to do.'

'The stamp said seventeen forty-three when the fire first lit,' Picaut says. 'When was it reported?'

'Seventeen forty-six. If they'd been half an hour earlier, we'd have been all over them, but pretty much everyone here goes home at five-thirty. I'm guessing they knew that.' Evard is staring at the screen. 'Can you get the registration? Maybe trace them that way?'

'Patrice is on it.'

Picaut glances across at Patrice, who makes an 'almost there' gesture with one shoulder. Because she is watching him, she sees the moment he finds out, and the sudden shock.

'What? Who?'

'Abayghur Amrouche.' Everyone, even Picaut, looks at him blankly until he says, 'Algerian. One of Cheb Yasine's cousins. He lives three doors away from the man himself.'

'Oh, Jesus, fuck.' Picaut falls back against a wall. 'Fuck,

fuck, fuck, fuck, *fuck.*' She opens her eyes. Martin Evard is staring at her as if this is the first time he's heard a woman swear. Everyone else is either studying the floor or spitting curses of their own.

For the fire chief's benefit, she says, 'Cheb Yasine is third generation French Algerian. Badder than bad. Rémi's drug squad spent two years on an undercover op and in the end they lost three of their people, one tortured to death with a power drill, the other two shot in a firefight. They still didn't get enough on Yasine to hold up in court. He's beyond hard and if he's found God and decided to wage a religious war on Orléans, we're fucked from here to midnight.'

'You think he's behind Jaish al Islam?'

'I really, really hope not.' She turns away. It's not a good lead, but it's a lead, and that's way beyond anything she expected. Now, at last, she can act. *'Alors, mes amis . . .'*

Garonne and Rollo have been here before, more or less; they know what she needs. Garonne is smiling. Rollo looks as if he's already striking bargains with his war gods, promising sacrifices of life and blood. Picaut only has to nod and they'll be off, back to the station to arm and pick up the vests, the long-range cameras, the flasks and empty bottles they will need to piss into if they have to set up a long watch.

There's a moment's tension. She nods. 'Sylvie, get back to the office and keep up pressure on the two priests.' Everyone is relieved by that. 'Patrice, you're with me. I need an address that overlooks Yasine's place, where we can set up a hide.'

'Chief, you can't go there.' That's Garonne, sounding almost like he used to. 'The press are on your tail like dogs after a bitch in heat. Sorry, but it's true. If you go anywhere near this, Yasine will know it in seconds and we'll lose any lead we have. It has to be me and Rollo. You can send the others in one at a time if you want.'

If you want us to teach them how it's done is what he

244

means.

He's right.

'Go.' She nods to the door. 'I'll get rid of the press and come for the night shift.' It's not right, and it may not be possible, but it's the best she can do for now. 'Patrice, you and I will head back to the station. Most of them will follow us. Sylvie, you go next. See if you can get whoever's left to follow you, so they're not after Garonne and Rollo. If the bastards stop you, make a point of this fire being a change in the pattern: it's daylight and they're targeting the work of a man. Both are new. It might not be the same group. We can't afford to assume that it is.'

'What do you really think?'

'I think we're about to get another phone call.'

Picaut is cutting her own three-point turn on the tarmac when Patrice takes the call on her mobile and puts it on speaker phone.

'*Ici Jaish al Islam . . .*'

CHAPTER TWENTY-FIVE

IT IS MORNING. Brother Tomas stands at the head of the French army as it lines up on the broad plain of Montépilloy to face the English. Unmounted, he stands in the front row, not far from the Maid.

He was with her at Mass, and afterwards, for the first time, he heard her confession: litanies of men dead and others injured, of curses vented against the king. She is clean now, clear of taint, and she is where she wants to be, on a battlefield, with her king behind her. She shines.

Just now, the sun is their most pressing enemy. Already, barely halfway to noon, the heat is killing. Even his white robes are a cauldron. Heaven knows what it is to stand in full armour.

Dust is his benediction; all along the lines, the bright colours of honour wilt, drab and dry and dirty. Heat boils up in shimmering panels from the rows upon rows of men. They shift from foot to foot, test their blades, the run of iron on leather. Bowmen worry about their strings. Everyone worries about the flies. A man three rows back pulls out his cock and pisses where he stands and the air feels fresher for it.

Nobody complains. The men know God is with them because the Maid is with them. Against them is Bedford, who calls himself regent of France, brought to bay after nearly a month of hunting across the country.

He will not give them an easy battle. He has done what his brother did at Agincourt, which is to say that his men have dug a ditch around the edge of their chosen stand, and every man has set his stake pointing outwards to cripple the French horses. Their carts are pulled up within, making shields against French arrows, and their longbowmen wait in that shelter to rain their own shafts on French heads.

Tomas knows the strategy, but he is not sure it will work this time. The Maid gave a speech after evening prayer last night and before Mass this morning, saying to the knights, who said it to their men at arms: that under no circumstances were they to charge the English position. 'We shall learn from the mistakes of the past, and not repeat them.'

So the French will not charge the English. And the English will not charge the French. For hours, therefore, nothing moves between them but dust.

Brother Tomas stands not much more than a good bowshot from the English. The Maid is to his left, bright in her white armour. She has slept in it, eaten in it, fought in it for three months now and it has moulded to her, or she to it, so that she looks easy, as any knight might. Still, she wears the bassinet with the open face, that all might see her, and know her for who she is.

The king sits his dull gelding to her other side, and of all of them, he is the least willing to be here. Therein lies their deficiency.

Once, if he were captured, Charles VII might have been ransomed, but these last weeks Bedford has dashed

247

off proclamations by the score naming him traitor and promising to behead him as a common criminal when – not if – the English catch him.

All of the French nobility who have set themselves against England face the same fate; this war has gone beyond the niceties of chivalry. They have known this since they broke out of Orléans, but Charles de Valois, it would seem, only came to understand it last night in his tent, with all talk gone, and England camped at his feet, when honour demanded that he fight.

He looked sick with fright last night and was no better this morning: a startled fawn caught at bay by mastiffs, with nowhere left to turn.

The Maid, of course, makes the move. Of a sudden, turning, she wrests her standard from de Coutes, her page. He opens his mouth to protest, catches sight of her face within the open circle of her helm and closes it again, with a click of his teeth.

On either side, knights grip their reins tighter, causing their horses to fidget and stamp. D'Alençon is there, and La Hire; they go nowhere without her now. Jean de Belleville is somewhere further back; he has not yet earned a place at the forefront of any fray. Father Huguet will not be far away; those two are never parted, and neither is ever far from the Maid.

Tomas watches her and those closest to her. He sees the moment she meets d'Alençon's eye and gives a small nod. La Hire doesn't understand.

'Girl, where are you going?' He's the only one who doesn't speak to her as a knight. He treats her as one, though. Where she leads, he will follow.

'I'm going to draw them out.'

'Jehanne, you can't . . .' René d'Anjou, Yolande of Aragon's second son, grabs her wrist. He is the son of a queen; he can do things the rest would not dare. He says, 'You can't go near them. It's too much of a risk. Bedford's said publicly he'll burn you.'

She tips her head, in the way she has that says 'What of it?' Aloud: 'But he has to catch me first, and to do that he has to come out, and he won't come alone. Trust Xenophon; he is the better of any English horse.'

Once more, René d'Anjou says what everyone else is thinking. 'Your horse is better than their bowmen? I know you think a lot of him, but really . . .'

The Maid pats his arm. 'He's good enough, you'll see. Let La Hire come and get me if they try anything. He'll enjoy that.'

She thinks to go alone, but Tomas follows behind on foot. He is a priest; even with the acrimony of both sides, he does not believe he will be the target of anyone's bowmen, gunners, or men at arms. He is clad in white, and his head is shaved. One arm is in a sling. The other holds a staff that Huguet found for him. To all who see him, God carries him close; they will not risk the wrath of heaven.

He walks through the hot, hard dust until he is level with her and he, too, can see into the ranks of the English: his brothers. Or at least his countrymen. His half-countrymen, then. Well, anyway, he is on their side, did they but know it. They don't. They look on him with hate.

The Maid, as far as he can tell, knows no fear. She stares directly at Bedford, at his knights and men at arms, at the English bowmen who are too busy making the sign of the cross to lift their bows against her. Not only the archers, but the knights. Tomas can see them, see the furtive signs to ward off evil, the amulets twisted, the crosses kissed. They know exactly who she is, but there is not one of them cares to come out to fight her, man to . . . woman.

She stands before them breathing in the war-stench of

England, which is not so different from the war-stench of France, and then she puts her mount through its paces, just as she did when last he watched her on the water meadows outside Rheims.

She shows the traverse, left to right and right to left, the perfect bend to the heel. She shows a passage, though only a little, because it is hot and he has carried her in full armour all through the day and it is hard for the horse to trot on the spot.

She shows a pesade, forelegs slowly raised on a perfect angle, because she can. At the end, she shows the strike to the rear that so discomfited the herald at Jargeau. They have heard of this, the English; he told them. Tomas feels the ripple of anxiety pass through the lines. Somewhere far back, a man raises an ironic cheer and is swiftly hushed.

D'Alençon can't let her do this alone. He presses forward, and then La Hire, and together, all three, they shout challenges to the English knights to come out and ride against them, hand to hand, to show who is best.

This is not a new thing. In other wars, in long campaigns, even in sieges, the knights of one side often ride out to offer challenges one to the other. They fight and feast and then retire behind their lines for the duration of hostilities. In truth, the knights on opposing sides are closer to each other than they are to their own peasants and villeins.

Surely, then, this is the time when Bedford will come out. If he were to kill this woman, one on one, it would change the whole nature of the field. The English might be outnumbered, but they were outnumbered at Agincourt, at Verneuil.

Come *on*! Tomas stands in the dirt and watches three French knights put on a display of riding worthy of the great masters and all the time he wills Bedford, his master, his lord – the man whom, in a world of disrespect and cant, of broken loyalties and treason, he holds in highest regard – to step out and match the challenge.

He does not.

Not Bedford. Not Warwick. Not Gough. Not Percy. Not one English knight has blood red enough, hot enough, sure enough to ride against this Maid. It's as pitiful a display of cowardice as has been seen on the soil of France since their annihilation at Crécy, and that's saying something.

In the late afternoon, with the sun sliding for shame behind the horizon, the Maid and her train ride back, disgusted. In the dark, like the craven he is, Bedford marches his men away.

If the French were to follow him now, they could turn them at bay, at the very least, and have the battle they want. To assault a retreating army is almost always a victory. And if England loses Bedford they lose France; everyone knows this.

But the king is afraid. There is no other way to look at it. Charles VII, by grace of God King of France, most badly does not wish to fight. And so he will not let anyone else fight. Harsh words are exchanged between the Maid and her king, in the unprivacy of his tent, but Regnault de Chartres is in there making sure he will not change his mind.

Thus Bedford escapes.

Bedford, who is also afraid.

Afterwards, Tomas stands for a while by the horse lines, weighing his next action. In the current chaos of the French camp, it would be easy to sneak away, to follow the English army, to catch up with the lord who leads it and ask him why he chose not to fight.

He bridles his horse, but does not slide the saddle on its back. What would he say? I saw the fear in your eyes and I despise you?

He wants this not to be the truth, but he was there. He

knows it wasn't just the men at arms who were afraid of her, with their superstitions and their herd panic, but also the knights, the great men of England: Bedford, Warwick . . . Everyone.

And so in the evening, when he stands at the camp fire and calls God's scorn on the English in the company of Frenchmen, he does not silently apologize within.

He prays with the Maid at sundown and then, at her invitation, joins her in her tent for a meal. They are five in addition to the Maid: d'Alençon and La Hire, as ever, plus de Belleville and his priest Father Huguet, are made welcome. And, newly among them, Brother Tomas, the Augustinian friar.

She is different with them, less victorious, less cheerful. In fact, Tomas sees anger for the first time in the sharp, clipped measure of her step as she paces the length of her tent, in the terse restraint of her language. She will not curse the king, but by heaven she wants to.

Their conversation boils down to this: the army is dwindling. The king in heaven tells her to take Paris. She counts on these men present to help her so to do and they willingly promise their aid. Brother Tomas gives his oath with all the rest.

CHAPTER TWENTY-SIX

La Chapelle Saint-Denis,
15 August 1429

They move back to the village of la Chapelle Saint-Denis to the north of Paris and plan for action. And throw the plans away because the army is smaller now. And plan again.

Brother Tomas is party to all the planning. He has proved himself useful and continues so to do, offering suggestions that make sense.

'If you're going for a gate, go first for Saint Honoré to the west. It's the least defensible, though I have heard that Bedford has bought in Genoese crossbowmen to bolster the courage of those inside.'

'Have you, Tomas?' La Hire looks at him, narrow-eyed. 'You hear a lot.'

'I'm a priest.'

'You wouldn't break the confidence of the confessional?'

'Never!'

He is sweating when he leaves, but d'Alençon lays an arm across his shoulder. 'Don't mind him, he's on edge for lack of fighting. He hasn't seen action since Patay.'

'None of us has.' Everywhere has surrendered, even Soissons. Compiègne threw open its gates before the Maid ever reached them, and the people celebrated in the streets. Bedford ran rather than fight. Only Paris is holding out.

D'Alençon says, 'We'll be well when the king gives permission for the attack on Paris.'

'Will he?'

'He must. We can't bring up an army and then just stand here and do nothing . . .'

But the king has Regnault de Chartres whispering in his ears, telling him how close is a treaty with Philip of Burgundy, and now wants this more than anything. Burgundy is his cousin. He wants France whole and his family whole and he has been given to understand that God will not love him if he does not achieve this.

The men are restless. D'Alençon has been back to Compiègne once to beg for permission to attack, and has been rebuffed. D'Alençon, it seems to Tomas, is close to mutiny, and d'Alençon has a reasonable claim to the throne, being a distant cousin of the king's and married to the king's uncle's only living child. Bedford would smile to hear of possible mutiny in the French ranks, but Bedford is in Calais, calling in more troops from England.

Tomas walks through the village, past lines of tents and fires, listening to the murmurs of discontent. He knows the sound of an unhappy army, and this is it. Each day, men slip away back to the harvest and the comfort of their wives. Another month and there will be no army at all. Delay and delay. That's all it will take to destroy her; a constant stream of delays.

He was offered lodgings in the village inn, but, like the Maid, he has refused, and camps with the rest in a tent. Through the evening, they listen to the golden notes of young Raoul de Coutes, younger brother to the Maid's page.

He has begged to join the greatest army in Christendom, and how could anyone deny him when his brother has served her half a year?

He is a songbird, so they discover, pouring out clean, high notes in praise of God and France. The Maid gives him gold, and promises to let him hold her standard when the fighting starts.

They sleep soundly, and wake, and still the king has not given permission. The day promises to be a long one.

Tomas is standing at his own fire gnawing at a hunk of hard cheese, when a small man with a lazy left eye shuffles past and offers the observation that the Brother's horse is lame in the near hind and did he want it seen to?

Really? If this is the best Bedford has got, Paris is in trouble. 'Give me a moment and I'll come and see. She was sound enough yesterday.'

He flexes his left arm back and forth. His elbow pains him hardly at all during the day, and is held now by a loose cord that loops about his neck, not pinioned to his torso. He strips off the cord and tests it. Usable. He has a knife strapped to his forearm. He tests the draw and finds it smooth. It's not that he doesn't trust Bedford but . . . all right, he doesn't trust Bedford. Nobody in his right mind trusts Bedford and Tomas has been out of touch for over a month; there's no telling whether he'll be deemed to have outlived his usefulness.

He walks easily down to the tethering yards and finds a big, bluff man, with eyes that at least look in the same direction, pretending to examine the wall-eyed chestnut mare that is his current mount. The boss-eyed messenger leans on an oak stump, cleaning beneath his fingernails with his knife, whistling, the very picture of un-innocence.

The bluff man says, 'Bedford wants to know what you plan. It's been over two months since you said you had a way to get rid of the Maid.'

'If he'd taken the field at Montépilloy, all this would be over by now.'

'You want me to tell him that?'

'If you like.'

The man spits. The mare lashes out. She's been even-tempered up until now and Tomas wants to keep her that way. He catches the bluff man's fist as it swings back, clenched. 'I'll thank you not to hit my horse.'

They straighten together; two men of a height, eye to eye, chin to chin, fist to fist. He slides his hands into his sleeves and takes a step back, making space.

'Your plan?'

The knife hilt fits to his palm. The handle is cherry wood. He rubs his thumb on it, loosely. He has a plan. Of course he does. 'Go to Regnault de Chartres and tell him this . . .'

He gives it in short, easy sentences that cannot be confused, and has them both repeat it back to him. When they can do it verbatim, he lets them stop.

'Then find Bedford, and tell him that he needs to get King Henry's squalling son to Rheims, or he won't be acknowledged as king by the French.'

'Rheims is in French hands.'

'Then he'll have to take it back, won't he? Because the French have remembered where their kings are made in the eyes of God. And it's not Paris. If you'll excuse me?'

CHAPTER TWENTY-SEVEN

'BRACE IT THERE. *There*, damn you!'
'You shouldn't swear.'

'Oh, for— Right. Thank you. Just fix the brace there before the whole thing comes down on our heads.'

This is nearly the last brace. Tomas has been building this bridge since noon and now it is midnight. The harvest moon, a week off full, stands high overhead, spilling pale gold almost-daylight on to the river, the land around, and the bridge he is building. He stands in the river, his habit hitched high. His balls have drawn up halfway to his navel and still the water laps at them. He is happy.

'One more and we are finished. Put it here, between the bank and the first upright.'

Three men act on his order. The sound of hammers on nails is loud enough to wake all the men of Paris, sleeping in their fastness a quarter of a mile away, behind the thickest walls in Christendom. At least now he can curse without being hushed by Maurice and the other carpenters. He does so, leaning back against the baked mud of the river bank.

'Brother Tomas?' The Maid is on foot, not on her devil-horse. She appears on the heights of the bank, looking down. 'How much longer?'

'We are finished, lady.' He has had steps cut in the bank, and ascends them now, pulling his habit out of his belt as he goes. The moon spins his shadow ahead of him. His bridge casts black lace on to the milk-moon water, a ripple of possibility. A direct hit from a gun the size of the Rifflard might destroy it, or a keg of raw gunpowder strategically placed. Two kegs, actually, one at either end, would break its back, and Tomas knows exactly where he would put them.

Failing that, it will hold against anything the armies of either side can throw at it, and while it stands it gives d'Alençon a chance to flank round and assault the Porte Saint-Denis while the Maid is setting all she has at the Porte Saint-Honoré. All they need now is the king's assent.

'My lady . . .'

The Maid has her back to him, looking away. If he still wanted to kill her, it couldn't be easier; her men are spread out around in a ring, facing out. He says, 'Would you try your bridge?'

'In time.' He expects her to turn, smile, walk across his planed planks, offer a compliment or two. She stares away from him, into the night. 'La Hire will escort the men back to la Chapelle. You may go with them if you wish.'

Which means, obviously, that he may choose to remain. 'You will stay here, lady?'

He feels her smile more than he sees it; she is still turned from him. 'Do you think the Parisians know that we're here?'

'I'm sure they do.'

'So, what would you do, were you them?'

'Well . . .' If he were behind the walls, knowing that Paris had never been taken by direct assault but always fallen to treachery from the inside, he might spend his time and his money rooting out any possible dissent, sew the odd churchman in a sack and throw him in the Seine, behead a few butchers, flay a few flayers, hang a few stewards from the gateposts of the various lordly hotels.

He'd build up the fortifications and bring in powder and mercenaries and make sure the latter were well paid, all of which Bedford has done, and as far as he knows there is nothing else planned.

On the other hand, given the basic principle that one does not wish one's enemies to gain any kind of victory, and the men inside, the Frenchmen into whose hands the safety of Paris has been entrusted, might not know what is or is not planned . . .

The Maid is watching him.

He says, 'I would have destroyed the bridge before it was complete.'

'Or?'

'Or I'd wait until it is finished, and then blow it to pieces.' He speaks the thought as it takes shape in his mind. 'That would be the better boost to the morale of the defenders, and inflict the greater damage to those who would attack my city.'

'Where would you place your men?'

He swings round. To his left, the river winds back towards Paris. Somewhere distant is la Chapelle.

All around is open countryside with bands of thorns and the occasional oak. The only wrinkle in the land is to his right, where the meadow dips away in a shallow groove.

'There?'

She nods.

He feels like a boy again. Looking away from the mercury sheen of the water, his eyes grow more used to the dark. Still, he sees nothing.

'Lady?'

'Men. At least a dozen, but there will be others.' She strips off her gloves with her teeth, puts her thumbs to her lips and makes the call of the owl that is her night signal. Shapes grow out of the ground; two men, then three, then six and more.

She has a permanent detachment of a dozen French men at arms who will kill for the privilege of escorting her, and half as many Piedmontese mercenaries, led by a gunnery captain called Pietro di Carignano, who has brought them across Europe to fight with the Maid.

At her silent signal, they begin to move towards the dip in the ground. Her glove is back on, and her blade now free. Tomas checks the knife under his sleeve as he follows.

The moon makes a mirror of her plate. She is a beacon, traversing the countryside. She sends out her men in a broad sweep, half to the left, half to the right. By following the trajectory of their movements, he sees what she has seen: a clump of shadows too dense to be thorns, moving with such slowness that they could as easily be stationary.

Tomas's mouth dries; his head grows light. Like all the rest, he has not fought since Patay. Oh, for his hammers. Or a longer blade. And not to be wearing a white habit under moonlight. He would be better naked. The Maid and her men are within bowshot of the enemy. If they have bodkin tips that can pierce armour . . .

This is not the plan. He cannot breathe.

And then he can, because the two groups are within closing distance and nobody has fallen. He hears a shout. In German. Mercenaries. The Germans are better than the English, better than the Genoese or Venetians or Poles; more disciplined, better trained, fond of the big *zweihänder* blades that are lethal in spread combat.

They are more expensive than the Piedmontese, who

might be able to match them. Bedford, it would seem, is putting considerable gold into the defence of Paris, which may be wise, but suggests a distressing lack of faith in his servant Tomas Rustbeard.

He hears a crisp command, no attempt at concealment now. 'Links. Geh' Sie *links!*'

'My lady, have a care! They are flanking to your right!'

Running towards the fight that has not yet begun, his sandalled feet slither on tussocky grass. His knife is out, but he is watching for the first man to fall, for the first dropped blade, axe, hammer . . .

He angles to the right, listening for the brisk, clear, foreign commands. He is slow, and yes, men have fallen. He scoops up an axe; not perfect, but better than nothing, and soon after, a heater shield with the mark of Luxembourg on it, the lion rampant *queue fourchée* in saltire gules. He runs to the far end, where he can outflank the flankers, but the Piedmontese are already there, curving round the back, and he is redundant, left to watch for solitary men trying to leave the field. There are none.

The fight is short and relatively straightforward. The Maid has brought crossbowmen. A simple expedient, but he doesn't know they are there until he sees the glint of the bow to his left, and hears the particular hard-spring *whup* of a shot. He cannot possibly see the bolt, but his eyes furnish him with an imaginary flicker of silver and shortly after, satisfyingly, one of the big Germans deflates, making short choking noises, like a dog that has swallowed a too-big bone.

Three men dive for the *Zweihänder* that falls as a result. There's a sense of invulnerability that comes from wielding so large a blade, even if it needs training to do it well. The crossbows take out four more and then there are only a handful still fighting around their captain, who is, by the sound of him, French, or Burgundian, or a Luxembourgian, these three being the same in all things but those that matter. At any rate, his blade is of ordinary length.

The Maid is opposite him, and nobody will shoot a crossbow while there is any chance they might hit her by mistake. They match, Maid and man, blade to axe, axe to blade.

Tomas has not, now he thinks about it, seen her fight one on one before, with men standing back to watch.

It is hard to focus on the individual moves in this dance. Their blades are sparks of living silver. The sound is crisp on the warm night. He hears a sigh from the watching men, sees the Maid sway a long way to her left, and, coming upright, cut a clever backhand to the knees, that is blocked and turned with a flick of the wrist; whoever he is, her opponent is good.

But not good enough. Perhaps here, when she is under moonlight, on French soil outside Paris, nobody would be good enough. There's a twist and a slide and a crack, hard, of metal on metal and a sword spins across the turf.

It comes to rest near Tomas. He picks it up, feels the weight, the balance of pommel and blade. It's broad at the hilt, with a clean guard and a strong handle, bound in oxhide, resilient and not likely to slip. The pommel is solid silver, or so it looks. This is German-made, but there is no questioning the identity of the captain who held it: the lion rampant is stamped on the head and after all, Luxembourg is allied to Burgundy.

'A blade fit for battle, lady.' He gives it to her as they ride back to la Chapelle. 'God's gift, perhaps, to replace your Crusader blade.'

She has given her miracle-blade to the shrine of Saint-Denis, patron saint of France. Himself, he wouldn't have done something quite so ostentatiously pious, but then she was petitioning the king for permission to assault Paris: she had to do something to counteract Regnault de Chartres.

And it has worked. They arrive back in the small hours of the morning to find d'Alençon pacing outside her tent, his face alive with battle-joy.

'He said yes! The king is coming from Compiègne. He says we can attack in two days' time. If we are ready.'

You could see the shine of her smile from the heart of Paris.

'We shall be ready.'

CHAPTER TWENTY-EIGHT

ORLÉANS,
Tuesday, 25 February 2014
21.30

S OON.
    Soon Picaut must have answers, because only four full days of campaigning remain until the polls open and if she was in any doubt that the arson had a political motive, the assault on Luc's project has quashed it. She has no idea how the fires might escalate in the short time left, only that it will happen.

She has spent two hours with the forensic teams in the burned-out warehouse, but the wreckage has told her nothing that the CCTV had not already done: that her best and most fertile lead points to Cheb Yasine, the drug dealer who lives in the nearest Orléans has to a slum.

So now Garonne is down at street level, sitting in a car near the private apartment in which Yasine is spending his evening, with a directional microphone pointed at the windows.

And Picaut is in the lookout set up by Rollo on the third floor of a block that looks directly over the bulk of Yasine's territory. The floor is hard under her abdomen. Binoculars press red rims to her eyes. She could feed on the tobacco smoke in the air and not go hungry. She could pillow her head on the hip hop beat pulsing up from the floor below. Insofar as it is possible these days, she is at peace, wrapped in the focused attention that she can never sustain in the chaos of the outer world but always comes with a stakeout.

Sylvie is here with her, monitoring the wire taps on Yasine's landline and his three known mobile phones. In theory, Rollo is asleep. Certainly, he has accepted the order to leave and go home, but everyone says he becomes undead in times like this, that he stands in his kitchen with one hand on the kettle making and drinking coffee after coffee until she summons him again. He inhabits a place apart, invincible, immortal; only a silver bullet will kill him.

There are no silver bullets here, only young Algerian men in trainers and hip-slung jeans who slide back and forth under the streetlights on skateboards; young women with scarves on their heads and great brown eyes whose gazes linger nowhere for long; children and grandparents, harassed mothers and working fathers; Cheb Yasine's drug dealers work openly throughout the ghetto.

It wouldn't be hard to pick them up, but there would be no great value in it. They'd be replaced within the day and Picaut would be no closer to discovering whether he is lighting the fires, and why.

They haven't located the car that Patrice identified on the CCTV yet. It hasn't been reported stolen or missing, or found burned out or crashed or dumped in the river. Garonne keeps looking. Nobody else dares to go out on the streets; they'd be too obvious, and the last thing Picaut wants is to spook Cheb Yasine when she has this one tenuous, beautiful lead.

Her mobile quivers to an incoming text from Patrice.

Picaut holds it up for Sylvie, who shrugs. Neither of them has seen him come near, which is probably just as well. His kingfisher hair is a beacon that would mark him out here as different even faster than a leather jacket on a woman. She walks over and opens the door.

'What on earth are you doing here?'

He's there on the doorstep, a long, lean youth in a hooded sweatshirt and tattered trainers, with jeans slung so low they show a three centimetre rim of tanned skin and lean muscle above the waistband. He's got a bag slung over one shoulder and a skateboard with a luminescent stripe balanced on the other. If he hadn't texted her to say who he was, she'd have her gun out, ready to take him down.

He grins. 'I've found it.'

'Found what?'

'The Civic. Are you going to let me in?'

Pushing past her, he sinks down in the foul armchair that is one of the few pieces of furniture left in this deserted apartment. He unhitches his satchel and brings out a flask, heavy with the scent of Éric Masson's Peruvian coffee.

He holds it out. 'Want some?'

Her own supply ran out an hour ago. 'If you can spare any.'

'You can have it all. I wasn't planning to stay.'

A laptop follows the flask out of the bag. Opened and fired up, the screen displays three photographs of the Honda that was used in the arson attack on Luc's Project.

'It's about four blocks away, parked behind two others. I'll look to see who lives near here when I get back behind a firewall, but I need to leave you with this so you can check on it while I'm away.'

He has already closed the images and is typing fast, his

tongue trapped between his teeth in concentration. Text stutters across the screen with many line breaks.

'What are you doing?'

'Hacking.' He speaks without looking up. 'I put a tracker on the Civic. With a bit of tweaking, Google Maps will let you know if it moves and give read-outs of where it is every fifty metres. Just hold your breath a bit . . .'

Picaut and Sylvie go back to watching the street. Patrice gives a huff of satisfaction, stands, and brings the laptop over to show them what he's done. On the screen, a red dot blinks within a map of the ghetto.

'If it moves, it'll grow larger. The further and faster it goes, the larger it'll get. I could set up an audible alarm, but—'

'But not while we're trying to keep quiet for the sake of those below. Thank you.'

'My pleasure.' He's ready to go, flipping his skateboard up with as much ease as any of the youths on the street. 'Let me know if they move it. I can follow.'

'You're not going down there again?'

'Why not? I can skate better than any of these guys.'

'Patrice, they'll tear you to ribbons.'

'Only if they find out I'm working for you. Which they won't, unless you tell them. Which you won't, so I'm safe.' His grin is brilliant and carefree. He blows her a kiss and is gone.

Picaut is not relaxed now, watching the street; she is watching the lean, hooded figure of Patrice and trying not to imagine how he will look if Cheb Yasine practises on him with his power drills.

Patrice wasn't working for the department when Rémi's drug team lost their man; he never saw the body, he just heard about it afterwards, which is never the same. There's a raw terror that he lacks.

It's not a good train of thought and it doesn't get better

when Patrice skates out of sight and she's left watching a nearly empty street. Cheb Yasine is having dinner nearby, but that apart, the ghetto is in party mode, with loud music and the stink of cannabis layered through the air.

Yasine himself is quiet to the point of being introverted. Picaut is beginning to understand why Rémi had such a hard time reeling him in. Mid-thirties, hard, with a penchant for gold chains and cigarillos, he is none the less the epitome of the successful businessman, husband and father, outwardly at least, careful in his work as the owner of a string of mobile phone shops, adoring of his two teenaged daughters, carefully respectful of his wife.

He may be a pimp's pimp, but he has not been known to use prostitutes of either sex or any age. He sells drugs, but never takes them. He runs bars, but doesn't drink anything more potent than fresh peppermint tea laced with a near-fatal dose of sugar. He is a model of the community he rules, and everyone knows it.

He's out there with his wife, Jasmina, and their two daughters, dining with his cousin Ferhat, eldest of the sprawling Amrouche clan; one of the middle-ranking ones owns the car that Patrice has just found. Garonne is nearby in his car, watching the places she can't see, pointing his directional microphone at the windows, taping the conversations taking place within. He has a radio link to Picaut that Patrice swears is untappable.

It hisses to life now as Garonne says, 'Moving.'

'How many?'

'Three adults, two children. Coming your way.'

They are relaxed, happy, peaceful, like any other family taking an evening stroll. Picaut watches them go past, notes the time in the log, initials the entry. It is this precision that brings results in the end, but she would do it anyway; time matters. Garonne comes in soon after, drops in a recording of the evening's conversation, takes a look at Patrice's laptop and leaves.

Finding time on her hands, Picaut slips in an earpiece and begins the transcription of Garonne's audio files. Hours of family chatter are tedious and she skips through, barely listening.

There's a brief moment of interest when Yasine moves away from the table to talk to a cousin who is also his lieutenant, and they set up what she thinks is the delivery of twenty kilos of cocaine, which might at least pay for the wiretap if she passes it over to Ducat, but there is not a word about the fires.

She takes the headphones off, drinks the last of Patrice's coffee, goes into the next room, pees silently on to a sponge in the base of a bucket, and settles back for the night.

Downstairs, the hip hop beat is toned down a notch or two to make way for the late evening news. Picaut winces as the sound of her own voice follows the headlines. It could have been worse. The press caught her on the way out of Luc's burned warehouse, but they were relatively respectful in their questions.

Until now, the fires have been directed solely at women. The men of the press, therefore, were able to ride out on their white chargers to defend their damsels. They may be, to a man, sexist boors, but they are virile in their defence of their women; they see no contradiction in this.

Now, though, a man has been assaulted. And not just any man, but Luc Bressard. The message from Jaish al Islam condemned him for his 'conciliatory hypocrisy'. The enormity of this is lost on no one: Jaish al Islam, whatever it may be, has now set itself against the Family.

The press is silent in the face of this, lost for words. Outside in the real world, courage and wisdom are added to Luc's list of attributes, as if he has personally faced down the

Islamic jihad, while at the same time calling for calm and reconciliation.

There is nothing Picaut can say that will change any of this, so she says that she has a lead on the fires but nothing definitive and please will anyone who has anything that might prove useful report it immediately to the following address?

Luc's slot follows hers and is live. All evening, he has been on one channel or another, giving his response to the attempted destruction of his Project, swearing that he will rebuild it bigger, better, further-reaching. With each repetition, the sense of the Family being the lifeblood of Orléans grows. There were those, perhaps a decade ago, who thought they had over-reached themselves in coming here, that they should go back down south to their ancestral lands east of Lyon. Nobody is saying that now.

Listening to Luc is an exercise in media-craft. His voice is carefully modulated for the studio, not the hustings, but the message is the same: he will not be cowed, nor will he succumb to the siren calls of those who would cleanse France of the kaleidoscope of races, creeds and beliefs that help give her the vibrant culture that makes her great. In the past the Huguenots, the Cathars, the Jews were all hounded, many of them slaughtered, but nowadays we despise those who did it. 'Kill them all. God will know His own.' We don't think like that now; we know it's not civilized . . .

He's good. His poll ratings are soaring. His campaign team is visibly buoyant. On the whole, lying on the floor of a seedy, empty apartment with her eyes pressed to a set of binoculars, Picaut is probably as safe as anywhere else in Orléans. She looks forward to a night's unbroken sleep. She is not given it.

CHAPTER TWENTY-NINE

Porte Saint-Honoré, Paris,
8 September 1429

'FOR FRANCE! FORWARD! Go! Go! *Go!*'
A surge of men. A glitter of arms. An obliteration of
cannon fire. The Rifflard and its brethren bellow all at once,
hurl their tons of shot against Saint-Honoré, the weakest
of the Parisian gates. They spew stone across the walls,
destroying blockwork, killing the first handful of defenders,
because at last, after weeks of waiting – and d'Alençon sent
twice to fetch him – the king is come from his fastness at
Compiègne to give the Maid permission to assault the
biggest, best fortified, most glorious heart of his kingdom.

It is September, four months since the lifting of the siege of
Orléans. Tomas has spent the days hearing the confession
of an army that is at its smallest since Orléans, less than
half the size it was at Troyes. But at five thousand men it
is still substantial, and those who remain nurse a hatred of
England that curdles more with every passing dawn.

And they still have the gunners. In spite of a flurry of
small skirmishes against men sallying out from the city,
Jean-Pierre hasn't lost a single man from his team. This is

271

one of the many signs the French take to prove that God is still with them.

That wall stretches before them now, a mountain of stone the height of four horses stacked one atop the other. A moat wraps around, a great festering wound in the earth the depth of another two horses and half a bowshot across. This the French must cross before they can reach the men of Burgundy and England, Picardy and Germany, Luxembourg and Poland who line the walls against them with their guns and their maces, their swords and shields and hammers and hot, blistering oil.

There is not wood enough in France to fill the whole of this ditch as the Maid did at Troyes, but in the time Tomas has been here, her men have gathered half a forest to bridge the narrowed gap that lies before the gate of Saint-Honoré, where, by strength of arms, by their faith in the Maid and by the grace of God, they intend to pierce the fastness of Paris and give the king his capital to rule.

Brother Tomas is with the Maid now, part of her inner circle. He, La Hire, d'Alençon, d'Aulon, de Coutes, they fight so close to her that you could throw a cloak across them all and have space free at the edges. Young Raoul de Coutes holds her standard; he alone is not used to battle. She sets him behind her, rakes the rest with her glance, and raises her captured sword.

'For France! Bring the wood.'

Whips crack. Harness strains. Horses and bullocks drag fifty laden carts to the lip of the moat. From behind, the big French guns fire over their heads.

'Forward!'

Wood goes down, men stamp it solid, arrows hiss and thrum, crossbow quarrels stutter wickedly.

The Maid summons forward the pavisse-men, who bear on their backs great shields that make them like turtles.

They are safe, except when they stand up. They are sent beetling on and Brother Tomas follows with the rest, his boots amongst the mailed feet stamping, a wall of men and armour, bringing sword and axe and mace to hammer and cut at the gate.

Soon, at her order, the shield-men bring a great tree trunk to batter against it. The men at arms keep their shields aloft in protection. Tomas is in the group closest to the gate, staff in hand, calling benedictions on the men, sighting the guns, signalling back to Jean-Pierre if he thinks the angles need to change.

The Maid and d'Alençon are to his left. La Hire is wide to his right, a raging bull, smashing the wood with his great war-hammer, but he is too obvious. The English above recognize his colours, and want his blood. Tomas hears a yell in English, and the name within it and turns, shouting, 'La Hire, watch out!'

The cannon fire renders them all deaf, but La Hire feels the shape of the words enough to make him look up, and see the danger, and spring away.

He is fast in his responses, as a knight must be. Spinning, he drags a crossbow from a man who has just loaded it and shoots one-handed up into the battlements. Three of them, Tomas, the Maid and La Hire, hear a hit, a death, exchange a look, bare their teeth, flex their fingers, send out the cry that will draw the army on.

'For the Maid! For France! *For France!*'

The day wears through in heat and noise and pain. Tomas listens to the song of the gate, the rising notes of wood under torture. The men can hear it. Their hammers rise effortlessly in their hands. Their armour is as silk; their rage is holy, and fierce.

'My lady!' A cry from behind and to his left, twenty yards back from the wall, beyond the edge of the moat. It is young

Raoul de Coutes, stricken. From his foot has grown a bolt, and bright blood blooms around it. He is weeping; a child in pain. He takes off his helm, and kneels, and tries to pull out the quarrel that pins him to the floor.

'Raoul! No!' The Maid throws herself at him, but her legs are of lead, too slow, too slow, and no one on earth could be fast enough, for she knows what is coming. They all do.

Tomas shouts, 'Raoul! Get down!'

But the boy is not made for war. He has only played in the meadows, where his brilliant gold hair does not make a target such as the men on the walls have prayed for all day. He doesn't hear; or, hearing, doesn't understand the urgency.

The second quarrel takes him between the eyes. He topples, and takes the standard with him. The Maid catches them both, the boy in one hand, standard in the other. It must not fall. It does not; Jean d'Aulon, at her side as always, takes it from her as she cradles de Coutes in her arms.

'Raoul!' She howls his name, in fury at the English, at the king, at God who lets boys die. He is so beautiful, and he looks barely dead, just a little affronted by the insolence of it; at any moment he might open his eyes and show his white peg teeth and dimple his cheek and say something a page should never say to a knight, which will make them all laugh.

She should not be standing there: she is too exposed. Tomas is with her, at her side, the closest. 'My lady! You must step back!'

She cannot hear him. The Rifflard has just fired, and two others. Everyone is deaf. Tomas drops his staff and searches frantically for a shield. There is one just nearby, vert and argent quartered, the colours of Orléans. He runs for it, scoops it up, turns to see her lower the boy down, close his eyes. Still, she should not be there. Not there, not now. Especially not now. 'My lady, *move*!'

Too late, she sees what he has seen. She jerks left, away from the quarrel that is coming her way—

—spins a full circle—

—it misses her chest—

—and hits her leg.

She falls, her face starkly white, framed by the polish of her helm.

'My lady?' Tomas is beside her, shield in hand, giving scant shelter, but it is all he has. D'Alençon, praise be to God, has the sense to grab a pavisse from a dead man and hold it over them, shielding them from other men's eyes as much as from more bolts and arrows.

Still, he thinks she may be dead, and for a moment his world is adrift, as bad as when he was under the poppy. Not here. Not now. This is *not* his plan.

Sense catches him up. She cannot be dead for a bolt in the leg only. Surely she cannot?

'My lady? Can you hear me?'

By force of will, she drags her eyes open. He sees the clash of pain and fury in her gaze; she has been hit before, but never incapacitated. She tries to speak, but pain is a river that holds her, might drag her under. He slides his shoulder under her arm. She grinds her teeth. In the sudden hush, he hears them, and because of that, knows the field has stopped fighting, to watch.

She knows it too. 'Get me up. They have to see me up.'

'Up, then.' He helps her. 'But don't go outside the shelter of the pavi—'

Too late. The second bolt misses her but strikes her hard-won German blade square on. The sound of breaking steel rends the air.

He feels the shock, spreading outwards. A sword is a sacred thing and everyone knows how she won it in a fight, one on one, with a knight. To see it shattered before the walls of Paris . . . such things have turned the tides of too many battles to count. It is this, the breaking of her blade, that lets the dam break.

'The Maid! The Maid is down!'

French voices and English shout it across the field and upon the walls; only the tone is different. In something approaching terror, he waits for the cataclysm of Jargeau, for the French to gather breath and swear vengeance, for the power of five thousand men to join in one single unstoppable force.

And he waits.

And he feels only the ruin of loss. Delay after delay has rotted the core of this army. Its self-belief has gone. Its belief in the Maid is not what it was. The men love her, but if the king, who is God's anointed, does not want to fight, where is the certainty of God's help?

The Maid feels it. She is white as fire ash, but she will not leave. 'Help me to stand.'

La Hire ducks in under the shelter of the pavisse. 'Girl, we have to get you back to la Chapelle. If you die here . . .' He shuffles round, takes hold of her other shoulder, ready to drag her back.

He should know better than that. She knocks away his arm. 'Better that I die here than in a tent behind the lines. The men must see me up. They must know I'm alive, or all is lost. Tomas, tell him.'

'She's right.' He braces himself, holding her full weight up, armour and all. 'The ranks will fall back if they think she's dead.' And if they fall back now, they may regroup and find their heart and that would never do. 'La Hire, take her other arm. I've got this side. Careful now . . . make her steady. Give her your sword. She must appear armed. My lady, can you stand without us?'

'Give me the standard.' She reaches out, blindly. Tomas

grabs the banner from her squire and thrusts it into her left hand, the side where her leg won't hold her.

Her pain comes in waves now; he can see the flood and blanch across her face. She grips the standard left-handed and raises La Hire's blade with her right and shouts, 'Onward for France! Onward! *Onward!*'

The men put up a tattered cheer and rally their efforts. 'Don't stay, we'll take the bastards without you!'

Which is good, because he thinks pain has made her half blind. She can't see which way is forward and if she blunders any further into bolt range they'll have her again. They know they can now; she isn't magic any more. At last it is clear to them that neither God nor the devil is protecting her.

'We have to get her back across the river.' He begins to turn her.

She resists, pushes him away. 'Tomas, stay on the field. You're needed here. I'll get back on my own.'

Hardly. Not now. He says, 'You won't get back to la Chapelle like this, and we can't pull any of the knights off the field. I'll take you. Your squire will help.'

The friends of her childhood are gathered round her now. D'Alençon takes the standard back and hands it to Jean de Belleville. He lays a hand on her shoulder. 'My lady, you were hit before, at les Tourelles, at Jargeau. We won there, both times, and we shall win here, now. Nobody will say God has abandoned you.'

Around them is a moment's darkness, a keening desolation. She hovers on the borderlands of death.

Her eyes grow dull.

She says, 'The king, maybe. But not God.'

CHAPTER THIRTY

La Chapelle Saint-Denis,
8 September 1429

At dusk Tomas is alone at her bedside, in her sick room in the inn at la Chapelle.

She would have preferred her tent, but she is royal in all respects that matter and there are appearances that must be maintained. Thus Tomas has brought her to this room with its stone floor, and windows shuttered against the ill humours of the day, and dark, heavy furniture, a hundred years old, pushed back against the walls. Candles fret and droop in the four corners of the room, and a brazier sulks by the bed, barely hot enough to cook more valerian and melt the honey into it.

Brother Tomas is the epitome of compassion and practical care. He has had the mattress dragged out and burned and a fresh one filled with straw they brought from Rheims; it carries neither lice nor mould.

He has had water drawn from the well, and his medicine box retrieved from his tent. He has had her page remove her armour and then sent the lad off to grieve in the chapel for his slain brother.

He has mixed poppy, hemlock and henbane, juice of lettuce and gall of a gelded boar into a mix that sends her so completely to sleep that her squire is not required even to hold her shoulders still, and can instead help to hold the tourniquet on her leg while Tomas works the honeyed Musselman spoons down around the bolt's head, until he can grasp it and draw it out without doing further damage to her thigh.

The tourniquet, once released, spews out gouts of dark blood, but he plugs beeswax and linen in the wound and binds it tightly and makes sure he can still feel the throb of life at the crook of her ankle that will keep her foot vital. He thinks she will not die of this if he can keep the wound from festering. She must not die yet; it would undo all he has worked for.

It is evening by the time they are done, and her squire is as grey as his mistress, with fatigue and hunger. Tomas sends him off to see to the Maid's devil-horse and then feed himself, and is left to care for her alone.

He is mixing possets of lavender and honey with the bitter poppy beneath when d'Alençon knocks and enters. In the gold-red light their eyes meet, two men united in grief.

Tomas asks, 'How went the day?' He keeps his countenance sober, but his heart thrums with the nearness of everything. It takes more effort than it has ever done to keep his knowledge tight to his chest.

D'Alençon leans back on the door, holding it closed. 'We have not broken through, but we shall. The men are in good heart. My lord of Montmorency has joined us with fifty men at arms and their retainers.'

A day before and that might have turned the whole battle. Montmorency is good, but he comes too late. Tomas says, 'With their help, and God's, we will prevail.'

'Indeed. And the Maid?' D'Alençon crosses to her bed.

Without asking, he pulls up a stool, a clumsy, brutal affair in heavy oak with a padded seat that might once have been velvet, but has since seen the slide of ten thousand buttocks and is worn to threads. He sits at her side and picks up her hand as if he were her husband, father, brother. He has known her since childhood. It never does to forget that. If anyone knows her truth, d'Alençon does.

Tomas says, 'She sleeps. I have given her that which will keep her free of pain until morning. My lord, have you eaten?'

'Not yet.' The duke waves his other hand. 'There was rumour of a goat stew out there somewhere.'

'Stay with her. I shall see to it.' He wants d'Alençon relaxed and he won't be relaxed until he has eaten, and Tomas has heard the same rumour.

Men are clumped near the door of the inn. He tells them what they need to hear. 'The Maid is well. She recovers. She hears how you fought and is pleased with it.' This is true in spirit if not exactly in fact. She has that skill of the best commanders, of making each man in her army feel as if she has singled him out for her especial attention.

The goat stew has been boiled with barley meal and beans. He tracks down better wine, clean well-water, pewter goblets. Returning, he lays them out on a board, with a linen cloth beneath.

'My lord . . .'

A spoon. A bowl. Good, plain, mouth-aching food. He knows how it is after battle, the desperate gnawing hunger that hits as soon as the threat is gone.

'Tomas, what would we do without you?'

'Much the same, I suspect. She is the one we cannot do without.'

She is unconscious, black lashes stark against white cheeks. D'Alençon is eating and cannot reply. Then he is

280

drinking and cannot reply. The moments tick past. Soon, it will be too late. Come on. Come *on* . . .

At last, he looks up, and Tomas can ask the first of his questions. He has to ease into this with great caution, but doors are open now that were not before.

'Does the king know that the Maid was a ward of his father?'

D'Alençon looks down at his hands.

Tomas says, 'Claudine came to me for confession. She had been . . .'

'Servicing the men?'

'That, obviously. But she had also drunk too much. On my life, I have told nobody.' He raises his right hand. This is the truth: he has not sent his knowledge to Bedford yet; some things, he must deliver in person.

D'Alençon looks at him squarely, thinks for a while, nods. The duke has grown into himself these past months: he is better fleshed, his skin no longer prison-jaundiced, his heart shows in his eyes. 'If he doesn't, he's a fool.'

'I'm not certain, my lord, that the question is therefore answered.' He could die for that; beheading is the wages of treason.

D'Alençon doesn't look like a man planning an execution. He eats more of the stew, sucking the juices off his spoon, drumming the index finger of his left hand on his knee. 'I think he must do. Why else did he prevaricate over Paris?'

'Does he think she will be a challenge to him? To his kingship?'

'Don't you?' The bowl is on the floor and d'Alençon is up, pacing, restless as a tethered bear. He reaches a wall and blindly spins. 'The old king didn't make her what she is, but he saw the potential and nurtured it. She has every part of his understanding of battle, of his martial valour. He may have been mad, but he was a great knight, a great horseman, a great tactician. She is all of these, and they are not tainted by his madness. She hasn't lost a battle yet, unless she loses this one, and if she does it'll be only because she wasn't allowed to attack when the army was at its strongest. If she were a man, she'd be on the throne by now. As it is, the man who marries her, if he has any royal blood in him, if he has ridden once into battle this year, is clearly more of a king than the man who hides behind the robes of his archbishop and claims that he wants peace through treaties. Treaties!' D'Alençon's laugh would strip the skin from the king, were he here.

'His godforsaken treaties have given Bedford time to bring in three thousand more men and build up the defences of Paris to the point where it is well-nigh impregnable. If we'd attacked in July, with the holy oil still wet on his skin, we'd have taken it without effort. Now—' His closed fist rebounds off his palm. 'Now we are going to have to rely on Jean-Pierre and his gunners to pound the gate of Saint-Honoré tomorrow to draw them all away from Saint-Denis so the rest of us can endeavour to break in. I tell you, if you hadn't built us that bridge, we'd be in sore—'

A knock at the door.

All talking stops.

Briefly, the shadow of a shameful death stalks the walls; they both know this is treason and even dukes may be executed for *lèse-majesté*.

Tomas rises. Can whoever is there hear through this door? He thinks not. It is so old, so heavy, so intricately carved, that it must be a barrier to all but the most forcefully projected words.

The Maid's squire sways from foot to foot in the doorway. 'A message for my lord d'Alençon. One is here who would speak to him.'

'He's too busy.'

282

'Not for this. It's Regnault de Chartres. He comes directly from the king.'

The king has gone back to Compiègne, where he is safe from possible assault. Nobody has named this cowardice. Not aloud.

D'Alençon is standing by the bedside, his hand on the shoulder of the sleeping Maid, his gaze upon her face.

Tomas turns to him. 'My lord, you must go.' D'Alençon looks up. His whole heart is in his eyes, his yearning, his fierce, prideful ache and want.

With care, as one in the presence of an unknown hound, Tomas says, 'Regnault de Chartres, my lord. Go to him. Find what he wants. Find a way to . . .'

He loses the words. How often has he imagined this? How hard is it now? Much harder than he ever imagined.

He flaps a hand towards the door, a useless gesture. D'Alençon reads into it what he needs.

'Yes. Of course. D'Aulon, lead me.'

They go. Tomas sits where d'Alençon lately sat, on the ugly, threadbare stool, by the low bed in the stifling air. The candles seethe in the corner, giving off light the colour of goat's urine. The brazier is all but dead. He lifts her hand, lays it down again, covers his face.

He waits for elation to hit. And waits. It must come, surely, because this is it, his final stratagem, the keystone in the arch of his planning.

Somewhere in a room not far from here, Regnault de Chartres, archbishop of Rheims, is sitting in close conference with Duc Jean d'Alençon, prince of the blood, unwinding at length the final denouement, the knife in the back that will finish the Maid and all she stands for.

He thinks of his bridge. It isn't a miracle of engineering, but it is solid, and competent and built to exacting specifications, with places at either end under which a man or two might hide, or a gunpowder keg be left. Blown in these two places, its back will break and fall with some neatness into the river. He would like to have seen it, just to know he had done it right.

The Maid stirs on the bed. He did not plan for her injury, but it does mean that he, Tomas, the architect of her downfall, might yet be the one to break the news to her.

He rehearses the words in his head. My lady, you have lost everything: the bridge, battle, the war, your credibility as an agent of God. Your army has been stood down. Your campaign is over. You are nothing now but a chimera, a girl who dresses in armour and fights like a man. You cross halfway to heresy simply by rising from bed each morning, and when they discover your lies the crossing will be complete. How long before they burn you?

Not yet; she sleeps still, although her face is regaining its colour. Life blooms on her cheeks. Images cluster in his head, float in the forefront of his mind: the Maid at Jargeau, laughing after her fall; at Patay, before the charge, locked in white armour, lance aloft, joy alive in her eyes. And something more: the touch of royalty, a mind tutored by a king.

He thought she was the young Henry, coming to her Agincourt, and he was not so far wrong. He remembers Troyes, and the filling of the moat. He stands again before Bedford's massed armies at Montépilloy and watches her put her devil-horse through its paces while not a knight in the entire English army dares accept her challenge.

He hates Bedford. More, he despises him. The understanding of this has been for some time at the edge of his awareness. He does hate Bedford. And he does not hate the Maid as he did.

Sitting at her side, he lifts her hand again. As at Jargeau, the jolt strikes him to his heart. Unlike at Jargeau, he does not let go. Counting the passing minutes, he wonders what part Regnault de Chartres has reached, whether d'Alençon knows yet that it is all over.

They will have to send the good duke away. Normandy will do; anywhere far from the Maid where she and the duke cannot conspire. D'Alençon loves her. Is it any wonder? What man wouldn't, having seen her at war? What man wouldn't, having seen the spark of her courage? What man . . . ?

His heart is suddenly empty, aching, wretched. He feels as d'Alençon looked, and when he rubs the knuckle of his thumb across his cheek, it comes away wet.

He blows his nose on his sleeve. He grips her hand. Without any great thought, he lifts it, kisses the knuckles, just a brush of his lips to her cracked, bruised skin. And thus is he lost.

In the space of one breath, his heart turns over. His guts invert themselves, inside to out, outside to in. The marrow of his bones, which is writ in its oaken heart with the names of Bedford and England, breaks apart and comes together anew and the names it writes are no longer English.

The Maid. France. Jehanne d'Arc.

My love.

He feels himself falling; an old sensation, newly returned.

Once, a long time ago, when a nine-year-old boy named Tomas de Segrave thought he knew who his father was, before he understood the meaning of the word bastard, or how to fight others who used it as an insult, before he saw his mother die, before he left Normandy for England and a better life, long, long before he grew a beard and was named for its hue; back then, in his innocence, he played with other boys through summer and into winter.

There came one white winter, with water made stone, and the lake solid as a limestone cliff, laid flat out between the hills. The boys carved skates from the leavings of the carpenter's shop and raced each other from side to side and back again, swan-gliding across milky ice under a sky of such perfect, aching blue that it might have been poured by God from His own vessel.

He does not know what it is to be unhappy, and so he does not treasure the happiness, but he does sing the song his not-father has taught him and it is like this, skating, singing, laughing, that he comes to the cracked place in the ice.

He does not see it. He does not know to look for such things. It comes on him suddenly; one moment sun, sky, ice, warm, brilliant, cheerful – and the next cold, black water. So very cold. He can't breathe. He can't think. He panics and, panicking, may die; he knows boys do, who fall under the ice and cannot find air.

This single thought clamps down on his panic: if he does not think clearly, he will die. He stops fighting, makes himself still in the water. He bobs up until the crown of his head taps on something solid. He stretches out his arms and finds that his left hand has met something living; the arm of his father (not his father, but he doesn't know and at this moment, even if he did, he wouldn't care: he loves this man) reaching into the black water to find him. They link hand to arm and he is pulled up from the drowning.

And so he is out again, under the sun, but cold now, and older, and wiser. A line has been crossed that cannot be uncrossed. If he were to put a time on the start of his natural caution, on his need always to think ahead, to his ability to quell his own panic, it would be here, this moment, and the long, slow thaw in front of the fire afterwards.

But here, now, sitting in a stinking inn within striking distance of Paris, he drops once more from fire-bright-warm into black-ice-soul-sucking-cold and this time, he is alone; nobody is here to lift him out.

He wrenches his hand from hers, but it is far, far, far too late. He spins, rendered clumsy by shock and grief, hauls open the door, crashes into the page, Louis de Coutes, whose brother is dead. 'Where is my lord d'Alençon? Find him. I must speak to—'

'Here, Tomas. I am here.' D'Alençon is a revenant; a monster come back from the dead to taunt him with the success of his own plan. The duke is white, dead-eyed. His hands hang by his sides, useless. His words are wrought in dust.

'It is over. The king has ordered the army to stand down. We have not permission to continue the attack on Paris. Tomas, the King of France has had his sappers blow up your bridge . . .'

CHAPTER THIRTY-ONE

ORLÉANS,
Wednesday, 26 February 2014
06.30

THE SIXTH FIRE IS called in at 06.09 on the Wednesday after Iain Holloway's death. The target is the offices of Orléans! 24/7 and the fire is broadcast live by Henri Aubel and his producer who manage to keep a camera rolling for each step of the fire-fighting retreat out into the streets.

Every media anchor in France is on the scene long before the flames reach their zenith and the rest of the world's newscasters are there before they are finally quelled. The networks are sending their big beasts out now; men – and a few women – who might otherwise be reporting from Syria, Iraq, South Sudan, Nigeria, find themselves on the Loire, watching fire lick at the sky.

Picaut is on the site by quarter past six. The world's media feast on her presence. By nine, they are reporting the fact that Marianne Roche, one of the interns, is missing, and may have been inside. Her name flashes round the world. Picaut sends a team to find the young woman's parents and protect them from the scrum, but they arrive after the media masses and have to fight their way through to an already grieving couple. It's a PR disaster and can only get worse.

'We need to get in,' Picaut says to Martin Evard.

'Not until it's safe. They used incendiaries on this one, and I want to be sure there aren't any more waiting to go off.'

A booby-trapped building would break every pattern, but that's not a reason to assume it can't happen. She waits. The cameras roll. The news anchors interview anyone who will stand still long enough. Picaut is not one of their targets.

Shortly after ten thirty in the morning, the fire chief finally gives his permission for her to enter. The images on the lunchtime news are of her in white overalls, hard hat and closed breathing kit, standing by the technician whose job it is to open doors that locked shut when the power went down.

She is about to go in when she feels a tug at her sleeve. Lumbering, she turns, and Trudi is there, Marianne's friend. Her pink-blonde hair is smeared now with soot and the fringe has been scorched back to half its length. Her perfectly oval sky-blue nails are scratched and broken. Her red dress is filthy. She has been weeping, and may do so again.

Picaut says, 'I'm sorry, you can't come in.'

'I know. Colin . . . that is, Mr Graves, asks if you will wear this.' She holds up a spider's lace of webbing with a lens attached.

'Is that a helmet camera?'

A shrug. Half a smile, all apology. 'There's a microphone as well. It'll stream to us live whatever you see and say.'

Picaut shakes her head, aware that every move is being broadcast worldwide. 'I can't.'

'I am to offer you half a million euros to be paid to the charity of your choice.'

'It's not about money. It's about safety and sanity and not turning a catastrophe into reality TV. It's about Marianne's decency, if she's even in there.'

'She is. She was on shift with me.' Old tears already weld Trudi's lashes together. New ones ripen, ready to fall. Picaut signals for Garonne, who has come from the stake-out of Cheb Yasine and is hovering, waiting for something useful to do. He's good with the bereaved; surprisingly compassionate.

To Trudi, she says, 'Wait out here with Lieutenant Garonne. I'll let you know as soon as we find her.'

'The camera . . .'

'Not a chance. If Colin Graves needs me to explain why, tell him it's time he found a new job.'

She turns back to where Martin Evard and the technicians are waiting. The door is open.

'This way.' Her voice echoes through the microphone in the helmet. She pushes past the others, through the door, and then has to wait in the foyer while the no-longer-whispering inner door screams back, wrenched in slow motion by a pulley and chain. At least none of the reporters tries to follow her inside. Danger has its uses.

A corridor stretches ahead, scorched and black, full of smoke and warped metal. The tiled floor has bucked and cracked. Evard says, 'Round to the left, then third door on the right.'

'Where are we going?'

'To the start of the fire.'

In her mind's eye, Picaut can see the green room as it was on Tuesday morning. Marianne ushers her in, sends Trudi for coffee, Suzanne for magazines. Esteban, the make-up technician, is at work. A prickle at the back of her neck says that whoever started this fire knew she had been here. Whoever did this, they set the incendiaries where she was. Every step closer makes her more sure.

She wants to run and can only shuffle in the wake of the technicians. An age and an age and they can creep on round, taking photographs at every step until they reach the door and force it open and there, amidst the shattered mirrors and plastic chairs melted to doorstops . . .

'Oh, God.'

Curled up on the floor are the charred remains of a corpse. The clothes are burned away, and the hair. The eyes have long since boiled to nothing. It's not even possible to tell if it was male or female. Only that it was once human.

Picaut stands, stranded, in the middle of the floor. Her memory of Marianne vanishes in a whisper of smoke: the shape of her face, the colour of her eyes, the angles of her teeth, all gone. She remembers only the dynamism, the vivacity, the utter, unquenchable *life*.

She walks out. Behind her, Martin Evard speaks into his headset to the listeners outside. 'Call Ducat. Tell him we have a body.' He listens for a moment, shrugs heavily under his protective gear. 'They can speculate all they like. We won't have any information for them in less than twenty-four hours.'

Picaut is in the corridor. Ahead, the door to the ladies' lavatory is being winched open. And so she is there when the body that has been pressed against it tumbles out into the corridor.

'Martin!' She kneels, as if there were something useful she could do. But this corpse, too, has been burned beyond distinguishing. Still, she would bet her rank on its being Marianne.

'Marti—!'

'I'm here.' His hand heavy on her shoulder, his

white-wrapped bulk a comforting presence. 'There'll be a feeding frenzy on the steps if they see we have two dead.'

'Which is exactly why we won't tell them. Get the ambulance to back right up to the door. I want this kept quiet until we have some idea of who they both were and why they were in the building.'

Standing, she phones Éric, and then Ducat, and breaks the news. Later, blinking in the daylight, she finds that Garonne has succeeded in pushing the press back behind a crime scene tape. Now they can shout questions all they like, and she can ignore them.

Someone – Ducat? Luc? – has arranged for an escort to get her back to the station. On the radio is news of a fresh wave of demonstrators gathering at the *Front National* offices across the river. They plan to march in force north across the bridge, giving vent to the fury of a France under siege, bolstering with every step Christelle Vivier's chances of election.

Four days remain until the polls open for what is now the most heavily reported mayoral election France has ever seen. It is impossible to imagine how anything worse could happen by then, only that it will almost certainly do so.

CHAPTER THIRTY-TWO

Orléans,
Wednesday, 26 February 2014
11.30

Maître Ducat! Is it true that a fingerprint was found at Orléans! 24/7 that might lead you to the people who perpetrated this atrocity?'

It's true, yes, they have a fingerprint. A single, perfect, absolutely clear-as-newsprint set of swirls. They have a 98 per cent probability match in the local database that has given them a name. The press know about the print, but not the name. They scent something, though, and are not about to let it go.

From the cool of Éric's lab, Picaut watches on a wide-screen TV as the BBC reporter asks his question. The camera pans to Ducat, harassed, sweating, standing on the steps that lead up to his office. He gives his gap-toothed smile and replies in perfect English.

'It is true that one hundred and fifty different prints have so far been identified in the Orléans! 24/7 building. The police are sampling all the staff from the cleaners to the CEO. When they have ruled them out, they will begin to look at who else might legitimately have been there. Only when we rule out all of those can we consider that the print might belong to one of the perpetrators.'

'Maître! Is it true that not one but two bodies were found inside, and that therefore one of the arsonists was caught in the blaze?' This is *Die Zeit*, but the question comes in French. Ducat could probably answer in German. So far, as well as French and English, he has spoken Italian, Dutch and a Scandinavian language that Picaut thinks might have been Swedish. She had no idea he stretched this far. She is impressed.

'You all saw the ambulance. We cannot comment on identity until we have a pathology report.' That's clever. He hasn't mentioned a number, so, later, he can't be accused of lying.

'But you did find the missing intern from Orléans! 24/7 staff? Marianne—'

'As I said, we cannot comment.'

Ducat's face is thunderous. He can't comment, but they can keep asking questions, can play out the entirety of Marianne's biography on their rolling news channels, her Pinterest, Instagram, Twitter and Facebook streams, the Facebook page set up in her memory, the trolls already lurking at its nether margins, spinning webs of hate.

More than ever before, Picaut is working in a goldfish bowl. The forensic team was filmed going in and coming out, and when they found the fingerprint on the inner door frame the long-lensed cameras broadcast the fact before they had time to call in the news to the station, never mind identify whose print it was.

Picaut, meanwhile, is waiting for the moment when someone asks, 'Is it true that your police captain is the target of the last two attacks?' Luc's warehouse and now the studio that hosted her. Everything at one remove, but coming closer.

On the steps to Ducat's office, the questions press on.

—When will you bring a case against the perpetrators?

'When Capitaine Picaut provides me with sufficient evidence to do so.'

—So we can hope for a report later today?

'You can hope, as we all do, for an end to the fires and peace to be restored. We're working as fast as we can, but nothing is as simple as we'd like it to be. And now, if you'll excuse me, I have work to do.'

Ducat turns his broad back to the pack and stalks in through the doors to his office. Nobody makes any attempt to follow. The men and women of the press are no longer cowed by the Family or by the prosecutor, but terrified of their own story. If a television station can be torched, any one of them might be the next target. And now one of their own has died, or so it seems. The knowledge of this shrouds every report.

The doors close behind him. The shot cuts away to the studio where serious people wear serious faces. Picaut taps her elbow on the control that mutes the sound. Without it, the room rustles to the shallow echo of white tiles and stainless steel and death.

Today, two burned bodies lie on adjacent tables.

Éric stands between them, clean in his pale blue theatre scrubs. Radiographs are displayed on screens on either side.

Picaut says, 'We need IDs soon. Ducat won't be able to keep the sharks at bay much longer.'

'We're getting there.' Éric pushes down his surgical mask. It hangs from his ears, loops like a hammock just below his chin. He looks tired.

'On the left we have a Caucasian woman in her mid-twenties. I'll need to check the dental records to be certain, but I'll give you ninety per cent odds that we can tag this one as Marianne Roche, the missing intern. If you can give me another hour before you send someone to see her parents, I'll have definite proof. She died trying to get out of the door. We can say she died swiftly, of smoke inhalation. Her parents will need that.'

Her parents, of course, are already broken. Her name was broadcast from the beginning by a courageously tearful Henri Aubel, who is wearing black now, in mourning. The parents are newly under police guard in a small, select, immensely discreet hotel. So far, they are being given a modicum of privacy. It's hard to imagine that it will last.

Éric turns to his right. 'This one inhaled a lot of smoke, but he didn't die of it. Something else killed him first, and then he was in the fire's heart. This is serious damage. If we start with basic morphology, we have—'

'A history of youthful body-building?'

Éric is about to set off in full flow. He brakes hard, gazes at her. 'How do you know that?'

She lets herself smile. 'My father thought my education wasn't complete unless I could tell the difference between a trained knight and a peasant by picking up the femur. If nothing else, I know the signs of extensive load-bearing before the growth plates close.'

'Right.' Éric stands back. 'Get anything else from this?'

'Nothing that matters. I can't see what killed him.'

'Nor can I, and it's occupied a deal of the past couple of hours. I'm running tox tests, but the rest will be on the PM.'

'So tell me what you've got.'

'Male, early twenties, one metre sixty-five, a lean sixty-one kilograms and of North African descent.'

'Fuck.' The fingerprint was from one of Cheb Yasine's cousins. This is too close for comfort. 'Are you sure about the race?'

'Take a look.' Éric turns to the radiographs on the wall, speaking as he goes. 'Skull lateral and AP: we're looking at the size of the supraorbital margin, bony glabella, largeish, squareish mastoid process, et cetera et cetera ad nauseam. No question as to gender: this one is male. Early twenties because the growth plates in the femur are closed, which puts him over twenty, but the sagittal suture of the skull hasn't closed yet, which puts him under twenty-six. Race is trickier, but the zygomatic arch is halfway between the narrow of the Caucasian and the wide of the negroid and I've only ever seen that in the northern African communities. We need to find a relative and get a DNA match. Until then, I'm stabbing in the dark.'

'So he could be Algerian?'

'Algerian, Moroccan, Tunisian . . . Whichever, he was at the fire's heart and it's the hottest yet: he's far more badly burned than Iain Holloway was. If you want my guess as to whether the rogue fingerprint is his, my money's on a positive. Whether he put it there is another question entirely.'

Indeed. Her phone rings: Ducat. She hits the elbow patch that brings him on air. 'Maître, you lied to me. The cameras love you.'

Ducat snorts. 'Do you have any IDs yet?'

'The girl is Marianne Roche. We're waiting on dental confirmation, but she's right height, right age and in the right place. The other . . . Éric says he's North African.'

'And the fingerprint?'

'That's a perfect match for Tahar Amrouche, one of Cheb Yasine's myriad cousins and youngest of eight brothers. It may be a plant, but if it's from the dead man, then there's no doubt he was present when the fire was lit. The thing we have to remember is that Iain Holloway was present when the fire that destroyed the Hôtel Carcassonne was lit, but nobody thinks he lit it.'

'This is the value, no doubt, of being white and having a

medical degree. You will not tell our friends in the media I said that. Does our current body have a fractured skull in the way Iain Holloway did?'

'Not that Éric's found, no. He was alive when the fire was lit. He may not have been conscious.'

She can hear the tap of Ducat's pen on his desk. 'You don't sound to me like a woman on the verge of a major break-through, Capitaine Picaut.'

'I'm not. Our best lead was Cheb Yasine and I had people on him all night. We have him on a tape from Garonne's listening post that's time-stamped from nine thirty to nearly midnight, after which he went to bed and slept in silence. He and his cousin set up a coke deal for next week that I've passed to Rémi in Drugs. They also talked about the fires and the *Front National* and how fast they'd have to clear out of Orléans if Christelle Vivier were to be elected and Troy Cordier were in charge. They talked about long-term plans for shipping AK47s from Romania to some other branch of the family in Syria. They were relaxed and open and thoughtful. They were not men planning to light the sixth in a series of fires within hours of parting. And they didn't know that one of their own was about to die, I'd bet my job on that. These men are like the Bressards: family is every-thing to them. They wouldn't sacrifice one of their own.'

'So—?'

'So I'm waiting for Éric to give me a cause of death on the unknown body from last night, but I think he was a victim, not a perpetrator. And if he did light it, Cheb Yasine didn't know he was there.'

'Amrouche is a minnow in a pool of sharks. Maybe he thought it was time to set up on his own?'

'I don't think so. Would you be inclined to go self-employed if big cousin was there offering easy money and free use of his whores when the alternative was being tied

298

to a chair with a sixteen-millimetre drill bit ripping holes in your kneecaps? I wouldn't. Cheb is still our best link. Just now he's our only one. I need to put some pressure on. If he's being set up, he may know who's doing it and why. I need to push him and then see what he does.'

'If you need a twenty-four-hour extension on the wiretap, let me know.'

Picaut blinks. In the entirety of their joint existence, she has never known Ducat to offer an extension on a tap; she has been bracing herself to beg.

She says, 'That would be useful, thank you.'

'Excellent.' He is briskly, sharply, earnest. 'Don't do anything precipitate.'

'I'm sorry for your loss.'

It is the middle of a hot afternoon. Picaut is alone, without either Garonne or Rollo – or the entourage of the press – standing in Cheb Yasine's front room.

What she has seen so far of his residence is a careful hybrid between contemporary France and ancient Algiers. The sideboard in blond wood, with clean, almost Scandinavian lines; the pale leather sofa, with the muted, expensive look of Maison Lafayette; the polished parquet floor: all and each of these could sit in one of the Bressards' many homes and not look amiss.

What could not be are the heavily padded thick-silk cushions with the single central button in royal blue and gold, the carpets hanging on the walls, the wide, sweeping archways decorated with Arabic script in gold lettering on blue paint.

The air is light with spices, tobacco and peppery incense. Picaut sips sweet, scalding mint tea from a glass. Cheb Yasine stands opposite her, slack-hipped, one hand on the ash wood sideboard. Behind him, the script-mounted arches lead through to a kitchen, and other rooms she cannot see. The women are there, invisible and silent.

Yasine is dressed in Ralph Lauren jeans and a marine-blue hooded sweatshirt of the kind that were worn at the Palme d'Or last summer. His gold is limited to a thick cable chain at his wrist. He is smooth-shaven, with a boyish, open face and perfect teeth. His lips are sensuous, full; on a Caucasian, they'd be proof of silicone and expensive surgery. His brows are strongly horizontal. He emits a sense of studied courtesy, fragile as fine porcelain.

'Are you wired?'

'Of course. My colleagues are monitoring all that we say. It's safer for us both.'

A slow nod; he knows the law and what counts in a court. 'The man that is dead. Are you sure it's Tahar?'

'Not certain. We'll need to take DNA from the closest relative to be sure, but we think it's likely. I can show you photographs, but you may not want to see them.'

He shrugs, holds out a hand. She passes over four images of the blackened body that Éric Masson printed off before she left. She didn't tell him she was coming here; his response would have been the same as Garonne's and harder to deal with.

Cheb Yasine's pupils flare as he studies his cousin's remains; it is the only response, but it's genuine and when he looks up she says again, 'I'm sorry. Did you know he was missing?'

'His mother called this morning. I have three people out looking for him.' With deliberate slowness, he draws an iPhone from his pocket. 'If you'll allow me?'

She nods. He hits a single key. He doesn't give his name, makes no introduction, only says, in strong French, 'Stop looking. No, in the fire . . . Yes, here, now. No, that won't be necessary.'

300

He shrugs her an apology as he hangs up. 'They wish to come and protect me from you. I am safe. I have told them so. Now you tell me why you are here. You could have sent anyone with this.'

There are very few advantages to being a media celebrity, but Cheb Yasine's appreciation of her rank is one of them. Choosing her words with care, she says, 'It seems that there are people who wish me to believe that you are both the leader of Jaish al Islam and the primary arsonist. I am not currently inclined to believe either of these.'

He takes out a slim, black cigarillo, asks a question with a raised brow, lights at her nod. The texture of the air changes. 'If Jaish al Islam existed, and if I led it, would I tell you?'

'Not in words.'

He hooks up one brow. The silence stretches. 'And in not-words, what have I told you?'

'That you didn't know your cousin was dead. Whoever lit the fire knew he was there, therefore you didn't light the fire, or order it lit, and you didn't order someone to plant Tahar's body at the location. Also, I don't think you're stupid enough to let anyone leave a perfect set of prints on the entry door of a burning building. Nor are you stupid enough to use a car registered in the name of your family to light a previous fire when there were half a dozen CCTV cameras trained on the door of the building in question. Particularly not when whoever lit all the previous fires was well aware of the cameras and their timings. We were allowed to see the Honda. I don't think by you.'

He's not used to being read, or to that reading being spoken of openly. He glances towards the window, as if he expects Garonne or Rollo to be sitting in easy view. When they are not, he leans back against the wall, shoves his hands in his jeans, loses a decade. 'How did he die?'

'The pathologist isn't sure. There's no damage to his skull. He thinks perhaps a stiletto to the heart.'

'Why does he think that?'

It was Éric's last comment before she left, said with some uncertainty. 'Because it's incredibly hard to discover at post mortem. The flesh closes over the wound and if the body is burned enough—' Picaut spreads her hands. 'He is performing histology on the left ventricular myocardium, but—' How to say this? 'The fire was hot. We may never be sure.'

'So he thinks it because he's found nothing else?'

'More or less.' This is kind. Actually, Éric thinks he was sedated, but not unconscious. That, too, is a hunch that will be difficult to prove and she sees no reason to let this become common knowledge. Her cover-up starts here. She drinks her tea, lets him think, waits.

Then: 'Who's doing this?'

'If I knew that, I wouldn't be here. Do you have any enemies?' A stupid question; she deserves the scorch of his stare. 'Have you any particular enemies who would be interested in lighting six fires in Orléans with the express purpose of framing you for the havoc they've caused under the glare of maximum publicity?'

He gives a thin smile. 'All my enemies use SIG-Sauers and shoot to wound, not kill.'

The SIG is the police weapon of choice; Picaut has been trained to aim for the right shoulder except in dire emergency. This is not a serious answer.

She waits.

Relenting, he says, 'If someone wanted to damage me, Tahar's body would have been left on my doorstep and it would be very obvious how he had died.'

'Not a stiletto?'

'Nothing so merciful.' He considers something, rolls it

round his mouth, tests the taste and then, hesitantly, the sound of it. 'There are some Somalis from Marseille. They think they will make a new base for themselves here. If anyone might try to intimidate me, it is them. I don't think they would burn half of Orléans to do it, but . . .' He stubs out his smoke. 'I will ask some questions.' His eyes promise things about the nature of the asking that he will not say when she is wired. One way or another he will get answers, and they will be true. 'Is there a number on which I can reach you?'

She gives him the number Patrice, Garonne and Éric Masson use. Nobody else has it.

At the door, they shake hands. His grip is firm and light. He says, 'Will you tell the press about Tahar?'

'Not until we have to. At some point, we'll have to give a name, but we won't offer any link to you. I'd like to think they won't make that connection themselves, but I can't promise it.'

Walking back to the car and Garonne's bad temper, she feels oddly light, as if she has made a breakthrough, when in reality she is no further forward than she was before the fires started.

Garonne is not where she left him. Nor is Rollo. Patrice pulls up just as she begins to dial his mobile. He throws open the passenger door and guns the engine. She climbs in. 'We need that man sewn up tight. Where is everyone?'

'Sylvie is in the watch-room keeping an eye on Yasine. We didn't get a tab on the number he called, it was too fast, but we got the conversation in the can. If he moves, we'll know about it.'

'Where are Rollo and Garonne?'

'Tailing Monique Susong. She took a call ten minutes ago from Father Cinq-Mars, the bishop's heroin-chic assistant, inviting her to meet him at the basilica at Cléry-Saint-André.

They're following her; they went less than three minutes ago. If we leave now, we'll catch up.' He casts a sideways glance. 'We thought you'd want . . .'

'Oh, I do. I really do. Thank you.' Picaut blows a kiss at the sky. Maybe there is a God. 'If anyone knows why Iain Holloway died, it's Monique Susong. It's time to bring her in, and the priest with her.'

CHAPTER THIRTY-THREE

La Chapelle Saint-Denis,
18 September 1429

'Have a care. A *care*, damn you!'

The palliasse is Tomas's own design, stuffed with horsehair and slung on a hessian stretcher with loops for two poles. Jean de Belleville, Father Huguet and the Piedmontese captain, Pietro di Carignano, are amongst those lifting the poles. The rest were chosen by lot from the men at arms who still surround the Maid, half of them Piedmontese.

The rest of the army is gone, dispersed at the king's command. The king, in his contrition, has sent his own covered wagon to transport the Maid away from la Chapelle which, now that her army has disbanded, is no longer safe.

Eight horses pull it, all black. Tomas considered sending them away, bringing in oxen, great grey carthorses, anything that wasn't black, but there are limits to what a priest can do to offend a king, and it matters more that the Maid is transported in safety. He still is not sure they will be allowed to go where he thinks they should.

At his instruction, they lift her from the dank, shuttered

room, out across the untented campsite to the wagon. Inside, he hangs bunches of rosemary from the hoops, and posies of small yellow flowers he found near the river bank when he went to weep over the destruction of his bridge. He has heard that the colour helps to balance out the henbane and hemlock and she is still sleeping under their influence, although he is running out of boar's gall and without it he dare not give her the rest. He has seen men die and will not take that risk.

He gave her a half dose at dawn and has enough to repeat it on arrival, but that's it until he can restock in Rheims. Rheims loves her. It must be to Rheims they go, or at worst, Orléans. The king may yet intervene.

'Lay her here, on the right, the south side as we travel east. Put the testament at her head, and her sword and armour on the left. She will not want to be parted from them.'

He has never taken this care with anyone; not a lover, not his mother, not his father as he lay dying. Even d'Alençon stepped carefully round Tomas in the days before the duke was sent north to Normandy, partly for his temper, and partly because he knows things they do not.

Here is another irony: for years, Tomas hated his father, and the godly men who took in the unwanted youth who arrived knocking at his gate. Now he is daily glad of their teaching, and considers the price they extracted a pittance, willingly paid. 'Leave me with her,' he says, and they do.

D'Aulon rides up front with the wagoner. Louis de Coutes sits on the tail boards. Like that, ponderously, with their horses tied behind – not the devil-horse, of course; some unfortunate groom has that in charge – they roll east.

She wakes sometime after noon. He is grinding cloves with goose grease to make an ointment for the wound and, feeling her stir, looks up. She is watching him, or he thinks so. Certainly, when he lays down the pestle and mortar, her eyes track the movement of his hands.

'My lady?' Does she know? Has she heard any of the night-long, acrimonious row at her bedside? 'My lady, I can give you—'

Her hand is a rank of talons, striking his wrist. 'No. No more. I need to rise. Are we going to Rheims?'

'Rheims, yes.' He nods. 'Unless the king orders something different. He may do. We have not seen him.' He loosens her grip, finger by finger. 'My lord d'Alençon has been ordered north. He asked me to—'

'He refused you. Why?' So she did hear the night's muted conflict in the dark, dank room in which he, Tomas de Segrave, endeavoured to put right the wrong he had wrought and d'Alençon, knight of the royal blood, refused to put aside his wife, marry the Maid and lead a coup against the king.

'He said it was not his duty to break France on the wheel of his own ambition. Nor mine.'

'Nor, evidently, mine.' Her black gaze slides away from him, to her hands. She picks at the counterpane, finds a thread of gold, teases it free. 'Did anybody hear?'

'I am still alive.'

A faint smile, a nod, and her eyes flitter shut. She is blue about her mouth and on the high bones of her cheeks. Her skin has an unnatural sheen. He reaches for his satchel, finds the henbane and the hemlock and poppy. Maybe, if he can reduce the proportions, and find some mandrake root—

'Tomas, put that away. I will take no more.'

'Lady, your leg—'

'Is it unclean?'

'It wasn't this morning.'

Every day, at sunrise and sunset, he lifts the bandages and lets the odours rise, sifting through the notes of healing, raw-red flesh for the telltale scent of mouse urine that is the advance herald of gangrene. Not yet. Not yet. And not yet. If

307

she stays clean, he might find God again.

She flexes her ankle, an interesting experiment. He watches the flush of colour cross her face, the sweat leak from her temples. He thinks she will stop, but she is who she is, and the next he sees she is bracing her palms against the palliasse.

'My lady, no! Please, I beg of you, lie still. You must not exert yourself.'

'Then lift me. I grow weary of looking always upwards.'

She has lost weight. He is not remotely at his full fighting bulk, but even so he is twice her size, at least in girth. He could lift her one-handed. He uses both hands, with care, over many minutes, until she is sitting upright, cushioned on three sides, hugging her arms across her chest, staring out of the back of the wagon. Her teeth are locked, her fingers white at the knuckles, where they grip and counter-grip.

The king has sent heavy silks for her blankets. He wraps one about her shoulders; it is blue, with the fleur-de-lis eternally repeated in gold.

'I could make you—'

'No.'

'Rosemary, valerian and elderflower. Trust me. Just those. You shall see me put them in the water and heat it.'

He has a travelling brazier, such as they use at sea. It rocks with the roll of the wagon. He heats the water, drops in a hand's length of dried rosemary branch, and a loose fistful of dried elderflowers, small, brown flecks, and valerian, rolled into balls. He stirs them clockwise and speaks aloud three Ave Marias in slow succession over the rolling boil, pours two beakers, lets her pick one and drinks the other, first. 'My mother taught me this. It helps, I swear.'

They watch each other through steam. A fine line grows

308

between her eyes. He has seen it before, when she is thinking through a strategy from end to end. He waits. He is good at waiting. Even so, when she speaks, it is not what he expects.

'Have you told Bedford who I am?'

What? He nearly knocks the brazier over. 'Bedford, my lady?'

She stares at him. He has never been afraid of a woman before. He has rarely been afraid of a man. Except Henry, of course, the late king; everybody was afraid of him.

She glares at him. Her lips press in a hard white line. She says, 'You know who I am. How long have you known?'

His bowels lurch, but he has made promises to himself. He squares his shoulders, as in battle. 'Truthfully? I wasn't certain until the day of the king's coronation.' He is about to mention Claudine, but Claudine is dead, and he does not know how much responsibility he bears for that. He says, 'But I knew before then.'

'How?'

He meets her gaze. 'Did you ever meet the old King of England? Henry?'

Her mouth hardens. Her drugged eyes dip and widen. 'I was at Troyes, at the signing of the treaty. He didn't know who I was.'

'You were a maid in the retinue?'

'I served as the old king's squire.'

Of course you did. He is beginning to feel a sneaking respect for the old King of France, this man who made a fool of everyone while they thought he was the fool. He stifles a laugh, too high and nervous. 'What did you think of him?'

'Henry? He was arrogant. I wanted to kill him. I was aggrieved when he died too soon for me to do so.'

'Arrogant? Yes, but with reason. He was the best warrior England has ever seen.'

'I am better.'

'Which is how I knew you had been trained by the king.'

'Don't flatter me, Tomas. We have passed beyond that, surely.'

Oh, my lady, I hope so. He locks his clasped hands on his elbows, gauche as an apprentice lad. 'My lady, I have witnessed both of you at war. You are perhaps as good as Henry. You are not better.' Honesty. Claudine notwithstanding, he has promised himself that.

She lets it pass, closes her eyes, finds whatever it is that is keeping her awake, opens them again. 'You didn't answer my question. Does Bedford know?'

Sun into iced-black water. Too many more of these and he will cease to breathe. He shakes his head, and then has to hold it with his hands, fingers wrapped about his temples, pressing the plates of his skull together. He has heard of men who cut circles out of their skull, to let out the vapours. He thinks, just now, that it might be a good thing to consider.

'I told him you were a ward of the king. I did not tell him that the king had trained you in all the ways of war.'

'Why not?'

Because after Montépilloy I learned to despise him? Because even as I built the bridge, with the places by which it might be destroyed, a bit of me hoped you'd see it? Because even after you fell, and the king did all that I had planned, if I could have persuaded d'Alençon to marry you and seize the throne, France could be the place we all want it to be?

Because I have, I think, loved you longer than I know.

How many men love her? How little does she care? He finds the wine that he has brought, empties the beakers, pours, adds water in generous measure, drinks. 'How did *you* know? When?'

'That you are Tomas Rustbeard?' She shrugs. 'When did I not?'

'Is it that obvious?'

'I fought with you at Jargeau and back to back at Meung. There is no greater intimacy than that.'

She may be right, although at this moment, in the intimate space of the wagon, he does not wish to believe her.

'So you knew me when I came back? At Troyes?'

'Of course. And if you had gone to the lengths of counterfeiting your own death, it must be for a reason. What could it be except that you were Bedford's agent? I had you followed afterwards. Bertrand wanted to kill you, but I was taught never to let an enemy out of my sight if I could avoid it.'

Tomas looks to the wagon's foot. The page has not moved. It may be they are not overheard. He has to believe so. 'Who else knows? Besides Bertrand?'

'Jean de Metz, who brought me from Chinon with Bertrand. The lady Marguerite de Valois, of course; she knows. And her betrothed, de Belleville. And Huguet, the priest.'

The lady Marguerite. There was a time when he thought he was in love with her; he did not know what depths his heart could measure. Of course they all know. Of course.

'They will kill me now.'

'Not unless I tell them to. Answer me: why have you not told Bedford? He would use it to complete his destruction of me. Certainly Regnault de Chartres would.'

'Which is why I will not.' His hands are clasped between his knees. His shoulders are drawn so tightly together they may crush his chest. 'Lady, I erred. I gave my allegiance to my father's people, when I owed it in my heart to my mother's. I know this now: I love France. I will work to make her whole. I cannot expect forgiveness, nor will I ask for it, but I will give my life to undo the harm I have done.'

'Did you know they were going to destroy your bridge?'

'Lady, I ordered its destruction before I ever built it.'

Her eyes fall shut. He thinks she has left him, and frets. Sometime later, flat-voiced, she says, 'Tomas, some things cannot be undone.'

'Nevertheless, I will spend my life in trying. But first we must make you well and I fear the king's physicians may not minister to you as we might wish. We shall take you to Rheims, to Marguerite, who loves you. Maybe the king's mother-in-law, Yolande of Aragon, may be persuaded to come. She knows the truth of you, I think? Yes, so with her and de Belleville and Father Huguet, all who have known you since childhood I believe, we can keep you safe and make you whole again. If you can . . .'

But this time she really has left him. Her fingers lie pale on the blue silk, her head tilts on to the cushion. There is colour in her cheeks. He takes the mug and sets it down before it spills, slips his own hand into hers and like this sits with her through the day, that he might know when next she wakes.

At midday, the wagon turns south. He stands, goes forward, pokes his head through the covering. 'This is not the way to Rheims!'

D'Aulon says, 'We're going south. The king has ordered us to Gien-sur-Loire.'

A three-day journey. He subsides back into the shade. Charles, by grace of God King of France, is planning to give Rheims back to Bedford. He feels it in his water, in the sick marrow of his bones. The magistrates will be hanged for treason. All those revellers, the infants conceived in joy, will be broken.

When the Maid wakes, and he tells her, she lapses fast into fever. He gives her the remains of his hemlock and poppy and sends ahead into Gien for the bile of a gelded boar.

CHAPTER THIRTY-FOUR

GIEN-SUR-LOIRE,
18 October 1429

HERE IN GIEN is another rented room, taller than the cell in the inn at la Chapelle, broader, sweeter smelling. Set along the walls are a dozen sconces filled with Venetian oil that burns with a bright, smokeless flame, and on the bed a goosedown mattress, layered with satin sheets in blue and gold.

Everywhere is blue and gold, everywhere lilies: on the bedhead and the tables; the floor tiles and the cabinet of lapis-inlaid walnut that has been given to Brother Tomas to keep his medicines in; on the poker and the linen and the bowl that holds the comfrey for the compresses. Everywhere, as clearly as if it were the king's thumbprint, is the Valois mark. She is mine. Mine. I am king. The Maid belongs to me.

Tomas wants to throw them all out, and cannot. The Maid cares nothing for the wall hangings, but reacts to confinement the way a bear reacts to the cage.

'He is never going to let me go, is he?' She paces the room, the radius of her circles inverse in size to the number of

313

people around her. Small now, when here is Tomas, and Yolande of Aragon, Marguerite de Valois, de Belleville and Huguet Robèrge, all come, as he had wanted, to care for her.

Together, these few make up one faction of the king's court. Periodically, the door of her sickroom is darkened by the other faction, by Regnault de Chartres and Georges de la Trémoïlle, who bring apples studded with cloves and strong-smelling unguents and stand as ghouls over the bed.

—How fares the Maid, my dear chancellor? Is her colour not better?

—I think it is, my good archbishop. The king's care suits her. She must remain under his watch another month at least, I think.

—But then the fighting season will be over.

—No loss. How can she fight, who has no army?

She sleeps while they are here, or appears to, and wakes when they have gone, to spit curses into a mug of watered wine and gall, that she might not taint the air.

Her friends come more frequently, and with gifts. Always, Tomas hears Yolande before he sees her, a sigh of silk and satin. He smells her too: a light, flowering scent of citrus, lavender and rosewater and a top note of something sharp-light-sweet that he cannot name.

Today, she is caught in dry October sunlight, taller than the tallest man, stretched to it by a confection of veils and wire, so that she approaches God with her height, can petition Him for favours.

She comes prepared for battle, girded in midnight blue damask, bright jewels and gold. Her eyes are dark pits, reflecting a thousand points of coloured light. He cannot truly see her face for the dazzle.

By contrast, de Belleville remains the very epitome

of self-effacement. When the rest of the court is gaudy, he is clad in doublet and hose of near-black English wool (in some things, England cannot be bettered) with a cambric shirt and a jacket of tawny silk, stiffened at collar and cuffs by Belgian lace and Italian pearls. His boots are calf hide, neatly fitted, with pointed toes.

Marguerite, of the alabaster skin and black hair, is midway between these two. Her veils are not overly high, her brocades are good but not exceptional – Italian, he thinks – in muted gold and blackened blue, with lilies here and there but neither the restraint of her husband nor the bludgeoning magnificence of Yolande.

Once, Tomas thought she had eyes for Huguet, but now he has a chance to see more deeply, and to understand, for in the Maid's waking moments, Marguerite sits always beside the bed, unless the Maid is on her feet, when she finds a place that does not block her walking and follows her with her eyes. Whatever the company, it is to the Maid that she turns, the Maid's embrace that she seeks. Nobody else matters.

They are like *this*. So said Claudine, her fingers scissored together. Claudine who resented their closeness. Claudine who . . .

Stop. Look to the Maid. She, likewise, does not see the rest of the room when Marguerite is here. They laugh together now, over some small murmured intimacy.

Tomas catches de Belleville's eye. They share a shrug. What can be done when the die was cast so young? Nothing. We live with it, as do they. Tomas takes his jealousy and scatters it into the darker corners, to spin its webs and die for lack of food. It is his penance. He has much to repent. He will not feed it.

'What can we do?' Marguerite asks the Maid. 'You will lose your mind if you are confined thus for another month.'

'Another month? I will be barking with the moon if I cannot ride within the week!'

She smiles as she speaks, mellowing herself for the sake of the present company, but he has wondered this past week about the balance of her mind. He offers the idea he has been incubating since the wagon ride from Paris.

'The king will not let you fight against the enemies of France, but he might let you assault the enemies of his friends. At the very least, those friends may add their voices to his persuasion.'

'Which friends? Which enemies?' Yolande, her fingers steepled, head slightly bent, catching the late light. She is like Bedford, possessed of a vast, sharp mind to be wooed with intelligence and swift thought. She is their best hope in the turning of the king from spineless puppet into monarch worthy of the name.

And so, to Yolande, he says, 'Perrinet Gressart.' The name drops as lead into an ocean, straight down. Nothing happens.

They stare at him, except the Maid. Her look is his reward. She ceases to pace, sits on a stool. Not for here the thick, black ugliness of the inn at la Chapelle. The king's furniture has elegant, cup-shaped legs that cross over, and bear the sitter as on a small throne.

The Maid says, 'Perrinet Gressart leads his own company. Burgundy funds him.'

Tomas corrects her. 'Until recently, my lord of Burgundy funded him; now he is his own man, fights his own battles, takes the towns that please him. Specifically, he has taken those lands to which Georges de la Trémoïlle lays claim. The king's chancellor, I hear, is most discomfited by the loss of his tax revenues. He has complained bitterly to the king, who has, as yet, done nothing.'

De Belleville: 'De la Trémoïlle might ask of the king that we retake his lands?'

The Maid is one step in front. 'Better that the suggestion comes from Regnault de Chartres, who must believe it comes from Bedford.'

Guerite asks, 'How will such a thing be done?'

Tomas's heart takes wings. This is what he was born for. He sweeps an extravagant bow. 'Leave it to me.'

CHAPTER THIRTY-FIVE

'ARE WE READY?' Picaut asks Patrice as he drives into Cléry-Saint-André.

'As we'll ever be.' Garonne, answering, is in Rollo's car outside the basilica awaiting only Picaut's order.

Patrice drives on past, turns right and parks a hundred metres further down the road.

Picaut: 'Do you still have the directional microphone from last night?'

'Already out.'

'Any sign of Monique Susong?'

'Her car's the yellow Clio three in front of mine. She just walked inside. There's no sign of the priest, but he might be inside already.'

There is a moment while Rollo turns the car and drives back to park out of sight around the corner. She keeps the line open. Garonne murmurs, 'Gotcha,' and there's a scrape of plastic on plastic as he balances his mobile by the output speaker of the directional mike.

A murmur of conversation hisses down the line, too distant, too fuzzy-thick to be coherent. Patrice says, 'Wait,' and pulls a mini USB lead from his satchel, connects her phone to his laptop and tweaks the software.

A hiss of white noise and Monique Susong's voice emerges from the fog. She sounds muffled, as if she's speaking through a gas mask, but it's good enough to pick out the meaning and Patrice is recording every word.

'. . . that he didn't die for nothing. I don't expect you to understand the science or the need to set history right, but I do expect you to understand that a man *died* for this. Isn't that what your religion is all about? A man who died for a cause?'

'Our Lord died for our sins. Yours as well as mine.' The priest speaks with the dry, husked whisper of a man who is losing his voice, or regaining it.

He could be on the tail end of a cold, but Picaut has heard that particular rasp before, and the pathology behind it was far more malign than a virus.

She wants to know the man behind the sound. At her request, Patrice pulls up an image from the Internet and mounts it on the right half of the screen.

In his online identity, Father Cinq-Mars is lean, wiry, surprisingly youthful. His hair is dark and thin and falls straight to below his ears. His profile is angular and angry.

Today, he sounds like a man with little time to spare. 'What do you want?'

'I want to see whatever Iain Holloway saw that made him fear for his life.'

'That won't be possible.'

'You would rather I went to the police?'

'It's not a question of preference, it's a question of possibility. What Dr Holloway saw no longer exists. It has been incinerated.'

'You destroyed human remains because someone with a modicum of qualification wanted to take a proper look? You *burned* them?'

The enormity of this stabs through the walls, blows the sensors on Patrice's microphone off the red end of the scale. In their separate cars, Garonne and Picaut sway back, put their hands to their ears.

In the basilica, Father Cinq-Mars says nothing, and nothing, until, eventually, 'Some things are better left undisturbed.'

'You mean the Church wants them left that way?'

'Not just the Church; the whole of France. We will not let one man's obsession – or one woman's – destroy our heritage.'

'That's . . . vandalism . . .' Monique Susong sounds defeated. Inside the basilica, there is a rustle of clothing as if a woman of extravagant means has lifted her handbag and slid it over her shoulder.

'What will you do?' the priest asks.

'What I was going to do in any case: find out why Iain died.'

'The police are already doing that.'

'No. The police are searching for whoever is lighting the fires in Orléans and they are failing to find them. They don't care about one man, a foreigner, and his death.'

'Whereas you care about his death, but not the fires.'

'I am trying to convince myself that a priest of the Church has not lit half a dozen fires in Orléans merely in order to kill one man.'

'Then you must succeed in your endeavour, because I give you my word, in the name of God, that we neither lit the fires nor killed your friend. I don't know who did.'

'I believe you about the first, if only because they started long before Iain Holloway set foot in France. If I thought otherwise, I'd have gone to the police long ago.'

'I am grateful for your insight . . .'

A brief pause. Perhaps a handshake?

'I will be back.'

'I could say that I look forward to that with pleasure, but what I can do with honesty is wish you well in your quest.'

They part.

Into the microphone, Garonne says, 'Do we take her?'

'Not yet. Follow her. If she goes to Orléans, bring her in. Otherwise, I want to know where she goes, and— Fuck . . .'

Patrice has been trawling through the net and has pulled up one of the most striking images of Monique Susong, sub-editor of the fashion pages of *Vogue Paris*. Seen in full screen, she is tall, black, astoundingly dressed – and not the woman who is now walking out of the west-facing door of the basilica. Her facial structure is similar enough to confuse them in a thumbnail; they may be cousins or sisters, but they are not the same woman.

'Rollo, Garonne, she isn't who she says she is. Follow her and pick her up at her hotel. Patrice, keep the tap on her phone. I want to know who she calls and what she says.'

The woman calling herself Monique Susong is dressed in scarlet and black. On the grey winter streets of Cléry-Saint-André she stands out like *Vogue* amongst the broadsheets. Picaut watches in the side mirror as she returns to the Clio, sits for a while in thought, then pulls away and heads back towards Orléans. Garonne reports soon after that he and Rollo have her in sight.

Picaut steps out of the car. To Patrice, she says, 'Stay here. I'll call if I need you.'

'Where are you going?'

'To talk to the priest.'

He is at the far, eastern end, beyond the altar, when she

reaches him. She doesn't need to show her police ID to prove who she is, the television coverage has seen to that. He nods a greeting, as if they had a longstanding appointment to meet.

'Monique Susong,' she says. 'Who is she really?'

He has the intelligence not to look surprised. If anything, he seems tired.

'Iain Holloway's lover?'

'That would be one part of it, I imagine.' His voice is still husked, but she was right, this is not simply a viral infection. The rest of him bears only a ghost of a resemblance to the man in the online images. With a precision that is not purely professional, Picaut notes that his fingernails are yellowed, with ridges and troughs ploughed along their lengths, his face is lined, his hair far thinner than the photograph and damaged by radiation or drugs; he has been mortally sick and may never be well again.

He sees her looking. 'Laryngeal carcinoma.' He gives a thin smile. 'Your father and I share afflictions. I suspect we also shared an enthusiasm for the same cigarettes in our youths.'

'Do you have pulmonary secondaries?'

His eyes skid away from hers. 'I will not meet my maker just yet.'

Her father went through exactly this; the remissions and re-admissions and false hopes that turn out to have been better than no hope at all, and were, in fact, the best he'd get, and looked back on later as oases of sanity in the final crumbling.

She says, 'What did Iain Holloway see that you have since destroyed? No, really—' She holds up a hand. 'I heard what you said to Monique Susong. She might accept it, but I don't. If I have to, I'll present a file to Prosecutor Ducat this afternoon and we'll hold a press conference on the steps of his office this evening. All we have to do is breathe a suggestion that you're linked to the fires, and I promise you, the press will wreak havoc with what's left of your life.'

He stares at her. The scleras of his eyes are yellow with jaundice. Still, there is some fire there, some spirit. He chews on his lip. When at length she reaches for her phone, he says, 'He saw a collection of bones, old bones, bones that were purported to be, amongst others, the monarch Louis XI and his wife.'

Louis XI: son of Charles VII, the king made by the Maid. A pattern nudges at the edges of her mind; not one she wants. 'Purported?'

The priest spreads his hands. 'Our nation, you might remember, has suffered more than her fair share of revolution and strife. English, Spanish, Huguenots, revolutionaries, Nazis; times without number, men armed with fire and axe have swept through this church. Each time, the priests have saved that which mattered most, which is to say the mortal remains of the men and women who were interred here. The stone and brick and marble they have left to those whose pleasure is destruction. In the process, human remains are not always labelled as accurately as we might like. Those in our care were said to have come from the king's tomb,' he gestures back towards the marble monstrosity that sits inside the northern door, 'but one can never be sure.'

'Why did you burn them?'

'A precaution.'

'In case they were real?'

'You could say that.'

'What would you say?' She is growing tired of this. It must show on her face. He looks down at his feet.

'I would say that Dr Iain Holloway was a very intense, focused and driven man; that he had an agenda and would have followed it anywhere; that he would have made his

323

facts fit his narrative, and his facts were not ones that would be useful to France.'

'What facts?'

The priest studies his nails. She waits; she can wait all day if she has to. In time, he says, 'The doctor was a man for whom the identification of ancient remains was a vocation. Accordingly, he was given unprecedented access to bones of our royal lineage, in part to establish the exact identities and relationships therein. He read into the collection theories that fitted his own inclination. They were not necessarily based in historical veracity. Capitaine—' He reaches out a clawed hand. 'I will not say more, and whoever they once were, the bones in question are now gone. You can make as much of a fuss as you like, but in the end, hounding a dying man may not help your husband's appeal to the people. The elections are on Sunday and it matters to all right-thinking people that Christelle Vivier not win. Do not add to her chances. Instead, do what you do well: find the arsonists who would burn Orléans. And know that nobody in this church was responsible for the death of Iain Holloway.'

He takes a step back, lays his right hand on the copy of the scripture that lies on the altar. 'On that, I give you my word.'

He's right at least in the first part; it takes no imagination at all for Picaut to see what the headlines will say if she drags a dying priest to the station and charges him with . . . what? Destruction of ancient relics of questionable provenance? She would have to prove they existed in the first place. Already, she can hear Ducat's laugh.

'Where can I find you?' she asks. 'Apart from here.'

He pulls a small card from his inner pocket, scribbles a mobile phone number on it. 'I sincerely hope you never have occasion to use this.'

She calls Garonne as Patrice pulls out on to the Orléans road. 'Can you still see Susong?'

'Three cars ahead. She's going straight back to Orléans.'

'Good. Bring her in.'

CHAPTER THIRTY-SIX

Orléans,
Wednesday, 26 February 2014
17.38

ANOTHER DEMONSTRATION FILLS THE STREETS. Orléans's youths are not just taking back the night in the name of the *Front National* by their thousands, they are taking back the days, too.

They are marching peacefully thus far, but are creating monstrous tailbacks in the evening traffic. Patrice and Picaut are caught in the mother of all queues when Garonne calls in to say that he and Rollo have arrested the Susong woman and will hold her incommunicado until Picaut can reach them.

'You might want to come in the back way,' he says. 'The entire French press is camping out on the front steps, waiting to smother you in media-love. They know you went to see Cheb Yasine. If they thought you might be our national hero before, they're bloody certain of it now.'

'Oh, Jesus, *fuck*!' Her fist bounces off the dashboard. 'How the fucking hell do they know that? Garonne, if you told them . . .'

'Do I look like I want to wear my balls for a necklace?' She can see his grin in her mind's eye. Truly, he is thawing. He says, 'Trust me, I want to see Yasine brought down, and telling the media is a fast way to see him skip the country. My money's on your ex-husband. The Bressard media machine knows everything.'

'Whoever it is, I'll kill him.'

'We're right behind you, chief.'

She throws her phone in her pocket. 'Fuck them all.'

Patrice rolls his eyes, but he flicks on the indicator and pulls out into the left lane. They are at least moving forward when her phone rings again: Luc.

She is ready to eviscerate someone and here is the perfect target. 'What the *fuck* are you playing at? Who told you, and why the hell did you have to spew it to the press?'

'I haven't told anyone anything, Inès, I swear. The first I knew of it was from the Deux–Quatre bulletin. You shouldn't—'

'Luc Bressard, if you even think you have the right to tell me what I should or shouldn't do, I'll break your—'

'I'm sorry. I'm sorry.' He is close to panic, which is novel. She's heard him irritable, sullen, morose, exultant, frivolous and happy, but never within touching distance of panic. 'Please, you must believe me, I didn't say anything to anyone.' He swallows. She can hear the breaths he takes to calm himself. He says, 'I don't want to lose you.'

She has no answer to that. Beside her, Patrice murmurs, *My Preciousssss* . . . She fights not to laugh.

'Why are you calling?'

'To make amends. Don't go to the police station; it's mayhem. If you can get to the hotel where we held the press conference, we can try to divert the press mob. At the very least, you and I can do another small event and calm them down.'

'"Small" being a hundred and fifty men and women in a dining-room suite with television cameras on every wall? Get real. I might fall for that once, but never again.'

'Please. Think about it. We'll keep it really, really small. On-the-steps small, with Landis keeping it tight. No more than a couple of sentences each. Inès, they're scared and they want someone to rescue them and you're their hero of the moment. They're ready to crown you saviour of Orléans and you know what comes after that. It's madness out there. Someone has to do something.'

'Fuck you.'

She hangs up.

'Fuck. Fuck. *Fuck!* Fuck him and his fucking mind games. I hate that man, and all his family, did I mention?'

'Not in words, but your body language is pretty eloquent.' Patrice is manoeuvring through a chicane of parked cars, still heading towards the station. 'Shall we book a flight to somewhere safer? Iraq maybe? Or Syria? You'd have to wear a black sack with an eye slit and they'd cut my hands off with a blunt pair of scissors for having wrong-coloured hair, but the press would probably find they had better things to do than follow you around.'

It's impossible to be angry for long in his company. Picaut leans her fist on the glass and her head on her fist and stares out of the window. 'And let whoever is pretending to be Monique Susong get away with it? I don't think so. We're going to the—'

Her phone rings again, and, again, it's Luc.

She answers wearily this time. 'Luc, give up. I'm not doing another press conference however much you beg, so do us both a favour—'

'Inès, please. I hate this as much as you do, believe me. But you *can't* go back to the station. There are over a hundred paparazzi waiting outside and they've gone way beyond sanity. They'll beatify you on the steps and then tie you to a stake in a marketplace. If you come to the Maison, I'll see you're kept safe, I promise.'

'Oh, God . . .' She raises a brow to Patrice, who shrugs and starts to cut back across the traffic.

To Luc's taut, waiting silence, Picaut says, 'We're on our way.'

They park two blocks south of the Hôtel Jeanne d'Arc and walk up. Picaut takes off her leather jacket and slings it over her shoulder; it's not as good as swapping with Lise, but it's better than nothing.

It works until they draw into sight of the front steps of the Maison de la Pucelle, but there's a TV camera crew hanging around outside with no obvious intent but an eye to the main chance. Picaut sees them just too late, a fraction after she has been seen.

'Captain!'

'Capitaine Picaut! Is it true that you went—?'

'Inès!' A woman's voice: friendly, assured. 'In here!'

The sound pulls her into the narrow doorway to her left: the entrance to the museum of the Maison Jeanne d'Arc, where the Maid is reputed to have stayed during the lifting of the siege. After the cathedral, this is the second most famous building in Orléans.

Patrice bundles in beside her. The door closes. A lock turns. They are in darkness only briefly. Lise Bressard flips a light switch.

'I'm so, so sorry.' Luc's cousin is standing by the door wearing a five-thousand-euro Saint Laurent biker jacket that is nothing at all like Picaut's, but is probably as close as Lise can get. It suits her.

She is crisply, blisteringly angry and that, oddly, suits her too, particularly given that Picaut is not the focus of her ire.

'Inès, my entire family should be lined up against a wall

329

and shot. I swear to you, if we get through this in one piece, I'll have Landis and Luc deported to a penal colony.'

'I don't think we have any of those left.' Picaut is amused, in spite of herself. 'They went out of fashion after the last war.'

'Then I'll create one. The Americans will help me; they know how. In the meantime, can the two of you wait here and trust me if I lock you in? I know it feels like a dungeon, but the door's thick enough to keep the press out, at least for a bit.' She gives a brisk smile. 'I'll bring you Luc's head on a plate when I come back.'

Picaut and Patrice are laughing as she leaves. And then not. The interior of the Maison turns out to be a short, dimly lit hallway with a reception desk just inside the door and an oak-panelled display room to the left where the lighting is barely worth the name. Stairs lead up from the end of the hall, but they are roped off and Picaut has no reason to think that she'll find anything more interesting up there than down here.

'Down here' is the museum, a place oddly muted in its praise of the city's saviour. A short film runs in a continuous loop with commentary in English or French – *your choice!* – describing the myth of the peasant girl who saw visions of saints and angels that ordered her to save Orléans, and so France, from the depredations of the English. Moving on from that are depictions of her life and death and all that has grown from them.

'You'd think they could do better than this.' Patrice makes a circuit of the room, lifts things from the walls, stares through thin glass at mock-ups of Orléans under siege. Next to one of these is a presentation showing the many images of the saint herself as she has been seen in the time since her death: always lean, brightly armoured, monumentally over-horsed. Only her hair changes: sometimes long, sometimes short, sometimes dark, sometimes fair. As Christelle Vivier pointed out, at no time has anyone suggested she was a redhead.

Picaut slides down the wall to sit on the floor by the entrance. Patrice gazes at her, owl-eyed, then back at the pictures. 'The resemblance is perfect.'

'Drop dead.'

'Just saying.'

Cheerful as ever, he abandons the displays and folds down on to the floor across from Picaut. Her skin prickles in a way she has nearly forgotten. There is a moment's stillness that lengthens as she scours her memory for other times when they have been alone in each other's company like this. In the car, obviously, but that doesn't count; they were both looking at the road.

She tries to think of something to say. He doesn't rescue her until the silence has stretched for too many heartbeats. Then his eyebrows flick up and down (does he pluck them? She thinks not, they are too strong) and, pulling his laptop from his bag on to his crossed knees, sets to work.

Within half a dozen keystrokes, vivid, vibrant colours – cerise, magenta, emerald, citron – leak up from the display to throw kaleidoscope patterns across his face and the metallic blue of his hair. Eerie orchestral music fills the small room.

Today's T-shirt proclaims that REAL MUSIC ROCKS above a photograph of a long-haired rock climber – it could be a woman, Picaut hasn't decided – executing a move that defies the laws of physics.

Picaut screws up her face. 'Am I supposed to believe that's real music you're playing?'

'Sorry.' Patrice hits a button. The noise stops. The cascading colours don't. 'Jewelcrafting dailies.'

He says it in English. It doesn't make any more sense when

her brain parses it to French. He helps her out. 'Warcraft.'

She gives a strangled laugh. 'You're playing a computer game in *here*? Is that not some kind of sacrilege?'

'I wasn't really playing. More like housekeeping. Finished.' He hits a few more keys and the swirling colours mute to a faint pearlescent white.

He studies this a while, clicking an occasional key. 'The comments on TripAdvisor totally slate this place. "The most boring museum in Europe." Shall we add something to spice it up?'

'Mostly boring?'

'Yes!' His smile is measured in megawatts.

Picaut feigns nonchalance. 'I had an English teacher who thought the *Hitchhiker's Guide* was a better way to learn than reading Shakespeare or Dickens.'

'Now I have teacher envy. We had Sherlock Holmes. It wasn't quite the same.'

'It brought you to the police, though, didn't it?'

'I think that was more a deal my father made to keep me out of gaol.'

'Do I want to know the details?'

'You really don't.' He types two words, dizzyingly fast. '"Mostly boring" it is.'

With a flourish, he kills the power and closes the lid. The colours in the room die away. His wild kingfisher hair is lying free today, not braided. He pulls it from its band, shakes it out, runs his fingers through, loops it up again. The whole movement is completely unselfconscious. He catches her looking. She feels like an intruder.

He gives the half-smile she is growing to know. 'So we could talk about our English teachers, or—'

'Or we could find out what Iain Holloway's obsession was. The priest said he came with his own agenda. It might not be what killed him, but we need to know what it was before I talk to Monique Susong. How many forums was he on? What else was he doing?'

'He was one of the eight thousand people who downloaded your father's paper when he made it open source.'

'You can find that out? How?'

His smile is sad, and guarded. 'I have a friend who works for TAO, also known as Tailored Access Operations, the cyber-warfare wing of the NSA.'

'You mean he's a hacker,' she says. 'Like you.'

Patrice shakes his head. 'Better than me. And he has resources we can only dream of. He pretty much knows everything that happens, to anyone, anywhere. The trick is to know the right questions to ask.'

'Is that as scary as it sounds?'

'Technically, we're on the same side, and they should be keeping us fed with information so we can do our bit in the war against terrorism. So no, you don't need to be scared. Unless Christelle wins control of the police, in which case you'd better get used to the view . . .' His long fingers frame an oblong around his eyes.

She laughs. 'Iraq?'

'Probably safer than anywhere in Western Europe. Or the US. Or Canada. Or Australia. Norway might be OK, for a bit.'

He isn't entirely joking. Picaut covers her face with her hands. 'So Iain Holloway downloaded my father's paper—'

'Which said that if the record of her life had been accurately assessed, it would demonstrate that the Maid was a fully trained knight, but nobody in the fifteenth century could handle that, so they passed her off as a miracle.' Patrice is watching her closely. 'Do you think he was right?'

'He was my father. I was listening to this before I could walk. So, yes, I think he was right. I can argue the details if you want, but that's not the point. What matters is that it sounds as if Iain Holloway believed it. He came to France. He spent time at the basilica. And he died. The priest swore the Church didn't light the fire, so—'

'I'm not sure that narrows the field much. Who sent death threats to your dad?'

'Troy Cordier. Or at least, one of his staff. They weren't serious. Cordier might be a political shark, but he wouldn't burn Orléans.'

'Somebody is doing their best, though, and neither of us thinks it's Cheb Yasine.' He shuffles sideways until he is opposite her, the soles of his feet pressing lightly on hers. 'And closer to home, somebody outed you to the press. Someone on the inside knew you'd gone there and told them.'

'Ducat.' She has already thought about this. 'He hates the Bressards, and this is his way of usurping their agenda.'

'He doesn't hate them enough to damage you. He's a fan.'

'Ducat?' She laughs. 'I don't think so.'

'Who else does he share his press conferences with? Ever?'

'You're not old enough to know what Ducat's ever done.'

'I'm old enough to have watched his archived newsreels.'

'You watched Ducat's newsreels? Patrice, when do you get time for that?'

He shrugs, not quite loosely. They are too close, suddenly, and there is too little air. Picaut stands. There's nowhere to go but out into the hallway and that feels too exposed, too close to the baying press. She makes a circuit of the room. It takes no time, and doesn't help.

Patrice crosses his legs, checks the texts on his phone. Only when she comes back does he look up.

'You OK?'

'Fine.' She sits down. 'If not Ducat, then who?'

Patrice says, 'My first thought was Rollo, but he's as

desperate to get Yasine under wraps as Garonne is. So now I'm thinking it's more likely Rémi.'

'Rémi from Drugs?'

'That very one.'

'Because I'm pissing in his coffee?'

His nod is halfway to a shake. 'He's a vindictive fucker at the best of times and Garonne didn't help, throwing all the Maid stuff back in his face. And now you've been to see Cheb Yasine, who is his personal territory.' He leans back and laces his hands behind his head. The figure on his T-shirt *is* a woman. She stretches out now, across his ribs, endlessly reaching for an overhanging rock. 'And Rémi doesn't care about you the way Rollo and Garonne do.'

This is the second time he's spoken of someone else's care for her, or lack of it, and his gaze has a new quality to it. Or perhaps she is just seeing it differently.

Somewhere deep inside, a switch flips over and makes sense of the world, even as it wreaks havoc with her stability. Her breathing grows tight. Her palms flash hot and then cold. She fights a need to get up and walk out.

Patrice pulls a face. 'Now you're not OK.'

'Patrice, how old are you?'

His brow twists. 'Twenty-nine. You?'

'Not quite old enough to be your mother. Not legally, anyway.'

Patrice shakes his head. 'You were nine when I was born.' And at her look, 'Your date of birth's on your wiki page.'

'I have a *wiki page*?' Her shock is real, and it shatters the moment. She wonders if it was meant to.

Patrice grins. 'Do you think the Bressards would let you go without? They've got their PR people on it round the clock. I put up a test post at two thirty yesterday morning that said you didn't want your husband to be mayor. It lasted seventeen seconds.'

335

'Christ on a bike . . .'

She should laugh, but she can't. It may be that she's forgotten how. Patrice, too, is taking care with his breathing. His air of dry amusement is a mask he's forgotten to change. Underneath run other things she does not want to name. Her throat is parched. Her heart is too big for the cage of her ribs.

The silence lasts too long. She has to break it. 'Patrice . . .'

'I know. You don't have to say it.' He doesn't move, but in the fluid place they inhabit the essence of him is backing away. His face is closing.

'No!' She reaches out, lays her fingers on the back of his hand. 'Don't go.' Just one finger stays in contact.

He says, 'We don't want to make your life more complicated.'

She manages one painful laugh. 'Is that even possible?'

'We could walk away.'

'Certainly we should, yes.'

He isn't laughing. Nor, now, is she. He says, 'On the nights when you're not home, do you stay with Éric?'

'Is it that obvious?'

'Lucky guess. Is that also "complicated"?'

'Not in the least.' It is safe to let go of him now, and dangerous to stay. Picaut leans back. 'It's one of the few things that isn't. He has a spare bed. I use it. Used it, past tense. I'm home again now.'

He looks vulnerable, which is not how she has known him. She has no idea how she must seem to him: ravaged, probably; tattered, over-tired, worn. 'Patrice . . .'

He is rummaging in his laptop carrier, tearing up a sheet of dark grey paper that isn't paper, because he peels a paler film from the back and rises, wandering round the room as he speaks. 'There are three CCTV cameras in the walls: one up . . . here; one behind you . . . here; and one behind where

I was . . . here.' He sticks his patches to the wall: three dark squares, two centimetres across. 'So now they can't see us, but a basic rule of thumb says it's not the ones you can see that are the problem.' A flicker of a smile. 'I thought you should know.'

'Right.' They may be blind now, but she wouldn't have known they were there. She believes him, though. She trusts him, which is rare enough to be remarkable. She stands up. She can taste the iron-electric closeness of him. 'Do we care?'

'I don't if you don't.' He reaches out. She meets him, palm to palm, fingers interlocked. It matters that they are equal in this. It does not matter at all who may or may not be watching.

His hands are bigger than hers, and more careful. She is careless of his T-shirt, of his jeans, of her own, when he is too slow; of his skin, of his lips; she crushes them. Their teeth clash. She wants to bite, to taste blood, and has to rein herself in.

'Don't.'

'I'm sorry.' She draws back.

'No.' He pulls her back to him. 'It's fine. Let go.' His searching hands have reached her breasts. She can barely hear through the rushing blood in her head. His fingers are mapping her, span by span. His breath is hers. His words streak down to coil and curdle and lay waste to her sanity. 'Don't stop. It's fine. Really. Trust me. It's fine.'

It's fine.

It's fi—

Her phone shrieks in the gap between their breaths.

She freezes.

He curses, using words she has never heard him use. She fumbles for the phone. The message is from Lise:

Patrice reads it over her shoulder. He is standing rigid, biting his lip. His teeth make a line of even prints in the flesh. 'I did say it was the ones you couldn't see that were the killers.' He is breathless. He may be laughing. She thinks he isn't.

'Luc wouldn't . . .'

But he would, and they both know it. Patrice takes a step back. She can feel his heat, scorching. She is the one swearing now, a long stream of quiet, potent invective. He does start to laugh, not quite in control.

She catches his hand. 'Promise you won't switch off on me?'

His gaze searches her face. 'If you think I could, something is badly wrong.'

She shrugs. She is older. She would like to say she has been here before, but she can't think when. She's been close, though, and she knows the perfidy of human reaction. 'Anything can happen.'

'Good.' He kisses her hand. 'So that's a deal.'

They head for the door, straightening clothes, hair, faces. Light footsteps approach the other side; Lise, not Luc; she can tell them apart. But that doesn't mean Luc isn't watching. She leans up and kisses him, full on the lips. 'Fuck them all. By Sunday we'll be free of this shit.'

338

CHAPTER THIRTY-SEVEN

'TELL ME ABOUT THE OLD KING. What was he like?' The king in heaven. The king who ordered you to help his son. He didn't know that his son would turn against you? Or did he know, but not care? Kings are notoriously single-minded in their drive to power.

'Kind. Always kind.' They are riding side by side, the Maid and Brother Tomas, who is acknowledged now as her sole confessor, her physician, her companion as she rides south to assault the enemies of the king's advisers.

Her devil-horse accepts him, after a fashion; he can ride at its withers almost without concern that it will snake its head round and rip his ear from his skull, or his fingers from his hand.

Few others can come this close unless they are armoured knights, and there are none of those in this cavalcade. This in itself is a testament to the king's intent: he has sent neither arms for a long siege nor armour for a quick victory. Nevertheless, he has sent an army of sorts, and the Maid is riding as she did in the spring, in her white plate, with an axe in her left hand and a new blade in her right, gift of Yolande of Aragon. Things are not as they were, but they are close enough.

And here, under the squally sky, with the wind shredding the words half-formed, they can speak as they have not been able to since the wagon out of la Chapelle, without the risk that a servant lies in the roof space, listening, or a steward dallies behind a curtain.

He knows he is privileged. She may not trust him, but what harm can he do that is not already done? She thinks he has told Bedford and no amount of denying on his part will change this. But no arrest has come, no charge of heresy or treason, and she is relaxing, day by day, so that he can inch towards the question that haunts his nights and his days: Who are you? Whence do you come? Why did the King of France choose to teach you, above all the others: not his son, not his cousin's children, not the sons of lords who clustered round him?

Why you?

Cautiously, then. 'When did the king teach you to ride?'

'When I was young. I was not one of the royal children. I did not have the tutors or the jewels, the fine foods and the silks. But I was not kept from the king's company as they were. Did you know that he once asked Charles, who is now king, when he had last seen his mother? The answer was, three months before, and I would doubt if he had seen his father any more often.

'Me, the king could see every day, if he chose, and he did. He took me on his horse and rode out into the country. I was a girl, and a bastard, and he was king; why should he not do with me as he pleased?'

A girl, and a bastard. So we have that much in common, our bastardy. She looks ahead, but she is not watching the ruts on the path, or the thorns that line it; her horse is taking her and she is letting it and she asks her questions of a ghost. If it answers, Tomas cannot hear it.

He feels on the edge of discovery, and is afraid that if he once pushes her in the wrong direction, he will find he has closed for ever a door that he should like open. This is a courtship of the mind. Never has his wooing been so delicate, or so slow.

Carefully, when she seems more present, he asks, 'Do you remember it, the riding? He must have taught you well.'

'No. I have tried to, but . . . no. Not the early days. Not the first time or even the second.' She runs a hand along her mount's flank. 'Rouen,' she says, slowly. 'I remember Rouen. I was eight years old, and it was raining. It did not always rain in Rouen, but of all the times in my childhood, this was the last, and the one I remember: Rouen, rain and the end of innocence.'

'The day of Agincourt?'

'Yes.' She is startled, a little. 'How did you know?'

'Claudine told me. You were fighting in the yard. You and Jean de Belleville, and the priest Huguet. Then Matthieu and Claudine came, and d'Alençon who was four years old. And then the angel came, the king's daughter. And then the king himself.'

'The angel? Claudine called her that?' She smiles. 'He took me to ride Poseidon, the best horse he had ever bred. This one's grandfather.' Once more, her gloved hand soothes the devil-horse. It lifts lighter on its feet. 'I fell off so many times. I thought I had broken every bone in my body. I thought I would never walk again. But I learned that day what it was, really, to listen with my bones to the feet of the horse as it moved. I learned . . . and then the messenger came, and the king never knew that I had learned it.'

'The messenger?'

'From Agincourt.'

She is gone. If he speaks now, he will break something precious. He holds silent.

She says, 'He had a cap on his head with a feather in it, which was the mark of a message from the Duc d'Orléans, who led our army. The king didn't see him at first; he was watching me ride, laughing. Then he did, and all the laughter fell away. It was the first time I had seen him thus. We knew that a great battle had been fought for the honour of France, but for over an hour, I had forgotten. The king, of course, had not. He walked to the man as he might have done to his own execution.

'I thought to follow him, and, because I thought it, that was what we did. Poseidon walked on air, the reins as silken moths in my hands. I had worked a year to feel such a thing and now it was there I was too afraid to celebrate, too caught up with watching the king crack open the seal and read.'

Tomas knows what the message said. He was there when the Duke of Orléans wrote it, held flame to the wax, pressed on the cooling blob the imprint of his own ring, handed it to the messenger who was himself trusted to return to captivity. The battle over, the laws of chivalry had been reinstated. Except they never were, not fully.

He hates himself. She goes on.

'I had always known that words have power. That afternoon, in the late sun, I discovered they could crush a man's soul. The king read through to the end. His face was ashen, his eyes lost in an otherworld of horrors. He could not speak. He handed the message to me, and because my tutors had not all let me go outside to fight, I was able to read it.'

I knew it! You were taught to read and write. Claudine, he is prepared to bet, was not so taught. Who were you? What made you special? He cannot ask yet, but perhaps soon. Very soon.

'So I learned of a battle fought almost by accident against

the small, disease-ridden army of Henry of England, caught while trying to lead his men to escape at Calais, and of the terrible destruction they had wrought.

'I read of battle without quarter, of English villains slaughtering French knights with no mercy, no thought for the laws of chivalry. I learned of the destruction of the flower of France, of the Admirals, the Constable, dukes, counts, knights. All the great warriors of France were dead; the king's friends; the backbone of our nation. Without these, how could we ever fight again?

'I pressed the letter back into his hand. I slid down from his horse, looped the reins on his arm, and, together, we walked back through the alley and the black gate to take the news to the men and women who waited, thinking still of victory. France did not just lose the best of her men that day; she lost her heart and her reputation. In the minds of all Europe, her name was defeat.'

What can he say? I, Tomas de Segrave, fought on that field, and I killed men whose death you mourned. I was there when Charles d'Orléans was taken prisoner. I was party to the decision to hold him in England until the young king, Henry VI, reaches his majority and can decide for himself whether it is safe to let him go.

He could say all of this, but he prefers not. They ride a long time in silence. She glances across at him. He feels the touch of her gaze. Is it any wonder she loves France? That she hates England? In her place, would he not do the same?

The silence cannot hold all this. She shakes herself like a hound out of water, and tightens her lips and turns to him, and, seeking consolation in other avenues, asks, 'Who taught you to ride? Was it your father?'

'My father?' He wants to laugh, but this is not the time. She does not know him; the question is innocently asked. 'My father was the bishop of Bordeaux, although I didn't know that until I was older than you were on the day of Agincourt. I grew up thinking I was sired by an English archer, settled near Bordeaux with some gold and a bit of land as a gift from the king, a good yeoman of a good family; the old stock who used to patrol the Marches back in England in the old days of the Black Prince. They were called Red Men, once, long ago, and rose almost to be knights. I was proud of him. I thought he was proud of me.'

'How did you find out you were not his son?'

'I heard my mother scream it at him. They were fighting, as men and women do. He was not . . . he was not a man for women. But I didn't know such a thing existed. I thought every man tupped a woman, that every woman was tupped. So did my mother, I think, when he agreed to marry her. She got a husband when she might have faced shame. He got a child to call his own, and if I came sooner than nine months after the marriage, nobody thought less of them for it.'

'Except you.'

'He lied to me. So did she. How could I not think less of them? I stayed a year longer, but it seemed that everybody knew. I crippled a boy who taunted me with it and so it became time to leave. I sought out my real father. He had been granted a new see by then, of Exeter, in England. I thought he would welcome me.'

He thinks that's the end to it, but some half a mile further down the track the Maid says, 'Children are allowed to believe things of the world that, grown, they find to be wrong.'

'Indeed.'

'But he trained you to be a churchman, your real father?'

'Not him. Those who took orders from him. They were not unhappy that I had come. I was a red-headed boy with fair skin, tall for my age.'

'You were beautiful?'

'I was told so.'

They come to a difficult part of the track. The day is blustery; the clouds jostle across the face of the sun, sending spiked shadows to spook the horses. There is a corner, full of darkness and danger, that they must persuade the Maid's devil-horse to pass, and then Tomas's chestnut mare. Pushing on afterwards, putting clear distance between them and the evil, for the first time he feels her circling him as he has been circling her, testing how she might ask what she needs to know.

Eventually: 'Have you . . . sired any children?'

He has been asked this how often? But rarely so delicately. A laugh catches in his throat and comes out more harshly than he intends. 'Did the priests infect me with their ways, you mean? No. I favour women over boys or men. But I have not sired any bastards. I know what it means to grow with that blight. I take my women carefully. Not every tumble need lead to a child.'

He looks sideways, at her profile. Something has shifted; the scales of her trust are tipped a little in his favour. It occurs to him that to gain her fullest confidence, he may need to show himself worthy.

On a risk, he says, 'I have been in the company of my lord of Belleville. He, it seems to me, is not a man for women.'

She does not turn his way, only says, 'If a man lies with another man, as with a woman, he shall burn for it.'

'Indeed. So we shall not speak of Father Huguet, priest to the de Bellevilles, who, if I understood Claudine correctly, has known my lord of Belleville since boyhood. But it seems to me that Marguerite's virtue is safe, married to such a one.'

She does not answer. He thinks he has burned his bridges; that she is never going to speak to him again. In silence they pass a small stream, a well, a charcoal burner in his

345

hut, sweet smoke rising in strings to the sky. Fallow fields lie rutted, still creased with morning frost.

Past the hut, she says, 'If you tell Bedford this, I shall uproot every tree in France to hunt you down. If I die, the hunt will not stop. You and everything you care about shall be taken from this earth in ways that men will speak of for generations.'

Jesu. If Bedford said that, he would smile, wryly, and know it true. Why does he not smile now, never doubting it? 'Lady, nobody shall hear it from me. I will swear that on anything that will lead you to trust me.'

She turns to him, eyes black, brow furrowed. 'But there isn't anything, is there, Tomas? There is nothing you could lay your hand on that would be sacred to you, to seal an oath.'

He wants to say: your hand, your knee, the plate of your armour; any and every part of you is sacred, and will seal my trust. She won't believe him. He is distraught. They ride the remainder of the way to the night's camp in silence.

CHAPTER THIRTY-EIGHT

'I WILL KILL HIM.'

It is November, two months since the siege of Paris, half a year since the relief of Orléans. The Maid is pacing the poor, torn earth outside her tent. Her armour is buffed to a painful brilliance.

Tomas can see himself twinned; on the breastplate, on the nearest arm. He looks thinner than he has ever done; the remnants of Tod Rustbeard are long gone. He sees his own head shake twice over. 'Lady, I think you do not need to risk the charge of treason in this way. It would seem that my lord of Albret has realized the depth of his ignorance. Look, he is coming to speak to you.'

November is not the worst time to fight, but it is far from the best. They know this, Tomas and the Maid, but leaving the court it had seemed a worthy gamble. A quick run south, a swift battle, a swifter conclusion and back to the king and his advisers, aglow with the patina of victory. The king promised to knight her at Christmas. What better prelude?

Thus did her men march through mud. They camped – still do camp – in wet tents, watching mail and plate rust before their eyes. They ate cold, slimed, blue-furred food over cold, spitting fires. They slept in their hose and tunics and woke damp, with stiff necks and frozen feet, rotten between the toes.

All of this for love of her. They are her men, but she cannot give their orders. The king has given command to Charles d'Albret, half-brother to the present chancellor, Georges de la Trémoïlle, whose land they are due to liberate from the bandit Perrinet Gressart.

Nothing against d'Albret, but he has no understanding of warfare. He has just wasted nine days and virtually their entire stock of gunpowder, hurling shot at the walls of Saint-Pierre to no noticeable effect.

He and his cohort of lace-decked lords are the dregs of Agincourt; men who either did not fight or escaped without injury, which says all about them that you need to know. They think they will win this by the power of powder alone, with Jean-Pierre as their mascot.

They are wrong. Saint-Pierre may not be huge, but it has huge walls, recently repaired, and Jean-Pierre does not have Rifflard or any of its major cousins. Jean-Pierre has been given an assortment of culverins of various sizes and none of them shoots a stone bigger than a cabbage. Around now, those in command have realized the little gunner was not being uncharacteristically bashful when he said it would not work.

Charles d'Albret, if he is bashful, does not show it. He held something glittery at the anointing in Rheims and has behaved as if he were the king's brother ever since. Addressing the Maid, he does not even bow. In other circumstances, this would be a mortal insult. 'My lady, we think it may be meet to assault the town directly.'

'How?'

He steeples his kid-gloved fingers, as if to a child. 'A charge by the men?'

Jesu. She *will* kill him if he keeps this up. Tomas considers whether he can place his body between the Maid and the lord, but he does not want to die for someone as trivial as d'Albret.

She tilts her head. 'I ask again, how? The moat is three lance-lengths across and one deep. If they go armoured, they will drown. If they do not, they will be killed by quarrels from above. If you give that order, the captains will sign it with a circle.'

D'Albret frowns. It is custom amongst the army that an order signed with a cross must be followed and that signed with a hoop or circle is to be ignored. It would appear the good lord does not know this.

The Maid clearly has no intention of explaining it to him. She comes to a halt squarely in front of d'Albret. 'My lord, may it not, rather, be wise to assault Saint-Pierre in the way the king assaulted Troyes? It was, after all, a similar situation. And a notable success. The king professed himself well pleased.'

In d'Albret's eyes, a flicker. He wasn't at Troyes. In the king's court, the detail of the assault is clearly not discussed; certainly not enough for his chancellor's almost-brother to know what was done by whom or how or when. 'Indeed,' he says. 'Very much so. Indeed.'

The Maid is fighting not to laugh. At least she hasn't stabbed him. 'In that case, I believe it may be politic for me to speak with the men, and repeat the orders of Troyes. By your leave, my lord?'

'Of course. Go. Do as was done at Troyes. This is our command.'

'I will still kill him.'

'You won't have to. He'll leave. He hasn't the stomach for this much mud.'

It has taken three days to gather wood that could have been cut on the way and brought with them if anyone had bothered to ask about the defences of Saint Pierre-le-Moutier. Three days in which the weather deteriorated and the rain began in earnest. It was soft at first, a smear on the horizon, little more than a heavy mist that layered like sweat on mail and plate, but by the eighth day of the month it has become a river pissed by God upon the earth.

On the ninth, the men fill the moat. They march across wood and break open the gates of Saint-Pierre in a wave of dogged fury and the need to be dry. That night, they sleep in beds under solid roofs, but they have not made themselves rich, nor sated the passions of their flesh, neither their stomachs nor their loins. There has been no theft, no rape, no plunder; none of the dues to a victorious army. The Maid is in charge and this is not the Loire. She tells the men that they need to know that God is with them, and God does not condone cruelty to women, or theft from honest Frenchmen.

She has to place herself in the doorway to the church of St Peter to keep them from sacking it. They grumble, but what can they do except walk away and find another meal? She has not told them not to eat, and there is a wealth of food in the town.

When they are gone, and not coming back, Tomas follows her in, and kneels beside her as she prays. It's hardly the first time, but today, she has a fervour that is new. She clasps her hands, raises her gaze to heaven. There's a particular yearning about her, a tension of her shoulders.

Tomas watches with new eyes. He has not seen her pray since Paris, not like this. He is sure now that all along she has been asking questions of the one man she can trust; the king in heaven, who led her, at the very least, to Rheims. He believes also – and this disturbs him far more than the notion that she is conversing with a dead monarch – that she is no longer hearing an answer.

Nevertheless, she is a thoroughly competent commander and the ranks are in good heart. After the victory at Saint-Pierre, they march south to Moulins, which is friendly. Charles d'Albret no longer pretends to be in control. The Maréchal de Boussac rides in with fifty men at arms. He reports directly to the Maid. They plan the assault on la Charité, the highly fortified base town where Perrinet Gressart holds court and flies his banner of three cinquefoils and a band across.

La Charité was fortified by the old king. It is not Paris, but it is not so very different. It is hard to find time alone with her. Tomas has to wait until after Mass, when he hears her confession. I had ill thoughts about d'Albret. I feared we may not take la Charité. I do not have faith.

As if they had always discussed such things, he asks, 'What says the king in heaven?'

She shrugs. We have to take it.

He wants to ask, did the dead king tell you that? And if he did, can he explain how he proposes we might do it, now that we are without powder, shot, quarrels, arrows? Without food and henbane and poppy; without leather for boots and wood for the fires, how can we?

'Tomas, I will not have it said that we lost for lack of courage. Write this to the people of Riom:

351

Dear and good friends,

You well know how the town of Saint-Pierre-le-Moutier was taken by assault, and with God's help I intend to clear out the other places which are against the king. But because so much gunpowder, shot, and other materials of war had been used up before this town, and because myself and the lords who are at this town are so poorly provisioned for laying siege to la Charité, where we will be going shortly, I pray you, with whatever love you have for the welfare and honour of the king and also all the others here, that you will immediately send for use in the siege gunpowder, saltpetre, sulphur, shot, crossbows and other provender of war. And do well enough in this matter that the day will not be prolonged for lack of gunpowder and other war materials, and that no one can say you were negligent or unwilling. Dear and good friends, may Our Lord protect you.

Written at Moulins the ninth day of December. Jehanne

D'Albret has grown weary of this: no glory, no riches, no honour. He is discovering what Tomas already knew, that war in winter is a ghastly, cold, mud-slick affair. All the little lords and petty earls have ridden away to their warm, dry chateaux. They have not sent more food to the army they have abandoned, nor medicines, nor powder, shot, or horses. Thus is the king's destruction of the upstart Maid complete. Bedford might have a hand in this, but truthfully, he doesn't need to any more. The Valois boy has seen his competition, and he will not let her prosper.

The people of the Loire hold faith; they send the Maid what they can, but they have little to spare and it is not enough. The army moves on to la Charité.

LA CHARITÉ,
14 December 1429

'May the Lord Jesus Christ protect you and lead you to
eternal life.'

The tent is a sweep of stitched hides set on rotting poles
that barely offers a roof and three walls. Sleet rolls over in
freezing shoals, breaks on the men beyond, the horses, the
cannon stuck in the slurry that was once a pasture. Cold,
wet, starving, each is pushed as close to death as the living
may reach and yet step back from it.

Inside, cold, wet, starving, are those who cannot step
back. Here, Tomas murmurs the viaticum, dabs holy oil
on the dying palms, temples, breast. He lays the wafer in a
just-living mouth and holds his crucifix forward, where the
dying man can see it without turning his head.

The dying man is called Alexandre. He holds the Maid's
hand. His eyes are fixed on her face, and when he has
confessed his last few sins to Tomas – I wanted to kill the
English, Father, but I nursed a greater hatred in my heart
for those who had sent us here; I wanted to throw the king
from the throne and set on it someone who would rule in
fairness and not at the whim of men who know nothing of
war – when he has said all this, his red-shot eyes reach for
hers and he searches for words.

'Tell me of the king in heaven. Will I be with him this
night?'

The king in heaven? Do they all know? Tomas feels his
stomach plunge and sickness tumble into the ache it leaves
behind.

The Maid must not weep. She must not rage or she will
let loose the horror of this place, the desolation and despair.
Tomas has nothing else to give but this, his presence. He
steps forward, his shoulder solid against hers.

She grasps Alexandre's hand: a bundle of kindling; stick-brittle fingers and no warmth. She holds his gaze. Words flow, and who knows what the cost? 'The king sits in the golden light of heaven. He sees all. He knows all. He cares for each of us equally. And he loves France above all. He loves France. He *does* love France—'

'My lady, it is over. Come away.'

Tomas himself is not the man he was, hale, hearty, broad of shoulder and girth. He comes to her stoop-shouldered. The bones of his face make caves of his cheeks and his skin flaps loose over the shadows. He turns away from the vision of himself in her plate.

'Who?' she asks. 'Who's next?'

'Guillard.'

Guillard fell and broke his wrist three days before. The bones showed white through his skin; the only white they had seen in over a month. They were brown, soon, with filth, and then crawling green.

She turns, frowning. He watches her struggle to remember which Guillard, where he comes from, what he has done that she can talk about, can praise, so that he goes to his Maker with her approval in his heart. She turns and turns and cannot see him, and—

'My lady . . .' Tomas's hands bring her to a stop. 'It's too late. He's gone. And the next one also.' He pulls her to face him. 'Listen to me. We cannot stay here. Not unless you want to condemn three hundred more souls to the same death as these. It's my fault. We should never have trusted the king to send provision. I didn't see this. I am sorry. But apology won't break the walls, and it won't keep your men alive.'

She closes her eyes. He sees her reach for help, and the desperation of receiving no answer.

Why does the dead king not come to her now? Is there

some barrier that arose after the failure at Paris that keeps them apart? He brought her this far, whispering ghostly encouragement, and now he has abandoned her. If one could assault a dead man, he, Tomas, would seek him out in heaven or in hell and wring his scrawny, half-mad neck.

The Maid opens her eyes. Tomas stands like a fallen rock. Sleet shatters on his shoulders.

He meets her gaze. 'If we leave, they will say the Maid has failed,' he says. 'This is why they have done this; to break you, to prove you are not sent by God because God would not let you fail. Your army knows this. Every man here will die in the mud for you if you ask them to. But I think their deaths will not prove that you are right and the king is wrong.'

He and the Maid look together beyond the lee of the tent. The men, standing in stricken rows, all avert their eyes. It is a month since they had full bellies, longer since they had a drink. They tried to sack Saint-Pierre and she wouldn't let them; she thought God wanted French men and women to be left; she thought her father wanted it, that he would speak to her if she kept them off.

And the men listened, because they believed in her, believed that if she wanted it God must want it, and they must forgo the women, the gold, the velvets, the horses, the arms, the armour, all the comforts and riches of war.

Now they all look the other way, giving her a pretence of privacy in the heart of this stinking field. She looks to the sky, whence came her glory once. Tomas looks with her and sees only black clouds, and more sleet.

'We're going home.' She says it first, as if to test the feel of it, then shouts it loud enough to reach the walls. 'We're going home! Leave the cannon. Leave anything you do not need. Only take care of the horses.'

At her side, Tomas gives an infant cry and catches

her hand. 'They shall not take you. We shall not allow it.'

He is wrong, of course. Regnault de Chartres no doubt plans to let Bedford have her. But those who care for her will not make it easy for him and Tomas is foremost amongst them.

JARGEAU,
Christmas Day 1429

The Maid is the saviour of Jargeau, the one who rescued it from English rule. The people welcome her into their town at Christ's Mass as if she were the risen Child Himself. She and her men at arms are given rooms and clean linens and mattresses of duck down and hot food. There is tar for Xenophon's foot that has thrush-rot, and hot linseed boiled in a mash to put the condition back in his coat and flesh on his back. They offer her a chapel, bring her to Mass.

She is the destroyer of Jargeau. She led the siege, sent guns against their walls. She did not hold back the army as she did at Saint-Pierre. There is not a family that was not touched by the pillage that came after their surrender.

Their well-wishes hang sour on their lips and their eyes slide sideways when she and Tomas talk of war and England and the truces the king still hopes to make with his cousin of Burgundy. They fear that, like the cities around Paris, the towns of the Loire, too, will be given back to English rule, and English punishment will fall on them anew for daring to open their gates to France, for all that they did it under duress. Far worse for those towns who opened willingly; they tremble now at every letter that passes between the king and his cousin.

The Maid has a letter of her own, written by the Comte de Bourbon, who in turn writes on the orders of the king.

Tomas reads it out, in the quiet of their lodgings, over a potage of rabbit and beans. She is still thin. They all are.

'"Desirous of giving thanks for the diverse and signal benefits of divine greatness that have been brought to us by the actions of the Maid, Jeanne d'Ay, we hereby grant and donate from this day forth . . ."'

'He makes you a knight, lady.'

She is a knight. Her issue will be knights be they male or female. If she marries. If she has children. He cannot imagine it. Nor, he thinks, can the king. But her father, her brothers, their issue, shall all count themselves amongst the nobility of France and bear the lily on their arms. Her promise from the summer is made true. He remembers the oaf, Jacques of Domrémy, in a hovel, and the scorn in the Maid's voice.

'He makes me a knight. I should be grateful of this great honour, but I have been a knight since Jean d'Alençon gave me a horse and the king paid for my armour. I have been a knight since I rode down the English coming out of the bastille des Augustins outside Orléans. I have been a knight since Jargeau fell, and Meung, and all the towns to Troyes. I am a knight, whatever the king might say, but I have no income of my own, no gold I may give in largesse. I am dependent on a man who finds it amusing to give my keeping over to la Trémoïlle.'

They lodge with la Trémoïlle's wife's brother. The people nearby are kind. They bring her their rosaries to bless and will not have it that they could as easily bless them as she could. These notwithstanding, she is, in effect, under house arrest.

Tomas sees her through Christ's Mass and into the New Year 1430. On the fifth day of January, he saddles his chestnut mare and rides along foul winter tracks for Chinon, where is Yolande of Aragon.

357

He has one last idea, and does not know if it can be made to work. It will require Pietro di Carignano to remain true to his word, which may be asking too much, but he intends to try.

CHAPTER THIRTY-NINE

'You have two choices: you tell us the truth, or we charge you with everything up to and including the murder of Dr Iain Holloway.'

Picaut is good at this.

The cells are in the station's basement: chill, damp and unappealing. Monique Susong is visibly relieved to have been brought upstairs to the interview room, but her reprieve is short-lived. There are no windows here and the walls are painted a cloudy grey with exposed water pipes highlighted in the dull red of opened veins.

Garonne has the digital recorder set in a neat line with his iPad and he's taking notes with the enthusiasm of a new recruit.

Picaut leans across the table. 'Who are you?'

Brown eyes meet hers, flatly. 'I want a lawyer. I have that right.'

'Only if we charge you. If you're helping us with our investigation, you don't need one. Of course, if you push,

359

we'll make this more formal. And to do that, we'll need your name. Your real name. No—' Picaut pushes forward a single perfect portrait, laser-printed from the web. '*This* is Monique Susong, who works as assistant to the fashion editor of *Vogue Paris* . . .'

She waits.

'Yonita Markos.'

'Yonita?' Picaut feels her world grow sharper. She glances to her right, to the camera feeding a screen watched by Patrice, Rollo, Sylvie and Ducat. She slides the iPad across the table. 'Can you write that for us?'

The woman's typing is fluent. The first letter is enough.

Jonita Markos.

Picaut holds the Pad up to the lens. 'So we can stop looking for a Jonathan who works at Cornell.' Turning back, she says, 'Who is Monique Susong?'

'My sister. I can pass for her if you're not looking too closely.'

'Does she know you're using her identity?'

'No, that was Iain's idea. He thought it might keep me safe.'

'Has it?'

'I'm still breathing.'

'That is not always the best index of safety. Or the only one.'

'No.' Jonita Markos looks down at her perfect magenta nails and up again. 'What do you need to know?'

Picaut leans back, letting Garonne catch her eye.

'Start at the beginning,' she says. 'Tell us how you know Dr Iain Holloway, and why you came to France last week to meet him.'

Thus do they learn that the woman who is not Monique Susong is a molecular engineer, a fellow of Cornell University in New York State, who specializes in the extraction of DNA from old or corrupted samples.

She met Iain Holloway in Bosnia when they worked together on the identification of bodies from mass graves and their shared interest blossomed into a relationship, conducted across the Atlantic. She speaks fluent French because her stepfather was a French national. Her father was Greek; she barely remembers him.

She came to France because Iain Holloway asked her to, but she only arrived on the Saturday afternoon and he had become unrecognizable by then. Between Thursday evening, when he first called, and the Saturday evening, when she landed in Paris and rang him from the airport, he had changed from a man caught up with the thrill of a new investigation to one in fear of his life.

When she arrived at his hotel, he looked straight through her, as if they'd never met. Their only contact was a note pushed under her door.

'You have the note?'

'It's in my handbag. Which your officer took.' Garonne rises without comment and goes to fetch it.

Picaut says, 'What was Iain Holloway working on, that needed your help?'

'I don't know exactly. He was . . . secretive. He would get obsessions, and run them into the ground, and then drop them and pick up a new one. This one . . . Did you know he was corresponding with your father?'

Picaut's brows rise.

Cautiously, the woman says, 'Your father. Charles Picaut. The one who was—'

'Retired.'

'Yes, of course. Iain wrote to him. He had a theory. Your father seemed to like it. Iain was ridiculously pleased; like a kid given first prize in the spelling test at school. He—' She swallows, stares hard at her hands. 'He was not a dangerous man, or unkind. But he hated people who didn't think clearly. Which meant almost everyone. Except your father.'

'And you?'

'I tried my best. I didn't always succeed.' She spreads her hands. 'I truly don't know what he was doing this time.'

'You knew enough to go to the priest at Cléry-Saint-André?'

'Only because that last note told me to.'

'What about the email?'

'What email?'

Picaut looks to her right. 'Patrice, have you got the email from the chip?'

She's focused now. She can talk to him and not feel as if a flower is blooming behind her eyes.

Her iPad hums to an incoming mail. Opening it, Picaut says, 'When was the last email you got from Iain Holloway?'

'He sent something on Sunday night, about an hour before the fire started. I didn't see it until Monday, but in any case it came through as gibberish.'

'Like this?' Picaut spins the iPad round. On the screen is the undeciphered hex file that Patrice found on the USB chip.

'That's it!' The woman's eyes widen. 'How did you get it?'

'Dr Holloway left us a USB chip with a number of ciphered files on it. We've only been able to open one. The key was a list of names from the grave you both worked on in Bosnia.'

Picaut swipes the screen across to a new page. 'This is the translation.'

Jon – Too much to say, too little time. Know that I love you, and wherever we go after death, I will wait there for you. Don't hurry.

As my gift to you from beyond the grave – and with apologies that it's not more exciting – I've sent you two samples. A is from lii [*note from P: I have no idea what this means, but I have checked it twice*], B is from the subject. I would bet rather a lot that they're related. If it transpires that I am right, I would appreciate your telling as many people as possible: tell the whole world. Call it my legacy, or hers; either way, you will be safe when it's fully public. Until then . . . there are those, clearly, who will kill to keep this secret. Stay somewhere very safe. Don't trust anyone.

Keep well, beloved. Don't mourn me; just be yourself in all your wonder.

I love you. IH

Tears sway on the sheer points of Jonita Markos's lashes.

Picaut says, 'I'm sorry.'

'Don't be. I'd rather know. He was so . . . thoughtful. Clever. Careful. Caring. I keep thinking I'll pick up my phone and there'll be a text from him and it will all have been some kind of elaborate joke.' She closes her eyes and opens them, slowly. 'What did you mean, he left you a chip?'

'I mean he swallowed a USB chip just before he died. It was our only clue to what he was doing. Everything else had been stolen.'

'But why? *Why?* He was a *good* man.'

She is fighting hard for composure. Picaut must clasp her own hands together not to reach across the table and embrace her. If Patrice were to die now . . .

She says, 'We don't know. If we can find out what's on the other two files, we may have a chance to work it out, but in the meantime we have to work with what we've got. Does this make any sense?' Picaut taps the iPad screen and highlights **A is from lii**. 'What does lii mean?'

'I really have no idea. Believe me, I'd tell you if I did. He worked in Vietnam once, before I knew him. Could it be Vietnamese? A name, maybe?'

Picaut doesn't even glance at the camera. She doesn't need to look at her iPad either; she can hear Patrice's voice in her mind saying 'On it'.

She lets it drop and asks instead, 'He says he sent you a sample. It may have been labelled more clearly. Or there could have been a covering note?'

'If there is, I haven't seen it. Nothing had come before I left Cornell in the early hours of Saturday morning, so whatever happened it won't have got to the lab before Monday.'

'But he called Cornell on Sunday evening. He was heard to do so by a German resident of the hotel.'

'I suppose he could have been calling to alert the techs to look out for what he'd sent.'

'Would someone open it in your absence?'

'Possibly. But they might not know what to do with it. If you give me my phone, I can text the chief tech and find out.'

'Please do.'

There's a knock at the door and Garonne returns. At Picaut's nod, he slides the bag across the table and Jonita opens it. She removes her iPhone in its pink cover and a scrap of paper.

'He pushed this under my door on Saturday night.'

Ma chérie

Don't come to my room. Don't look at me. Don't know me. I am not currently safe to know. We must move to another hotel tomorrow. With luck, this will blow over and we can have a drink and laugh at my paranoia. But if I'm right, and something untoward happens, go to Father Cinq-Mars at Cléry-Saint-André and tell him I sent you. He may take some persuading, but he knows what this is about. Be safe in all things and remember that I love you.

Aye,
Iain.
PS Stay as Monique Susong. They don't know that name.

Go to Father Cinq-Mars at Cléry-Saint-André . . . 'You went. What did he tell you?'

The woman is writing a text, tongue trapped between her teeth, thumbs flying. She shakes her head, not looking up. 'Nothing of any use. He's a tight-faced little shit who has no intention of telling me anything I don't already know. His best advice was that I leave and never return. Don't darken our door again. That kind of thing.'

'He knows more than that, though, the priest?'

'Iain obviously thought he did.'

'Obviously.' Picaut's eye falls on the postscript. 'How many people in France know that you and Monique are sisters?'

'Her husband. Her son. And neither of them knows I'm in France. Monique and I don't have much in common. She doesn't know either.'

'But you have her driving licence?'

'I don't, actually. I have the European driving licence that Iain set up for me in Bosnia.'

'A fake?'

'Is that a crime?'

'If we need to hold you it will do. What was it for?'

'Not everybody wanted us to find the names of the men in the graves. There were death threats . . . We had protection, but Iain said I might need to disappear in a hurry.' She smiles. 'Clearly, it works . . .'

Garonne, whose responsibility it was to check the documentation, colours an ugly pink.

Picaut says, 'If Dr Holloway was right, then it may be that for your own safety you should continue to be Monique

365

Susong while you are in Orléans. Will you be able to do that?'

'As long as nobody looks at my bank cards. They're all in my real name.' She opens the bag, slides her hand down into a zipped pocket along the base, draws out an American Express platinum and a Bank of America cash card, both in the name of Jonita Markos.

'You didn't think to tell us any of this before?'

'I didn't know if I could trust you. Iain didn't say who was threatening him.'

Picaut opens the door. 'Thank you for your help. Obviously I can't compel you to stay in Orléans, but . . .'

'I'll stay. I want to know what happened to Iain as much as you do. I'll contact you when the results come through from the lab. If we find a genetic link between the samples, what then?'

'Then we talk to the priest,' Picaut says.

Later, in her office, the coffee is hot and bitter and perfect. The pizza is thin and well spiced.

Monique Susong has taken a taxi back to her hotel, and Garonne, who followed her, says she is safely in the dining room. He bought the pizza on his way back.

Patrice, Ducat and Éric Masson are all here, spilling out through the doors into the deserted office space. She is sitting on her desk, knee to knee with Patrice. He is absorbed in his laptop, she in her pizza. The place where their knees touch is alive, but nobody is looking askance and she realizes they have been this easy in each other's presence for some time now, she just hasn't realized.

'So.' She picks up her coffee, and hugs the mug to her sternum where it vibrates to the rhythm of her heart. 'Which of you is going to tell me why it took twice as long as it should have done to get Monique Susong's handbag into the interview room?'

Patrice breaks away from his screen, blinks once at Ducat who is staring fixedly out through the door, and says, 'I was cloning her phone.'

'I thought cloning went out when analogue died?'

'Copying the data, then.'

'Because . . .'

'Because I thought that one of their previous emails might be the key to one of the documents on the USB chip. Iain Holloway obviously wanted us to work with her. She's integral to the coding and she had a copy of the email. So it seems possible that their other emails might be the keys we're looking for that will open the remaining two files.'

'Are they?'

'Not yet. I'm testing each email and then combinations of them. I'll let you know if I strike gold.' Patrice tilts his head. 'Do you have your father's laptop? If we could look at his correspondence with Iain Holloway . . .'

'My father reformatted the hard drive just before he died.'

'Doesn't matter.' Patrice is grinning at her. In public. This is so very dangerous. 'The data's all still there and I can get to it. Trust me.'

She does. But . . . 'I gave it away.'

'*Gave* it?'

'At the funeral. The Bressards called in just about the entire family. There were over a thousand of them, showing solidarity. I talked to . . .' She screws up her eyes. 'I don't remember. A cousin of a cousin sixteen times removed. He was about fourteen, and not nearly as well off as the rest. I gave him the laptop.' She holds up a hand, blocks off his incredulity. 'I'll text Luc and see if I can get it back.' Her phone is in her hand. The number comes more fluidly

367

than she wants it to. 'I'm on it, Patrice. Don't hassle me.'

The air loses its charge. Ducat recovers from his momentary bout of deafness, and turns back into the room. It's hard to know at what point he stopped being the enemy and became instead an ally, but it's definitely happened. If nothing else, this is the first time he has ever been in her office for coffee and pizza.

Picaut fires off the text, then: 'Maître Ducat, I want to bring in the priest, Father Cinq-Mars. Do we have your permission?'

'Absolutely. He's a suspect in the murder of Iain Holloway. The threat of a murder charge should open him up.'

'He's dying of throat cancer. But we have to try. Next . . .' She finishes the coffee, fixes Garonne with a stare. 'What have we got on Cheb Yasine?'

Garonne says, 'He hasn't left his house. He's had three visitors, all of Algerian origin, all with form. Two were drug dealers; the third's from Marseille, and the police there think he's a hired hit. They're pretty sure he killed four Slovenians who were moving in on the coast, but they can't prove it. Sylvie and Rollo are watching now. I'll take over at midnight.'

'So we continue the watch on Yasine, and we continue electronic and actual surveillance on Monique Susong. We will continue to refer to her by that name for the time being. She may be in danger from whoever killed Iain Holloway; just because she hasn't been targeted yet, doesn't mean she won't be. I want armed officers on her, ready to intervene if there's any sign of danger. Garonne, I don't want you doing it, but I want you to organize it. Patrice, if I get my father's laptop back, I'll courier it to you. Let's go, people. We have work to do.'

Luc's press conference on the steps of the Hôtel Jeanne d'Arc has done its work; Picaut is not accosted in the street and not followed back to the flat.

She considers texting Patrice that she's going home, perhaps to invite him over. Sanity stops her, and common sense, and the fear of having his image next to hers all over tomorrow's papers. Still, even to consider the possibility leaves the day feeling sharper.

She falls asleep knowing that her world is not empty. Three more days until the polls open. One after that to count the ballots and announce the results. So, four days to freedom and a life that is already immeasurably better. Against all expectation, she is happy.

CHAPTER FORTY

Orléans,
Thursday, 27 February 2014
07.00

PICAUT IS HALFWAY THROUGH her second coffee of
the morning when the doorbell rings. However much
she loathes Bressard efficiency, their fanatical attention
to detail allows her to open a panel in the kitchen fascia
and check the live feed from two hidden cameras that are
focused on the area around the front door, three floors
down.

Currently, they show Cheb Yasine dressed in his designer
sweatshirt and jeans. She hits the microphone.

'Do the press know you're here?'

'I don't see any, but they may be developing better
camouflage than they've had in the past. It would be good
not to wait out here too long. May I come in?'

Ducat would go mad. Luc would have fits. Patrice would
. . . laugh, probably. She hits the entry button.

He runs lightly up the three flights of stairs. She stands at
the open front door, waiting with her Nokia in her hand. 'I
can have a dozen officers here inside four minutes.'

'I know.' He is fit; the stairs have barely winded him. He glances past her into the flat. 'Bressard money?'

'Certainly not a police salary.' She stands back to let him in and leads the way to the kitchen. He accepts coffee, but will not sit. He spends his time studying the view from the windows.

Picaut asks, 'What have you got?'

'It's more what I have not got that matters.' He leans in the corner furthest from the door. Like this, he has a wall to his back and a window to his left. His gaze ceases to roam the world outside and settles on her face. 'It seemed to me yesterday that you would know if and when I spoke the truth.'

'I wouldn't guarantee it.'

'Then you will have to decide now whether or not this is the truth. I will tell you that I believe it to be so.' He presses his hands together, looks out again and back at her. 'There is not a single group affiliated to Islam, not the jihadists, not the secular groups who use religion as a front, not the mosques, not the imams, not a single living soul who can put a name to the arsonists of Orléans. *Jaish al Islam* has not a single member in the Muslim community of this city. Nevertheless, we are all afraid of what will happen to us in the backlash from the fires. We are already seeing it in the demonstrations, and how soon before those demonstrations become riots in which innocent lives are lost? I cannot prove this, but I do not believe these people would tell me untruths.'

If he is lying to her, he is good at it. She doesn't dismiss the idea. 'Who do they think is behind the fires?'

'Who stands to gain most if we are vilified? Who wanted to be the new Maid of Orléans before you stepped into that role?'

'You really think Christelle Vivier would light fires in her own city?'

371

His smile is slow, and sad. He pushes himself away from the kitchen counter and heads for the door. 'I will leave you to ponder why your first instinct is to believe that this is her city more than it is mine, or that it is too precious for her to burn it for political ends, but not too precious for me or men like me to burn for religious ones.'

He turns on the threshold. 'I wish you well in your bid to bring the guilty to book, but my cousin has died at the hands of people who would destroy us all, not just me. Or you. Au revoir, Capitaine Picaut.'

When the downstairs buzzer rings and rings and rings again soon after he has left, she thinks he has come back, that the paparazzi are on his tail, that Christelle Vivier has set the attack dogs of the *Front National* on to him.

She activates the screen that opens the eyes of the hidden cameras. Patrice is staring up into one of them, his hands over the other, so that she might not be confused by the multiple images. He is not laughing. He isn't even smiling.

'Let me in.'

She does.

She thought Cheb Yasine was fast. Patrice takes the stairs three at a time and is at her door to meet her as she opens it. His T-shirt says EDWARD SNOWDEN FOR PRESIDENT over an image of an 'Anonymous' Guy Fawkes mask.

He slams in through the door and spins round in her hallway. 'What the *fuck* was Yasine doing here? Don't shake your head at me. I watched him come out.'

This is a new Patrice; blazing. She matches question with question. 'Where's he gone?'

'Back to his lair. What was he thinking? What were *you*?'

'He wants me to know that he's hunting for the killers of his cousin and he'll get there ahead of me. Have you slept at all?'

'Sleep is for losers. Current company excepted, of

course.' He exhales, hissing, through his teeth, and looks up towards the kitchen. 'Coffee?'

'Are you sure that's what you need?'

'No, but I'm guessing you don't keep stores of Red Bull.' He pulls a tight smile, and she can relax and, relaxing, think.

'Have you been staking out Cheb Yasine all night?'

'No, as instructed that was Rollo or Garonne, and either they didn't know he was coming here or they did, and I'm not sure which is worse.'

'I'll ring them later.'

He hitches one hip on to a tall stool at the breakfast bar. Sunlight paints him in shades of gold and mercury. Her guts roil, just to have him this close. She hands him a mug of coffee. Their fingers touch. He lifts her hand, kisses her palm, folds her fingers over. Her blood is an electric current. He smiles an apology. They are so fast, his mood changes. Luc could simmer for weeks when he was angry. 'Are we OK?'

She runs her fingers through his hair. Already it is familiar. 'Not if Garonne and Rollo find out you're here.'

'I came to advise you on security. Which I have done. My advice is that if you want to be secure, the last fucking thing you should do is let Cheb Yasine into your apartment.'

'I don't see why not when he let me into his, but I don't want to fight over it. Have you cracked another of Iain Holloway's ciphers?'

He stops, mug halfway to his lips. 'How do you know?'

'Why else would you come . . . ?' It's her turn to smile. 'Can you eat when you're like this? Or do you just mainline neat caffeine?'

'What have you got?'

Less than she had when she was Luc's wife, that's for sure. There is bread, of a kind, although she bought it before Iain

Holloway died. The cheese is older still, but has survived better. She puts them together and Patrice eats as if it is his first food in days and talks with his mouth full.

'The key to one of the texts is the numbering of letters from the last three emails that Iain Holloway sent to Monique Susong. I lifted the mails from her laptop while she was talking to you. Put together, the mails make almost a PGP cipher, but not quite. And even then, we don't get text. It took me till an hour ago to work out what he'd sent. It's an EXIF file.'

'*Patrice!*'

'Sorry. It's been a long day.'

'It's not half-past seven yet.'

'An exceptionally long day.' He laughs, leans forward, wipes a crumb from the side of her mouth, kisses his finger. 'EXIF is the transfer protocol for smartphone images.'

'So the file is a picture?' That really does surprise her.

'Not just any picture. A skull. See?' He opens his laptop and spins it round. On the screen is a colour picture of a skull, green with mildew and missing fragments from around one eye socket, but otherwise intact. Beneath it are a few cervical vertebrae, lined up in order, and beneath them is a black and white chequered marker for scale, and a small white-topped plastic pot of the type that medics use for sending samples to the lab.

'Iain Holloway's email said he was sending samples to Monique Susong's lab.' Patrice's fingers drum lightly on the screen. 'Et voilà! A sample pot.'

'And a woman's skull.' Picaut is learning to look for the supraorbital ridges. There are none, and the shape of the nasal bones is distinctly female.

'I'll take your word for it. So we think this is of Iain Holloway's sample subjects?'

'Pass. A name would have been nice.'

'If he knew it at all, he'll have put it in the last of the files; nothing too easy in case the wrong people start breaking the ciphers. I don't suppose you found your father's laptop?'

She had forgotten that. 'No. Luc texted while Cheb was here.' She opens her phone, turns it round.

SORRY. LONG GONE ONTO E-BAY. HE WAS G-BRANCH, WHAT CAN I SAY?

'G-branch?'

'All the names begin with G: Guillaume, Gérard, Georges. That kind of thing. It's family practice. It's why Annelise calls herself Lise. L-branch, obviously, is the top of the pile.' She shrugs. 'They came from Lyon.'

'Is this some kind of psychosis?'

'It feels sane enough when you're in the middle of it.'

'I don't believe you.' Patrice is eating more slowly now, bite by bite, bringing himself back to earth. Even so, Picaut can feel heat radiating from his skin, as if his metabolism has been racked up beyond human tolerance.

He is, if this is possible, too alive, and he is watching her, too-alive with possibility. She can count in her mind the steps between here and the bedroom. Her body sings to the thought.

She fills the kettle, clicks it on to boil again, says, 'Have you sent the image to anyone?'

'Besides you?' He hasn't even done that, but he does it now. The message pings into her phone.

'Send it to Éric, just to make sure I'm right that it's a woman. Then . . .' Her self-control is abysmal. She has crossed the room, is standing behind him, her fingers locked in his hair, pressing her lips to the crown of his head. She breathes him in like a drug, breathes out heat and need.

He stops eating. With wonderful deliberation, he lays

down his bread, pushes the plate away and turns round in his seat. His eyes are level with her breasts. His breath is fire, burning her heart. Of this pain, she is not afraid.

He says, 'If you want me to leave, now might be the time to say so.'

She takes his head between her two hands and draws him up. Her lips trace dry patterns along his cheekbones, the lids of his eyes. Her fingers loop through his, and lock there. She takes a step away, and another, drawing him with her, and like that, wordless, leads him the thirty paces to the bedroom.

A single finger pressed on his breastbone is enough to topple him backwards, on to the bed. He falls fully clothed on to the duvet. His eyes feast on her for a long, last moment, before he reaches out and grasps her wrist and pulls her down on top of him.

Later, unclothed, sated, she lies on him, skin to skin. Her ear is pressed to his sternum. The slowing drum of his heart beats up to meet her. His legs hook loosely over the backs of her knees. He kneads her palm with his thumb, traces her life line with his tongue, and on up to her elbow.

She turns her head and sees her alarm clock: eight thirty. Already she is late for work, she who hasn't been late any day through her father's death and all the recent chaos. She wasn't late even in the earliest days of Luc, when tearing herself from his bed felt like tearing off her own skin. To think of that now would be sacrilege, and anyway she can't think past the hour just gone, and the wild, cataclysmic soaring. Was it like this with Luc? She doesn't remember it if it was.

Patrice is pressing his lips to her brow. She closes her eyes, makes herself think of something other than the taste of him, the feel. In the swim of her mind is a thought with hard edges. She speaks it before she can decide it's too much trouble. 'My father had a Dropbox account. He might have kept his emails in there.'

She feels him tense beside her, sit up. She pushes him down, presses a kiss to his sternum, feels him stir. 'I don't believe this.'

'All you have to do is mention email.' He pulls her up, kisses her head. He is not entirely unserious. 'Tell me you have his login details written somewhere?'

'Burned into my brain.' She leans over the bed, finds her phone in the catastrophe of clothes, types with one hand: *crp@gmail.com/margueritedevalois*

Her phone hisses a send and sings to its arrival on Patrice's phone. He picks it up. 'Password is all one word, all lower case?'

She nods.

'And Marguerite de Valois is who?'

'Charles the sixth's bastard daughter. My father believed she was the most likely contender for Jeanne d'Arc. The only problem is that she lived until 1458, so she couldn't be. He ignored small details like that . . .'

She pulls him close, kisses his eyelids, feels the different layers of tension and exhaustion through his body.

'Patrice?'

'Hmmm?'

'If I asked you to go home and go to bed and get some sleep, would you do it?'

'When you've just given me the key?' He lifts his head away from her. 'Are you kidding me?' His eyes are alight with fires she cannot source.

'The email address is the key?'

'No, the password. It won't be in plain text, but there'll be something based on this, I can feel it.' He angles up on one elbow, searches for his jeans.

She catches his arm. 'Patrice, you need to sleep.'

He pulls away from her, only half laughing. 'I can't.'

'Patrice!' She is not laughing now, either. 'Please.'

He raises her to standing, wraps his two arms around her, kisses her brow. 'I'll do a deal. Give me six unbroken hours' work, and if I haven't cracked it by the end of that, I'll sleep, I promise.'

'Why not the other way round?'

'I work best when I'm wired.' He stoops for his T-shirt, hauls it over his head. 'Trust me, I can do this. Then I can sleep.'

She raises her hands. 'Six hours.'

'I'll call you at three with whatever I've got.' He is at the door. His mind has already left her. He hauls it back. 'What are you going to do?'

'I'm going to visit Father Cinq-Mars and see if the threat of a murder charge gets him talking. With a bit of luck, I might have the answers before you do.'

CHAPTER FORTY-ONE

SULLY-SUR-LOIRE,
16 March 1430

WRITE THIS TO THE CITIZENS OF RHEIMS:

Very dear and great friends, know that you are greatly missed and that the Maid has received your letters stating that you live in fear of assault and siege. Please know such an assault shall not occur; and if it should come to pass that I do not intercept your enemies and they come against you, then shut your gates, for I will be with you presently. And if they are there I will make them put on their spurs so fast that they won't know how to attack you, and very swiftly I shall come.

I will write no more now, except to say that you should always be obedient and loyal. I pray that God keeps you in His care.

Written at Sully this 16th day of March.

I would send you some additional news which might bring you good cheer, but I fear that the letters would be stolen along the way and our enemies would see this news.

Jehanne

What changes is how Tomas feels.

His heart is not a stable thing. His nights are sweaty, dark, lost in impossible desires and all too probable nightmares. Knotted in damp linen, he dreams of fires that eat the Maid living, and not a thing he can do about it.

The king has got her back. He has made her a knight, but he will not let her fight. He is holding her on the tightest of leashes. She must remain under his roof, as a part of his household, ready, in theory, to give her advice to His Majesty, except that her advice is never sought.

In March, the court moves near to Sully-sur-Loire the better to see how it is being assaulted by England; in particular, by a mercenary captain, Franquet d'Arras, who is raping women, slaughtering boys, stealing horses, all in the guise of helping Bedford retake the lands lost to the Maid.

The king watches. He does not intervene. In her chambers, the Maid paces.

Her father no longer drives her, no promises now, no oaths un-fulfilled, just a desperate, burning desire to mount Xenophon, lift her blade and take to the field. Her need is eating her alive; each day she is thinner, more fraught. And so, against the pull of his better nature, Tomas has found a way to make it happen. Now. Tonight.

He seeks out Marguerite, alone, before the time of parting. These past weeks, she has been the only one who could calm the Maid; she brought her small things to eat that diverted her attention. In the past days, she it was who argued most strongly that the Maid must go to safety, not danger. Nobody else would have dared say it. She did, and was overruled. Her purity sears him, and her pain.

He wants to say, I am sorry, but it would not be true. He cannot meet her eyes.

A porphyry statue stands on the table, a foot high. It is Saint Catherine of Siena, who evaded marriage by giving herself to Christ, and lived, for a while at least, only on the host. Her eyes are Marguerite's eyes, her hands Marguerite's hands.

He asks, 'Did you sit for this?'

'No. I would not make of myself a saint.'

Yes, you would. He has seen in her the fervour, the way her lips part when the priests speak of martyrdom. He has seen how she cleaves to this saint, patron of young girls who starve themselves half to death.

There was an epidemic of half-starved girls as the fourteenth century gave way to the fifteenth, and nobody had resolved thirty years of Great Schism. It seems that having more than one man claiming infallibility in God's name caused the gentle-maids of Europe to seek stability in hunger. Certainly, now that there is only one pope, they seem to be feeding themselves again, but not Marguerite. She looks thin. He thinks she has barely eaten these past few days, since his plan was fleshed out.

'I'm sorry,' he says, and in this moment, he means it.

'Do not say so. This is what she wants. She is afraid that the king will give Rheims back to the English as proof of his "good faith". Already he has ordered Compiègne to surrender to Bedford's forces.'

Tomas says, 'Compiègne will not surrender, whatever the king orders.'

Marguerite lifts one shoulder. 'It might if the Maid does not go to stiffen its resolve. And so you will take her.'

He nods. 'I will.'

'And you will keep her safe, while she does what she must do to make France whole again.'

'Yes.' And then I will bring her back to you. I swear it. He kneels. She lays her hand on his head. Her palm is cool, her touch surprisingly firm. 'Go well, Tomas. Do what you can. Do not make promises that you cannot keep.'

* * *

Later, in these same rooms, the two women embrace: both dark, slim, slight. They could be sisters, but that the Maid is taller, broader in the shoulder, with the arrogance of a knight.

They are framed by the light of a fire, and the lesser light of the wall sconces. The air around them crackles with regret, loss and longing, and it is not all from Marguerite; the Maid looks as heartbroken as Tomas has ever seen her. Minutes draw past, and might become hours, which they do not have. He takes a step forward. 'My lady, it is time to leave. The king's guards are distracted for a very short time only.'

The king's guards are presently being given a somewhat long-winded report by a scout as to the latest progress of this bandit, and all he has done. The Maid is not invited to this council, nor any other of the king's. She is not permitted to ride out with him. She is not really permitted to ride out at all, although she has done so, perhaps once a week, since Christmas. As one might imagine, she is going mad with inaction.

She rounds now on Tomas, her priest. 'You don't trust Pietro di Carignano?'

'I trust him as much as I trust any man who offers himself for hire.'

'We have not paid him.'

'Exactly. So I say again, we must leave swiftly, while there is time and before he changes his mind.'

Step by step, he prises the Maid away, draws her towards the door. His lasting memory of Marguerite is of colour and light, the liquid dapples of the sconces rolling over her green damask, her hair loose about her shoulders; her skin is clear, her eyes bright.

Truly, she is an angel. A part of him hurts to leave her.

382

She smiles for him, through tears. 'Take care of her, Tomas.'

'I will do my best. God keep you safe.' He bows. He has been unchaperoned with two women, but he is a priest; nobody cares. He steps back and closes the black-oak doors.

No guards stand there. He has no idea for how long they will be diverted. He hefts the pack at his shoulder; he has dark cloaks, and other things they will need if this night is successful. And he has a small pewter flask, containing a distillate of hemlock, in case it is not. He does not wish to burn.

'This way, lady.' He holds up a lantern of tin and thin, translucent ox horn which scatters light pale as buttercups in summer. His cupped palm shields the flame as much as do the shutters. By varying the tightness of his grip, he can let the light leak out between his fingers, not enough to scare the rats, but enough to see that he and the Maid don't risk treading on them. He swallows on spit the texture of egg white, kicks at a scurrying tail, pushes on.

'Tomas, you are worried. Did you not bring a knife?'

'I brought two, lady. But if we kill the king's men we will die for it, and not swiftly.' She may be a knight, but he has met their kind; they will kill her as a peasant.

She knows. It would appear she does not care. 'The Earl of Salisbury lost his jaw to a stray shot outside Orléans in the winter before we relieved it. He was eight days dying. Will it be longer than that?'

Probably not. I am not sure that it will seem like a blessing, though.

Again, he says, 'We are not here to kill guards. We need to be out of here and gone before they realize it. To the left here, and down. We go out under the wall.'

Every town in France, it seems, has tunnels going out under the walls. This tunnel is supposed to reach clear to safety. One has been dug from the outside expressly to meet it. He has not tested this assertion. It is one flaw in the plan; not the only one, but by far the biggest. If Pietro di Carignano has lied, if he has told one single untruth pertaining to all that is planned, Tomas will eviscerate him.

Thinking of this helps fire his belly as the tunnel narrows, the ceiling drops. They have the choice of crawling or crouching and the Maid won't crawl so they bend double, hobbling.

The air is stale and smells of terror and rat urine. He has never been a tunneller; he can admit without shame that he would never have the courage. He has never fought below ground either, although others do.

Twenty paces and an obstruction ahead. The width narrows so there is only room for one. He gives the Maid his lantern, lets her go ahead. His heart pounds. 'Turn right ahead, lady.'

Thirty more paces and he feels the bite of frost and wind, sharper than the cellar-chill. His bowels churn. 'Lady, the lant—'

She has already thought of it. One swift smother and they are in darkness, blundering by feel, fingers on mud, on wood, on stone, on—

'Stop.'

Her voice in his ear. He stands where his last step took him, on uneven ground, with spoil of the new tunnel under his feet. This much is done, that someone has broken into the tunnel coming out from under the wall.

He seeks stars, the moon, the light of men's eyes: anything. His hands slide up his sleeves. He is going to abandon this pretence of priesthood; it does him no good. Both knives are loose, then they are in his hands, ready. He can throw if only he can see something to throw at.

'Tomas . . .' She grips his shoulder. 'Here.'

Here, if he makes a quarter turn to his left, is starlight,

enough to see by. And here, Pietro di Carignano, soft-soled, face darkened with fire ash, smiling.

'My lady.' He is not a big man, half Tomas's girth, a head shorter, dark-haired, dark-skinned, wiry. He handles his blade well. And since the hell of la Charité, he has been back to his home and raised a new company of men to come and fight with the Maid, or so he has said.

No money has been paid, or asked. These men come, allegedly, for the honour of fighting in the Maid's company, although there is an understanding that there will be plunder; never again the restraint of Saint-Pierre.

From tonight, the Maid no longer fights for the King of France. She is a mercenary captain, no better – but no worse – than Perrinet Gressart, whom she fought in the winter's mud, and failed to defeat.

Tomas can see no sign of the Piedmontese. How would you hide two hundred men in the meadows of Jargeau? Are they lying flat on the soft spring turf? Where, come to that, are Jean d'Aulon and Louis de Coutes, who were sent ahead on a pretext of finding a smith capable of shoeing Xenophon without being killed? They took the horse, of course; that was the point, so it's possible they're dead and the horse gone. He doesn't want to be near her if she finds that has happened.

'Lady, may it please you?'

Pietro di Carignano is insufferably polite. It pleases the Maid. She follows close enough to wet his neck with her breath. Tomas trots after them, down a slope, up again. They crest the hill. Below, a mass of mail and arms, padded for hush. Horses shift and twitch. Their scent is a floor, a solid thing he passes through as he steps down the slope's far side: warm, dense, mellow-sharp. A big white-grey lifts its snake-head and snores out a greeting, not quite a whicker. Xenophon is too well trained for that.

She runs. In near dark, the Maid runs to her horse. He is glad Marguerite is not here to see this, her heart would shatter.

A man offers his looped hands for her to mount. Another lights up a torch, sending flickers of sooty flame across the assembled mass of men. A third passes up to the Maid her breastplate and helm. D'Aulon is here, after all, and Louis de Coutes. Somewhere close are the two brothers d'Arc. Since Christmas, they have been made knights, and their village is free of taxes for ever. They have remained with the Maid, though; they want to fight on.

For Tomas, her priest, the men have brought his wall-eyed chestnut mare. He is secretly pleased; he has come to like the beast. He mounts. Now is the time for him to give what he has brought. He opens his pack, draws out his gift, rolled, tied with a riband of blue silk. Even in this light, the gold glimmers.

'My lady.' He holds it forward.

She eyes him a moment.

He says, 'It is safe.' He reconsiders. 'Almost safe.'

She laughs, and he laughs with her, and then doesn't, because she has taken his gift and shaken it out: a surcoat in cloth of gold. It is not the one she wore at the coronation; the king has taken that back. She knows this. Her brows dance, asking a question.

They are in public. They have to be careful. Aloud, for everyone to hear, Tomas says, 'The fabric is a gift from the people of Rheims. The king's sister, Marguerite de Valois, stitched it with her own hand. The lady Yolande thinks you should wear it, and so do I. You should be seen, now, for who you are.'

He sees the sudden shine at her eyes, the prick of tears unshed. She has fixed her own breastplate. And now she fixes her own surcoat, sliding it on, tying the loops at the side with the dexterity of a lifetime's practice.

Two men bring forward the blazing resinous torches. She is a vision in gold. She looks out across the men, surveys their mass. Two hundred Piedmontese, plus two hundred loyal Frenchmen raised by Jean de Belleville.

When Montmorency came a day too late to Paris, he brought fifty men at arms and was considered a strong commander. She has eight times as many.

She sets her horse three paces back, so she is apart from them, and, lifting her hand as priests do, and kings, casts her voice out, cold and clear across them. 'While you are in danger, I will not flee. While you fight, I shall fight at your head. While you sleep, I shall be vigilant.'

It is a knight's oath. They cannot cheer her, not here. Scabbards hiss and creak, harness chimes. In a quiet that presses on them all, four hundred men lift their blades in the yellow light and now he, Tomas, cannot speak for the tightness of his throat. Henry was like this. Nobody since.

He heels away tears. She turns her horse towards him. She is smiling as he has not seen her since before Paris. Two months of planning, paid in a moment. 'Well, Tomas, where do we go that our men may make their names and their fortunes?'

'Where the fighting is thickest, my lady; where Bedford seeks to retake French towns. North, I think, towards Compiègne. Lagny-sur-Marne is on the way. There are those in that town who will aid you, however many men you bring.'

CHAPTER FORTY-TWO

'Go!'
The sudden end to waiting. The sway-into-stillness of the lance, the sword, the mace, the axe. The soundlessness of too much sound, of four hundred men – the Maid's men – all armed, armoured, horse-bound, implacable in their purpose; free.

For a moment Tomas too knows the freedom. He has no lance, never has had, never will have, but in this moment he comes as close as he ever can to being a knight. He is a horse's length behind the Maid when she singles out her target: a flashy rider on a flashy bay sporting a blue velvet cloak and swan feathers in his hat who shouts to the men on either side of him, raises his sword and circles it clockwise in the flashing air so that there is no question but that this is Franquet d'Arras, the bandit captain whom the king has ostensibly come here to hunt. But the king is not hunting him. And the Maid has seen him. D'Arras too has no lance, and his archers are fumbling their strings and he is caught between the stream and the hedge with nowhere to run.

He has some courage; in the last three strides, he brings his shield to the fore; gules and argent chequy, no other signs. She aims her lance for the centre. Caught in a place where time has become syrupy, Tomas sees the fine adjustments that bring her tip true, sees the tension of the brace, the breath that will hold through the impact.

His own breathing stops. His horse gathers itself. It, too, is coming new to this, but learning fast. Together, they ride through the contact and do not wince or veer away.

The Maid's lance is built for war. It does not shatter; rather, her enemy soars back over the nearside quarters of his horse.

D'Arras is not fully armoured: a breastplate, greaves, a helm, gloves; no great weight. He can rise, and does, but this is the Maid, and she is mounted on Xenophon. She is not going to ride past him and engage someone else.

She slews her horse to a halt, throws its weight back, lifts its forehand, turns it on its quarters, and as it comes round to face him she has already hurled her lance to her squire and drawn her blade, the new one, got for her by Yolande. This one will not break.

She bears an axe in her off hand; no shield. Her enemy knows, then, that he is done. He flings his own shield away, brings his sword to the guard, but he is slow and war sings through her veins.

Her blade cracks his away, and stops right on the brink of his throat. The skin parts, releasing a thin thread of blood.

'Yield.' A clear, crisp word, singing out across the field.

'You are the Maid?'

Of course she is the Maid. Who else rides with cloth of gold surcoat on her breastplate and fleur-de-lis on her shield? The king could do so, but is it likely that the king might ride against an armed knight?

She says only, 'Yes.' And takes her blade back a hand's

breadth, enough to kill him if she makes the stroke.

'I yield.' He raises his blade, balanced across his hands. 'To you. Only you.'

Thus is Franquet d'Arras taken; the bandit who has been terrorizing the surrounding area for months now. He is not a big man, and while he has not made himself wealthy on war, his sword is the best on the field. She takes it from him, feels the balance, tries it in the sheath at her side, and chooses it over the one she has been using.

It feels like an omen. The king made her a knight, but by her own actions she is giving her men plunder and honour. From this skirmish alone, they will raise ransom and horses, arms and armour the worth of half a thousand livres tournois.

The Maid could ransom d'Arras. He would like that; it is said he came here only to match against the Maid on the field, and having done it, he can pay his ransom and go on his way.

She has other ideas. She turns to Louis de Coutes. Her page has grown in the almost-year he has served her, and not only with the death of his brother. He is a young man, now, not a boy.

'Send to the Duke of Burgundy. Tell him that I will exchange Franquet d'Arras for Jacquet Guillaume, who led the revolt in Paris over winter.'

There were those in Paris who did not want the Maid to give up her assault on their city. They banded together and attempted a revolt from within, but one of their number was captured and gave up their names to Bedford's torturers. The uprising was crushed before it could begin, its leader arrested. The Maid, not unreasonably, considers herself responsible for his welfare.

The page goes at her word. The Maid's company waits in Lagny-sur-Marne, eating, drinking, swapping stories. The

Maid prays that Burgundy will treat her page as a herald, and not as a traitor. She looks always to the sky, awaiting the word of her father, which does not come.

On the third day, de Coutes returns, lean and cautious, while the Maid is in conversation with the magistrates of Lagny. The town, now that the king has gone south again, has offered board and keep for all four hundred of her men. The page bows to the Maid, hand on his heart. He is a good, godly boy. Youth. Young man.

'My lady, the duke sends me to tell you that Jacquet Guillaume died a traitor's death in Paris.'

He swallows. His eyes flick left and right. They alight on Tomas. What can I say? He nods. Tell the truth. Tell what you are told to say.

The boy takes a breath. He *is* a good, godly boy. 'I am to tell you that the same awaits you when you are taken.'

She carries d'Arras's blade at her hip. For a moment, it seems as if she might seek him out in his boarded room and drive it into him, for rage, not for the threat against her, but the death of Jacquet Guillaume.

Tomas lays a hand on her arm. 'Lady, there are others for whom he may be exchanged. We must but ask the men of Paris who else still lives that we may—'

'No. My lady, if it please you, we should have him; the men of Lagny-sur-Marne.' The chief magistrate of Lagny steps forward. He is a sturdy, black-haired father of six, strong in his affection for the king, stronger in his hatred of Burgundy. 'This man, d'Arras, is a traitor to France. Before you came, he committed many acts against us. He murdered our sons, raped our daughters, left our wives as widows and children as orphans. He stole our horses, our arms, our provender. Lady, if you love us, you will give him to us, to show that the king's justice rules in Lagny as much as it does in Tours or Chinon.'

What can she do but let them have him?

A court is summoned. Franquet d'Arras is brought in. Without his armour, he looks like a petty thief, caught stealing bread of a morning. He would beg, but he has his pride. And in any case, he can tell that there is no point.

The people of Lagny try him of their own volition, and in their own way they find him guilty of treason, theft and murder. The Maid plays no part, not in the sentence, nor when they hang him at dawn the next morning.

They leave Lagny and head north, towards Compiègne. The King of France has ordered the citizens of that town to surrender to their enemy, to Bedford or his vassal, 'our cousin of Burgundy'.

With polite – so very polite – regret, Compiègne has declined. Its citizens wish to remain French. That is, they wish to remain subjects of the king so recently anointed in the eyes of God at Rheims cathedral, should it please him.

It does not please him. You will surrender to Burgundy. It is our wish. The king names them all traitors for defying him. The massed armies of Burgundy grow by the day and the townsfolk are stocking up on powder and shot. This is the next Orléans, and if the Maid wants to win fortune and favour for her mercenary troop, if the Maid wishes to crush Bedford and make France wholly French, then Compiègne is the place to be.

CHAPTER FORTY-THREE

ORLÉANS,
Thursday, 27 February 2014
08.30

A T THE STAKEOUT IN the northern ghetto, neither Garonne nor Rollo has any idea that Cheb Yasine left their care earlier in the morning. Both are suitably chastened by the news that he has been to visit Picaut and returned under their noses, but their being chastened doesn't plug the gap in their surveillance.

Picaut calls in Sylvie and the team begins to set up ways they can watch more closely.

'Things may be bad, but if he starts wreaking vengeance on Christelle Vivier, the past few weeks will look like a holiday. Do I make myself clear? I want to know when he picks his nose, when he kisses his kids, when he writes his emails. And I want to know what he's telling his people.'

Rollo says, 'If Patrice taps their emails, we could—'

This is dangerous: even the sound of his name makes her guts roil. 'Patrice is working on the unsolved ciphers. He'll be back on stream tomorrow. Today, we use old-fashioned policing.'

Picaut takes Sylvie with her to visit the priest. She feels the heat of Garonne's gaze on her back as she leaves.

The drive west proves, as nothing else has done, that the press really are leaving her alone. In Cléry Picaut parks outside the basilica's northern entrance, leaving Sylvie in the car.

'Watch the priest's house. Let me know who comes in, who goes out.'

'Are you going to be safe on your own?'

'Cinq-Mars is dying of throat cancer. He can barely stand up. If I can't handle him, it's time to find a new job.'

Inside, the basilica Notre Dame at Cléry-Saint-André is deserted, as it has been on every visit she has made.

She has the phone number the priest wrote on his card the day before. On the third ring, he answers.

'Cinq-Mars.' The last shreds of life have left his voice. If a ghost could speak, this is how it would sound. Picaut takes a breath, makes herself look around at the grey stone, the hideous marble tomb just inside the entrance.

To the listening hush, she says, 'Prosecutor Ducat sends his best regards. Shall I come to your house to arrest you? Or would you rather meet me at the basilica where you can start telling me the truth?'

He stalls just long enough for her to think she's lost him, then says, 'I'll be there in five minutes.'

She waits.

Sylvie sends a text.

PRIEST ON HIS WAY. HE LIVES OPPOSITE. CAN'T SEE ANYONE ELSE.

Picaut lingers by the tomb that is a copy of a copy of the one Louis XI made for himself before he died.

Louis XI.

In English: 11. Picaut feels that singular sensation of

pieces coming together, of a blurred image coming into focus. She is thinking more clearly this morning than she has done for months. She doesn't have a whole picture, but she has at least a forward step, which is better than nothing. It's gloriously, magnificently better than nothing and she wants to share it. She thumbs open her phone and writes a text to Patrice.

lii = Louis XI?

'Can I help you, Capitaine?' The priest's footsteps sound like feather-fall. He comes up behind her, slim as his own shadow; a knife-edge of a man, with translucent skin to match his voice. His eyes have sunk into his head and his hair looks as if it is falling out with every step he takes.

He is carrying something in both hands and for a brief, charged moment she thinks it's a gun, but he moves into the light and it becomes a flask, from which foul-scented steam rises.

He smiles crookedly. 'Chinese herbs have to be taken to a particularly rigid timetable. And yes, before you ask, they taste every bit as bad as they smell.'

'I thought your God disapproved of anything unFrench and unChristian?'

'Not according to our new pope. Now, we recognize that what God makes He cannot despise.'

'But you're not in any hurry to meet Him in person, your God?'

'He will call me when He needs me. Until then, I have a duty to remain where I can do His work. Why are you smiling?'

'I was wishing my father were still alive. He'd have enjoyed you.'

'Do I take it we won't meet in the hereafter?'

'At least one of you will be wildly disappointed if you do.'

He does his best to show amusement. 'My life is doubtless the lesser for having missed him. And perhaps what comes next will surprise us all. I spend rather more time considering the possibilities of this than I may have done in my youth.'

'And do you spend time considering how obstructing the police makes the world a better place?'

'Capitaine Picaut, I have not lied to you.'

'You haven't told me the whole truth.'

'I have told you the two things you need to know: I did not kill Iain Holloway. I don't know who did.'

'But you do know why. You know that what he found cost him his life?'

She waits. He looks down, looks away, looks back at her. 'This is possible, yes.'

'Something he found here, in your basilica. Something to do with Louis XI?'

'Yes.'

She waits. He waits. At length, 'You are going to have to tell me what it was.'

Father Cinq-Mars studies the floor a moment, sweeps it cleaner with his foot. 'You are aware, I imagine, of the Nuremberg defence?'

Picaut leans back against the wall, arms folded. 'I'm surprised that a priest wants to draw parallels between his Church and Nazi Germany.'

'Which, of course, I do not. And yet, however unseemly, there is one notable similarity: I am under orders and they constrain what I can tell you.'

'No.' Picaut moves to stand directly in front of him. 'They don't. The Church does not have authority over civil law, as any number of recent child abuse cases in any number of countries should have taught you. You can tell me here, or you can tell me in custody, but you *will* tell me. Unless you'd rather I went directly to the bishop? Assuming he's the one giving the orders?'

'Unfortunately,' his cavernous eyes give the lie to the word, 'you can't.'

'I think you'll find there is very little I cannot—'

'The bishop has just been made a cardinal. He is at the consistory in Rome. He was summoned last week by the holy father and he left twenty-four hours before Iain Holloway met his demise. Unless you wish to issue a summons to the pope, you will have to make do with me until the end of this week.'

Which is exceptionally convenient, except that even Picaut, atheist and daughter of an atheist, does not believe the Church would make a man a cardinal simply to get him out of France.

'So then . . .'

He studies the floor again and when he looks up he is older, in greater pain, infinitely more weary. 'Capitaine Picaut, I am a man for whom each moment is precious. What can I do that will persuade you to leave me in peace?'

'You can tell me – in detail, missing nothing – why Iain Holloway came here and why he left in such a hurry. You can tell me what he found that led to his death, because whoever cared enough to kill him is very likely also lighting the fires that are destroying Orléans, and I would like to find out who it is before anyone else is burned to death.'

He ponders a moment, as if asking the questions of his god, and then gestures to the pews. She wants to know what answers he heard, but all he says is, 'Shall we sit?'

'You may. I prefer to stand. It's easier to move fast if I have to.'

He eases himself down on aching joints. When he looks

up at her, a small smile lights his face. 'Do you enjoy living in this state of heightened awareness?'

Nobody has ever asked her this, but the answer comes readily, and not altogether surprisingly.

'Of course.' This is why she does this job, because it keeps her at the edge of herself.

'Well then . . .' He makes himself comfortable, sips at his herbal concoction. 'You are a professional, and this is your job, so it will come as no surprise when I tell you that Iain Holloway has an international reputation as a man who can build a face on to skulls of great age, even those that are incomplete.'

'And you have Louis XI, who ended the Hundred Years War, and next year is the anniversary of Agincourt, that war's most famous battle. Did he offer to come to you or did you invite him?'

'Do you know, that is one question you would have to ask the bishop? I only know that he arrived, and I was instructed to render him every service. I was not—'

'You didn't know you were dying.'

'I thought I might not be, which is not quite the same. At any rate, Iain Holloway quite evidently had the artistry, perhaps one might say the compassion, that computer programs lack. We wished him to create for us the face of Louis XI, the king who rebuilt our basilica, who rescued it from desolation and destruction. As you so rightly say, the anniversary of a certain battle is nearly upon us and we are required in these times of austerity to do what we can to attract interest to our church. You are observant. You can see that we would benefit from some . . . largesse.'

It certainly could. With necessary tact, she says, 'It's not quite the cathedral.'

'Indeed not.' His smile is soft and sad. 'So: Iain Holloway came with a reputation for making a success of partial remains, of bodies whose constituent parts may have been mislaid, perhaps mixed up with others of a different . . .' He coughs, drily, and recovering, loses himself in spitting into a handkerchief.

Gently, Picaut says, 'Dr Holloway can reunite a person with himself?'

'Indeed. Or herself. It is a singular skill. As I mentioned on your last visit, the tomb that stands behind us is not the original and the bones of the man to whom it is dedicated no longer lie within it.

'Over the years, they have been moved often to preserve them and each movement took its toll. Bones became separated, skeletons broke apart and were mixed with others of unknown origin. I had done my best ahead of time to gather those parts that I believed all came from the same individual.'

'They didn't?'

'Capitaine Picaut, please let me tell this in my own way. I am endeavouring to tell the truth as you require it while maintaining my oath and this is not entirely easy. I presented him with the pieces I believed should be together – a cranium, a jaw, bits of a spine – and Dr Holloway went to work with an enthusiasm that carried him through the first day. On the second, he ran aground on what we might call aesthetic issues.'

'The king was not who you wanted him to be? Or the bones weren't from the king at all?'

'They were definitely the king, just that . . .' He taps his fingers to his lips. 'They say a picture is worth a thousand words, and in this case a model of a dead king's head may save you and me time we can both ill afford to waste. Come.'

He leads her back to the small chapel on the left by the main door. At first it looks empty, but there, in the dim space behind the door, is a clutter of discarded boxes, amongst which a drape of black cotton covers something that stands at chest height.

'This?'

'Indeed. If you will take off the cover?'

Wide black eyes, polished dome, depth markers dotted about and fleshed with plasticized muscle. The orbits are here, surrounding glass eyes with a wide brown iris, and the firm lines around a mouth, the beginnings of a cheek. For a moment she thinks she's found another key to the puzzle, but this is not the skull in Iain Holloway's picture; it's too clean, too whole, too white.

'This is the king?'

'It is.'

He is not an appealing man. Picaut turns him towards the poor light from the windows. The glass eyes are friendly enough, but they are caught beneath an unbecoming frown that is not remotely enhanced by the rings of skinless muscle that surround them. The nose is of unseemly length, and the chin vanishes back into the larynx. He is not finished, by any means, but there is enough to see that Louis XI, the Provident, was not a man of beauty.

Aesthetic issues indeed.

Tentatively, she says, 'Good looks were clearly not a pre-requisite to successful kingship in the Middle Ages.'

'Indeed not.' Father Cinq-Mars smiles thinly. 'Not a single one of the eye-witness accounts of the time suggests to us that Louis was beautiful by any measure. This is not necessarily a defect; even today, few men are truly beautiful and those in power often least so. But as Iain Holloway brought our late king to life, it seemed to us both that by contemporary standards, where all judgements are made on external signs, Louis was beginning to look at the very least mendacious. He has, as you can see, a long nose and a weak chin and he looks, as Dr Holloway said, like the kind of man who would rip the eyes from your head and sell them back to you for money you no longer had. He asked if I wished him to exert a judicious "sleight of hand" that might restore some sense of dignity to our king, at the expense, perhaps, of verisimilitude.'

'That doesn't sound like the man I am coming to know. He wasn't a liar.'

'Nevertheless, he had a generous spirit, you must have learned that of him. And he wished us to celebrate the greatness of our past. Louis XI achieved great things, of that I have no doubt; France came to wholeness under him. After the madness of his grandfather and the craven behaviour of his father, he was a king we could all respect. It is to our regret that the present day is so shallow as to see only the surface. So yes, Iain Holloway offered us a small white lie. A shorter nose, a better chin, a skull not so domed, more generous eyes.'

Enough work has been done that it is possible to picture the improvement. The king will not become another Luc, not even a Patrice, but— Think of something else. Think of Iain Holloway, burned, and why it might have happened?

'Did you accept his offer?'

The priest pulls a face. 'It is not within my power to accept such a thing. I told him that I must consult with the bishop.'

'And the bishop was being made a cardinal at the consistory in Rome?'

'Not then, no. But he was not immediately available. We found ourselves with time to spare and, as I am sure you already know, the devil finds work for idle hands.'

He pauses.

Picaut has nothing to say. She fails to imagine either this man or Iain Holloway colluding in evil.

The priest continues more slowly now, as if the memory adds to his pain. 'Dr Holloway, finding this abundance of time on his hands, offered to build the face of Queen Charlotte without charge. We believed, you understand, that her body lay with that of the king, her husband. She was not acclaimed a great beauty, but still, it would have added a feminine touch. It took us some time to find her; the bones of which this church has charge were not all in the same place. If you look down there, to the left of the king's plinth . . .'

The box is old and scruffy and has seen use for other things. It smells of mildew and dust. Inside, a second skull rests on an identical square wooden base, but there is no plastic rod holding it aloft, rather a web of fine wires that secure it in place, or perhaps they hold it together. It's hard to tell which, but either way time has not left to posterity a great deal of Charlotte, queen of France.

Gingerly, Picaut carries the skull down towards the altar. It is barely intact; at some point it has been split through the nose and the left half is largely missing, with only a few teeth remaining in either jaw.

This, too, is emphatically not the one from Iain Holloway's encoded email. It occurs to Picaut that the priest has lied at least once and she holds the evidence in her hands.

'You told Monique Susong that you'd burned the bones on which Iain Holloway was working.'

He meets her gaze, wide-eyed. 'How could I burn such as these? They are our heritage.'

So who did you burn?

He is still not telling all of the truth; Picaut can hear a rush in the valleys of his voice, but over the years she has learned that if she lets those who lie to her go their own way, she learns more than if she tries to force them to follow her own sense of truth. She sets the latest skull on the floor beside the king.

'Did Iain Holloway say this was the queen of France?'

The priest looks at her aslant. 'You think perhaps he did not?'

'If he did, he was a great deal less competent than you believed him to be. This is a man's skull.'

'Very good. Very good indeed. Someone has taught you well. Your father, perhaps? Well, anyway, someone good.' The priest folds his hands. 'So I will tell you that no, he did not say it was the queen of France. He laughed a little and then was kind and broke to me gently the news that I held in my hands the skull of a man who had died in his dotage, when what we sought was a woman who had died in childbed in her early middle years. To the best of my knowledge, the king and his supposed wife have lain in close proximity for nearly four centuries. I was not proud of this.'

Father Cinq-Mars drains the last of his herbal mixture, swallows against an evident wish to gag, and sets his flask between the two skulls.

'The prospect that we might have lost Charlotte was unconscionable, and so we proceeded to search with some fervour through all the remains in our possession, looking for a woman who died in her thirties, of slight build, brought to bed of many children. If you will now take the lid from the box on the right, I can show you what we found.'

She lifts the lid from the box and looks again for the skull in Iain Holloway's picture. She does not find it.

She does, though, find the skull of a woman of slight build; her skull has teeth missing, and signs of rodent damage.

'This is the queen?' She is back with the priest.

'Dr Holloway believed so. The age and build are right, so I am told.'

She lays the skull back in the box. Around it is a collection of other bones. Some are fighting men, knights. She knows the thickening of the long bones, the angles of the femoral

403

heads, the specific arthritis of knee and hip that her father taught her in her teens, when she still found his obsession charming. 'What did Iain Holloway make of these?'

'He was like a child in a confiserie. Most of the day was taken up with sorting the bones. By the evening, he believed he could identify six distinct individuals, one of which is this woman of slight build who died in her thirties and is, we earnestly believe, Queen Charlotte. Among them, however, was one other woman, and she nearly twice the age Charlotte had attained by her death.'

Picaut looks back into the box. There are three skulls, all of them male. Her palms prickle. 'She isn't here?'

'She is not.'

'You burned her?'

'I did.'

'Why?'

'The Nuremberg defence, Capitaine Picaut: I was told to. Why, I do not know. If Iain Holloway told me the truth, it is because he believed he had found the mortal remains of Marguerite de Valois, who was—'

'The woman my father thought was the Maid.' Her mouth is dry. Blood surfs in her ears. 'My father sent him here to find them.'

'But it can't be . . .'

'Obviously. But my father had death threats for simply suggesting she wasn't a helpless virginal peasant, so . . . Did someone believe him?'

'I don't know. Iain Holloway spent his last morning here – the Friday – taking pictures and measurements and talking to himself. By noon, he demanded to speak to the bishop, who was preparing to leave for Rome. They spoke for an hour. Their voices were raised almost from the start. Whatever you choose to believe, I am not a dishonest man: I did not try to listen, but I could not keep from overhearing the accusations of calumny and destruction and the dishonour of France and the Church, the potential influence on our electoral process.'

'Who else but the Maid? Even then, the *Front* had taken her as their mascot.'

'In retrospect, you may be right, but I didn't know that at the time, I swear it.'

'What happened?'

'Iain stormed out of the church. I was summoned immediately by the bishop and told that the relevant bones must be burned and that all "interference" must stop. I was told also that Dr Iain Holloway was leaving to return to his homeland and would not sully France with his presence again.'

'And you really did burn the bones? For God's sake, why?'

'Please, let us not revisit the concept of authority. Some orders I must follow to the letter and this was one of them. Do you really need to ask why that is? You have already pointed out what happened to your father. It is less than a century since she was made a saint, a heroine of France: our greatest, most beloved, most widely known woman. We need her to be who she is. As, of course, do the various political parties who have claimed the Maid as their own. If you are looking for your murderers, there are many beyond the Church who should be your first—' The priest's head snaps round. 'Who is the young lady at the door?'

'Sylvie. She's one of mine.' There's a rhythm to her footfall that spells urgency and distress. Picaut reaches the doorway, running. Sylvie meets her; panic lights her eyes.

'Not another fire?'

'No. Cheb Yasine has disappeared again. And nobody can find Christelle Vivier.'

CHAPTER FORTY-FOUR

'I'LL FUCKING SKIN THEM ALIVE.'
'Who?'

'Whoever is leaking everything useful to the fucking press.'

That Picaut had thought the press frenzied before was, she understands now, a measure of her own naivety.

Battling her way through the mob that is blocking her route to the front doors of the police station, she discovers that however scared they may be of the recent developments, they still have deadlines to meet and editors to please and that nothing will keep them at bay now that some idiot has seen fit to leak two facts: first, that Cheb Yasine has slipped his surveillance and his current location is unknown; second, that Christelle Vivier has disappeared and may be about to reclaim her role as the new Maid of Orléans, particularly if she is found dead.

If she is found dead in a fire, there will be no doubt at all: she will be a martyr to Jaish al Islam and her party will reap a landslide in the polls. This shouldn't be Picaut's problem, but she has made a promise and so it is, and it is here, in the form of her soon-to-be-ex-husband.

'Inès, the polls open on *Sunday*. If Christelle's been kidnapped, either they'll cancel the election or she'll get a sympathy vote that'll leave the rest of us in single figures. You have to find her.'

Luc is a wreck. His skin, once so bronze, so smooth, is blotched a muddy red around his eyes. He looks dishevelled, which only adds to the surreal nature of the day.

Worse, the press pack no longer respects him as it did. Men and women with microphones and earpieces jostle him just as they jostle Garonne and Rollo and, heaven forbid, Prosecutor Ducat in their effort to get to Picaut, to get a picture, to get her, above all, to offer some pithy sound-bite that they can file for the next bulletin, the next blog, the next report.

Ducat is thunderously angry. Truly, the newshounds have no idea what wrath he can call down upon them, or how close he is to doing so. Actually, Picaut hasn't much idea what wrath he can call down either, only that it will be terrible and she would dearly like him to get on with it. Now, in fact, would be perfect, so that she can get into the station and talk to her team and make some kind of plan.

She reaches the door, which falls open before she can push it. She half expects Patrice to be holding it for her. But no, it's Rémi from Drugs.

She feels her face tighten. She can be thunderous herself if she has to. 'If you fucking told them that Cheb Yasine—'

'Wait.' He holds up his hands, warding her off. 'I've called everybody in. I thought you'd need help.' His face has grown thin. His eyes dodge and weave, never settling in one place. He's the leak: she would put money on it. 'Peace, OK? We can't let them crush us like this.' It's an admission and an apology, all in one. Today, clearly, is a day in which the normal order of things is exploded. He thrusts a hand out. 'OK?'

'OK.' They shake. His palm is damp. He is as scared as he looks. She feels her own small lurch of terror. 'Who else is missing?'

'Six Algerians from Marseille; the one who visited Yasine yesterday and five others who drove up last night and arrived this morning. They're his hit team. We have no proof, nothing that Ducat' – he nods towards the door where the Prosecutor is holding back the tide – 'would let us use in court. But he's planning revenge for his cousin. Of that I have no doubt.'

'*Shit.*' It's ten o'clock in the morning and already Picaut feels as if she's lived the day twice over. 'If he takes on the *Front*, we'll have war on the streets.' She pulls out her phone. 'Get everyone to my office. Not only do we have to fix this, we have to be seen to be fixing it.'

Her office is three flights up. She runs up the back stairs, avoiding the elevators, which are full of listening ears. She rings Cheb Yasine as she goes. Call it intuition, a stab in the dark: it works.

'Capitaine Picaut, what can I do for you?' He's in a car, driving with the windows open; she can hear the traffic noise and a radio poorly tuned to an Arabic station.

'Tell me where you are. Tell me you're not about to use imported Algerian muscle to launch a war on the *Front National*. Particularly, tell me where I can find Christelle Vivier.'

'You have lost her?' His voice is stripped of its humour. He is not a stupid man. He can work out the implications of this.

She says, 'You need to listen to some of the French-language stations. The press are already making her a martyr, dead at the hands of Algerian Islamists. The *Front National* are gaining a point per hour in the rolling polls.'

He doesn't answer, but he doesn't hang up. She hears clipped, rapid Arabic, a quiet curse, the distress of tyres cornering hard.

He says, 'I don't know where she is, nor do I wish to. Whatever is happening to her is none of my doing. I apologize if I upset Lieutenants Garonne and Rollo by leaving, but you must understand that I am an innocent man and unless Prosecutor Ducat has invited you to press charges I am not, in fact, required to let you, him or anyone else know where I am going and what I am doing. Which is not outside the law. On that I give you my word.'

'The Algerians from Marseille?'

'Are here to make sure I live to see tomorrow. I advise you to find people of similar calibre who will ensure your own continued good health.'

He hangs up. She reaches the third floor. Rémi has excelled himself: every serving officer not currently on sick leave, maternity leave or abroad is here, in the open-plan area around her fish tank of an office. Patrice is the only one absent, but then Patrice is sleeping. She hopes he is sleeping. There must be limits to how much Red Bull anyone can drink and stay sane.

There's no room in Picaut's office so her vastly expanded team is in this outer room, which has space for five times this number. They part to let her through, waiting in silence, as if she has all the answers. She climbs on to a chair, the better to be seen and heard.

'Cheb Yasine is near the main railway station, I heard the station announcement on his phone. He's driving a large vehicle, probably his Toyota Hilux: there's one registered to his name that he keeps in the garages two blocks from his house. If he has Christelle Vivier, then he knows we're on to him: he'll act soon. I want traffic patrols out looking for his car now. Follow him, don't take him in without word from me.'

The Traffic Department is eight men strong. She favours them with an encompassing nod and they drag their gloves from their pockets, check their phones and leave. She turns her attention to the rest.

'Right: the first thing you need to know is that Iain Holloway thought he had found the mortal remains of the Maid. We all know that's impossible, but I have a priest who thinks this is the reason he died – and he may be right. Whoever is doing this, these three things are linked: the fires, Iain Holloway's death and now Christelle Vivier's disappearance. We cannot rule out her own campaign manager, he has form. So who has the details of Christelle's last known movements?'

'Me.' That's Rollo, who lost Cheb Yasine and is now over-compensating. 'She had a breakfast meeting with Troy Cordier, who is her campaign manager, and as you say may now be in the frame. They were at the Jean-Jacques Rousseau Hotel near the cathedral and then they separated.

'Cordier stayed there to coordinate today's photo-calls. Christelle's car picked her up from the front of the hotel at eight forty-five and was due to take her to a children's day care nursery, ETA nine twenty-five, ready for a photo-op with the kids at half past. When she didn't turn up the nursery called Cordier, who sent his own men out to look for her. He didn't call us until six minutes past ten. He says he's personally driven her route twice and there's no sign of Christelle or her car.'

'Right.' Picaut presses her thumbs to the bridge of her nose in an effort to find clear thought. 'We need a car of our own to check the route. Look for signs of a shunt: broken headlight glass, tyre marks on the road. You know the kind of thing. Rollo, Garonne?'

They nod and prepare.

'Sylvie has run a trace on her mobile phone and that of the driver. They both switched off soon after they left the hotel so there's no help there unless they switch back on again, in which case we'll be notified of the time and the place. I want all the news channels to shut the fuck up. Given that they won't, the next best thing would be for them to put out an all-points appeal asking anyone who may have seen her to call into the station. Rémi, can you get someone on it? Thank you.'

The phone rings on her desk. Sylvie picks it up for her. 'It's Éric Masson. About a photograph of a skull?'

'I'll call him back.

'I want everybody else to go to the hotel and fan out from there. Go in your cars, and keep in touch with everyone else. The chances of finding her walking the streets are close to nil, but we need a massive police presence out there being seen to be looking. There's an election in three days and whoever wins will own us. If it's Christelle Vivier's replacement, whoever that is, from her grandfather down, we don't want to be the ones who sat on our backsides while she was being burned alive. Sitreps every fifteen minutes. No lunch breaks, no coffee breaks, absolutely no smoking. If I see one picture on the twenty-four-hour news of one officer taking one break, that officer will be out of a job, is that clear? Go.'

The room empties with gratifying speed. Soon, only Picaut and Sylvie are left. 'What are you going to do?' Sylvie asks. 'Besides talking your husband down from whatever heights of anxiety he's scaling.'

'Fuck him, he's got Lise for that. And Uncle Landis to talk him back up again. I'm going to go to the hotel and talk to Troy "I have a holiday house in Switzerland and a penthouse flat in Hampstead" Cordier, and see what he knows.'

Somewhere in her desk is a packet of chewing gum she keeps stored for the days when she's not going to be able to stop to eat. She keeps a tidy desk, but the gum isn't there. She's easing the drawer out, ready to tip it upside down, when the first phone call comes in to Sylvie.

The gum is in the back of the second drawer and it's a lot newer than the one she put there. This one isn't nearly past its use-by date. The chances of anyone's stealing it are nil, except for Garonne. So he's been 'borrowing' it and replacing it. She's weighing it in her palm when Sylvie comes to find her, office phone in hand.

'It's Troy Cordier from the Hôtel Jean-Jacques Rousseau. Christelle Vivier's driver just called in to say they're at the school, and why are there no press there to make the most of the photo-op?'

'*What?*' Something sharp and hot detonates behind Picaut's eyes. 'If this whole thing has been a hoax—'

'It's not. That's the thing. The school they were supposed to go to is south of the river, not far from the hospital. The one they're actually at is halfway to Tours. The driver swears he went to the address on his itinerary. He says his satnav was preprogrammed. They're there now. They want their photo-op. Do we let them call in the press?'

'Fuck.' Picaut wrings her hands across her face. 'I don't think we can stop them. No, wait, yes we can. We have to. Tell them Prosecutor Ducat is already dealing with the press and he'll make appropriate arrangements. I'll call Ducat. He can make it bloody clear that we were not the ones to fuck up on this. You start calling in the teams. As soon as we're done, you and I are going to the Hôtel Jean-Jacques to have a serious word with Troy Cordier. Either something's gone catastrophically wrong with his communications or he's trying something really, really clever that we need to stop before it starts. Or someone – maybe him – is trying to distract us from something more important. Which means we must not be distracted. I want a maximum police presence through every part of Orléans. Get everyone who can walk or drive out on the streets. If there's going to be another fire, I want us there before the smoke reaches knee height.'

'Are you still going to see Troy Cordier?'

'Absolutely. And you're coming too.'

CHAPTER FORTY-FIVE

Compiègne,
22 May 1430

The Maid is in Compiègne.

The city has not yet surrendered to Burgundy and so to England, and shows no sign of doing so, but the king has not yet gone so far as to send his armies against them: Bedford is doing that well enough. The Maid is among those who have come to the aid of her countrymen.

She is not alone. Over winter, her reputation has spread to the far corners of the continent. The pope in Rome has written his approval. The Scots adore her. The people of Italy are entranced.

More important than these, are the men at arms who are daily coming to join her. Now that she is a free agent, a mercenary captain in her own right, with successes to her credit, they are flooding to the plains of Compiègne to fight beneath her banner.

Only those expressly forbidden by the king have stayed away. D'Alençon is not here, nor La Hire, but there are amongst her retainers, knights of almost equal calibre. The way things are going, by summer Bedford will face an army of a size that will make last year's purge of the Loire valley look like a pack of unruly schoolboys on an afternoon's jaunt.

He has therefore abandoned his assault on Rheims. He will have to take it back if he is ever going to anoint the snivelling boy for whom he is regent, but nobody will believe that God might anoint two kings and just now, Charles VII is monarch in the eyes of God, brought there by a Maid who works at God's right hand. If Bedford wants his nephew to wear the French crown, he must destroy the man whom the Maid has elevated, and to do that, he must destroy the Maid.

Lacking the help of Tod Rustbeard, he has abandoned subterfuge, and is resorting to a bludgeoning violence. He has given the Duke of Burgundy every one of his field guns. The scouts say that the assaulting force has five large bombards the size of Rifflard or bigger, two veuglaires, one large and one small, uncountable numbers of culverins of all sizes and two engines which hurl rock overhand, and can kill. All of these he has brought to bear on a city which once thought itself impregnable.

Compiègne is well defended. The River Oise is its moat. The walls are a mile in circumference and thick enough to withstand a sustained bombardment. Towers and turrets keep watch on all sides and the drawbridge works with buttered smoothness. There is only one bridge. It has a gatehouse at one end and a boulevard at the other.

The city has a new governor, Sieur Guillaume de Flavy, a favourite of the king, recently appointed. A big, hard man, he has a history behind him of bloody battles, feuds and scores settled by violence. He is also the personal friend and confidant of Regnault de Chartres, archbishop of Rheims.

Tomas doesn't like the feel of this. He didn't like it when he heard de Flavy had been appointed, and he didn't like it any more, when de Chartres himself turned up to join the Maid's company.

Over the past ten days, the archbishop has become one of her constant companions. Nobody has suggested that he is Bedford's paid man, but everyone knows that he spent all last summer negotiating a series of pointless treaties with Burgundy that expressly prevented the Maid from assaulting Paris when she could have taken it.

In the eyes of the world, if anyone is the architect of her failure, it is Regnault de Chartres, but he claims now to have seen the error of his ways.

He no longer hates the Maid. He certainly doesn't believe she is a fraud. *Au contraire*, she is the saviour of France and it is his duty to watch over her spiritual welfare. He joined her company on the month's first day and follows her as a fawn follows a doe, nose to tail. Tomas hates it.

He is here now, in the governor's dining hall in the keep at Compiègne, where they have been brought by a sleep-dazzled chamberlain, after a day's excursion that has seen them add a hundred men to their army. It is late. Boys run for kindling and heartwood and soon the fire spits and sighs and climbs up the chimney.

Over the hearth, red light gives life to the dusty tapestries, to Moses, parting the sea; to Joseph, reading the dreams of the pharaoh; to Lazarus, rising. The Maid's company gathers close, and the archbishop closest. He stands with his arms wide, his chest turned to the flames, hogging the heat. He has mud in his hair and moss stains on his elbows. His hawk's nose is blue with the aftertaste of fear of the dark spirits that gibbered in the forest as they led their horses through; he was not happy then. He is not happy now, but warmer.

416

'I shall bid you goodnight, what's left of it.' He rolls his hands into his sleeves. As if struck by a fresh thought: 'Is there a boy with lights, perhaps? A rush light? A lantern? And someone to build up the fire in my chamber? I find I am in the heights of the tower; closer to God, but colder, I think.'

Of course. For the archbishop, anything. Boys are called, with rushes, a fire basket, tinder, kindling, logs. They troop together out of the room. The governor himself goes to fetch heated wine; for the archbishop, nothing is too much. De Chartres bows once again and departs for his chamber in the heights of the castle.

'He is gone,' says Tomas heavily. 'To work out how he can betray us.' He has thought this for days now, but this night he is sure; call it instinct, call it the shadows around the archbishop's eyes, call it an old memory, rekindled, he is not sure whence it comes, but he is certain. 'Bedford and Burgundy know too much of our movements and he is the one most likely to be telling them. If the governor is helping him, he's got it easy. If he isn't, then he has some other way of getting the information out.'

There is a brief, explosive silence.

'Guillaume de Flavy loves this city. He'll be walking his line with care, doing what de Chartres demands, and not a whit more.' Pierre d'Arc speaks, from the place beyond the firelight where he sits with his back to a wall and one knee drawn up to his chest. He is older, by far, than the day when Tomas met him by a river; a better rider, a better fighter; a man now, versed in politics, not a green country boy.

'He'll do what de Chartres tells him to do. We can't trust either of them.' That's Jean d'Aulon, the Maid's squire. He, too, has grown in the past twelve months.

A year ago, he looked shocked if a man died in his presence. Now, he would kill the archbishop with his bare hands if only someone asked it of him. He watches the Maid with naked hope in his eyes, but he knows well enough that she can't: the king is turning a blind eye to her being here. Regnault de Chartres' presence is the price.

So she does what she always does, which is to ignore the archbishop and focus on the ways by which they can assault Burgundy, and so Bedford.

Leaning on the wall by the fire, she says, 'We need to break the encirclement or they'll lock us up in a siege and the town won't hold against it. The Burgundians hold Margny under Baudot de Noyelles. Jean of Luxembourg is a couple of miles upriver at Clairoix; and Montgomery holds Venette for the English an equal distance to the south. We must take each of these if we are to break them: Margny, Clairoix, Venette, in that order.'

To d'Aulon, 'Find someone awake who knows the lie of the land and have him sent to me.'

Tomas looks across at her. He is oddly hollow, clear-headed and tired at the same time. 'It is yet night. Do you not wish to sleep, lady?' He can ask this, now; they are close enough.

'No.' She is distracted, thinking of too many things. 'Sleep will not come tonight. We must plan for tomorrow.' She leans over, taps him on the arm. 'I would go to the chapel to pray. Will you come with me?'

Of course. He would follow her into hell and back; she knows this. He follows her into the small, cold church, kneels on cold stone, mouths cold prayers to a God who may still be listening. All the while, he watches the Maid. She may be busy-headed, but she seems happy, at peace. She is fighting. She is leading men. This is what she was born for.

Later, she speaks to men d'Aulon brings to her who know the land, and they make plans: Margny, Clairoix, Venette. How to take them, and with what, and when.

*   *   *

Guns. Everywhere, the engines of war turn the air black with their powder. They punish the ears, drown the cadences of Mass. After, Tomas and the Maid go to the top of the wall and look out. D'Aulon and Pierre d'Arc follow up soon.

They have not slept, any of them. They do not need to speak now; from moment to moment Tomas knows what the Maid needs, what she wants and what he can give her.

He follows her up and they stand together atop the tower, looking south, towards the River Oise. In the meadows, the thorn blossom is out. Petals fall in snowy drifts with each cough of a gun; today, blizzards. Above, the sky is an aching, desperate blue. Already the crows gather. They taste blood on the winds of tomorrow.

From the belly of Burgundy's line, a bombard heaves and grunts. They watch the shot soar, weightless, see it break apart on the wall, see the whole wall shiver at the blow. The stone beneath their feet bucks like a bull.

Pierre d'Arc joins them. He and his brother are the least used to guns. He flinches at its power and has barely recovered before another follows, and another. Yesterday's bombardment was less than half the ferocity. He pats his hands over his ears, checking they are still attached to his head. 'They surely know you are back here, lady.'

'They do, don't they?' And how could they know that unless someone has signalled them?

Last night, Regnault de Chartres asked for a room in one of the highest towers and Tomas did not understand why. Put it down to lack of sleep and a night spent creeping through the dark trying to see where he was putting his feet; put it down to carelessness, or stupidity, but he did not think to send someone out to see if lights flickered from the casements through the last hour of darkness. This morning, though, he will wager his life that if there were no signalling lights, then a boy went willing through the postern gate with a message. An archbishop can command a particular loyalty on little more than the strength of a smile.

There is no point in laying this out. What's done is done, but she is looking at him as he looks at the tower, and there is a question in her eyes. He says, 'Lady, Regnault de Chartres remains your enemy.'

'He will betray me if he can.' She nods, smiling. Later, he remembers that smile; the grief within it.

Now, something sharp twists in his chest. He is like Jean d'Aulon. One word from her and he'd push the archbishop from the top of the tower. He asks, 'What will you do?'

'Fight. What else do I ever do? We should arm ourselves. Today, I think, will be bitter. We should break fast.'

The archbishop is in the dining hall, his hands clasped behind his back, watching the preparations with apparent fascination. He holds tight to a cloak of vair, bundled against the morning's chill. A hundred squirrels died for his comfort; their fine white belly fur glistens in stripes between the black of back and flanks. He still hugs as close to the fire as he did in the night.

The hall is lit with wax tapers ingrained with sweet oils. Their light melts in shades of blood and amber across his shoulders. Seeing the Maid enter, he tilts his head, presses one long finger to his cheek. 'My lady, cloth of gold!' He speaks like this often these days, in tedious exclamations.

As she passes, he reaches out to grasp at her chest. Were she not armoured, this would be an indecency that would require someone to call him out. Tomas, in his guise as a cleric – he will have to drop this, soon, he so very badly wants to fight – cannot touch him. D'Aulon is an optimist; this might be his chance. He raises a brow, leans his head her way. She signals him no with a shake of her head.

The archbishop seems to reach in, piercing flesh and flat

white bone, knifing through to her heart, but is only testing the fabric of her surcoat, folding it between his fingers.

De Chartres's smile is serpentine; is her sin pride or hubris? He will not say. 'Such a glory! Perhaps when you are done with the day's travails you will tell me whence it came? I might have one like it perhaps, to give to the king?'

She tilts her head. 'I will tell you now; it was a gift from the people of Rheims, for bringing their king to them for crowning. I'm sure they would happily give him a like one themselves, did they think he might have use for it.'

'Ah.' A revelation. Rheims, of which he is archbishop, is bestowing gifts upon the Maid. A hardness flickers behind his eyes. He might speak, but beyond the walls the great gun coughs again. Even here, in the heart of the citadel, they feel the tremor as the walls hold against it. Pierre d'Arc crosses himself. The archbishop does not.

The Maid tips her head towards the door. 'Perhaps you would like to go out and tell Burgundy, now, how much he needs to join with France? Then we can all go home and plant our crops and enjoy our summer in peace.'

What can he say? De Chartres's shrug is the very soul of regret. 'My lady, you know where my heart lies. Were it possible . . .'

'You would do it. Of course. And so Burgundy's obduracy must be held back by other means. We shall not let Compiègne fall. That is clear. Do you understand?'

Burgundy. Not 'my lord' or 'the duke'; she addresses him as an equal. More and more, she skates close to claiming royalty. De Chartres, always sallow, yellows to the tint of rat's urine, but her words were not for him, they were for Guillaume de Flavy, the governor, who has entered by the side door to the chamber. His, this city, his the tapestries that cover the walls – Moses, Joseph, Lazarus – his the pain of assault, redoubled because the Maid is here. He must be torn, surely, if de

Chartres is his patron, but this town is his ward? Where does his loyalty lie?

Of him, the Maid asks, 'Have your guns begun to fire back?'

'Lady, they are making dust of the enemy.' He is solid, blunt, unyielding.

She nods to him. 'Let me go to them. There are things we can do to ensure their safety.'

Under her tutelage, his men spend the day rearranging the guns of Compiègne in the way they did outside Jargeau. Three shots and move, then one and move, then two; never more than four, and no fixed rhythm: they spin a dice for the numbers and spin again if they roll a five or a six. They score several strikes against the great bombards and are happy.

In the late afternoon, with the sun lying bright and low, Tomas is sent with fresh orders to the men of the town. He summons the archers, crossbowmen, gunners and sets them about the north side of the walls and on the barges that are strung across the river.

All about, men string their bows, set foot to stirrup and load their machines of war. Bolts and arrows bristle. Strings are taut, and faces behind them. All day they have fired their guns, but they are no more comfortable with this distant killing than they are with suffering its consequences. They ache for the Maid to bring the enemy within range of a decent bowshot. At the drawbridge, the windlass girns.

Tomas calls across to Louis de Coutes. 'Make ready my lady's horse!' The other pages run to the call.

When they reach the bridge, the Maid's grey-white devil-horse is not there. 'Where's Xenophon?'

'He's lame, lady. He trod on a stone and bruised his sole.' The page holds the reins of her second horse, a dark bay courser. It is big enough and well-schooled, but it lacks the fire of devilry.

She chews her lip a moment. Tomas says, 'Lady, if you wish to remain here, we can send out my lord of—'

'No. We ride out. You may stay back if you wish.'

'Never, lady.' It stabs him, that she can still say this.

They mount. She casts her eyes over the men. They are about two hundred, all mounted, four men per lance. Above Louis de Coutes floats the fleur-de-lis in gold on white. She is gold. Her horse should be white and instead it is the colour of old blood. This isn't right.

'My dear and loyal friends.' Her voice takes flight on the still air. 'The men of Burgundy have spent all day on the guns and they are weary. They have come to skirmish in the meadows and they have taken their horses home now, with orders they be fed and watered. This is our chance to hammer them into the ground, to show Duke Philip that he dallies with France at his peril. Are you with me?'

'Aye!'

Louder. 'Are you with me?'

'Aye!'

Once more, the loudest. 'Shall we do this together?'

'*Aye!*'

On which, they sally out across the bridge of eleven arches, on to the causeway that leads across the water meadow, towards the Burgundian emplacements.

Stone chimes under shod hooves. Sun strikes helm and vambrace, breastplate and shield and lance. They are the might of France. The Maid turns to salute Guillaume de Flavy. Tomas turns with her, sees the governor's arm raise in response, sees the black and white vair of Regnault de Chartres at his side, thinks this is wrong, my Lady, my Lady, it is not right, but it is too late to speak aloud, for they are in the charge and he must set his thinking forward,

forward, steadily forward, not yet at a gallop, *mon brave*, we shall go steadily, and *there* – ahead – they have seen us! Thanks be to God, the Burgundians are coming out to meet us.

'For France!'

Once more, the devastation of hoof beats. The shimmer of armour. Here is a thicket of lances, iron points unwavering. Soon, the moment when she lowers her lance and picks her man. His shield bears crossed quarters, gules and vert, with something Tomas can't quite see – a lion, perhaps? Half the English have lions in their arms and there could easily be English knights here – on the two red quarters.

An outbreath, held, the shudder of impact, the crisp strike, the shattering of bone and flesh as the enemy's chest is crushed. Her horse gathers the force of the strike. It's not the quality of the grey-white devil-horse, but it's still one of the best on the field.

She draws clear, passes on even as the light dies from the surprised white-gone-purple face. Tomas is after her, looking down at the remains of a man newly dead. Surprise, he reads, not fear; a death so swift there is no pain. This is why they fight, the men of France, of any nation: that they might die like this, in glory, with their friends around.

He swears himself an oath that tonight, before them all, he will relinquish the cloth of his order and become again a man at arms. He may not be a knight, but he is as good as the d'Arc brothers; better.

The enemy scatters before the might of French arms and the feet of French mounts. They are run down, and again, but it matters that they not go too far into enemy territory; there lies ambush and disaster.

'Collect!'

The routed troops are running back into the rows of

whitewashed stone and timber that is Margny. The Maid's troop gathers, comes together, raises palms in breathless greeting. Nobody is lost.

Behind is a ridge of high ground; sunlight catches iron on the heights. Tomas says, 'We're being watched.' He has the sharpest sight of them all. He narrows his eyes, gains more depth. 'Four men,' he says. 'And one just gone, riding hard to the north.'

'They'll be sending for Jean de Luxembourg at Clairoix.' The Maid bends her mount round her heel, lifts it into a canter. 'Fall back. Let them come out again. We'll get in another assault before their reinforcements arrive.'

The second charge is a repeat of the first. The Maid drives Burgundy's men back to their own lines, kills a handful, cripples the morale of the rest.

'One more drive. Just one more and we'll break them!' She is joyous, a hawk loosed from the fist. She is all that any man could wish to be, to hold, to love. Tomas wants to raise her fist in his hand and shout, 'This is France! See? See! This is the true France!' God, if only d'Alençon had put aside his wife and married her . . .

Others see something different. 'Lady, we must retire.' D'Aulon is at her elbow. 'See, over there? Luxembourg's men.'

He is right. Reinforcements have come; a mounted company, riding hard. They are perhaps five minutes away; there are knights amongst them, some lances raised, some bowmen.

She says, 'We can fit in another charge. We can—'

Tomas says, 'No, lady, look to your left.' Men. They are too far away to see the colours, but they are in force, three or four hundred, perhaps, come from Venette, maybe, or somewhere else close.

'Lady . . .' Her squire dares speak against her now; out

of friendship, she has granted him that power. 'You must retire. Come back in to Compiègne.'

'No! We have them on the run. We can force them out of here. We *can*—'

But they are gone, her knights and men at arms, edging back, horses sidling across the drying causeway flags, not knowing if they are charging or retreating.

D'Aulon stays. And Louis de Coutes. And the d'Arc boys, Pierre especially. Perhaps half a dozen altogether mill around her, unwilling to leave.

'Lady, please come back.' Louis de Coutes is tugging at her reins. 'Please. They are too many. Everyone else is going back. We'll be caught out here. They want you more than anyone.' His eyes are wide with fright. 'What will it do to those inside to see you taken?'

They are off the causeway now, in the harsh, sour water meadow. Ahead are the Burgundian forces, behind and to their left are the English who could hail from anywhere within a five-mile radius. There's enough noise here now to draw the crows from the sky, and the carrion feeders of Bedford's army are hungrier than crows.

From entirely the wrong direction, Tomas hears a voice he knows bark an order. The tone is unmistakable. He does not hear the content, but terror fills it for him. Frantic, he spins his horse. He has been looking outward for the enemy, towards the English, the Luxembourgers, the Burgundians, but of course the enemy is behind: Regnault de Chartres, spilling poison in the ear of the governor.

'Lady, they are closing the bridge! *Jehanne!*'

Never has he said this name. She spins to the sound. And so she, too, sees that at the bridge into Compiègne the archers are hopping off their boats; the men with guns are already in through the drawbridge. Men are waving their arms, their bows, their guns.

Somewhere high up is Guillaume de Flavy. They feel his words, if they cannot hear. Hurry, hurry, for the archbishop has ordered me to close the gates and he outranks me as the sun outranks a candle. I cannot go against his order. Hurry, before it is too late. Only come in, Lady. Come *in*.

The Burgundians are running up out of Margny now, scenting a possible victory after a day of losses. Men at arms converge on all sides. So it's a fighting retreat.

'Lady, you must—'

'I must see my men back safely inside. I will not leave those who fight for me outside to die while I run for safety: a captain's first conscience is for the men.'

'Body of Christ, woman. They will *burn* you.'

'They have to catch me first.' She grins. His heart will break. 'Go in, Tomas. I'll follow.' She glances across at her page. 'Take the standard back in.'

De Coutes will not move. 'No, lady, I will stay with—'

'Go! For your mother's sake. For the loss of your brother, please go.' He would stay but how can he when she invokes these two? The look he throws her is all pain, but he turns about and the Maid switches her attention to Tomas. 'You too. Go.'

'Lady, I will not—'

'I order it. If de Chartres wants me dead, I will not give him your life too. You know enough, now, to make sure France is made whole. Besides, you can't fight, not as you are. I won't have you hamper me. *Go!*'

He does not have the will to stand against her. He just . . .. doesn't. He turns away and the last he sees is d'Aulon and the man who is not her brother, Pierre d'Arc, who has not turned his horse, but is grinning savagely, swinging his sword, screaming, 'Come on, you bastards! We're not beaten yet!'

It's not so far back to the bridge, and not far across it, ten

427

arches, eleven, to the gate. Guillaume de Flavy is there, grey-white, shaken. Whatever de Chartres has said or done, the governor cares for the Maid. 'Why doesn't she come in? I have to close the gate. I *have* to. Burgundy has said he will burn us all: men, women, children. I can't let them in. It will be carnage. Why does she not hurry?'

'She wants to see the men all safe.'

'Who's left?'

'I'm the last, almost.' But he's not, there are still half a dozen out there, dallying, not wanting to be seen to leave her; men who don't understand how to take an order. Men with more – or less? – courage than he has.

Guillaume de Flavy is weeping, but his hand, once raised, falls. A scream of rope and iron. A dozen heartbeats, thirty, sixty, and the bridge is up and it's too late for Tomas to change his mind, or he'd throw off his habit and run out naked, sword in one hand, shield in the other. He cannot stay at the gate. He runs up to the top of the wall, three steps at a time. Bile fills his mouth, stings his teeth.

She is riding. Men are coming for her. She is bright gold against their verminous, mouldering dull-mud-greys and greens. He watches as she stands her lance upright in the soft soil, takes up her axe and draws the sword she took from Franquet d'Arras.

They go to join her, left and right, good men on both sides: d'Aulon and Pierre d'Arc. Good, but not the best. She holds her horse – God, but he wishes it was the devil-beast; Xenophon would keep her safe – one last heartbeat. A nod to her companions. She lets Tomas go.

She is free. As nowhere else and no other time, this is the *mêlée à outrance* that every knight lives for. He sees her released from the cares of captaincy. Here is life: an open meadow with knights and men at arms and archers and pikemen and all she has to do is kill. And survive.

And yet, they are so many. Why does she not turn and run? They are three hundred against her and she is lost in the sea of them, striking left and right, as men come at her stirrup. They know her. Their cries carry on the still wind. The Maid! The Maid! The Witch!

The words float up to the heights of Compiègne, to Tomas de Segrave, weeping. Her sword sings as she slices down at the hands that grasp her. Her axe is the chorus, iron on iron, on cloth, on mail. Her horse dances, spirit made flesh, but it is not the best.

A knight comes at her, full-breasted, face on, mace and shield. She lifts the horse and the knight's face dissolves in a plash of blood. She spins away, slash, chop, kick, courbette, capriole, kick out behind. Another man falls away, but there are more, coming on either side.

'Come back. Lady, come back.' Tomas is on stone, but he is on the field. He is shouting, and she is not listening. He will not believe she cannot hear.

'It's the fucking bitch! Get her!'

Someone tugs at her arm on the left. She wheels the horse, scatters men like spilled apples, cuts out and down, swings back, one in front, a swordsman with a great-sword swinging, right, and she spins, and there's a hand grasping her doublet to the right: 'I've got her! Get that fucking horse!' and hands laid on her bridle and the horse is not evil, it does not kill for the temerity of touching it, and she wrenches it round and there is a moment when she might break free and then she is sailing back and off and—

'Jehanne!'

'She's down! Get her!'

Pierre d'Arc's round valley vowels: 'Bastards, get back! Leave her be! Get off! Get *off*!' and her horse, somewhere, grunting in pain, because men are wrenching his bridle and

429

a single man's face looming over her, 'You're mine; do you yield?'

'*Jehanne!*'

Tomas is running now, down the stairs. Forget the bridge; there are other ways out of this godforsaken place. He has both knives in his hands. He is scrabbling at the gate. Big arms wrench him from behind.

'No, Tomas. Don't go. She wouldn't want it.'

Guillaume de Flavy was at Rheims when the king was crowned. He fought the English at Rouen, at the relief of Saint-Martin-le-Gaillard. He is as much a knight as Poton de Xaintrailles, as La Hire. And he is weeping as much as Tomas. But he will not open the gates of his town when there are four, five hundred Burgundians outside and more pouring on to the field every moment. 'Don't go. Do not go. I will not let you go.'

Tomas does not see her taken. Does not see the moment when she kneels and yields her blade. He is on the wrong side of four inches of oak, on his knees, howling.

And then he stands, and by the quiet inside, and the cheering outside, he knows there is nothing left to do.

Except one thing.

'Where is Regnault de Chartres?' His knives are in his hands. His blood, charged and ready. For this, he has the courage. 'Where is he?'

Nobody knows.

They search and they search and he is not found. Regnault de Chartres is no longer in the town. While the Maid was being taken on the field beyond Compiègne, the Archbishop of Rheims made his exit. Nobody doubts that he has safe passage, that he will journey through the English and Burgundian lines untouched.

'What will you do now, Tomas?' Guillaume de Flavy is tight with cold and fear. He knows where the blame for this will lie. And that Burgundy will not stop until he has punished Compiègne for its harbouring of the Maid. On both sides, now, his name is a curse.

'I will go to the king. We have Talbot, Suffolk, Scales languishing at our pleasure. We have half the English nobility in our prisons and she has taken them. They will make an exchange for her. They must. They cannot refuse.'

CHAPTER FORTY-SIX

ORLÉANS,
Thursday, 27 February 2014
11.15

THE HÔTEL JEAN-JACQUES ROUSSEAU, campaign centre
for the *Front National* in Orléans, is situated a block east
of the cathedral in a street whose northern end dates back to
the fifteenth century.

The hotel is the first of the late-forties buildings south
of the bomb line. Until recently, it was tidy but tired; a
reminder of post-war privations. A post-millennial EU grant
has recently transformed it into one of the most sought-after
venues in Orléans, and the fact that Old René made several
on-record comments deriding the grant as Nazi guilt-money
hasn't stopped Christelle Vivier's election coordinators from
using it as their base.

On a normal day, Picaut could walk down to it from the
station, but the press are still camped on the steps leading
up to the front door and are very likely doing the same
at the hotel. In the absence of Lise Bressard to lure them
away, she has little choice but to make a run for her car.
Sylvie sprints beside her, flash in new Nikes. They depart,

with press motorcycle outriders herding them like sheep.

Inside the hotel, the new decor is still fresh from the refurbishment. Spotless slate floors meet marble walls against which stand vast, waist-high vases packed with lilies that make Picaut sneeze. The elevators are silent, but for the hiss of a smooth ascent.

Christelle Vivier's press office is in a penthouse suite on the sixth floor, where giant windows run from floor to ceiling on three out of the four sides and the sun-polished air runs so thick with coffee it makes Picaut's head spin just walking in the door. Clusters of young men and women in sharp suits stop what they are doing to watch her.

Troy Cordier, taller than the rest and spectacularly blond, detaches himself from the farther group and strides across a dozen metres of snowy carpet to reach her, hand extended as much to stop her moving forward as in greeting. His white teeth gleam.

'Capitaine Picaut. We owe you and your force a wealth of apology. Please be assured we are informing the vampires in the media that the fault was all ours and your response was exemplary.'

She has seen him on television. She saw him in the foyer of Orléans! 24/7 before it became a crime scene. But she has never shaken his hand before. It is as coolly crisp as the rest of him. He's younger than she'd thought, too, closer to forty than fifty, but his south-coast tan and ghost eyes beneath the brilliant platinum hair give him an air of ageing decadence.

His suit today is palest grey, his tie a silvery blue to match his eyes; he is by far the best-dressed man in the room. His accent is high-class Parisian and in this alone he is not unique; it applies to all of Christelle's team with the single exception of Old René.

He's there, the war hero, rumpled and lined in his open-necked shirt and trousers that may well be relics from his war days, a direct contradiction to the rest of the team. And he is smoking, which they are not. A hand-rolled cigarette hides between his remaining thumb and forefinger, the tip tilted in to burn his palm. When he draws in, his cheeks cave with the effort. Exhaling, he turns his gaze slowly to Picaut.

'What does the officer think? Is it the pretty boy's fault?'

'Grandfather, don't. Capitaine Picaut is here to help. She doesn't need you to—'

Christelle is back in the office, which means someone moved quickly when they found her. You might expect her to be discomfited, or perhaps just cross, but she is flushed and tight-lipped and close to tears. Whether her discomposure arises from her grandfather's evident hatred of Troy Cordier or Picaut's presence, or just the ravages of the morning, is hard to say.

She doesn't like cigarette smoke; that much is evident. She hovers just on the margins of the blue haze that surrounds Old René with her hands on her hips, bridging the gap between him and Picaut, or blocking it.

Picaut says, 'It's fine.' And to Old René, 'We don't know if there is a fault or if there is, whose it is. That's what we're here to find out.'

Whatever Christelle and her grandfather think, Troy Cordier wants Picaut gone. His smile is ten thousands watts of blistering brilliance. 'As Prosecutor Ducat has already noted,' he says, 'mistakes were made. We shall address them. I really don't think we need to waste any more of your time.'

Picaut can polish her own smiles if she has to, but right now she doesn't bother. 'If someone is trying to stoke racial tension,' she says, 'it's not a waste of my time to find out who it is and how they did it, and, most important, why. We'll need to interview the driver, and I'd like to see the details that were sent to his laptop, which means I'll need access to your server to check the data and the backups.' She gestures to Sylvie, bringing her into the room and the conversation. She is as white-blonde as Troy Cordier, but her hair is cut into rough spikes and gelled, and she wears gothic eye shadow and chains on her sweatshirt, which probably reduces the Aryan appeal.

Smiling now, Picaut says, 'This is Lieutenant Ostheimer, our technical specialist. If you could furnish her with whatever she asks for, we'll be out of your hair all the faster. And meanwhile, if I could see your itinerary for today?'

'That's confidential.' Cordier's face droops into a frown. 'If I might say so, Capitaine, you are the wife of our principal opponent.'

Picaut sighs. 'I am entirely capable of separating my work life from my private life. If you think otherwise, you should take it up with Prosecutor Ducat. And as the entire world knows, I will very soon be the former wife of your opponent.'

She heads towards the computer set on the oak desk by the wall. Troy Cordier blocks her progress. He is so tall, and standing so close, she has to crane her neck to look up at him, squinting against the fierce sun.

'Just let me see the detail you had of the school, and exactly what was sent to the driver.'

'They are identical. He was ordered to take Madame Vivier to the Saint Francis of Assisi primary school for nine thirty where the press would meet them and take some photographs of Madame Vivier speaking to the children.'

'Very touching. And where, instead, did he take her, given that it obviously wasn't the right place?'

'To the Saint Francis of Assisi primary school. Only, the one on the itinerary was in Orléans, and the one he took her to was an hour's drive away.' Cordier gives a theatrical shrug. 'It would seem he was sent the wrong address. An easy mistake.'

'If it was a mistake. Who sent him the details?'

'My personal assistant emailed them to him last night.'

'May I speak to her?'

'She has been given the day off.'

'You mean she's been dismissed?'

'Her employment status is under review. It was a mistake of the kind that we can't afford.'

'She left her laptop behind?'

'Of course.'

'So have you checked whether what she sent out is what the driver received?'

Puzzled, he asks, 'How could it be otherwise?'

'Monsieur Cordier, you have no idea what a resourceful hacker could do with your data stream. The exact detail is beyond me, but I'm reliably informed that intercepting the output from one email stream and sending something marginally altered in its place would be, and I quote, "trivial". So perhaps if we could look at your PA's laptop together?'

The laptop is locked in a drawer in the desk set against the northerly wall. Cordier liberates it and then marches it and Picaut to a small desk by the most distant window.

Picaut keeps her back turned while Cordier keys in the pass codes and fires up the email client. She says, 'I don't need to see anything except the specific part of the email that relates to the school trip.'

'Here.' He slides the laptop across the desk with a single email open on the screen.

From: Christelle Vivier Campaign office <CVNF@mailscore.fr>
To: Yves Perusse <YP@mailscore.fr>
Subject: CV/driver Itinerary 27 February
Date: 26 February 2014 18:58:38

27 February

08:00	Collect car. Check tyres, fuel, water.
08:15	Arrive at HJJR. Pick up CV.
08:45	Depart HJJR, Destination, **St Francis of Assisi Primary School, rue de la Fontaine, Orléans South**. Park at rear entrance. Details already logged on your satnav.
09:15	Meet **Mme LaScale, headmistress**. Introduction to selected pupils.
09:30	Press arrives for photo shoot FFS. Make sure no blacks in shot.
09:50	Latest, press leaves.
10:15	Return to HJJR. CV has lunchtime interview with

Cordier says, 'The lunchtime interview has been cancelled. The rest, of course, is private.'

'Of course.' Picaut nods to Sylvie. 'Check the ISP and the servers. See what went in and what went out.' To Cordier: 'Can I see the driver's printout?'

'There isn't one. It's all on his phone.'

'Then I need to speak to him. Is he here, or—' She reads his expression. 'He's been given the day off too? Tell me you kept his phone?'

Cordier looks around. Eleven of the dozen aides shake their heads. The twelfth, a young woman with russet hair and flat, unplucked brows, crosses to the same desk as the laptop. The phone is locked in the lowest drawer. Relief swells thicker than Old René's cigarette smoke.

Picaut says, 'I sense a promotion coming on. Can someone open that at the incoming email, please? The one that relates to the school.'

It's different. The realization is written across every face. Shaken, Troy Cordier turns the phone so she can read it.

From: Christelle Vivier Campaign office <CVNF@mailscore.fr>
To: Yves Perusse <YP@mailscore.fr>
Subject: CV/driver Itinerary 27 February
Date: 26 February 2014 18:58:38

27 February

08:00	Collect car. Check tyres, fuel, water.
08:15	Arrive at HJJR. Pick up CV.
08:45	Depart HJJR, Destination, **St Francis of Assisi Primary School, Sury-aux-Bois**. Fastest route: east along the D2060 and on to the D909. School obvious on entering the village. Park at rear entrance. **Don't forget to switch off your mobile this time. We don't want phone calls on live TV feed**.
09:45	Meet **Mme Vernier, headmistress**. Introduction to selected pupils.
10:00	Press arrives for photo shoot FFS. Make sure no blacks in shot.
10:15	Latest, press leaves.

From the dense, tense silence, Cordier says, 'Who would do this? And why?' At least he is no longer asking how.

From the corner, Old René says, 'Who stands to benefit most from our apparent mistake? And who has invested most in fancy gadgets and the men who run them?'

Christelle Vivier has joined the gaggle of fretting aides. She flashes a glare at her grandfather. 'I'm sure Capitaine Picaut does not believe the Bressards would do this.'

'Capitaine Picaut,' says Picaut, 'will believe whatever the facts support. At the moment, your own campaign team are as high in the frame as anyone else.'

'*Us?*' Cordier is incensed. 'Why would *we* . . . ?'

'You are the ones with the poll bounce. You are also the

ones who might wish to see a man dead who believed he'd found the mortal remains of the Maid.'

'*What?*'

If he knew anything of this, he is an exceptional actor. Picaut is inclined to think he is not. Having stepped in this far, she has to explain. 'Iain Holloway found bones he believed were hers just before he died. He was the victim of the fire at the Hôtel Carcassonne . . .'

Troy Cordier steps in front of her, making the most of his height. 'Capitaine Picaut, you are entering the same fantasy land as your father. If you continue with this victimization of our campaign, I will request that the Prosecutor remove you from—'

'Which is why I won't. For the record, I think you'd have to be immensely stupid to amend your own server. But then the Bressards would need a particularly good reason, too. At the last poll, you had all the bounce on the back of sympathy for Christelle. The Bressards may expect a counter-bounce, but with only two full campaigning days left before the election, that's a particularly high-risk strategy and, his family's wartime conduct with respect to your grandfather notwithstanding, Landis is not the kind of man to take unnecessary risks.'

Eyes meet across the room and all of them avoid hers. Old René says, 'Notwithstanding his family's betrayal of an entire Resistance cell, that man is the worst kind of snake.'

'*Grandfather—*'

Troy Cordier moves towards the door. 'You'll forgive us if we still consider the Bressards to be top of our list of suspects. We respect your need for evidence and we will help you to gather what you can. We will notify the press.'

'No. Not yet. Please. As it is, we have a short enough window in which we might track down whoever did this. If they know we're on to them, they'll wipe everything beyond any kind of retrieval and we lose any advantage we might have.'

'We can't let them go on thinking we were at fault. It will hurt our poll ratings and the election is—'

'On Sunday. I know. But if you can say that there appears to have been a typographic error, would that suffice? We can come clean tomorrow if we're no further forward. Just give me twenty-four hours. If it turns out to have been the Bressards, I swear we will pursue it as hard as if it turns out to have been Cheb Yasine.'

Troy Cordier shakes her hand at the door. 'It's been a pleasure.'

'No, it hasn't. But it may yet prove useful in our search for the arsonists. I hope so.'

Back at the car, the press have largely disappeared. The story has lost its bite. No motorbikes follow them, nor any photographers. As they turn the corner, she says to Sylvie, 'Do we need Patrice?'

'No. I can handle it.'

'Thanks.' Picaut checks her watch; it's twenty past twelve. Her hands twitch. She wants to phone him, to hear his voice. She has more self-control than that. Really, she does. To Sylvie, she says, 'I'll drop you back at the station and you can at least access the servers and get a list of all the activity. See if you can find out where the backups are too. If we're lucky, they'll be time stamped and we can see when the changes were made.'

'Where are you going?'

'To talk to Éric Masson about a skull.'

CHAPTER FORTY-SEVEN

On the table in Éric's lab lies a young Caucasian woman in her twenties, with needle tracks on her inner arms and at her ankles.

'OD?' Picaut leans over the woman, and studies the freshest of the self-inflicted injuries: about eight centimetres long, a dull red track almost lost in pale, blue-grey flesh, with the crust of a scab at the base where the needle has dragged. The girl is heroin-thin. Her hair has lost its gloss; her breasts lie flat against her chest.

Éric Masson has completed his dissection and is coming out, closing the incisions he has made in chest and abdomen.

Quietly, she asks, 'Where's she from?' Not Orléans, obviously, or she would have heard about it. Even on a day like this, news of a heroin death would have reached her.

'Tours. Found dead this morning. Her father is some-thing big in the city administration, so they sent the autopsy out of town.' Éric lays the last knot and pulls off his gloves.

441

'She's been using for seven years and he swears he didn't know until he found her last night.'

He is a conscientious man. He draws a sheet over the body and pushes the gurney himself to the numbered racks of cold storage units. By the time he returns, Picaut has ground the coffee beans (Fortnum & Mason's Ethiopian Tchembe, promising *an explosion of fruit aroma and an unusual cocoa-banana flavour*) and is filtering the first cup.

'You got the picture of the skull?'

'I did. I never thought Patrice would be sending me pictures of old relics, but this is entirely fascinating.'

He nudges the mouse to clear the screensaver and she sees the skull again, enlarged on the one-twenty screen that takes up half the wall. The green mould, the break at the back of the cranium – she knows these, as an old friend.

Éric asks, 'This is from Iain Holloway's chip?'

'It's the second file. Apparently he thought it might be the Maid.'

'She was burned.'

'I know. So we have to work out why an intelligent man with an obsession for detail thought it might not be impossible.'

The coffee has filtered through. They drink it black, because Éric thinks that adding milk and sugar is as barbarian as watering your Scotch. It has taken Picaut nearly two years for her mouth not to ache for the milk, but now she's here it was worth the hell. She closes her eyes to the first taste and yes she can, more or less, taste a faint flavour of banana. She smiles, and finds Éric watching. 'So,' she says, 'tell me about the skull. It's a woman. I can tell that much: shape of cranium, ridge by the eyes . . . Those three cervical vertebrae look rough, as if she had arthritis in her neck, so I'm thinking she's in her fifties at least, maybe more?'

Éric looks as if he wants to hug her, gets halfway there,

thinks better of it and wraps his hands around his forearms. 'You're learning. I can't tell you how happy that makes me. So yes, she had arthritis in her neck, which, coupled with the dentition – she had all her teeth still, which is pretty good, though the teeth were loose in the sockets – makes her somewhere beyond middle-aged when she died. If I had to make a guess, I'd say possibly as far as mid- to late-sixties, but we'd need more of the body to go on and a proper forensic anthropologist. This is beyond my field. The right person could read this like a book.'

'Have you got someone in mind?'

'I did a preliminary search and came up with a certain Dr Iain Holloway, which is interesting, if not altogether useful. I can get you someone by this afternoon if it matters. Does it?'

'Definitely. Whatever he may or may not have found, I'd bet my career that Iain Holloway died for this, which means someone, somewhere, wanted him silenced. I am prepared to believe the priest that it wasn't the Church, but that still leaves a lot of people with a vested interest in maintaining the myth of Jeanne d'Arc, visionary peasant from Lorraine.'

'I'll find someone.'

'Do. Thank you. Patrice says he'll have answers from the chip by three. I'll send them over if there's anything relevant.' She pours the coffee into a lidded travel mug. 'Right now I have to sort out the clusterfuck that took out Christelle's campaign this morning. Somebody sent us out chasing our arses and I intend to know who, why and how. Wish me luck.'

443

CHAPTER FORTY-EIGHT

RHEIMS,
9 June 1430

Tomas's wall-eyed chestnut mare is breaking down.
He has pushed her too hard, over ground that is baked
to granite. He feels the jolt of an uneven pace when he is
still three miles out of Rheims and he flogs her on, keeping
the pace, watching the black sweat grow on her neck, smells
the rank, sharp odours of pain, hears the groan and shudder
in her outbreath, and pushes her on, and on, and on.

She is lame in both forelegs by the time he ducks in
through the gate arch at Rheims. He pulls her up, drops
the reins, throws himself off. The royal stables – which is
to say the stables used by the royal party during its sojourn
in the town – is on the left, three dozen stalls set in a square
around a central fountain, with a tack room to one side, and
grooms' quarters along the northern, shaded boundary.
He pulls at his purse as he runs in under the arch. A dark-
haired horse boy steps out to greet him, face shaded against
the sun.

'The mare outside . . . a silver coin if you can bring her
sound again. She'll need to stand in a river for half a day,

and she needs feeding. I need another horse to match her that I can ride out tomorrow. Four men will be here soon, bringing the Maid's battle-horse. Make ready stables for five mounts. Find me rooms for four men. And . . .' And find a tanner who calls himself Stefan, but that Tomas must do himself.

The boy is lean, angular, clear-eyed. His white teeth make indents along his lip. Was she like this once, the Maid? In her past, did she help men to find good mounts and send them on their way?

A shadow shivers in the sharp sun. It is nine days since she was taken. Tomas does not want to think what they have done to her since.

He throws coins to the boy, a tumble of wealth, cleanly caught. 'You will want food, lord?'

Is he a lord, now? He has forsaken his monk's attire, taken on doublet and hose, a clean linen shirt, calfskin boots, all sober, all the equal of anything Jean of Belleville might wear; or the Maid when she is not in her armour. 'Yes. Food for five. And good wine.'

The day is hot. Going out into the town, he takes a top coat only for decency, not for the warmth. The wool is Flemish, dyed a dark, unprepossessing blue; he will have nothing of England now. He heads east, away from the gate, to the taverns he knew, and begins to ask questions, quietly, of men he cultivated when last he was here.

An hour later, he is in a stinking back alley. It is not the tannery – that would be unbearable – but even here the stench is a wall. 'Stefan?'

'Here.' He is smaller, more stooped, his face more lined. And he is smiling. He steps out of the doorway that shelters him. 'Bedford is happy. There's a knighthood here for you if you play it right.'

'So I should go to him.' This is a jest and Stefan takes it as such; nobody goes to Bedford without a better reason than wanting to claim a knighthood. 'Where is he?'

'At Calais by now, I think. The whole of Europe knows about the Maid. Her trial needs to be a French thing: caught by the French, questioned by the French, executed by the French for heresy, and then where will be her false king? If she is a heretic, so is he, and his coronation last summer a sham. The day after she burns, Bedford will bring Henry of England to Rheims to be anointed with the holy oil. Until then, he will keep well away.'

'What if the French king ransoms her?' Tomas makes this sound like a bad thing.

'He won't. That door is closed. He will not offer ransom for her, and in return, the Duke of Burgundy will enter more fully into the "peace treaties" that the king has been asking for since his anointing last summer.'

'Which will go nowhere.' Of course. It is what he would plan, were he still planning this.

'As you say.' Stefan raises his palms, the very essence of regret. 'After many months of negotiations, sadly, Burgundy will find itself still at war with France, and we shall assault their holdings, whatever is left to them. But the whore will be dead by then.'

Regnault de Chartres; this is his doing. Tomas lost the first handful of days after the Maid's capture in hunting the archbishop, and failed to find him. One day—

'What are you going to do?' Stefan peels himself off the wall that has been holding him up, comes a step or two down the alley. There is barely space for the two of them, and barely light enough to see by, even in full summer afternoon sun.

Tomas shrugs. 'My work is done. I'll go to Bedford and collect my knighthood.'

He strives for nonchalance, but he is not as good as once

he was. Stefan's smile does not slip, the slant of his eyes does not narrow, his hands do not move to grasp the blade that must hide in his sleeve. Nothing is different, except that death hunts in the alley, where before it did not.

For one flickering moment, Tomas entertains the idea of death; the peace, the blessed release, not to lie awake another night with his eyes open, because in the dark, always, is the fire with the Maid at its heart.

It's a wire, not a knife. Tomas can see the loop, faint as a dawn-dewed web, between the little man's searching hands.

He takes a step back. Twenty paces round a left-hand bend to the alley's mouth; it may as well be in England. Two blades, one in each sleeve, but this is not a cassock: his shirt cuffs are tighter and they are not so easily reached. The alley is empty; no rock, no rope, no broomstick, stave or cudgel. Stefan chose it, knowing Rheims; very likely he cleared it ahead of the meeting. It was sloppy of Tomas to allow it, and he cannot afford risk now.

My dear . . . while you live, I will not die.

He ducks, which is a risk, given there is a wire seeking his neck, but he goes left, where is a recess, probably a latrine pit, but no risk of falling in because this is a feint, although he must make it seem real, and – yes! – Stefan's hands snap out, the wire sings of death between them, and Tomas is on the right, his own hands searching; he has no wire, but the way he's feeling now, he doesn't need one.

For just a heartbeat, the little man's neck is hot between his palms, and then gone again, slipping away, a trout in winter water.

At least they are no longer pretending. Stefan smirks. Between feint and counter-feint, 'Bedford knows you . . . are not his.'

'If he did, you'd have come with more . . . men and more blades . . .' Another miss, but closer; his hands sting from the wrench where Stefan pulled his woollen tunic free.

'Why, when I can kill you alone? I needed only to be certain.'

This is a lie. Bedford has never needed certainty to push him to murder; a half shadow of a suspicion has ever been enough.

Another feint. Fast footwork, and it is Tomas who has felt the wire snap up past his face. He could lose his nose to this. He laughs, breathless, and takes two long steps forward. And trips on Stefan's outflung foot, and falls into the filth of the alley's floor, not baked hard here; the sun never reaches it.

He is face down, which is fatal. His left arm is trapped beneath him. He flails back with his right, grabs a leg, could pull, but doesn't, slams on up to a groin not so far away – Stefan is a small man – and grabs a fist full of loose, dangling flesh.

A wrench, a twist, a shriek—

—and he rolls on to his left side, uses his handhold to pull himself up to his feet. Upright, he stamps on an outstretched knee, on the side, so that the bones angle away from him, the opposite of nature. He feels the grating pop of a joint snapped, hears the choked cry that goes with it.

And then his hands are about the other's throat. The wire snakes about his feet. He could reach for it, but here is the closest he will get to killing Bedford with his bare hands. His heart sings to the crush of cartilage, flesh and blood, the sense of it pumping between his fingers.

With a vicious joy, he watches the branching veins swell and burst in the whites of the eyes; feels his enemy thrash and kick and gouge . . . and die.

Too soon. Too soon. And not soon enough.

He snaps his hands open. Stefan bounces dead at his feet. The alley's far end is a midden. He drags the body back and stuffs it in under old fish bones, a hog's head, a dead dog. As an afterthought, he eases a blade from his left forearm, leans down and cuts off the small man's cock in the universal sign of an adulterer.

Later, at the stables, he greets Louis de Coutes. Here, too, is Jean d'Arc, whose brother is in captivity along with the maid he calls his sister. With them are two Piedmontese who have proved themselves good horsemen and can at least lead the Maid's devil-horse, if not actually ride it.

Tomas buys them a meal and wine, tells them what he has learned and sends them on their way: Jean d'Arc and Louis de Coutes to Chinon, to find Yolande of Aragon; the other two with him, heading west now, to Belleville-en-Poitou, where are de Belleville and Marguerite de Valois, sister of the king.

BELLEVILLE,
Nineteen days later

'They took her to Beaulieu-les-Fontaines with d'Aulon and Pierre d'Arc. They kept her in the cellars, alone, but near to the others, so that she could hear them. She knocked unconscious a guard who came to feed her and nearly freed the two men; the Burgundians only caught her because another gaoler came and found her as she was trying to break down the door. They will move her now, away from the men. I think they may take her to Beaurevoir, to the seat of Luxembourg: it is safely in unFrench territory and she is owned now by Jean of Luxembourg, whose man captured her.'

Tomas's news falls into a kind of horrified hush. He does not mention they will have mistreated her, they will have taken her armour and bound her limbs, they may have assaulted her; they are men and she a woman alone, who has angered them greatly. He is amongst intelligent company, these things do not need to be said.

He stands in silence, and waits. The meeting takes place in the library at Belleville, one of the few rooms of his host's chateau not currently undergoing renovation and remodelling. Everywhere else is scaffolding, the discord of hammers and whistling, the scents of sawn wood and resin and paint.

Here is quiet, solid as winter fog. The books make it, and drink it up. On the shelves are the illuminations of centuries, thousands upon thousands of hours of candlelit work.

To his left, the *Roman de la Rose* grapples with Jean Gerson's *Tract contra*. To his right, Herodotus, Homer, Horace, ordered by the alphabet. Their words slide out from the vellum folds, slink into corners, argue themselves into dust. Here is heresy. Here is piety. What man can tell the mind of God? What woman?

In the high-backed chairs on either side of the fire sit Marguerite and de Belleville, both of them lacking sleep. The lady, moreover, has patches on the knees of her gown, where she has knelt often and long in supplication. Her fingers are raw from telling beads, from touching icons, her skin is translucent from fasting.

Also in the room, not seated, are the priest Huguet Robèrge, who stands always a little to the left of his lord; and Yolande of Aragon, mother-in-law to the king. Tomas has not summoned her here – a commoner does not summon a queen – but Louis de Coutes and Jean d'Arc carried each the same message: if we are to save the Maid, we who care must act together. We meet in Belleville. We would welcome your presence.

And Yolande is here, a maypole of silk and satin. She

paces across and across in front of the fire. Tomas thinks this every time he is in her company: if she had been a man, there would have been no need for the Maid.

She stops in front of him. 'May we speak?'

'My lady.' With a scant bow, he yields her the floor. His etiquette is perhaps not quite what it could be, but he is not long arrived. He has stood a full quarter hour for the boot boy to attack his boots, cloak and hose with a stiff brush, in an effort to knock off the mud of travel. He still rocks with the rhythm of the roan gelding that was his last mount. He has changed nine times since Rheims.

He leans back against a mantelpiece and listens.

'We know the lady of Luxembourg; we shall write to her. She is not without power. While the lady lives, the Maid will not be ceded to her enemies. But the lady is old and not in good health. If she dies, then her protection dies with her. We cannot depend on it.'

'We can depend on nothing. Bedford will not let her languish in womanly company. We must undermine the trial.' De Belleville stands, walks to the fire, his hands behind his back. 'Who is to prosecute?'

Tomas says, 'Pierre Cauchon, of the University of Paris. He has just finished escorting the young King Henry from London to Rouen. He is as solidly English as if he had been born on the banks of the Thames. We cannot subvert him.'

'Then we must change the minds of the other men whose good offices he will need to draw on. Huguet? Whom can we count on?'

Huguet Robèrge takes the floor, their expert in canon law. 'By law, she must be tried where she committed her "heresy", which is to say where she was captured, outside Compiègne, or in the see of her accuser, which is to say Pierre Cauchon. Compiègne remains in French hands and is not safe, and Beauvais is no better. In either place, we might be able to

451

mount a raid to recover her. Thus they will seek somewhere safer, but to do that, they will need to change the laws. Cauchon has no writ beyond Beauvais.'

'Rouen,' Tomas says. 'It's where the English king is being kept. They have a big garrison there. Since the fall of Troyes, it's the most English town in France, more even than Calais.'

'Then Cauchon must gain authority there, and he does not currently have it. This may sound like a small thing, but the law is the law. He will have to get good men to turn a blind eye to his rewriting of it and there are sufficient men of good conscience who will not be party to that kind of calumny. We can make this hard for him.'

Yolande: 'We shall write to the inquisitor at Rouen. We shall write also to the knights of the realm, to d'Alençon, La Hire, all the others who support her. They are all French lords cognizant of French law. She shall not be alone.'

From her seat by the fire, Marguerite says, 'She is not alone. God is with her. He will not favour those who act against her. The bishop should be told so.'

Her words fall on a web of glances. How does one tell her that if Pierre Cauchon desires that God hates France and loves England, that He despises the Maid, then he will make it be so, and no one will dare stand against him.

'My dear . . .' The queen crosses the room. Her hand falls on Marguerite's shoulder. They lock fingers, the two women, and if you look with the right eyes the blood line is clear in the set of the jaw, the long, lean face, the colour of the hair, what you can see of it beneath the trains and veils and plucked, high brows.

Marguerite has on her neck the birthmark with which Charles the Mad stamped all of his children, but otherwise they could be mother and daughter, or close cousins, at least.

452

Yolande says, 'We shall do what we can.'

'If we fail, she will die.' Tomas has travelled nineteen days, and if he has seen any of the land through which he rode, it was for less than half of that. He cannot eat or drink except by dogged determination; he is no good to her if he wastes to nothing. He wants to tell this to Marguerite, and cannot find the words. She thinks God has imprisoned the Maid, and that fasting will change His mind.

De Belleville knows. With an effort, he takes his grey, grave gaze from his betrothed and fixes it instead on Tomas de Segrave, who is no longer a priest. The change has not surprised any of them. He wishes he had become a man at arms sooner. He might have saved her, or at least shared her captivity.

'Tomas, we will do what we can, but we need your guidance. You know the English better than we do. What can be done?'

'We need to get to her.' Over nineteen days, he has thought of nothing else. 'Where an army cannot go, one man may succeed. I will go to Bedford at Calais. He believes I am his agent. I will go to him, and assure him of my loyalty. I will find a way to get him to send me in to her. She needs a friend, and I will be that friend, a link from her to the outside world. Together, we shall find a way to get her out.'

CHAPTER FORTY-NINE

CALAIS,
July 1430

ANOTHER DAWN, ANOTHER STABLE. The stable boys have
been shooed off, partway through their mucking out.
A melange of horse dung, urine and fresh-cut grass layers at
head height. Bedford surges in, breasting through it, bright,
sharp-eyed, combative.

'Tomas, you've lost weight even since last we spoke. Don't
tell me you're pining for your little war-girl?'

'The one whose downfall I engineered?' He has practised
this; his life depends on his being better than when he met
Stefan in the alley at Rheims. Across his face is stitched a look
that combines satisfaction with dislike. 'I ate some bad fish at
Lent and I'm still shitting water. I am pining for no one.'

'I heard you threatened to hunt down and kill Regnault
de Chartres after he betrayed her at Compiègne.'

'And yet he remains alive.'

'Indeed. As I told him: if Tod Rustbeard wanted you dead
... Well. He should know. He does know. It's why he's afraid
of you.'

Good.

Tomas is clearer now, less ragged than he was. There will come a time when Regnault de Chartres will die a lingering death in a cage, with rats gnawing out his eyes, defecating in his mouth, dicing over his testes. But not yet. Not while the Maid lives and Tomas needs to get close to her.

He says, 'I heard she was in Beaurevoir, with the ladies of Luxembourg. Is that safe?'

'As safe as if she were in London. The French can't reach it. There is no army big enough to come within a day's range. Not even Jean d'Alençon. He blusters a lot, for a minor lord with no money. Just because he is married to the king's cousin does not give him rights to send letters demanding . . . this and that . . .'

Demanding that the English and their French puppets adhere to Church law, perhaps?

Armed by Huguet's assessment of canon law, pressed on by Yolande, if d'Alençon has written one letter he has written a hundred; the French king may have confined him to Normandy, but he cannot prevent him from writing in aid of the woman at whose side he fought.

Letters, of course, do not change the world. If the king wrote, perhaps, or the pope, but the king will not and the pope is dying and neither will move to help a girl who is named a heretic by some of the most powerful men in Christendom.

Tomas leans against a stall and makes himself look at Bedford, presses his fingers together, in the way of a priest. 'Three women reside in Beaurevoir, all related to the Duke of Luxembourg. His aunt, his wife, his stepdaughter; all three named Joan. I have heard that they are become enamoured of their charge. Do you really think it's safe to leave her there?'

'You hear things other men don't.'

A shrug. This is why he is paid . . . what he is paid. With

both sides paying him, he has enough, these days, to retire. He has no intention of retiring.

Bedford asks, 'What would you have me do?'

'Send in a spy.'

'You?'

'Who else?'

'How could you go to her now? She thinks you are French and she is held by the English. Why would her guards let you through?'

'I will tell her I am infiltrating the English side as I have done in the past. That you believe me your man, and have sent me to question her, while, in truth, I am sworn only to her.'

'And is that the truth now, Rustbeard?' The big, glaucous eyes search his. 'You are not the man you were when you left.'

'I am who I always was. The Maid is friendless in an enemy chateau. She will trust me. I can get from her what you want. Just tell me what that is.'

He is too desperate. He can feel it leaking from his bones, oozing like marrow. Bedford may be a coward on the field but he reads men better than most.

Luck is with him. Temporarily, Bedford isn't looking at him, but at the grey mare that is Tomas's current mount. This is a gift from Yolande of Aragon, not as good as the chestnut the Maid gave him, but still of the late king's stock. Bedford is a horseman before he's anything else, he knows quality when he sees it.

Bedford steps into the stall and runs his big soldier's hands along the mare's top line, kneading the spot in front of her withers that makes her stretch her upper lip and sag her hip. Thoughtful, he says, 'I want a confession. I want her to accept whatever charges Cauchon brings. I want her to sign her own burning.'

'Then send me to Beaurevoir. I shall get it.'

'Tod, she's a bitch who put on armour. She goes against all of God's laws, but she's not insane. Do you really suppose—' A scuffle outside the door. Heads turn, equine and human. The mare leans her chin on Bedford's shoulder. Traitor.

A rider barges in past men whose duty it is to keep him out. He is young, lean, swaying to the rhythm of a horse he no longer sits. The stable may be ripe, but the air is sweet compared to what he imports: rank, hot chaos.

He sags against the doorpost. In the presence of Bedford, he fails to stand straight and Bedford does not order him flogged. It is less than an hour after dawn. To arrive in this state, he's been riding through the night, and men are permitted some leeway who have done that.

Bedford snaps his fingers. The stable boys who have not, after all, been far away, run to see to his horse, to whip off its saddle and throw on a rug, to stand it in cold water to keep its tendons whole, to find it food and a straw strap. A lad with white-blond hair runs in with a pitcher of wine and a ladle.

Bedford scoops up a measure, hands it himself to the messenger.

'My lord . . .' He's good, well trained; he speaks before he drinks. 'The Maid of France. She got on to the roof of Beaurevoir Castle. She tried to climb down, to escape. She fell.'

Oh, dear God. He has seen Beaurevoir. It is seventy feet from the heights to the moat. Oh, God. Oh, God. *Oh, God . . .*

'Damn her!' Bedford slams his fist against a wall. The mare jerks back. 'She will *not* escape me. I will not allow it.' He spins, catches hold of himself, forces his temper down as he might force the head of a wilful horse. 'Is she dead?'

The messenger has drunk. He has closed his eyes, as if

he has just entered heaven, and wishes there to remain. From his distant place, he says, 'They say not, lord, no. She has cracked her ribs and her breathing is not good. But she lives.'

Tomas has read of volcanoes, of the slow simmer before the mountain explodes, spewing fire and rock and smoke. Nobody lives, who is close. He thinks it would be wise to remove himself from Bedford's presence, to think of other ways to get to the Maid. He can change the colour of his skin, find a wig, change his accent. Italian. That would be good. Tomaso di Carsoli, physician to princes; he has been that once before, in Poland. A beard. He will grow a short, spiked beard in the Italian fashion, and dye it black. He will—

Bedford grasps his arm.

He turns slowly. He is not at all sure that his heart does not show in his eyes. 'My lord?'

Bedford is crimson, dull at the angles of his chin, and up beyond his temples. 'Go to her. Heal her. Bring her to Rouen. Bring her alive, and well enough to stand trial. Do whatever it takes to get back into her credit. If you have to kill Regnault de Chartres to do it, I don't care. But see to it that she lives until we can burn her, or I'll burn you in her stead.'

Nine days later, he is at her bedside. She is bandaged, chest and brow. She wakes slowly, and incompletely. 'Tomas? They let you in?'

'I have Bedford's writ.'

Her face clouds. She seems to sleep, but he knows she is awake. He does not know how much pain she is in, but she is pale. Her pulse, when he feels it, is wiry, and bounds. He thinks the pain is great. 'What were you doing?'

'Escaping. It is my duty.'

'Escape how? You thought to fly?'

'I was climbing down the wall. I made it halfway.' Her smile is brief, a rare sun. 'Climbing down is always harder than climbing up. Jean de Belleville taught me that. Still . . .'

'You thought you could do it.' She is mad. He loves her madness.

'I had to. He is going to destroy them.'

'Who is going to destroy who?'

'Burgundy is going to destroy Compiègne. On Bedford's order, he is going to break into the city and put it to the sword: men, women and children. He will kill them all, and those he cannot cut open, he will burn.'

He would say that's not your fault, but perhaps it is. He says instead, 'Compiègne is holding firm. The governor won't let them in. The walls are thick and it's only one town. The English will give up in time.'

'Bedford won't.' Behind half lids, her gaze is disconcertingly sharp. 'The ladies here tried to buy my freedom.'

'I know.'

'The king could ransom me. Charles. He has Talbot, Suffolk, Scales in captivity. He could offer all for me.'

'I know.'

'He won't do it.'

'Lady, even if he wanted to—'

'Which he does not.'

'Even if he did, Bedford won't let him. He needs you convicted as a heretic so he can prove that Charles does not rule by divine right.'

'Fool.'

That could be him, or Bedford, or Charles; any or all. He says, 'I'm sorry.'

'It's not your fault. Did you kill Regnault de Chartres?'

'Not yet.'

He is a failure.
She sleeps.

The next day, she will not see him, or the day after. But by August, she is sitting up, talking to him, making plans for her defence, for her priorities, for how she can perhaps stay alive, and if not that, how she can be certain not to shame her king or lay on him the taint of heresy. It is December before the physicians say she is well enough for a journey.

By Christ's Mass, she is in Rouen, wholly owned by the English, kept in an unheated cell in a tower, chained.

CHAPTER FIFTY

MORNING HAS MERGED INTO AFTERNOON AND PICAUT is in the interview rooms at the station. Garonne has bought her a sandwich, which is the kind of thing he used to do in the old days.

The bread is fresh and hard and she gnaws her way through it as she questions Yves Perusse, Christelle Vivier's driver. She is expecting an older man, veteran of a dozen campaigns, but what she gets is yet another of the perfectly plastic aides whose only distinguishing feature is that he has an evident crush on Cordier's PA – older, wears her sense of purpose effortlessly – which is not remotely reciprocated. That apart, their stories corroborate and neither of them has the kind of technical knowledge needed to alter an email en route from her laptop to his phone.

It's just gone three o'clock by the time Picaut finishes the interview. Patrice has not texted.

Upstairs in Picaut's office, Sylvie is using Picaut's computer.

Picaut hooks up a chair with her foot, then leans on the back, looking down at the screen. 'What have you got?'

'Dead ends.' Sylvie pulls up three pages on separate screens. 'I've accessed the two Vivier backups either side of the email, but I can't follow the trail through to what was actually sent to the driver: it looks exactly the same, but it can't be unless the driver changed it himself.'

'Do you think he did?'

'Why would he? More to the point, how could he? He didn't have that kind of technical intelligence. I think someone else has been here, but that's only instinct. It's like walking through a room with someone else's scent hanging in the air. It just doesn't smell right.'

'Ducat doesn't count virtual scent as evidence.'

'I know.' Sylvie chews on a nail. 'I hate to say this, but we need Patrice.'

'Right.' Picaut dials his number from memory and can't think how long she has known it. It doesn't ring. She throws her phone down in disgust. 'He's out of signal. Can you email him?'

'That's not possible.'

'Why not? We have all his addresses.'

'No, I mean it's not possible that his phone is out of signal. Patrice has ways of linking to every mast in Europe. He's *never* out of signal.'

Picaut flips her phone to speaker. 'You try.'

Sylvie does. The tone is the same. She hands the phone back, pinches her nose. 'So he's either taken the battery out or wrapped the phone in aluminium foil so we can't reach him.'

'Email him anyway.'

Sylvie does. They wait. There is no reply. They send a text. There is no reply.

Sylvie says, 'He could have gone to sleep.'

'He wouldn't switch his phone off. I'll go. You stay on this.' Picaut tries to sound carefree. She's not sure she succeeds. The look Sylvie gives her could as easily be knowing as apologetic.

Sylvie says, 'I looked up his address. Do you know he lives in Blois?'

'Fuck.' That's an hour away. 'I thought he had an apartment in Orléans?'

'No. Blois. And not just Blois. He's in the old town, on the same side of the river as the castle. It costs upwards of five million euros just to put a roof over your head there.' Sylvie's brows tie complex knots. 'Do you think he still lives with his parents?'

Picaut grabs her jacket from the back of the chair. 'I'll get him. You keep working on the servers. Text me if you get anywhere. We'll be back before five.'

CHAPTER FIFTY-ONE

Château de Bouvreuil, Rouen,
February 1431

'FOR YOU, RUSTBEARD; FOR YOUR TROUBLE.'
'It is no trouble. I serve your lordship at all times.'

Another meeting, another lie. Not a stable this time to meet with my lord of Bedford, but a freezing, windowless room in the tower of the citadel at Rouen. Rush lights cringe on the walls. The shadows are fatter than the shapes they surround. If he looks up, he fancies snow drifts between the rafters.

A pigskin pouch sprawls across the table, big as a man's fist, twisted tight about the neck with iron wire: his payment in silver for bringing the Maid to Rouen whole, alive, able to plead, to speak – and to die. He is not sure he is right to have done this. Many mornings, he has thought that death would be a blessing, the way they are holding her. He has not found a way to get her out, nor even to lessen the horror of her captivity.

'My lord, if she is charged with heresy, she must be held by ecclesiasticals, by women of Christ, not by men who—'
'*Must?*'

Tomas holds still, sweating in the cold. His hand, resting on the table, not yet reaching for the bag of silver. Bedford's knife, slammed into the coarse-grained wood, his fist behind it, his face close now, smelling sour, eyes red as a boar's. If he has ever truly been close to death, he is closer now.

'Only that it will undermine the trial if she is seen to be treated outwith the law.'

'Rustbeard, you go too far. Bishop Cauchon is a man of the cloth. He is of the university in Paris. If he says the whore must be held in a cell, guarded night and day by English men at arms, I will not interfere. You will *never* tell me what I must or must not do.'

And that is how it is, and has been, and will be. Bedford, of course, has not been able to keep himself away from this, the greatest theatre of his generation, but he is keeping scrupulously clear of the proceedings. The French are doing this. The French are twisting canon law to suit their own ends. The French are ignoring all the legal precedents. The French, it has to be said, are making of themselves a mockery.

Bedford wrenches his knife from the table. It comes free with the crunching snap of breaking bones. 'Has she confessed to you?'

'I have told you her confessions. She says nothing to me that she has not already said to the inquisitors.' Inquisitors are becoming harder to find. The deputy inquisitor has already excused himself, finding urgent business elsewhere. This process has not all gone the way Bedford wants.

'You shall move her to a new cell, on the outer walls. It has a room underneath in which a man may secrete himself to listen. You will hear her confession before she goes to trial. She will speak to you. She trusts you. And we shall have its record to use against her.'

Eyes down. Hands clasped behind. To the hairs on his

head, the loyal servant. 'Who will stand beneath and write the record, lord?'

'A priest. A priest who can be trusted in this nest of vipers. Find me one.' And Bedford is gone.

Later, alone in the piteous cell they have found for her, where an unglazed window lets in the sleet, the rain, the snow. She is bunched up on the bed, wrapped in her topcoat, her nose red-blue and running, her hands up the sleeves of her coat for warmth, her legs tucked beneath her as far as they go. They are held by iron fetters, and those fetters linked to a chain that rises over a beam and down to a block of iron-oak so big that it takes three men to lift it.

If she moves, they hear it. If she wants to use the latrine, she has to ask them. Four English guards sleep in her cell, so close they can touch her, breathe on her, fart all over her. They are vile men, filthy, who call her whore and piss in her food. It is breaking his heart. He cannot let it break hers.

He brings her a wooden bowl of hot stew, free from contamination. He sits on the bed, and rubs her back while she eats. Outside, the guards huff and grumble, but Bedford has told them that Brother Tomas will win her confidences, that he must be allowed to be her friend.

Into her ear, quietly, he says, 'My lord the bishop sends to say that you are to attend the public court in the robing room of the Chapel Royal. It will be warmer there.'

'With you in attendance?'

'I can be present, but no, lady, they will not let me stand with you. They say the heresy is yours and you must face the court alone.'

'I will have counsel for my defence? Orléans would pay for it, I think?'

'Half of France would pay for it. You would have the best

counsel gold could buy, more men than Cauchon brings against you; but they know that, and they will not allow it. They say that you have claimed to hear the counsel of heaven and so no earthly counsel will be provided.'

'They would not treat a man thus.'

'They wouldn't treat a dog thus.'

She finishes eating. He takes the bowl and sets it aside, takes her hands in his to warm them.

She is well enough, now, as well as Tomas can make her. The irons gouge into her ankles, but he has done what he can to pad them. The rest of her maladies are to do with her fall from the heights at Beaurevoir. It was, indeed, seventy feet; he checked. And she fell from very near the top while trying to escape. Nobody will say she jumped. To attempt suicide is a heresy in itself.

Her ribs were broken in the fall; they still give her pain. And periodically, she has crippling headaches. He thinks her father is back. Sometime in the month of semi-consciousness after he reached her bedside she seemed to look past him, to someone not-there, who gave her greater comfort than anyone living. She goes silent sometimes, and when she comes back to him she is stronger, more sure of herself. 'Tomas, don't worry so. I shall not let them undermine me.'

Oh, my dear.

And tomorrow it starts. He releases her hands. 'Now let me take your confession.' This said loudly, so that Huguet, below, can hear it, and they can be sure that their stories correlate.

She knows of the man below, but not yet who it is. Huguet is his secret: that he is here, and Marguerite with him. They are among the hundreds who are come to Rouen to see the circus that is the trial: to be near her.

'What will they ask me?'

467

'I don't know. On the first day, they will take an oath only, I think.'

She gives a raw, cold smile. 'That will be enough.'

Wednesday, 21 February 1431

'Do you, Jehanne, who calls yourself the Maid, swear that you will speak the truth to any question that is put to you?'

It is not by chance that the first day of her public trial is Ash Wednesday, 21 February 1431. Cauchon seeks to make a point, although it is moot whether she is the child of Christ, persecuted by the Romans, or they are the agents of Christ, bringing the heretic into the holy fold.

Either way, as Bedford had said it would be, the court is convened in the Chapel Royal of the Château de Bouvreuil at Rouen. Painted windows colour the light, sending streaks of boldest blue, of red and green and butter-sun yellow across the floor.

She is wearing her doublet and hose. Her hair is cut short, the length of a helm. She is a small thing in all this great, vast space, facing forty men, forty minds, bent on her destruction.

The learned men of Paris are all about, trimmed in black and white striped squirrel hoods, white and black ermine collars. Their gowns are dyed so deeply black that light cannot escape them. They are pied crows, feasting on her soul, and Pierre Cauchon, England-loving bishop of Beauvais, is the greatest, most hungry of them, the most angry.

He knows himself in the wrong at the start, and it irks him. He has bent and twisted so many rules to bring her here, himself granted a fictional see which allows him to lead her trial. But he is thrashing around trying to find something to charge her with and after three quarters of a year he still has brought no witnesses, no accusations, no list of charges.

He cannot even prove she is not a maid. Twice, he has had her tested, once by the wife of Warwick, the English commander at Rouen, who has confirmed her maidenhood. He cannot impugn so great a lady, much as he would like to cry her false. He would check her himself, but what would that make him? He would never live it down.

In desperation, he seeks now to trap his victim solely in the net of her own words. No charges have been brought against her save the loose one of heresy, and that without foundation. So far, indeed, she has said nothing wrong, not in confession, not in public, not in private. It is without precedent. If he could accuse her of being too good a knight he might have a case, but since when was that a heresy?

Cauchon is beside himself and the proceedings have barely begun. 'Do you swear?'

'I don't know what you may wish to ask me and there are some things of which I am counselled not to speak. I will talk about my father and mother and those things I have done after I came to the king at Chinon. I will talk about my feats of arms, and the war against the English. But I will not speak about those things which are between me and my king and God.'

—You must swear.

—I cannot.

—You must.

—I cannot. I will not. You do not have the power to make me.

—That is not true, as you will find out.

Oh, my lady, have a care. You don't understand: these are forty of the highest trained legal minds in France and they think you a peasant. They will treat you as if you are stupid and you don't understand how much power this gives them.

—You must swear.

—I will swear to tell of those things I may tell. Of the rest, I may know later whether or not I can tell you.

Eventually, they bring a bible: a great thing, vast, bearing Christ in His passion in gold, and Saints John and Mary, encrusted with garnets and emeralds, sapphires and pearls, the jewelled heaven. They set it before her. She kneels, and in God's name swears to answer truthfully those questions concerning her faith; nothing more.

It is not enough; not nearly. Cauchon comes close, bending over. Even to Tomas, three rows back, he smells of old incense and new sweat. He smells of battles yet to be fought, and of garlic.

—Will you speak the Pater Noster?

Does he think he is her priest, this black crow, flapping? This is an assault on all the structures of the Church. Just for this, Tomas could kill him from here, with a single thrown knife. He could strangle him as he strangled Stefan in an alley. Blue veins writhe like slow worms on the backs of his hands. The pulse at his neck is fat and slippery. By its rhythm, not just Tomas but the whole court can count how much she angers him. Just now it thrums like a struck string, and the withered parchment-skin beneath his eyes is inky dark.

She looks Cauchon in the eye. *Lady, have a care.* 'Hear me in confession and I shall gladly say the Lord's Prayer to you.'

His veins will burst, and spread across his face. 'I adjure you not to escape, for if you do, we tell you now that you brand yourself a heretic.'

'That is not so, sir. For I have taken no oath not to escape, nor shall I. It is the duty of every prisoner of war to escape. I say now that I do wish to escape and shall avail myself of any opportunity. But you have dishonoured yourselves by leaving me in the hands of ruffians of the lowest sort. I should be kept by women, in a convent, as is proper.'

He might die now, of his rage.

—Take her away.

This is the day that Tomas remembers best; the first, in many ways the easiest. Cauchon does not know how to handle her. Do you swear? I will swear to tell you what I am permitted to tell you.

She doesn't vary, but then she can't. They are forty and she is one and they interrupt her when she answers, and interrupt each other, talking over themselves, throwing questions, questions, questions, with no order and no theme, so she cannot see where they are driving. All those questions Tomas had, to which he never truly got an answer: who is your father, who your mother? He knows Jacques d'Arc is not her father, but he does not know the truth and he prays now that he does not learn it here, in open court.

Under questioning, she relays with some reluctance vague details of her childhood: the names of her godparents, her brothers, her sisters, a certain attack by Burgundy on her village. She doesn't know whether it was her father or her mother who gave her the ring with the *Jhesu Maria* inscribed therein that was the basis of her pennants. She cannot remember her exact age. She swears she did not herd cows when all the witnesses swear that she did. If they were going to catch her out on failure to admit to herding cattle, she'd be burned and gone already. But that's not what they want. Herding cows – or not – won't bring down a king.

She will not cease her reference to her counsel, her voice. She taunts them with it. If you were well informed about me, you would wish me to be out of your hands. I have done nothing, except by revelation.

471

Oh, my lady.

He does not sleep. He can barely eat. The Maid alone is peaceful. In her cell, quietly, she says, 'Tomas, you have done all you can. This is not your battle. Do not put yourself in danger on my account.'

'Do you want to burn? You do understand what they will do to you?'

'I understand, and I assuredly do not want it.'

'Well then . . .'

She is lying on the bed, her wrists behind her head, watching him. She is thinner, her eyes bigger in her face. He cannot read beyond them. 'Go, Tomas. Find Marguerite. Tell her not to come again; it's too dangerous.'

'*What?*'

'She was in the court, did you not see? At the back, near the door. She and Huguet. They shouldn't be here, it's not safe. Tell them to go home and not to grieve.'

As well tell a pike not to hunt, a deer not to run, a falcon not to stoop to the kill. Marguerite's natural language is prayer, but God is not answering; He is not letting the Maid walk free, not striking off her chains and striking dead the enemy all around her. Faced with this lack, what else is there but grief, unless it is an impotent, murderous rage?

Marguerite is raging, who is not built for it. She is too fine, too fragile. Tomas, who watches her as closely as he does the Maid, can see the way it builds in her marrow, in the hollow places beneath her collarbones, pressing outwards, thickening her blood, causing her humours to rise and boil over.

Simply to stand near her is to be scalded by her fury. He aches to hold her, to fold her in his arms and kiss her hair and make her back to the smiling, radiant woman who nursed him when his own schemes had broken his elbow. He cannot. His heart breaks twice, for the Maid and for Marguerite. He loves both. He can have neither.

Marguerite is fasting again, if she has eaten at all since last May. He supposes she must have done, but the dark pools beneath her eyes are deeper, darker than the Maid's. If she were the one chained to the block in the cell, she could not look worse. 'What are you doing to get her out? There must be something.'

'If there were, lady, you have to believe me, I would have tried it. Even if I had to knock her on the head and carry her out sleeping, I would have tried it.'

A derisive snort. A raised brow that cuts him deeper than anything Bedford has ever done. He thinks that it's a good thing she's his friend or he'd be broken.

She says, 'Try harder.'

He leaves and the next trial day she is there, bearing witness, offering the support of her presence.

He, then, can only do the same. Day by day, nothing changes, except that the questions become more ludicrous, and the answers match them. Soon, the court is laughing more with the Maid than against her.

—Tell us about the angels who bring you counsel: what clothes are they dressed in?

—I have made no mention of angels. I have counsel.

He waits for her to say 'the king in heaven speaks to me', but she is not stupid; far, far from that.

—The angels are naked, then?

—You think God could not clothe His angels?

More laughter. Cauchon's veins grow fatter. In back rooms of the city, men lay bets on whether he will live to see her burn. The best odds Tomas has heard are ninety to one against.

They are obsessed with the matter of angels and saints and the many recorded ways by which men of the cloth might establish whether laymen – and indeed laywomen – who claim to have had visitations from holy figures are in fact being deceived by the devil. Or not.

Tomas thinks that this is the way by which three dozen learned men, having decided the rules by which an angel might dance on the head of a pin, will then question others on the finer points of those same rules, while keeping them hidden and secret. The whole thing is a sham, but he cannot say this aloud, and nobody else seems inclined to point it out.

Cauchon is determined that the Maid saw angels and no amount of 'there were no angels, no saints, only my counsel, which advises me' will satisfy him. He must know what they wore, how was their hair, how their countenance, the tone of their voice.

When, at the end of a hard day, she says that 'Saint Michael gave me some comfort', he fastens on it like a hound on a crippled deer.

'What were you thinking?' Tomas asks in her cell. 'He will never let this go.'

'I'm sorry.' She is white, drawn, lying on her bed with her ankles crossed and her hands behind her head, but she is not laughing at him now. Exhaustion drains the colour from her skin, makes weightless her body. If she could slip out of the shackles, he could carry her away. Her hair sticks around her head, held by old, dried sweat. When she was like this before, she had a headache that made her vomit, violently. He finds her water and gives it, and holds her while she drinks.

Gently, he says, 'Saint Michael is the patron of the Valois. They will know the old king trained you.'

'Tomas, all day the same questions, all of them, three or four at a time, until my head spins. I thought he might stop.

I thought it might get him to . . . I wasn't thinking. I just spoke. It was stupid. I'm sorry.'

'He won't let go of it.'

'I know.' Half a smile, all exhaustion. 'Whom should I have said?'

He searches in the breviaries and books of his mind. Illumination comes in the form of a memory: a taut face by his bedside, lips framing words of greater piety than has often touched his life. 'Who does Marguerite pray to?'

'Saint Catherine of Siena. Saint Margaret. Both are maids: safe, good, kind saints suitable for women.'

'Them, then. Speak of them.'

'And we shall make it exciting. What do you think a saint would wear? How would they style their hair? How would their voices sound? You haven't read Gerson, I suppose, on the topic?'

'Not recently. Not that.'

'A pity.'

On 10 March, they cease to question her in public. The humiliation is too great. They find themselves 'too busy' to appear in the great chamber of the chateau, and instead file into the chamber of her cell: Cauchon, Jean de la Fontaine, Nicolas Midi, Gérard Feuillet and others, plus the three notaries who transcribe the conversations each day and copy them clean in the evenings. Cauchon will prove this trial is fair, even in its unfairness.

Tomas would write his own account, more accurate, but he would be seen and what excuse could he give? My lord of Bedford requires that I give him an honest account because yours is rotten to the core? Nobody will believe that; Bedford doesn't want anything except a big, hot fire and a clear route through to Rheims at the end of it, and slowly, slowly, one misspoken sentence at a time, one mistake, one exhausted, frustrated, half-ironic answer that can later be caught and teased out and examined in ways that were never intended, Cauchon is giving it to him.

—Do you see the angels bodily?

'I saw them with my two eyes as readily as I see you; and when they left me, I wept and truly wished that they had taken me with them.' This by now is true, he thinks; she holds always to the almost-truth, that she might remember it better in the midst of their harangues.

—Do you know that Saint Catherine and Saint Margaret hate the English?

'They hate what God hates and love what He loves.'

—Does God hate the English?

'I have no idea whether He loves or hates the English or what He will do to their souls. But I know that they will be driven out of France, except those that die here, and that God will send the French a victory over the English.'

—What support and what succour do you look to from Our Lord with respect to your wearing of men's clothing?

'For that, as for the other things I have done, I have not wished to have any other reward than the salvation of my soul.'

Men's clothes. Is this the worst they can find, that she wears doublet and hose? Nobody has asked her how she came to ride a horse that few men would choose to mount. Nobody asks how she couched her lance on Ascension Day, how she knew how to direct the guns at Jargeau, how she humiliated all of England at Montépilloy. They don't want that in their court proceedings, but they will harp on endlessly about men's clothes.

—Did your voice bid you to put on men's clothes?

'Whatever I have done that was good, I have done at the bidding of my counsel.'

Later, Tomas hears that Cauchon has had an iron cage

made, that she might be tethered standing, unable to move, and might only eat and drink by the hands of others.

He has not used it yet, but it exists and he makes sure she gets to hear of it just before the hearing opens.

That morning, she says more things she should not say. 'I saw an angel holding a crown over the king of France at his coronation.'

Marguerite leaves the court after that. Tomas sees her go. He chooses not to follow; what is there to say?

CHAPTER FIFTY-TWO

CHÂTEAU DE BOUVREUIL, ROUEN,
March–April 1431

THERE IS A QUESTION to which Tomas thought he would
never learn an answer, and he was wrong.

The answer comes in late March, in the afternoon.

The Maid is lying on the bed, waiting for the old king to
appear to her, which is what she does, evidently, when the
days lie long on her.

Tomas hears afterwards how it happened, how she is
lying there, with the day creeping on; the rain, then the
rare spring sun. She has already told him that she measures
time by the changing angles of the shadows on the sill edge
where the narrow slit of a window catches the sun. The light
is angled sharply across the stone in late afternoon when the
door unlocks again.

She thinks, This is it: they have come to burn me. Tomas,
where are you? She stands and moves as far as she can before
the chains halt her. The irons drag at her ankles. She can
smell blood somewhere, iron-bright in the thunderous air.

The door grunts heavy on its hinges. Who comes in is
a knight: mail and surcoat with a badge on it quartered in

gules and sable, with the three lions of England in the red and a turreted castle in the black. A chevron shows him to be the younger son of a great house. Not Bedford; he is of Lancaster and his sign is the rose. Warwick, perhaps? A younger brother of the man who defeated the Welshman, Owain Glyndwr?

'So . . .' He is a bull, barging to a halt just inside the door, thumbs tucked in his belt. The buckle is silver, thick as a man's fist. His cloak is a soldier's, heavy with the weight of campaigning, crusted with mud at the hem. His boots have been worn through at the toes from long wear. Mud peels from them on to the floor.

She thinks, He has been hunting; this is where comes the scent of blood, of horses (oh, Xenophon, what have they done with you?), of terror and pain and the fierce joy of slaughter. It would be something hard; stag or boar: this man would not waste his time hunting hinds. He has matched himself against the biggest and the best and now he comes to prove himself again, against the Maid who terrorized Bedford, Warwick, the whole English army.

He heels the door shut, rips off his gloves. 'Fucking French whore. The piss-water bishop says you are too pure to have consorted with the devil. Tell that to Salisbury, hey? To Talbot's brother. To Scales. To Suffolk. To the defenders of Meung, of Jargeau. To the bowmen of Patay. How could a fucking whore beat real men if not with the devil's help?'

At each name, a stride across the cell, gloves hurled aside, fat fingers fumbling at his points. He chest-buffets her back. She is crushed between him and the wall, pressed there, held by his bulk. She is hobbled, unable to run. She has no breath to call for help; all her air has been stolen by his weight.

'I can't believe they haven't made you wear a gown, these worms who call themselves men. They need an Englishman to show them how to bring you to heel.'

His face thrusts at hers. Spit flecks the corners of his lips. His breath swarms over her, hot with fury. He is not drunk, unless an excess of lust and the thrill of slaughter be his wine, but he will break into her by force if he can.

His teeth are at her cheek again, pressing, crushing, driving her head back against the wall, sucking her breath. He is stuck at the forty points that tie her hose; always, she has had double the usual number, and this is the reason.

He rocks back, to look, and this is her chance. She brings up her knee, as hard as her fetters will let her. She thrusts her balled fist at his throat. And she screams. 'Help! Rape! Help! Talbot! Tomas! *Help!*'

'My lady?' By luck, Tomas is walking nearby, but he is outside, and must argue his way into the chateau. 'Let me in! No, don't go for Warwick! Actually, yes, do go for Warwick, but let me in first.' And up the stairs, to the guards' room, where five men shrug awkwardly; a lord has given them orders, what are they to do? But they would like to help. They have lived in her company for five months and they no longer piss in her food. He is a priest; he has enough authority to overrule some petty lord's second son. He sends them for John Talbot, cousin to the one in French hands, who has laid his hand on the bible and sworn to protect her. 'You would let them make an oath-breaker of you?'

In the cell, she is still under assault.

'Shut *up!*' Her assailant is fast: her knee did not reach the parts she aimed for. His fist slams her chin, her head smashes back against the wall. She bites her tongue, tastes blood, feels her nose crack and gush.

She is falling, flailing, grabbing out for loose clothing, for flesh, for anything she can hit and hurt, because she will *not* lose her chastity. She will not let them call her a whore. She cannot: only maids are immune to the devil. Without her maidenhead, she is as good as burned.

He falls on top of her. His points are open. He is strug-
gling, thrusting. She can feel the rigid end of his member
like a piston against her hose. He will force himself through
if he cannot work them open. She bites his nose. He hits her.
He is grunting, 'Whore! Whore! Whore! I will break you
apart, you little French cunt. I will—'

'My lord, you will not.' Tomas grabs his arm, fingers
biting into the flesh.

John Talbot takes his shoulders. 'Sir, you will stop this.
It does you no honour. Matthew, take his arm. Tomas, the
prisoner is in your care. If she is harmed, I will hold you
responsible. Send to your lodgings for someone to bring
your unguents.'

In short order, they are alone. Tomas has a bucket
of cold water and a cloth to make a compress, but her
nose is broken, and her lip is the size of her chin, and
there are bite marks on her cheeks and bruises the size of
a man's fist to back them up. The air stinks of sweat and
fury.

'My lady, lie still. Let me . . .'

He eases back the neck of her shirt, to clean a scratch
mark that goes down below her collarbone. And so he sees
it: the red strawberry mark below her right ear, exactly as it
is on Marguerite. The mark of the old king's get.

His world, already shaken, fractures. His hand will not
move. Water drips from the cloth.

'Tomas?'

'You are the king's daughter. The old king. You were not
just his ward. You were his *daughter*.'

She is too broken to smile, too bruised, but he sees a spark
deep in her eyes. She licks her lips, tries to speak. Stops. Tries
again. 'Are you going to tell Bedford?'

'Lady . . .' He is on his knees at her side, his hands clasping
hers, careless of her wounds. 'That you could think that of

481

me—' And because his mind is open, his thoughts flying too many different ways, 'You are Guerite!'

That at least raises a smile. 'My father was not stupid.'

He has never thought that. Mad, clearly, but never stupid. He named his daughter 'little war' because she was his warrior. And on her, it is as a glove made to fit the hand. She *is* Guerite, body and soul.

But then . . . 'Who is Marguerite? The king only had one daughter.'

'No, he had two, but one was never spoken of. I was acknowledged because my mother was La Petite Reine. My sister was got on a chambermaid if you speak to the dairymaids, or a dairymaid if you speak to the chambermaids. I don't know which of these is true, but she was the product of one of his bouts of madness. Her mother died when she was born. My mother would have taken her in, but . . . you don't know what it was like at court. She was safer, probably, growing up with her mother's people. And she came to visit us, often. My mother doted on her, and Yolande. All the ladies did. She was so beautiful, so pure. She still is.'

Two daughters, then, and one of them a warrior. The other . . . he remembers Claudine. *We called her the Princess. The king's daughter. The king's bastard daughter. We saw her hardly at all, and when we did she was with La Petite Reine . . .* Clever Claudine.

He says, 'Claudine let me think what I already believed was true. She didn't betray you.'

'I'm glad. Did you kill her?'

'No. That was an agent of Bedford's. I choked him to death and buried his cockless body in a midden.'

She laughs, breathlessly, painfully. 'Oh, Tomas. Thank you. Hanne will be pleased. She liked Claudine.'

Hanne. That name spoken with the same warmth he

heard in a hovel in Rheims on the night of the king's anointing. And so the last piece falls into place and the broken story is made whole.

'Marguerite is Hanne?' Of course. Of *course*. They are like this. Tight as crossed fingers. Claudine not a part of their closeness. So much explained.

She is watching him, the Maid who is the king's daughter. Laughter sparks her eyes. 'Properly she is Jehanne. I took her name, she took mine. We had to stay as close to the truth as possible so that if anyone – *when* everyone – started to ask questions, they would find what we wanted . . .'

She dries as much for pain as for the words. In a while, looking away, she says, 'It was always going to come to this.'

'No! No . . .' So many reasons why not. 'If the king had only . . . Body of Christ, he is your *brother*.'

'Which is exactly why he could not accept me; a woman who fights when he does not so much as tilt? It could never be. Yolande saw that from the start.'

'She made this happen? Yolande of Aragon?'

'The king's mother-in-law. Indeed.' A dry half of a smile. 'My poor brother is surrounded by women who would rule him. I had to wait until my mother died, but then Yolande was ready, and we planned it, she and me and Marguerite, so that when Marguerite de Valois returned to court in the middle of winter, it was not the same girl who had left Chinon four years before. Nobody noticed. They hadn't paid me any attention when I was young and they were far too busy making sure they were in favour with the new princess to ask questions. She fills the role well, don't you think?'

'As if born to it. You, however, are not a peasant.'

'And yet nobody asks. Father saw that. "If you claim God on your side, they will ask about that, not about the horses or the swords."' Her eyes close. 'They haven't asked, any of them. Not once have they asked how I was able to take the field against Bedford at Montépilloy and scare him into flight.'

'They dare not. The man who turns my lord regent into a laughing stock will find himself thrown in the river.'

'And I will burn.'

'My lady, no! Did not your father say you would be freed before the end? You told me he said so. Dear God, you even told Pierre Cauchon that your voice promised you freedom before the end.'

'He has not said it recently.' She closes her eyes, and is lost to him.

He presses the cloth on her neck, holds it awhile, dips it in the bucket, wrings it out, then goes down on his knees and lays his hand on her arm, where there is no bruising. 'I swear I will not tell them. I will not tell Bedford. I will not tell Cauchon. I will never tell anybody. I swear this on your life, which I hold more dear than my own.'

Through her bruised lips, past her broken nose, she manages a smile, of sorts. 'Thank you.'

CHAPTER FIFTY-THREE

Orléans,
Thursday, 27 February 2014
16.00

Picaut's drive along the Loire towards Blois is miraculously unattended. Christelle Vivier is no longer a story, therefore Cheb Yasine is no longer a story and Picaut may have run her full gamut of celebrity.

It's pleasantly liberating, although she is dogged by the sensation that something bigger is on its way, more damaging, something for which it was worth the effort of hacking into Christelle Vivier's campaign servers. Something, somewhere, will prove to have been worth distracting the entire police enterprise of Orléans.

She sifts through every sentence of her conversation with Father Cinq-Mars in the basilica, with Troy Cordier in the Hôtel JJR, with Monique Susong yesterday, with Sylvie, Garonne, Rollo. Nothing cracks the walls of her sub-conscious and the monster still lurks, but at least she hasn't spent the time considering the implications of being in love – there, she's said it now – with a man who still lives with his parents.

In Blois, she lets her satnav take her through the town and up the hill towards the castle. This, too, she last visited with her school, a day trip out to see the decadence of France's royalist past or the tragedy of its loss; her teachers were not entirely clear which.

Her father was entirely clear; she still remembers him reciting the bloody litany of fortunes spent on gold and diamonds, of lives lost and uncared for, of petty princes wreaking havoc with France's history for the sake of their vanity; the grim necessity of the revolution, and the blood-bath it became.

Sylvie is right. Here, where the houses date back to when England owned the land, where the roads are really not built for cars and she has to ditch hers in a parking space and walk, where the houses are built on a latticework of dark wood, with white walls and black-tiled roofs . . . here are properties owned by families with wealth nearly to match the Bressards. She had never imagined Patrice in one of these.

She is hoping there'll be a gap in the long stretches of magnificent medieval terraced mansions, that she'll find something else, a servant's cottage, perhaps, turned into a scruffy communal hideaway for the digitally obsessed.

But she follows the curve of the road to the address Sylvie has provided and it's identical to all the others: three storeys high, double fronted, of white stone under black tiles. A black-painted door gives directly on to the street. The window shutters are painted white. She glances in through the nearest window and sees a distressingly ornate chaise longue and two matching pre-revolutionary chairs all facing a wide-screen television. Something inside her shrivels.

She reaches the door. There is more than one bell: three, in fact, one above the other set to one side of a brass plaque on which, with the kind of arrogant permanence the Bressards would employ, three names are engraved: *P. LACROIX, V. TAVEL, S. SARLES*.

Courage is made of moments like this. Before she can walk away, she pulls her hands from her pockets and presses the bell, hard. No sound filters back through the black front door to say she has been heard. She counts a slow hundred and tries again, longer, harder. And then again.

Five minutes later, when a ten-second lean on the bell has produced no response, she tries the name below: V. Tavel. And receives an answer.

'*Oui?*' A woman's voice comes from a speaker set on the other side of the door. Young, perhaps twenty-something. She sounds warm, just in that one word: intelligent, friendly.

'Police. I'm looking for Patrice Lacroix. He's not in trouble; we need his help.' She has planned this approach in the five minutes of waiting. There has to be a reason Patrice has kept his work and home so far apart, and it may well be that the people who live around him don't know what he does for a living.

'Who is it?'

'Police. From Orléans.'

'You said that already. Who?'

'Picaut. Capitaine Inès Picaut.'

There is a moment's pause, and then the buzz that even here, in a place where the stones of the porch are over six hundred years old, signals the unlocking of a door. The woman's voice: 'Come up to the second floor.'

Inside is airy, and smells pleasantly of great age. Pale stone flags in the hallway are worn with the footsteps of centuries. Picaut follows their line to a wide spiralling staircase that sweeps up and round to the left ahead of her. Tall windows let in the almost-summer sun, washing to white the pale cream plaster. Everything is fresh and clean and painfully bright.

Running up, Picaut tries to imagine Patrice sliding down the gilded oak banister, or skateboarding down the grey marble stairs; something – anything – to break the perfect, bourgeois *neatness* of this place.

She reaches the second floor, on which is a small landing before the stair spirals on up. Ahead, a door hangs ajar. She's raising her hand to knock when a woman opens it and comes out; slightly built, with short, blue-black hair, she is wearing a white linen shirt that reaches just short of her knees, belted with calf skin. Her eyes are iron-grey and they scour Picaut from head to foot, take in the jeans and trainers and leather jacket that's not quite old enough to be vintage, not nearly new enough to be chic.

She reaches out a hand. 'Valérie Tavel.' She tilts a smile. 'Patrice has spoken of you.'

Her accent is Canadian, the old-French of Montreal. She kicks the door shut with her bare foot and nods up the stairs. 'I have a spare key. I think you'd be allowed inside.'

They head together up the last flight of the spiral staircase. Nothing changes, but Picaut feels as if she has passed through some kind of static membrane; that the world is more dangerous on this side than when she was safely downstairs. The sun is still too bright. She hasn't brought her gun. For the first time, this strikes her as careless.

The door to Patrice's apartment is identical to all the others in this house: solid – exceedingly solid – oak, painted white, with brass fittings. Valérie's key opens it.

'Wait.' Picaut catches her in the act of pushing it open. If he does live with his parents, this is her last moment of ignorance. If he doesn't . . . that might be more worrying still. She asks, 'When did you last see him?'

'This morning, around half past nine. He'd been to see

you. He was . . . very happy. Very pleased with himself. He thought you were pleased with him.'

She was. Did she say so? She can't remember and that, too, feels bad. Everything here feels not-right. 'Did he say he was going to sleep? That he didn't want to be disturbed?'

'No. He just said, "Life is good!" and ran upstairs. To here.'

'Who else lives here?'

'Me and Sebastien.'

'No, I mean, here, with Patrice? In this apartment?'

Valérie wrinkles her brow. 'Nobody. Just us.'

So he doesn't live with his parents. It would be pleasant to indulge in the relief of this. Later, maybe.

'Who owns this place?' Picaut asks. This apartment, which must cost more than his annual salary if he rents it, and more than his lifetime's salary if he tried to buy it.

'We do. Me and Trice and Seb.' Valérie flashes a grin. 'You think that's impossible?'

Picaut would clearly never make a poker player because that's exactly what she thinks. She is wondering if they perhaps all three are cousins and inherited this from some childless great-uncle, and wishes she had read more of Patrice's family background. She remembers a father in military cyber-intelligence, nothing else. She doesn't know if he has a sister. Or a lover.

Valérie Tavel, who could be either, pushes open the door to his apartment. 'You'd best come inside.'

Inside is . . . The first thing Picaut notices is that inside is pleasantly dark when compared to the blasting, unfiltered sunlight outside, at least until her eyes adjust to the subtleties of light. Then, it is reassuringly abnormal. Which is to say she has not walked into a chintz-flavoured drawing room, or a hallway with carpets of a depth to match Christelle Vivier's hotel suite. She has, instead, stepped into a long, echoing room that extends from side to side of the building and all the way from this end to the other – which is further than she'd imagined from the outside.

This is not one apartment in a terrace, but the entire row. Studying it, counting the tall sun-hazed windows, she's sure that this room extends through all four houses side by side; all the internal walls have been removed and the structural ones replaced by rolled steel joists. The result is a space that is easily sixty metres long, by fifteen wide. You could park aircraft in here, hide half a revolution. There's one solitary door set to the left of the entrance which she assumes leads to a bathroom.

In the main room, the floors are of plain wood, sanded smooth and sealed with something matt, while the walls are probably the same off-white plaster as downstairs, but they are covered in posters of skateboarding, snowboarding, base-jumping, mountain biking, sport climbing, capoeira, bushido, krav maga, wing chun . . . everything youthful, fast and dangerous is here, and if it involves dexterity and muscle and violent Day-Glo lycra, then so much the better.

There is more light than she'd first thought, just that it's filtered through muslin fixed across the windows, which acts to mellow the day's glare and makes it easier, she imagines, to work at a computer. Or to play.

The main part of the room has been converted into a skateboarding track, complete with built-in jumps and dips and ramps. Before she reaches it, Picaut passes a double bed against the far wall. Nothing complicated; a futon base topped by a duvet with a black cotton cover. But it's neatly made.

Beyond it is a kitchen area on the left, under the first of the windows. Here are no signs of breakfast, of half-finished food, unwashed coffee cups. She has never thought of

Patrice as being particularly fastidious, but looking back she can't remember a time when he failed to wash a mug, or left his desk disordered.

Carrying on, she crosses the last part of the skateboard track and comes to a workstation in which is a collection of computer equipment that would make Éric Masson weep with envy.

Six ultra-wide HD screens stand on a semicircular desk set around the treadmill, and these, in turn, are linked to an array of circuit boards, fans and heat sinks that looks homemade and powerful. Giant speakers sit between the screens, and behind them is a laser printer. Three iPads and a Samsung Galaxy lie in a rectangular arrangement on one table amidst the relics of a bygone era: an Apple Lisa, an Atari, an Amstrad, a BBC Micro . . . all the old names from the age when computing was new and memory was measured in kilobytes and backups were made to tape.

Each screen has a small sticker on its frame that reads, CTS TECHNOLOGY. Elsewhere is paper with the same heading, and a logo which she has seen before, once, on a T-shirt.

Picaut points to it. 'What's this?'

Valérie hesitates. 'Does Patrice get into trouble if he's got more than one job?'

'Patrice does not get into trouble, I guarantee it. Tell me what it is.'

'We're joint directors of a technology consultancy company. The company owns this building.'

'All of it?' Picaut's disbelief spans the length of the room. 'All the way along?'

'It came up at a very good price.'

Anything less than ten million would count as miraculous. 'What, exactly, do you do?'

'We test people's digital security, find the weak points, work out how to fix them before the hackers get in. Don't

491

worry – Patrice spends most of his time on police work for you. I've never seen it take him longer than half an hour to crack anything we've been sent.'

'Let me get this right. The three of you earn millions of euros for half an hour's work?'

Valérie smiles shyly. 'Experience comes at a price. It's like breaking into cars: it doesn't matter what the manufacturers do, there will always be somebody somewhere who is one step ahead. You must have men in your force who can walk up to any locked car and open it as if they had the key?'

Garonne can do this. There was a time when it impressed Picaut deeply. She says, 'Who do you work for?'

'Anyone with enough money. When we started five years ago, most of our clients were in the US. Now most of them are in China, some in India, Brazil, Africa, South America. We're just starting to look at South Korea: there's been an upsurge in interest since the boy in the north started executing his relatives.'

'I thought the East Asian countries had their own techno-genius graduates?'

'They have some very bright people, but they still aren't the best.'

'And you are?'

'Our clients think so. One day they won't. Then we'll put the whole building back as it was and sell it.'

Picaut can imagine what it must have looked like; she baulks at the work it would take to put it back. 'Is each floor like this one?'

'Seb and I share the floor below; it's not a skateboarding track, but it's not four apartments any more: we like open space. The ground floor is where we bring clients. It hasn't changed much.' Valerie has moved to the workstation. She nudges a mouse on the desk and all six monitors come to life. On the first five, the screen scrolls so fast Picaut can't read whatever is on it. On the sixth is an email.

Valérie studies it. 'Can you read English?'

'Yes. Why?'

'You might want to sit down. Pull up his chair. Here.'

Picaut does not sit. And then, after a moment, she does.

From: Charles Picaut <crp1955@gmail.com>

To: Iain Holloway <maidhunter@btconnect.com>

Subject: MdV and the Maid

Date: 15 October 2013

Dear Iain,

Further to our correspondence of 5 October, I offer my apologies for my delay in replying (if you are ever given the option, I advise you most strongly to avoid chemotherapy: death is a better alternative, and it comes to us all in the end). That apart, I have to say that I am immensely impressed with your work so far and the conclusions that you draw, and am proud to have played my part in this, however small.

To recap, we are both agreed that the Maid cannot have been what history suggests: she was a trained knight, not a visionary peasant.

We are further agreed that Marguerite de Valois is the most likely contender, and that Charles VI, called the Mad, is both her father and the knight who trained her. In a world where it was heresy for a girl to dress in doublet and hose, nobody but a king would have had the authority over the Church to arm a girl child and teach her to ride. Charles was obsessed with the tilt: he is known to have attended tourneys incognito, and could easily have taken his daughter with him as a squire. He had the means and the motive, and nobody else, frankly, was mad enough to try. Finally, he was surrounded by men who would indulge his every madcap venture as long as he wasn't actually trying to rule France: it can have been nobody else.

493

None the less, there *was* a maid: when Pierre Cauchon sent men to Lorraine to discredit her story, they found nothing that he would not have been happy to hear about his sister. Therefore a substitution was made prior to the Maid's arrival at Chinon in the late winter of '29: we are agreed on this, you and I. Marguerite de Valois departed the court on the death of her father in 1422 and *a different girl* returned five years later in 1429, sheltered by Yolande of Aragon, and later legitimized by the king.

So the obvious question therefore is not who was the Maid, but who was this new Marguerite de Valois, the woman who married Jean of Belleville and lived to a goodly age? Whence did she come and to where did she go? To this latter question, I may have an answer, or at least, the first part of one.

I believe that Louis XI, son of the craven Charles VII, knew the truth and Louis's bones reside in the basilica de Notre Dame at Cléry-Saint-André. Through a family link, I have gained access to records which few others have ever seen. If these are accurate, then *the bones of Marguerite de Valois lie with him*: a silent honouring for who she was, made in ways which need never have been spoken aloud, but which will have mattered to a devout king, who wanted to honour the truth.

These remains hold the key. If my theory is correct, then a DNA match against Louis XI should prove that they are not related. (Louis was the son of Charles VII who was widely believed to have been illegitimate, but if his natural father was the king's brother, then there should still be a sufficient familial link to connect blood relatives – or not, *if she was someone else*).

I shall not live to see this, but I sincerely believe that you will. Go with my blessing, and my hopes for your success: our nation deserves the truth, but more than that, we owe a debt of honesty to the woman who fought for our freedom and was

forced into lies from which her reputation has never escaped.
  CRP.

'Capitaine? Capitaine Picaut? Are you all right?' Valérie, at
her side, blocking her view of the screen. She makes herself
look away, look at the room, at the other screens, the pile of
cans, makes herself *here*, and not there, in his room, where
he wrote this.

'Do you want a drink? Coffee? Beer? We might have
vodka somewhere?'

'No. Thank you. I'm fine.' She will make it true.

'Did you know your father was corresponding with Iain
Holloway?'

'Not until this week.' She rouses herself, stands, walks
around, comes back to the desk, sits again. 'I gave away
his laptop, which was something of a mistake, obviously,
although I— What's this?'

She has run her hands along the edge of the desk. Beneath
the right-hand end is a flutter of garish yellow paper: a note
stuck underneath. She pulls it off, turns it over.

Your father's paper is the key to the last file. Email is the
first part. Second is an image. Decoding now. Screen 4.

The handwriting is Patrice's, hurried.

'Your father,' Valérie says. 'Not "the capitaine's father".
Not "Picaut's father". This is written to you. He knew you
were coming. Or he hoped you were.'

'He knew.' *Give me six hours.* Her eyes are dry, burning.
Her palms are sticky. 'What's on screen four?'

It takes moments to find it: on the furthest left screen,
another image is building.

Already the skull is in place: green with mould, teeth
intact. Picaut knows this one, she carries an image of it in

her phone, but this is taken from further away, and it's an entire skeleton. Only it isn't, yet; the image is emerging with excruciating slowness, pixel by laborious pixel. The first three cervical vertebrae are here, complete with signs of arthritis that would be consistent with a woman wearing a battle helm, but equally, they'd be consistent with falling from a horse, a high building – or wearing the kind of head-dresses that were the fashion in the court of mid-fifteenth-century France.

She says, 'If my father is even half-right, this is Marguerite de Valois, bastard daughter of the king of France.'

'Your father thought she was the Maid?'

'He did. But he was wrong.'

'Then why did Iain Holloway die?'

'I have no idea. And right now, finding Patrice has a higher priority.' Picaut turns her back on the monitors, makes herself think. 'Has anyone been to visit in the last few hours? Anyone who could have asked him to go out?'

Valérie spreads her hands. 'I don't know. I wasn't here. A few minutes after he got in, a neighbour of my mother's called to say she was ill: my mother, that is, not the neighbour. She lives on the other side of Tours. The traffic was bad. It took me over fifty minutes to get there.'

'And how was your mother when you got there?'

'Coughing fit to die, but she's smoked for sixty-two years, so that's nothing new. I called the doctor anyway and had to wait for her to find time to come and then run through a complete medical and then lecture us both on the evils of tobacco and the benefit of nicotine patches. I got home about twenty minutes ago. Trice was gone, but I thought he was with you, so I wasn't worried.'

'And now you are. Where's Seb?'

'I told you; in South Korea, with the men who make deals. He's the one who does the talking. You wouldn't send a man with electric-blue hair to Korea, and most of these people won't deal with a woman.'

'*Plus ça change* . . . Your mother's neighbour, has he ever called before?'

'He's not really a neighbour. He's just some random bloke who was staying at the hotel next door. He heard her coughing through the wall.'

'He told you that?'

Pale, Valérie says, 'You want me to check with the hotel?'

'Is he still there?'

'Probably not; he was calling from his car. And I didn't ask his name.' Her hands rise slowly to her face. 'Shit.'

Picaut can count the miles back to Orléans to get her gun. She leans back against the wall, seeking solace in solidity. 'Let's go back to the beginning. Patrice came home when he was expected to, and came upstairs. Was he here when you left?'

'I think so. The stairs are pretty loud. I'd have heard him if he'd come down again.'

'So he was still here when you went out. What time was that?'

'About quarter to ten this morning. I got back just before four.'

Six hours. She is doing her best not to become fixated by numbers. 'Is his bike still here?'

'I haven't looked, but it's kept in the garage at the bottom of the road, chained with three padlocks and two webcams, one hidden, one visible trained on it round the clock. You'd have to be mad to try to take it.'

'I'm not sure we're dealing with sanity here. Can you check the feed from the webcams?'

While Valérie clears all six screens and scrolls through the feed, Picaut makes a single rapid circuit of the vast room.

She checks behind the closed door at the far end and

finds a wet-room with high-pressure shower and toilet: empty. The kettle is dry. The fridge is stocked. The bed is cold and neatly made.

A wardrobe built into the wall has a rack of jeans and another rack of black T-shirts. The front one says NERDS 2^2 EVER. Without effort, she can imagine him wearing it.

Her circuit brings her back to where Valérie is checking the webcams in the garage. 'Anything?'

'Nothing. The bike's still there. Nobody has been near it.'

Patrice's workstation desk is busy, but ordered. The only thing awry is the spectacular three-dimensional pyramid of Red Bull cans built to one side; at least a hundred cans, arranged with mathematical precision. Three have fallen off the top.

'How long has he been building this?' Picaut asks.

'Since the start of the month.' Valérie gives a tight, half-shy smile, as of a sister with a mildly eccentric, but much-loved brother. 'He takes them all to the recycling centre on the last day of the month and starts again. He reckons one day he'll make it to the ceiling inside thirty-one days.'

'When he's with us, he's very precise. He wouldn't let cans fall off the top.'

Valérie nods slowly. 'Here too. He'd go mad if something was out of line. In fact, it should be a physical impossibility. That thing is structurally stable.'

She's right. Picaut takes the three cans and fits them back into place. She has to tap them hard to get them to move, but a larger disaster, like a physical struggle nearby would topple the entire construction.

Even more than the scribbled Post-it slapped under the desk, it's hard to escape the conclusion that these were moved deliberately, and harder to escape the idea that Patrice has done it to send a message. *I left under duress.*

I couldn't leave another note, but I leave you this, and trust you can read it.

Picaut closes her eyes. Her heart is a stone, sinking. To Valérie, she says, 'Have you somewhere safe you can go? Not your mother's; they know that address. Somewhere anonymous. A hotel, maybe? Not here.'

'There's a small hotel in Blois that we send clients to . . .'

'No. It has to be somewhere with no connection to you or the company. Somewhere small and out of the way. Go to Paris or Chinon. Don't stay in Blois or Orléans or Tours. If you can pay cash and use a different name, do it. Stay low.' Picaut is in a hurry now. She finds a used envelope and writes on it the number of the disposable phone that she keeps for emergency use. 'Don't use your own phone. Go to a kiosk and buy a pay-per-use one and text me on this number when you've done it. Keep off-grid. Keep away from people you know.'

'You'll be looking for Trice?'

'With everything we've got. We can—'

Her phone rings.

'Father Cinq-Mars, I don't have time just now . . .'

'Yes, you do. The gentleman currently pointing his gun at my head informs me that he is in possession of your friend. If you wish to see him alive, you will do as he tells you.'

'They have Patrice?' Relief punches into her solar plexus. At least there is this much certainty. And she has spent days, weeks, in hostage training. Keep them talking. Speak slowly. Keep them on the line as long as you can.

She signals silence to Valérie and scribbles *Can you track this call?* on the back of the envelope. It's a vain hope: it takes Patrice twenty-eight seconds to build the links that will allow a trace, and he's ready waiting when the call comes in. Today, here, now, it will take longer.

To the priest, Picaut says, 'I need to speak to Patrice. How else do I know he is alive?'

There is a pause, the silence of a muffled phone, then Father Cinq-Mars is back again.

'I'm sorry, but you will have to take my word for it. I swear I have seen him alive.'

'Describe him to me.' Each word is weighted, slow, sure. Valérie's fingers are flickering too fast to follow. It is possible that Valérie can type faster than Patrice, which is something to behold. The rightmost monitor in the bank of six has turned into a map of the Loire valley. A red haze spreads across it, becomes stronger near Meung-sur-Loire, not yet quite Cléry-Saint-André, but not far off.

Father Cinq-Mars, too, does not speak overly fast. Possibly, he knows this game, and is on her side. 'He has violent blue hair and a brilliant smile. His nose is perhaps a little large to be in balance with the rest of his face, but he is undoubtedly attractive, with the vitality of youth. His T-shirt is black and it features a cat in blue with beneath it the proclamation that computer games have ruined his life, and it is therefore a good thing that he has eight left.

'You should not count on those extra lives, Capitaine Picaut. The men who hold him, I believe, set fire to things, and they will use him as their tinder if they feel slighted. They may well burn my church in the process, which would, at least to me, be the greater catastrophe. I am told I must go. You are to leave the building you are currently in. Take your car. A new phone is in the front seat. You are to drop your old ones – both of them – down the drain outside. Goodbye.'

'No! Don't hang— *Fuck!*' To Valérie, 'Did we get it?'

'Out by about eight seconds. They know what they're doing.'

The map is still a disappointment of red. He could be

anywhere within a ten-mile radius of the basilica at Cléry-Saint-André.

'Right. We have to assume they're watching here. I have to do what they say. Can you make a phone call in a way that can't be traced?'

'Of course.'

'Call here.' She writes Garonne's mobile number on the envelope, and then Ducat's. 'Tell them both what's happened. All of it. Tell them that Jaish al Islam, whoever that really is, have Patrice and we know they'll kill if they have to. Their priority is to get Patrice out alive. I'll take care of myself. Got that?'

'They won't listen.' Valerie speaks as if she knows them. Or maybe she just knows their type.

'They'd fucking better. Tell them I said so. And then you get off-grid and don't talk to anyone, OK?'

'OK.' There is a short, awkward pause. Valérie says, 'Do you want to take Trice's gun?'

'Patrice has a gun?'

'He was given it the day he was recruited. He's never taken it out of the drawer. Wait.'

Valérie crosses the room. Below the bed, hidden by the fall of the duvet, is a full length drawer. She hauls it out and hands over a standard issue SIG-Sauer.

Picaut hefts it. It's nice, but it's too light. 'Where are the rounds?'

'Are they not in the gun?'

They had better not be: not if Patrice has listened even slightly to the regulations. She opens it. They are not in the gun. They are not in the drawer. They are not in any of the adjacent drawers.

'They must be somewhere.' Valérie is turning and turning, looking through cupboards in the kitchen.

There is no time. Picaut says, 'It'll do. Nobody but us

needs to know it's empty.' She slips it into the belt of her jeans. Following Valérie down the stairs, she chooses not to think of the circumstances in which it might become apparent that she cannot fire.

At the door, they clasp in a brief, awkward embrace. 'Good luck,' Valérie says. 'Bring him home.'

Her heart is lost. She remembers the pain of it from when her father died; the desolation. Patrice is not dead yet: she holds on to this. 'I intend to.'

CHAPTER FIFTY-FOUR

CHÂTEAU DE BOUVREUIL, ROUEN,
May 1431

IT IS EVENING. Tomas has done all he can to make the Maid comfortable after her ordeal and come away to the private room above the tavern.

Jean de Belleville is here at last. He entered Rouen in the afternoon, wearing the clothes of a merchant: poor Dutch wool, undyed, and shoes of horse hide with nails in the soles. He walked in through the gates bearing a skin of wine on his back and was not stopped by either English or French guards.

And so the Maid's closest family is joined again: de Belleville, Huguet and Marguerite de Valois, except she is not Marguerite, she is Jehanne, called Hanne, the one Tomas has been seeking since the day of the king's anointing: the angel princess who disturbed the fight amongst children on the day of Agincourt.

The other three seem relieved to be able to talk. And so he can at last have answers to the questions that troubled him. Did Yolande arrange this subterfuge? Is it all her doing? She is a strong woman, of discretion and power. He would not put it past her.

When he asks, Hanne gives something that is partway between a nod and a shake. 'It couldn't have happened without her. Yolande helped me to be accepted at court. She sent her men to bring the Maid from Vaucouleur, and made sure she was admitted to the king's presence at Chinon, to make her case.'

'That must have taken rare courage, to spin tales to the king, and all the time he might have recognized her.'

De Belleville bristles. 'The Maid never lied. She said, "My father in heaven has ordered me to bring France back to wholeness," which is true. If they chose to think she meant God, so be it. That idea was hers, and the making of it was Yolande's but the first thought was her father's. He made her swear on his sword three oaths: to take France back, to ransom Charles of Orléans, who was captured at Agincourt, and to liberate Paris.'

'He thought she could do all that?'

Hanne says, 'He was a king, she carried his blood. Of course he believed it. More than that, he was a knight, and he had trained her. From childhood, he saw what she was, what she could be, and he knew what Charles was. The king. Our brother.'

'Or not your brother, if the rumours regarding his parentage are true.'

She shrugs. 'It doesn't matter. That, too, is what Father saw: that she could unite the army, could lead it, could do all he asked, but she could never take the throne. She could not even lay claim to royal blood, because if she did, the peers of the realm would fight each other like stags at the rut to marry her and take the throne in her name. And then France would be torn apart again, because the losers would side with England.'

'Jean d'Alençon wouldn't marry her,' Tomas says. 'I tried to make him, at Paris.'

'Yolande made him promise not to,' says Huguet.

Tomas raises his head. 'He knows?'

'Of course, how could he not? We grew up together. He fought with her with wooden swords for hours when they were younger. He knows. La Hire knows. All those who support her, they know.'

'The king?'

'Not him, no. He was never at court when we were young. He'd gone to live with Yolande before we were born. He didn't meet her before that day at Chinon, and nobody will tell him; they wouldn't dare.'

Tomas wants to believe that Charles would not abandon his own flesh and blood, but the truth is that he has abandoned the Maid, to whom he owes everything, and it does not matter exactly what he knows.

A memory comes back to him, of a ditch outside Meung and Bertrand de Poulangy, a man who certainly knew. 'Was she ever a horse breaker? Before she came to Chinon?'

'Yes!' For the first time in months, he sees Hanne smile. Her eyes take on the same faraway look the Maid's do when she speaks of her past. 'That was later, after she and her mother left Burgundy.'

'Why did they go to Burgundy? Duke Philip is her enemy.'

Huguet says, 'Odette de Champdivers was Burgundian by birth. When the old king died, his mistress and his bastard daughter were driven out of court. There was nowhere else for them to go. I was at Sainte-Catherine-de-Fierbois. They came through and we buried her sword beneath the altar.'

Tomas sits bolt upright. 'The Crusader sword?'

De Belleville rises. 'The one her father gave her, yes. And the next morning, the Maid and her mother went on to Burgundy.' He goes to the door, shouts an order. 'And now, my lady should eat.' The tavern girls bring up onion soup, and bread, and small cakes of saffron and ground almonds.

Hanne is cheered; the reminiscence has brought colour to her cheeks. If she is ever going to eat, now is the time.

De Belleville ministers to her. 'Drink this soup, and tell Tomas the tale of Jean the horse breaker and his mother Marie who set up beside the stables in Sauvigny, and could have made their fortunes breaking difficult colts to saddle.'

Spoonful by spoonful, Hanne drinks. 'Father lost both his elder sons, and the third was . . . well, you know what he is. So he turned his attention to my sister. From when she first could walk, she would cry to be allowed on horseback, and so, in time, he taught her everything he knew. He made her ride and ride and ride without stirrups until she could sit any horse in his stable.'

Tomas says, 'In court, under oath, she said her mother taught her to spin and to weave.'

'It's true.' Hanne finishes the soup, lays down the bowl. 'For that one year in Burgundy, she wore gowns and pattens and high veils and learned spinning and weaving until her fingers bled. I wish I had seen her in a gown!'

Hanne comes to kneel by the fire, holding her wine. Her gown today is wool, dyed blue. Here in Rouen, she is a merchant's wife, but not a rich one. Her hair is unbound. It lies about her shoulders as a dark veil, threaded gold where the firelight leans to touch it.

Tomas prompts her gently. 'So after Burgundy, she became a horse breaker?'

'Yes. They moved to Sauvigny and began to make a name for themselves. As Jean, she took on the beasts nobody else dared go near, and her mother sewed bridles fit for a king. They liked the life, I think; at least the Maid did. Her mother lived only a year there, so perhaps it did not suit her. Odette died in the autumn of 1424, two years after the king.'

'The Maid could have stayed a horse breaker . . .'

'But she had given her word to Father that she would

see to her mother and then see to France. The spring after, she came to me in Domrémy. She sent a boy to find me in the fields with a message to say her mother had died, but he got it wrong and I thought it was my mother – that is, the woman who raised me. I flew to the house! Guerite hid amidst the nut trees, well away from Jacques d'Arc, the man who called me daughter; even then, he hated her.

'We met twice a month in the old chapel of Saint Margaret, in the woods three miles from the village. I walked there; she rode on whatever horse most needed work. She brought furs and wool and a cloak and cheeses and apples in the autumn and we talked of how life had been and how it would be when she had made France whole again. Even then, Father spoke to her, just as his counsel had spoken to him.'

'He heard voices?'

'Yes. I think not as often as he pretended, but sometimes the voices were real. They came always out of sunlight, I remember, and as children we had orders to find la Petite Reine if it happened when we were with him; he would speak to nobody else.'

The wine has worked its magic; Hanne is quiet, sleepy, warm. Huguet and Jean de Belleville excuse themselves and Tomas is left alone with her; they trust him this much. He comes to sit by the fire, keeping the flames for company, each lost in memory. As the darkness draws in, he takes her hand in his, and lifts it, and kisses the knuckles, and she smiles for him, and does not draw her hand away.

In the flame-lit quiet, she says, 'You love her.'

As it has been all day for her, it is a relief for him to speak the truth. 'I do.'

'As do we all. Even Jean and Huguet. Do you understand?'

'And she loves you?'

A sad smile. 'After Xenophon, yes.'

He sets down her hand. 'Claudine told me of the day of Agincourt, when you broke up a mock battle she was having with de Belleville. She said, "Even then, they loved each other, those two."' It is not quite what Claudine said, but it sounds as if she might have done. 'Tell me of that day,' he says.

He hears it as from the angel, the story of a child who blundered into a game and broke it, on the day their whole world was broken. In her memory stands tall the girl who threw herself into the rescue of the sister who sought only to be in her company. Even then, they were entwined, each with the other; the acknowledged daughter who bore her father's arms, and the untended daughter who had all of his beauty.

'You were never bitter that she was the king's daughter and you were the maid from Lorraine?'

'No. I was happy. And I could never have been what our father wanted. It was better that I did not have to try.'

He sleeps alone, always. That night, for the first time, in his mind he lies with the angel-princess who is really Hanne, and wakes soiled, and feels treacherous.

CHAPTER FIFTY-FIVE

Cléry-Saint-André,
Thursday, 27 February 2014
18.00

THERE IS A DRAIN by the car. As instructed in the phone call from Father Cinq-Mars, Picaut takes out both of her phones. A text has come up in the last few minutes, from Jonita Markos, aka Monique Susong:

> DNA RESULTS: A=MALE, B=FEMALE.
> FAMILIAL RELATIONSHIP STATUS: POSITIVE.

Which is, when she thinks about it, what Iain Holloway said in his note – and not the result expected by her father in his email. There is no time to work out the implications. Picaut drops both of her phones into the drain, hears the momentary silence and the double splash. Her guts churn at the loss.

Her car is locked. Nevertheless, a new cell phone sits on the passenger seat. It rings as she fires up the engine. Father Cinq-Mars sounds hoarser than he did before, less congenial.

'Capitaine Picaut. You are to drive to Cléry-Saint-André, to the basilica. Further instruction will be given you when you arrive. Drive directly away from your current location. Do not stop. Drop this phone out of the window as soon as this call ends. You will be seen if you do not and your friend, I fear, will lose a finger, if not his entire right hand. Goodbye.'

The line goes dead before she can speak. Picaut lowers the window, reaches out and drops this new phone into the same drain.

She starts the car and heads out of Blois. Traffic is light. It's not hard to see the team who are following her: a Suzuki GSX 1300 ridden by a biker in full black leathers and a black helmet with a darkened visor; a grey Audi S8: two occupants, both wearing dark suit jackets and sunglasses; a marine-blue Mazda RX8: one occupant, the same. Four against one is not great odds, but neither is it insurmountable.

They change places frequently with the slickness of much practice, but they make no real effort to remain invisible and as soon as she reaches the main road to Meung-sur-Loire, they move up until they bracket her, the bike in front, the Mazda behind, the Audi on the outside at the times when the road allows.

She does what she can to identify them, but the most she can see is that every one of the occupants of the cars is white. If this is Jaish al Islam, either it is composed entirely of Caucasian converts or it's a sham. Score one to Picaut: she told Ducat it was fake after the first phone call.

Like a sheep and its shepherds, they pass through Meung and on to Cléry-Saint-André. The spire of the basilica calls to Picaut long before they reach it. Her minders usher her into a parking space right in front of the northern entrance. The biker dismounts and jerks his head towards the door. He doesn't remove his helmet; she still can't see his face.

Picaut has tucked Patrice's SIG into the waistband of her jeans, hidden by her jacket. She has exactly the length of time it takes to remove the keys from the ignition and open the door to think about hiding it in the car, but the biker is too close, and in any case, there's no guarantee that it'll be possible to come back.

She leaves it in place and does her best to ensure that when she gets out, the flap of her leather jacket doesn't lift to expose it.

The door to the basilica is unlocked. Inside is cool and quiet and empty, or seems so until she walks towards the altar.

'Father Cinq-Mars!'

He is lying on his back at the altar's foot, with his hands crossed on his chest. She falls to her knees beside him, but her fingers seeking the pulse at his throat are a reflex born of blind optimism. There is no chance at all that he is alive; the bullet hole in his forehead has already told her that.

Her hand falls away from his throat. His body is already beginning to cool.

His eyes are still open and they would need coins, now, to weigh them shut. She wants to read peace in their depths, a release from the pain of his affliction, and knows she cannot.

She wants him to have left her a message, but the phone clasped between his dead hands is not his. It rings now, from a withheld number.

A man's voice says, 'So you know we are serious.'

'That was never in any doubt. Now you have me, you can let Patrice go. You have thirty seconds to let me see him alive and well or I use this phone to call Prosecutor Ducat.'

She hangs up. She has been taught never to let the opposition set the agenda, but to offer her own ultimatums;

her trainers never imagined a situation in which she would be her own bargaining counter.

She believes the men in dark glasses want her, not anybody else, and she is gambling Patrice's life on it.

She has had a twenty-minute drive to think it through. If he has seen their faces, if he can identify those holding him hostage, then he's dead; there is no other possible answer. If he hasn't, they may choose to let him go. If they shoot him, she will regret it for whatever remains of her life, but she can see no other way to get him out. Without doubt they won't let him go once she's dead.

She stands up and is about to head for the door when a glimmer of white at eye level makes her turn back. She steps over the priest and up to the lectern. The vast gilt-edged bible stands shut, but on it rests a note scrawled in a fast and shaking hand. *Marguerite de Valois: I did not burn her bones. Keep her safe. Please.*

He lied. This does not surprise her.

She does not care about bones. Patrice matters very much more.

Twenty seconds have passed since she hung up. She loses two more in sliding the paper underneath the bible.

At the twenty-eighth second, the Mazda driver appears in the doorway. A silk scarf reaches up to the lower edge of his wrap-around shades. He does not speak, but gestures with his Glock, a sideways flick of the barrel, motioning her towards the side door.

She is afraid she might have to go out ahead of him, and that he'll see the gun in her waistband, but he backs out first, keeping the gun trained on her torso.

She keeps her eyes down; they are doorways to her imaginings and at the moment the image of Patrice, lying across the path, pumping blood from his severed carotids, is too fresh to let anyone see; and the plans, the steps by steps, of what she might do if he is not. So don't look up. Not yet. Don't look up.

She feels the sunlight at the threshold before it hits her eyes, a knife edge of heat and brightness, and now she must look up, and see—

A flash of electric blue . . . Her heart leaps.

'Patrice!' At her voice, he wrenches round. He is whole, unhurt, unbound. 'The bike!'

Even as she says it, she hits the floor, rolling, pulling out the SIG. How often has she practised this particular manoeuvre? A thousand times. How often has she used it? Never. Not in anger. Not when a life depended on it. Not with an empty chamber that is a threat and nothing more.

She loops into a forward roll, head tucked in, right arm across her chest with the pistol sheltered by her body.

Her momentum takes her into the shins of the Mazda driver, bending them back in ways their anatomy was not designed to sustain. She hears a shout of pain. Several shouts. A body falls away from her.

She rises to her feet, gun out, arms straight, hands locked, head spinning. She wheels round, dry-mouthed. *Patrice?*

He is down on the ground, propped on one arm, his body sweeping parallel to the floor in a great two-legged round-house kick that strikes the legs from the Audi driver and his passenger, bowls them over like skittles.

Picaut swings the barrel left, threatening the biker, until he spreads his hands the way anyone does when confronted by the muzzle of a gun. She wants to tell him to take off his helmet but there isn't time. Patrice has hurled himself on to the bike, kicked it off the stand, is revving the engine so the noise blasts through the quiet village.

He turns. 'Come on!'

'Go!'

'Not without you.'

'Fucking go!' They are four to her one and they are recovering; the biker is to her right. Picaut clicks the safety off the gun, as loudly as she can, weaves right, left, right: biker, driver, biker. They are hesitant, but not stopped. 'Patrice! *Go!*'

But still he waits.

The Audi driver is armed, fast, recovering his balance. His weapon swings up and round. If her SIG were loaded, a double tap and he'd be dead. He must know this, but he's brave, or dedicated, or thinks she can't shoot. He is swinging round, pointing his muzzle at Patrice.

He's half a dozen paces away.

If she runs, if she throws herself bodily at him . . .

. . . she can cannon into his shoulder, play havoc with his aim. Over the kick of the recoil and thunder of the report, she can scream, 'Go! For fuck's sake, just *go!*'

She falls less elegantly this time, lands in a sprawled heap, and it is possible that her collarbone has broken and then not, because she can move her arm. She hears the rapid crack of single shots from several weapons, but over them the howl of an engine and the burn of rubber on the tarmac.

Her whole body cringes in anticipation of a crash, of the impact and the rending of metal she has heard so often.

When none of this happens she dares to hope and rolls over, pushes herself to her feet, looks around for shelter, for somewhere to run to—

And finds herself looking down the barrel of a Beretta.

While the other three have been firing at Patrice's receding back, the biker, who is perhaps the thinker where the rest are the muscle, has focused on her, and is standing now in the classic stance, feet shoulder width apart, pistol held out in both hands, but loosely; a practised manoeuvre; effortless.

As before, in the church, the Glock flicks sideways in a

get-moving gesture and the silent threat is more compelling than any verbal instruction could have been.

Picaut is shepherded towards the Audi. The driver opens the door. She slides in and is sandwiched between, she thinks, the driver of the Mazda and the Audi passenger. All three are armed; she can see the bulge of shoulder holsters under their jackets. There is nothing she can do. She waits and watches, and learns. The leather-clad biker drives the Mazda and follows them towards Orléans. There is a hierarchy at work here. Biker ranks above Mazda driver, but not as high as Audi driver.

They drive fast, heading east with the evening sun behind them. They follow almost the same road that Patrice has taken, although they drive safely within the legal speed limit. If the traffic police didn't pick up Patrice, Picaut will see them sacked.

It's never a busy road, and at this time on a Thursday evening, nobody takes any notice of them. They enter the city limits, keeping to the line of the river, and only turn when they reach the cathedral. It looms in her field of vision, vast, ornate, burnished gold by the late evening sun.

They come to a halt one street away. The Audi driver speaks at last. 'We will enter the cathedral. You will walk between us. Unless you wish to die, you will not call out or signal to anyone. You will not be seen.'

His voice is the texture of old gravel. His gun is his promise. She wishes to remain alive, and so she wishes to do what he says. But she is Capitaine Inès Picaut, and she has been on every television station and newspaper in the country for days now. Even on a good day people stop to stare at her in the street, and this is not a good day. She has no idea at all how she is going to avoid attracting attention. *Unless you wish to die, you will not be seen . . .*

At the cathedral, she finds that, like everything else, this been taken care of.

A mime artiste has taken up residence in the plaza that lies sunward of the cathedral. Lined with sun-washed stone, the open space is a natural theatre and in it, a white-painted woman dressed in top hat and tails is pretending to be a dove, joining a flock of trained birds that flit from wrist to head to shoulder to raised heel, to the end of a horizontal white cane.

The tourists have been drawn away from the grand entrance and are indulging in an orgy of mobile photography, focused only on what they see.

Flanked on either side by the suit-jacketed team that has taken her, Picaut is ushered past the signs that proclaim the building closed to all visitors and up to doors which open to a touch. Unseen and so alive, she walks inside.

CHAPTER FIFTY-SIX

CHÂTEAU DE BOUVREUIL, ROUEN,
May 1431

IN THE DAYS AFTER the assault, the Maid is too injured to be questioned, and the court is suspended for a while. Tomas goes to her each day, and in April there is a day when he brings home good news.

'Not everything is going Cauchon's way. The cathedral chapter loathes him to a man. They have refused to consider the articles he has brought against the Maid, and when he forced them they said they should be reframed in French instead of Latin and she should be given counsel so that she knows what they mean. He may be losing this battle.'

'He cannot lose it,' Hanne says. 'The English will sew him in a sack and throw him in the river. He *cannot* lose. What will he do?'

'I don't know.' Tomas delivers the soup he has bought, the bread, the cheese, and goes out again. After that one kiss to her hand, he has not touched her again, nor she him. He is discovering how much it hurts to love two women, neither of them open to him. The Maid has always been out of his reach, but Hanne . . . he tries to think of her as a sister. Sometimes he succeeds.

With Bedford's blessing, he becomes known through the town as a friend of the Maid's. He spends time with the men of Rouen, with the priests. He finds who her friends are, and there are more than he might have thought. In small ways, he encourages them.

For every scintilla of hope, there is a bucket of despair. A week later, news reaches them that the pope has died, who was her friend, however distantly. The new pope is not her friend. Cauchon swells visibly. He sends men back to Vaucouleurs, to Domrémy, to the Maid's childhood places, seeking any taint of untruth in her story.

Returning to the upstairs room, Tomas brings to de Belleville and Huguet a ham, and to Hanne lighter sweetmeats from the market, small things to pass the time.

De Belleville says, 'I hear she was ill?'

'Yes.' Again, after the assault. 'Bad fish, from Cauchon's table. He sent it for Lent.'

'He is trying to poison her!'

'If he is, it is a mercy, and to the detriment of his own soul. He swears not. Anyway, they bled her. She is better now.'

She is weak, but she is still speaking with care. She has said nothing incriminating, however they twist things to trap her. They fire words at her five at a time, sometimes, and she holds her ground and fends them off. He is astonished by her fortitude.

Hanne asks, 'Does Father still come to her?'

'Often.' This is true. The old king is her constant companion. Now that Tomas knows more of her history, he thinks that some of the old man's madness has infected her; that she is as present in the company of the dead as she is of the living.

Today, he has bought a cake of rice and ginger stuffed

with raisins. He watches Hanne tear off tiny pieces and roll them around in her fingers. He studies the curve of her jaw, the dark, pained line of her brow, the flow of her hair. She is, he thinks, putting on a bit of flesh, which is all to the good.

He says, 'Cauchon has sent men back to Domrémy to enquire again into your childhood.'

'I know. They will find nothing bad, I swear it.'

'Are you certain that Jacques d'Arc has been paid enough for his silence?' He remembers a hovel in Rheims, and a bitter man, not mellowed with drink, grasping for gold and rank.

A cloud settles on Hanne's shoulders. She says, 'It's not just the gold; she has threatened him. If he speaks, there are men who will do to him whatever is done to her.'

'I know, but all it takes is for him to drink too much and decide he is not going to let fear rule him.' It would take very little to kill this man. The question is whether it would attract more attention than leaving him alive.

He looks up. De Belleville is looking back at him. Huguet Robèrge is looking the other way; a man gone suddenly deaf.

'Bertrand de Poulangy,' de Belleville says. 'He would do anything for her. He killed Matthieu when he recognized her outside the castle at Chinon. He will kill Jacques d'Arc when we need it.'

'He will need to kill him *before* we need it. And in a way that looks like grief, not murder.'

'Leave it to me.'

De Belleville goes out. Huguet looks tired, or sad, or both. The atmosphere grows cold, dry, dead. Tomas understands why Hanne cannot eat. He takes the ginger cake, opens a shutter and hurls it out of a window for the first stray dog or urchin to find.

He hears a cry, and thinks he's hit someone, and ducks

back in, but Jean de Belleville is running up the stairs, hammering into the room and he has no fragments of rice about him, nor the smell of ginger.

'My lord, what?'

'The Maid. Cauchon has taken her for torture. She won't answer the way he wants and so the fucking bishop – sorry, my lady – has taken her for torture. Tomas, get to her. You have to get to her.'

'Really? You think those of us who go to war are afraid of pain?' Her voice reaches him from down in the dark, round a corner, clad in iron; hard, tight, coldly furious.

The stairs are stone, spiralling, and there is no light. The smell rises, thick as fog: tower-dampness flavoured with the iron tang of blood and layer after throat-burning layer of excrement and urine and fear.

Into this they have brought the Maid, alone. Tomas skids on steps so old he cannot imagine the feet that have trodden them. He hurtles into a dark-cornered chamber licked by pools of burning torchlight and the edged glint of blades, of prongs, of hammers and rasps, and a brazier that stinks of skin and hair and white-hot iron.

She stands against the wall, still chained at the ankles. They have not yet chained her fast. Her arms are locked tight across her chest, her shoulders press hard at the stone. Her skin is white as January ice, but her eyes blaze. Every line of her promises battle.

Geoffrey Thirage, the executioner, dominates the room, a hulk of foul oiled muscle whose vocation is pain. But the Maid is focused on Cauchon. It has come to this; he cannot break her any other way, and so he will use iron and rope, levers and angles, nails and blood.

She despises him for it and everyone present can see so. Scorn is her shield, as long as she can hold it.

'Truly, if you were to have me torn limb from limb so that my soul fled from my body, I would say nothing to contradict what I have already said. And if I did say something, afterwards, I would always say that you had it wrenched from me by force. Is that what you want?'

She is afraid. Tomas, who knows her features as his own, knows this. He is not sure Cauchon does. It may be that the bishop is beyond caring. Were he alone, it seems likely that he would give the order to proceed. But he is not. Nicolas de Venderès is there, lord of Beausséré and Archdeacon of Eu, and William Haiton, and Jean Dacier, Abbot of Saint-Corneille.

Dacier is in some disarray, breathing too fast, pink at the gills. It is not hard for Tomas to catch his eye, to quirk a brow, tilt his lips in silent, sober question. What *exactly* is the nature of your discomfort, my lord abbot? Are you like Thirage, perhaps, to relish the onset of pain in another? Is that godly?

A moment, a knife edge of possibility. He thinks he may have failed. He will kill her if he has to, a thrown knife in her heart, to spare her this, whatever they do to him afterwards.

The abbot flushes, shivers his jowls. 'Stop! Cauchon, this is unnecessary. The girl is right. How can you expect to get from her anything she has not said in public? Cease and desist. There will be other ways to get what you need.'

Once one has spoken, others follow; Jean Dacier, Nicolas de Venderès. Cauchon has authority, probably, but he doesn't have the majority. It's hard to tell who is more disappointed, Thirage or Cauchon, but they know when they are defeated.

'Take her back. Chain her fast. Do not speak to me of this. We shall convene a meeting in my chamber on Saturday to appeal this matter before the whole court.'

CHAPTER FIFTY-SEVEN

ORLÉANS,
Thursday, 27 February 2014
19.00

THE CATHÉDRALE DE SAINTE-CROIX is a mongrel of a construction. The foundations are laid on Roman remains that even now, twenty-one centuries later, still turn up surprises for the archaeologists, and every era since has striven to leave its mark, up to and including the tiny chapel of Jeanne d'Arc by the northern transept that was dedicated in 1920 to celebrate the canonization of Orléans' most famous maid.

For all that, it's still a largely Gothic masterpiece with vast, ornately vaulted ceilings nearly thirty metres high that dwarf every other endeavour of past, present and future.

They dwarf the people, too. There was a time when Landis Bressard wanted to hold Luc's wedding here, but even Hélène, lover of all things grand, was daunted by a space that is too big to leave an echo, where voices bounce to silence between the gargoyles and the tortured Christ.

Picaut has been inside only once, but it was enough for her to know that if the Family had pushed for a wedding in here, Luc would have been marrying someone else. Even then, when she was besotted, no amount of love would have outweighed the horror of this. Now she is here without choice.

Four men are grouped around her. They have brought their scarves down, except for the biker, who has pulled on a helmet again rather than be seen by the crowds outside.

The three Picaut can see are alike in height and colouring; well shaven, with olive skins that have enjoyed the sun. They are men who have the money for good jackets, good shoes, good guns, who wear signet rings on the small finger of their left hand. All four of them have one of these: a small but weighty lump of twenty-two carat gold with a pair of initials – AB – set within a shield. Luc has one exactly like this, save for the first initial. So does Landis. Lise's, now she comes to think of it, is identical.

Fuck.

Old René Vivier was right: it *is* the Family. All of it: the fires, the deaths, this.

For the first time since the phone call in Patrice's apartment, Picaut knows real terror.

Names. She badly wants to know the names of the four men who surround her but they are silent as monks, marching her down the aisle and then, just when she thinks they're heading for the sacristy, or – oh, dear God – the chapel of Jeanne d'Arc (*Inès, they've gone way beyond sanity. You'll be tied to a stake before you reach the front door . . .*), they turn off and down secluded steps that lead below the floor into almost-darkness.

A torch picks out a truncated cone of light, and a switch. Dim bulbs barely illuminate musty air; there is no height here in which to lose the echo, but rather a confusion of cold, clammy scuffing and the clog of old coal dust that coats her nose and throat and fogs her thinking.

The walls are yellowed stone or packed earth, she can't

tell which, but they bear the marks of long dead pickaxes in a rough-hewn counterpoint to the vast swathes of perfectly smooth stone up above. Just to feel the weight of all that rock pressing down . . . Picaut has never been good in small, confined spaces and while she might be able to walk upright this far, there's no guarantee that it won't grow smaller as they progress.

She trips. Someone catches her elbow, hauls her up; the biker. She sees lean fingers and that ring again, feels a leather-clad shoulder press to hers.

A voice – a *woman's* voice – says, 'Do mind the tracks. It's an old railrun. They had coal-fired burners under here for a while to keep the place warm, and had to move the coal from one end to the other. The kind of thing nobody thinks about until they're actually here.'

'Lise?' Picaut stops. Two men crash into her, cursing, but that's not enough to get her to move. 'Lise Bressard? What the *fuck* are you doing here?'

There is no question: the biker is Annelise Bressard. Possibly it should have been obvious, given the effortless panache with which she wears the leathers, but Picaut hasn't been paying that kind of attention.

Lise pulls off the black helmet, frees a long snake of hair from the scarf that binds it, and takes the sunglasses from her face.

Meeting Picaut's gaze, she says, 'Following orders. It's a Family thing. When our elders say "Jump", we jump. Please move on. Whatever my feelings for you, cousin Arnaud is rather too keen to shoot. If I were you, I'd do my best not to give him an excuse.'

Her voice is as acidly amused as it has always been. Her eyes flash complex counterpoints: anger, resentment, warning. Any or all of these. Picaut doesn't know her well enough to hang meanings on their messages.

She does as she is told and walks on, and the cavalcade marches down the rail tracks. Here is too much proximity to fire, however old it might be. She does not want to burn.

They come to a cavernous room carved out of the bedrock. The furnace is not here. Picaut comes to a halt and stands sweating in the cold. Around her, the three remaining men turn round, and so reveal themselves as minor cousins of the Bressard clan. A-branch: the kind who came to her wedding with their beautiful, well-bred, fantastically well-dressed wives, and then turned up to Luc's wilder parties with their mistresses. They drank, gambled, whored and spent money without restriction. She never knew how they earned their keep. She may be in the process of finding out.

Her many hours spent in hostage training had included remarkably little information on what to do if she herself were taken prisoner. She falls back on the advice they were told to give to the targets: build relationships, keep talking, be polite, unthreatening, positive.

She says, 'Why here? Why now?'

She doesn't ask 'Why me?' because when the Family has spent the past month framing her as the new Maid, and they are standing more or less directly beneath the chapel dedicated to the old one's sainted memory, in the city that owes her its freedom, 'Why me?' is a redundant question.

The polls will open in around forty-eight hours and the Family wishes to seal Luc's victory in fire and blood. So she has to keep them talking, and bland conversations about the state of the economy won't cut it, so she asks, and waits while they stare at each other and not at her and fail to answer.

Lise can't hold the silence. She says, 'Here, because it will make the most impact. Now, or at least in a few hours from now, because we have to wait until midnight so that we make the morning's news. The national outrage at your death, the sense of mourning, the wish to make it up to Luc, will all

525

peak when the polls open on Sunday. In the time between, he will have made impassioned speeches that sound dog whistles to the right while the left will be content that this is grief speaking and he is really their man.'

'I'm going to burn, so that Luc can win an election? I thought you were the sane one in your family?'

Lise's gaze traps hers, holds it, tightly. Whatever she is trying to say with that look, Picaut can't read it. Heavily, Lise says, 'Not just this election; this will carry him to the presidency – but then you know that. It will be painless, I can promise you that much. You won't be alive when the fire is lit.'

'A stiletto?'

'I don't know. They wouldn't tell me that kind of detail, but it will be something of that sort.'

This is not a small mercy. Picaut bites back the obvious retort but something must show in her eyes, because Lise says, 'If you had been less obviously heroic . . .'

'Lise, I didn't do anything! Not a single act of heroism. I didn't run into any burning buildings to drag out the children, didn't scale trees to direct the firefighters, I didn't work out who'd lit them until just now. I knew Jaish al Islam was a scam, but I didn't work out it was you. It was, I take it?'

'Not personally.'

'But the Family has done this? They – you – are Jaish al Islam?'

'So I am led to believe. Landis tells me that cousin Arnaud and his minions have thrown themselves wholeheartedly into the roles of Islamic jihadi—'

'Shut it!'

'Arnaud,' Lise's voice is the epitome of weary distaste, 'grow up. You've been war-gaming this for the past six months. Don't try to tell me you don't enjoy it.' Her gaze flickers towards the other two. 'You and your simpering catamites.'

It's a blatant attempt to provoke them into . . . what? Picaut has no clue, but it's a change in the dynamic and she is not the focus of attention, which has to be good. Her eyes are on the doorway; her mind plotting the route back as Lise ploughs on.

'Do you enjoy your time together? Landis tells me the three of you haven't been home to your wives since the fires began. I'd have thought—'

'Shut the fuck up!'

The Mazda driver – Antoine? Aurélien? Something like that – aims a slap at Lise, but he signals it too obviously and she moves with predictably fluent skill. Blocking his arm with her own, she makes a grab for his gun.

She has her hands on the barrel. She is not Patrice, with the core strength to sweep her body, board straight, a foot from the ground, but she is stronger than she looks and she is taking him down, round and . . . 'Inès, run!'

Picaut is already sprinting across the room like a hunted deer, but Arnaud, the Audi driver, is sharper than he looks; swifter, closer to the door.

He reaches it a fraction ahead of her. They meet in a body slam, flesh on flesh, bone on bone, and she is lifted and hurled back across the room to smash against the stone wall.

Her head snaps back and her teeth clack shut and she slides down and only muzzily sees Aurélien step up behind Lise and crack the butt of his own gun hard behind her right ear. She folds slowly at the knees and ends up lying face down, inelegantly sprawled.

The three men crow. There are debts and old, long-nursed resentments at play here that Picaut knows nothing about. And now a fresh betrayal. She has only an outsider's guess at how the Family might view betrayal, but it is not good.

She wants to ask questions. Why? What does this cost you? What can we do now? But Lise is either unconscious or feigning it. Even so, the men are taking no chances. Kneeling, Arnaud draws a cable tie from his pocket and fixes Lise's wrists behind her back. Picaut holds herself very still, eyes down. They have not bound her yet. While she has her hands free, there is still hope.

She draws into herself, hugs her knees to her chest, wills herself invisible, and the immediate danger passes. When she dares to look again, Arnaud has stepped back and stationed himself against the wall near the entrance, but not so close that someone coming in would be able to take a shot at him from the tunnel that leads here. The other two take other walls, lean back against them and retreat into whatever inner place it is that keeps them alert for hours at a time.

These are hard men, practised in the art of waiting, and their guns do not waver. Picaut is not hard, but she can wait as long as she has to. Midnight is not so far away. She endeavours not to think of fire.

CHAPTER FIFTY-EIGHT

CHÂTEAU DE BOUVREUIL, ROUEN,
May 1431

THE NEWS COMES WITH the rising sun, on the morning of the twenty-fourth of May. Hanne pounds her fists on his chest before he has broken his fast. 'They are taking her to the stake. They are going to burn her! Tomas, you must do something!'

Tomas has much in common now with the men of Paris who have publicly stated that this trial has gone on for far too long. He doesn't know how the Maid is staying as strong as she is. For himself, he would have walked into the fire by now, just to get it over.

'There is nothing I can do. Chérie, listen to me.' He catches her flailing hands. 'If there was anything, I would have done it. Bedford has threatened to remove Cauchon from the case and try it again with all English judges. There is nothing we can do except be there, to bear witness for her.'

Weeping, she says, 'I cannot. I cannot. I would rather burn in her stead. I am in God's hand. She is not. She has fought. Tomas, she has *killed* men.'

'She killed in battle. God does not forbid that. And

she has made confession. I swear to you, daily, she made confession.'

Her eyes are round, red and swollen. They rise to his from the shelter of her palms. 'With a proper priest?'

What can he say? There are those of us who think it doesn't matter?

He rises, throws on a coat. 'Wait here. I will go.' De Belleville is here now, and Huguet. They gather round Hanne, hold her. They are a family, welded together, and left unbalanced by the one who is not with them. He leaves her in their company.

He has to fight through the crowd to get to the market place, all the while searching the sky above them for the first feathers of smoke. Not yet. Not yet . . . Thank you, madam, thank you. And you, sir. Good day to you, sir. My apologies. Please? Thank you.

And through into a space and the stake, and the faggots piled high and stained with resin for heat and swift lighting, and Thirage in his element, oiled muscle and a blazing pitch pine torch.

But no one is at the stake, no fire lit yet. He searches round. Here a circle of men on a platform, and there, on its own, a platform for the Maid, and she is on it, but hidden.

Jean Massieu, the usher, holds her hand. Before them both, a slip of white paper, a *cedula*. It will have on it all they want her to say, as if, by signing, she will undo five months of careful argument.

Oh, my dear, have a care. You cannot read! Remember, you *cannot read*.

The Maid says, 'I cannot read. What does it say?'

'Never mind what it says. Just sign.'

She casts her eyes across the crowd, past him, past again, comes back, searching still. He lifts his hands. She is not here. Hanne did not come. She turns back, drops her head.

She signs. Not a long signature, just a cross, or perhaps a circle on the foot of the parchment. *Do not listen to this order.* He remembers it from Saint-Pierre-le-Moutier.

Cauchon looks stunned. This, he did not expect. What now? He cannot burn her if she has abjured her heresy. The English may burn him if he does not, but canon law is clear. By a simple mark of pen on paper, she is no longer a heretic. The crowd disperses. Silent guards lead her back to her cell.

'Rustbeard, she has to burn! I will not believe that the fainting clerics, after five months – *five!* – and seven months to prepare, cannot find a girl guilty of heresy. They say they have to take her to a convent, that she has to do penance, wear a robe, say prayers. As if penance and robes will see Henry anointed king of France.'

The same room, the rush lights cowering, the meaty fist, the dank, cold, unrelenting dark. Tomas is tired of this. He says, 'If she were to go to a nunnery, somewhere in England, maybe, far away from here . . .'

'Not you too? She must burn, do you not understand? The whole of Christendom must see her as a heretic. Only then can her petty princeling be unseated.'

'Lord.' Tomas bows out. There is nothing to say, nothing to do. He has no idea what will happen next.

'They say I have agreed not to wear men's clothes. They say it is on the document I signed, although that was only five lines long and the parchment they have brought me with my mark on it is a full page of close writing.'

It has taken a day to be allowed in to visit her, and then only by pressing favours from men who no longer trust him.

They must have made the robes for her ahead of time, for she is dressed in coarse blue wool to her ankles, rough at the seams, such as penitents wear, and a veil of undyed linen for her hair. This is as close as he will come to what she was in Burgundy, when her mother taught her spinning and weaving.

She sits on the bed. She is . . . unmanned is the wrong word, but she is undone, that much is certain. Her skin is blue grey. She has not slept. Her hair, for the first time, is not combed clear.

'Did you put a circle instead of your name?'

'Of course. But I am still doing as they asked.'

'They have to let you go. It's the law.'

She gestures down to her ankles. 'Tomas, I am still chained. I am still in the care of England.'

Still in the care of England, which is to say held by men when the law says she should be held by women, and these are new guards, who hate her afresh. He has seen the smiles, the sly, knowing winks. They will have her, but he is not party to how or when or where; they do not speak to him any more.

'I'll see what I can do.'

'They won't let me take Mass, or make confession. They won't strike off the fetters. Tomas, I cannot live encased in iron for ever.'

'I know. I'll see what I can do.'

He is a child, repeating phrases he has heard out of the mouths of adults, leaving them less meaning at each repeat, but what else is there? She is drained. He is drained. They are all drained except Bedford, who will burn the whole of Rouen before he will let her go.

CHAPTER FIFTY-NINE

Orléans,
Thursday, 27 February 2014
23.55

'Hello, Inès.'

Picaut hears Luc before she sees him. The injury to his hip is troubling him today. The drag to his left heel is amplified by the echo of the tunnel.

By the time he walks through the door, the shock has rippled through her, cleansing, excoriating. She feels liberated, which is ironic under the circumstances, but at least it deprives him of the satisfaction of seeing her shocked.

'Luc . . .' She manages a smile. 'So now you club us to death and set fire to the cathedral? Is that the grand plan? I had always imagined you to be more subtle.'

'But we are. And we shall be.' Luc is at peace with himself, not ready to be goaded by her. 'I shall grieve for you, Inès, truly. It won't all be a sham.'

'Unlike your protestations of love?'

Luc pulls a face. 'How else was I to get you on board? Particularly when the delightful Patrice had—'

There are three CCTV cameras in the walls, but a basic

533

rule of thumb says . . . There is nothing to say. She looks away, finds a blank space of wall and stares at it.

She wants to be calm and is not. However much she might want to be free of him, it is only now she discovers how much she still had invested in the idea that Luc was an innocent, drawn along in the slipstream of the Family's ambition; that he was not culpable, not involved.

Lise, on the other hand, she had always thought an instrument of her own ambition, her need so welded to the Family's as to be inseparable.

Which may not, after all, be true.

She glances across to where the other woman is now standing.

Picaut has watched Lise Bressard's slow return to wakefulness, to pain, to remembering, to rage that has curdled, over the past two or three hours, to an insidious, unsettling fear. Picaut cannot imagine Lise being readily afraid, but there is no question that she knows what is coming, and it isn't good.

She manages to regain some of her hauteur in Luc's presence, quite an achievement for a woman with an open wound from a gun sight down one cheek, filthy clothes, and hands cable-tied behind her back.

He glances at her derisorily and asks of Arnaud, 'Was I right?'

A nod. 'She went for Auré's gun. She was going to let the bitch go.'

'How distressingly predictable.' Luc favours his cousin with a blistering smile. 'Did you think we didn't know?'

What colour is left in Lise's face floods away. She is alabaster-white. Flatly, she says, 'Luc, there is still time to stop this. Just because Landis treats you as his glove puppet doesn't mean you have to jump to each twitch of his finger.'

'Oh, I shall miss you, cousin!' Luc slaps his thigh, but

Picaut knows him well. Lise has scored a point, or else he would never let her divert him. He chews his lip, thinking. Lise glares. The air aches for release.

And it comes with a soft tread down the corridor.

Landis Bressard.

His arrival seems to remove some of the oxygen from the surrounding air. The cousins lower their weapons.

Their uncle's gaze passes from one to one to one. It lingers last, longest on Lise. He shakes his head.

'Lise, my dear, you of all people should know that the needs of the Family come before any call of the heart. Even Luc understands that.' A nod to his left is the only indication that he has seen Luc standing there.

'Luc is a spineless puppet.' The scorn in Lise's voice would strip any normal man to the bone. 'Orléans may fall for his charade, but France has more sense. The world's media will see through you long before the presidential election.'

This has the ring of a long-standing argument. Landis's smile never loses its charm.

'So you have said. But we—' a circle of his hand includes Luc, 'shall be alive to usher our dream to reality. And if by some slim chance we are wrong, only the ghost of your memory will remain to tell us so.'

He turns away from her, as clear a dismissal as any Picaut has seen. His gaze, as if for the first time, returns to the lesser cousins. He nods to each a greeting and then to Arnaud, says, 'Don't leave her body here. Luc's grief must not be sullied by any hint of an alternative liaison.'

At last, he turns to Picaut. 'I could apologize for what is about to occur, but it would be hollow, and pointless. It will be little consolation, but I intend that your memory will live in the annals of French history for every bit as long as the Maid's. You played your part well, simply by being who you are. Luc was right. The Family is proud of you.'

CHAPTER SIXTY

ROUEN,
May 1431

'TOMAS! WAKE UP! Tomas, in God's name, wake!'

He is lost in the marshlands of exhaustion, where his dreams and his waking are interchangeable, and both are nightmares.

Weights hold down the lids of his eyes. Old blood sticks them shut, the bone-glue of dead men. With levers, he prises them open, clambers back to wakefulness.

'My lady?' The Maid is standing over him, shaking his shoulder, weeping. Behind her are de Belleville and Huguet the priest, red-eyed, discomposed. The sight of that wakes him faster than anything else.

He makes himself look at her. The light is bright and coming from the south; dawn passed a long time ago, and noon. Always, he wakes at dawn, except today. He tries to hold her in focus; fails. 'How are you out?'

'I'm not.' Crossly. 'That is, she isn't.'

He sees it now, or rather, hears it: Hanne's voice is a tone higher, more like a bell, less like a drum. In all other ways, they are almost identical; the last five months have hewn away their differences. They are both thin now, both drawn, both have shadows beneath their eyes, and the strawberry mark behind their ears. And both are now wearing blue woollen gowns, with a veil of the sort the merchant women wear.

He pushes himself upright, fumbles for his linens, his habit; the nights are still and muggy and he has been sleeping naked. Hanne flinches, but she doesn't leave; rather Huguet looks away, and then de Belleville.

He stands. Sleep still drags at him, drapes his shoulders. Sunlight pierces his head.

'They have taken her gown, her veil.'

'Who has? What do you mean, "taken"?'

'The English. Bedford ordered it. She sleeps in her shift, leaving her robe hanging over the beam. They put hemlock and poppy in her meal and took her clothes while she slept.'

'Why?' Hemlock and poppy, half the constituents of the dwale he used when she was injured. His mouth is furred, but he knows that taste. He ate with William Haiton last night; a potage of beans and pigeon breasts stewed in prunes and wine with many spices. So Haiton is against him. He will not be alone. If they have drugged him, then they know he is not for Bedford, so why is he still alive? What do they expect of him? Some last confession wrung from her?

'Why did they take her clothes?'

'They have left her doublet and hose. The clothes she has sworn not to wear. If she puts them on, it is against the terms of the *cedula* she signed.'

'Body of Christ.' His head in his hands. 'She will become a relapse.'

'Yes.'

'So they can burn her.' Not only can they, they must; relapsed heretics cannot be allowed to live or the entire fabric of the Church Militant falls apart. If one heretic flourishes, whatever will keep the rest in check? 'But she doesn't have to put them on, the clothes they have left her; the doublet and hose.'

'She does. The privy is along an open corridor. You know her pride. She will not walk it naked.'

He is dressed now; ready. 'I'll go to her.'

Huguet catches his arm. 'Tomas, it's too late. She will have woken at dawn. We tried to wake you, and failed, and we went ourselves. We can't get near her, but the English are celebrating. You can hear them in the streets.'

'Where is Cauchon? Has anyone see him?'

De Belleville says, 'Cauchon is with her now. He knows she's not a heretic; he damns himself by calling her one, but he dare not go against Bedford. He has made this happen.'

Huguet is pacing; a serene man no longer. 'They are going to burn her tomorrow. They will allow her to hear Mass, to take the Eucharist, to make confession. And then they will shave her head ready for the stake. Or rather, we will.'

'I don't understand.'

Huguet looks sick. Tomas has seen this look on the faces of men ready to go into battle, to face guns and archers they know will kill them. He has thought himself immune to this kind of horror. Now, his stomach roils and he tastes bile in his throat. His gaze flickers from one to the other and they all look away.

Desperately: 'Tell me.'

De Belleville says, 'The Maid's father in heaven has told her she will be saved. But she is not alone in hearing the counsel of heavenly voices and Hanne's have told her . . . something different.'

'I hear what God tells me.' Of them all, Hanne has the strongest tones. And so he hears her plan first from herself. And when he argues, he hears it next from Huguet, and last from Jean de Belleville.

538

At each iteration, he says no. You cannot do this. We cannot. She will not allow it, the Maid. I will not. It cannot be done.

Huguet says, 'We said that. All through the night, we have said that, but will you listen to Hanne? Will you see her lay her hands upon a copy of the testament and swear that what she hears is the true voice of God, with her father, the king, in agreement? And will you be the one to tell her she is wrong in it?'

CHAPTER SIXTY-ONE

Orléans,
Friday, 28 February 2014
00.15

Landis leads the way back up to the chapel of Sainte
Jeanne.

Aurélien goes next, driving Lise viciously forward, his
gun in the small of her back.

Luc takes Picaut. She is cold now, and stiff, and her first
steps are awkward. He grabs her arm and hauls her on, but
he does not bind her wrists as Lise's are bound. It occurs to
her that neither Iain Holloway nor Cheb Yasine's cousin had
marks on their wrists and that there is a point being made
here about willing martyrdom, a narrative being shaped for
the longer history.

They mount the steps into the cathedral. Faint moonlight
pierces the stained-glass windows, picking out in silvered
shades the stories of Jeanne d'Arc, Maid of Orléans, the
girl whose visions of saints and angels moved her to ride in
the name of France. The colours are muted whispers,
barely lit, but after the dark of the tunnels even this much
feels too bright.

Walking with care, Landis and his team navigate to the small chapel where it opens into the transept. Here stands the saint herself, wrought glorious in white marble, backed by a curtain of pale blue silk and set atop a pedestal worked in bronze relief that shows her victories.

Two great, gilded leopards flank her as she stands in prayer. Virginal, pure, simple, it would be hard to imagine anyone less like Inès Picaut, but it is to here that Luc brings her, to stand at the foot of the woman in whose image her own has been shaped.

The Family has been busy in the past hours: wood is piled here, bundles of white, pale carpentry timber in metre lengths that will burn like matchwood, and larger, heavier hardwood beams that will sustain a fire until it has eaten away all the wooden chairs and the altar, the blue silk curtain and the bronze relief, and feasts instead on the raw and ancient stone.

Here they will bind her. Blue silk ropes are set to one side, coiled and ready. A freak of moonlight highlights them, and the woman's skull, green but whole, that lies on top of them.

Picaut knows this skull, the shape of the teeth, the swirls of green on the cranium. 'That's her! Marguerite de Valois!' She rounds on Luc. 'You killed Iain Holloway for this?'

'Blame your father; he sent him.' Luc is round the corner, out of sight. His voice is warped by the distance and the high ceilings. 'Although it was you who gave us his laptop, which was immensely kind.'

'I gave it to Guy.'

'And Guy naturally copied the hard drive before he sold it. You could hardly expect otherwise when your father had been sending difficult letters to the bishop. Or, as we now have to call him, His Eminence the Cardinal. Landis is less than wholly pleased about that. It will be useful to have a man so high in the Vatican, but my uncle hates to be outranked.'

'The bishop is Family?'

'Distantly, through Annelise's mother's side. Don't look so distressed; you would have had to be particularly paranoid to have unearthed that. Your father knew of the link, but only very late in his life. We thought the matter closed when he died, but then Dr Holloway turned up and made his discovery. The timing was appalling. It could have derailed half a year of planning, and a chance for power that comes only once in ten generations.'

'A six-hundred-year-old skull?'

'Not just the skull; the entire skeleton is there under the ropes. Your father would have liked it. He was right in many ways. Lise found it very touching, didn't you, cousin? The love that gives itself in sacrifice.'

Lise is propped on the left, by the silk ropes. Picaut can see her from the corner of her eye: her colour is high, her lips sealed. She looks as if she will never speak again.

Luc is toying with her; with them both. Normally Picaut would ignore him, but now she needs to keep him talking. He is behind her and she can see a route out to the transept past Arnaud and Aurélien on her left, past the third cousin whose name she has never been sure of. He's the one who might catch her. In her head, she maps out a blow to his nose with the flat of her hand.

She says, 'My father thought the Maid survived and went on to become Jeanne des Armoises, the woman-knight who fought for the pope. But he never explained how she managed to survive, for the simple reason that she can't have done.'

'Are you sure? Even the nuns at Lise's excruciatingly expensive English convent school told her that there had been a last-minute switch: a drugged-out witch burned and thus saved her own soul while the Maid was spirited away down some secret tunnel that only the true French knew about. I'm not sure she believes it, mind you, do you, Lise?'

Lise turns away; the question is beneath her.

Picaut says, 'It's a story for school children: nobody believes it. The Maid stood at the scaffold and spoke for thirty minutes in full hearing of eight hundred English men at arms, plus the French clerics who had condemned her. They were all weeping by the time she finished and the flames were lit. They had questioned her for five months; they knew her. They were in no doubt that she was the same woman.'

'And yet . . . You really should take a look at the skeleton, Inès. When you meet your father, you want to be able to tell him he was right.'

She wants to say 'I am not my father,' but Luc, too, lived for half a dozen years in the shadow of Charles Picaut's obsession; he knew what it cost him, what it meant, and he is not laughing now.

In spite of herself, she glances down and yes, under the blue silk ropes is a flash of yellowed bone, a femur, perhaps, or a humerus.

Too late, she leans to look, for now Luc appears on the other edge of her eye line, holding a wad of cotton and a match. A great raft of paraffin sails to her on the still air. It clogs her throat, her eyes, her thinking. Don't panic. Don't panic. *Don't* panic.

She says, 'Patrice will find us. He broke the codes in Iain Holloway's chip.'

'I rather imagine he would have been here by now if there was any likelihood at all that he could work out where we might be. Did you know, he threatened to— André! Get up!'

André. The nameless third cousin is André. And he has just fallen flat on his face at Luc's feet, which might be amusing or irritating or just plain stupid were it not for the

543

fact that the back of his skull has been shot away. Nobody heard the shot, therefore it was suppressed. Therefore, too, there are those in the church whose first care is not for the Bressards.

Blood pools around the dead man's head, spreading on to Luc's Guccis. Clean bone shows wetly white in the mess of the dead man's hair. It's a paralysing sight, but Picaut has an advantage: she has seen these things often enough that her recovery is swifter.

'Run!' Her shout is for Lise, whose hands may be tied, but whose legs are not. Picaut herself is already careening out of the small chapel and into the transept, turning west, for the entrance.

In the dark, she is moving on instinct. There are thirty rows of chairs here, and then another thirty before the doors. Vast Gothic ribs tower over her, invisible, stretching to heaven. Behind is the altar, the organ, the statue of the suffering Christ. Even in daylight, the size and scale of this place is intimidating. In the dark, with faint stains of glass and moonlight irregular around her, she could be on the moon. She has to go slowly, feeling her way, bumping into chairs, pillars, possibly people.

She hears voices on both sides: Bressard men. Of course there are more than she knew about. Somebody moved the wood into the chapel while she was down below and that was never Luc; he doesn't sully his hands with manual labour. On instinct, she crouches down. Scant moments later, she hears a hiccough, feels the hiss of a round pass over her head.

The shooter is behind and to her left. From her right a voice she knows: 'Capitaine Picaut!'

She veers towards the sound.

Cheb Yasine is crouched amongst the chairs. Stained star-light paints him in muted reds and blues, a semi-automatic

544

in one hand, digital low-light binoculars in the other. He lets go of both for long enough to catch hold of her arm and draw her to safety.

'Are you hurt?'

'No. How did you find me?'

'Patrice called.' He looks up, takes a shot, ducks down again. 'And then I spoke with Old René Vivier who said that if I wanted to exact revenge for my cousin, I should follow Landis Bressard and he would lead me, eventually, to a fire.' He hefts his gun. 'Evidently, he was right. Look out!'

He catches her shoulder, presses her down. Picaut counts two muzzle flashes before she is too low to see anything. Rounds whine off stone. A man curses, but it is a living curse, not a dying one.

She says, 'Did you tell Patrice where we were?'

He rolls his eyes. 'This is personal, Capitaine, and beyond the law. I suggest you leave and let us put a permanent end to your family drama. Your friends are looking, I believe, at one of the Bressard warehouse projects east of the city.'

It's where she might have looked if she had suspected the Bressards, but it's too far away. She says, 'Landis has at least six men. How many have you?'

'Enough.' Cheb Yasine has a Bluetooth set in his ear. He speaks into it in a singing language Picaut doesn't know. Up near the Maid's chapel, Luc is issuing low, urgent orders; the rise and fall of his voice is a chanted litany. His men spread out among the chairs. Another shot pings off a wall somewhere south of where she hides, but the rest hold their fire; they're conserving rounds now, waiting for a clear shot.

Cheb Yasine, too, is moving. He lifts Picaut bodily up and pushes her towards the aisle. 'Get out. We'll cover you.'

'I'll bring help.'

'No!' He catches her wrist. His fingers are an iron band.

545

'The Bressards killed my cousin. They lit fires in the name of my god. The police shall not interfere.'

The set of his gaze does not promise her safety if she gets in the way of his vengeance.

She says, 'And in the morning?'

'There will have been a firefight between rival gangs in which men died. We shall all acknowledge that it was most unfortunate. I will have been in a club in Tours all night long. My mobile phone and my credit cards will show this to be true. You, I think, will have escaped under cover of the shooting at around one o'clock. Give me an hour. No one will know.'

He is wrong. The Family will know. And if she is to bring them down, she will have to tell what has happened. But to do any of that she has to get out alive, and nothing is certain. Three shots hiss close together from up near the chapel. She hears a body fall and has no idea who has died. She wants it not to have been Lise.

'Go!' Cheb Yasine's hand shoves hard in the small of her back.

She ducks down, keeping her head below the level of the chairs and begins to weave her way towards the door.

Behind her, pandemonium.

She knew the cathedral was big, but in the nightmare of glass-stained moonlight and gunfire it has grown to fill her universe, and it seems likely that Cheb Yasine may get his wish by default: it could take her another hour simply to reach the door.

She takes shelter behind a pillar. Rounds hiss; double taps and triple taps and pauses while men move.

At least two are dead and one is injured, moaning curses in French which is no help towards knowing who it is; in pain, all men sound the same.

She hears three shots and crawls out from behind her pillar. The floor is tiled in black and white, which is why she doesn't see the blood until she has put her hand in it.

'*Fuck!*'

It is warm, but not hot; sticky, not slick. She traces it back to the pillar she was heading for and finds a dead Algerian with a wound in his upper abdomen big enough to take four bunched fingers. So the Bressards are using soft-nosed rounds. Just when she thinks she can't hate them any more, some new discovery proves her wrong.

She runs her hands over the body. He has a shoulder holster, but it's empty. She begins a fingertip search of the floor. Eight more shots have been fired from the danger zone up near the chapel by the time she finds a Beretta, the gangster's gun of choice.

Armed, she feels whole again. Newfound confidence drives her away from the pillar, back into the maze of chairs, inching ever towards the door. Behind her, men shoot and die and call to each other in French or not-French. In this, the Bressards are at a disadvantage: they cannot understand their adversaries, while everything *they* say is heard and understood.

Even so, the not-French voices seem fewer than they were. If she were to pit Cheb Yasine against Landis Bressard, she has no idea whom she would back to win, only whom she hopes will do so. She crawls on.

With three more pillars to go, she is contemplating the risks and benefits of making a run for it when, partway through the next volley, a woman's voice keens in pain.

'Lise!' She may be a Bressard, but she was the only friend in a friendless place, and she did her best to help. Picaut checks the Beretta and doubles back towards the sound.

Retracing her steps to the chapel, and danger, she goes faster than she did coming out, but still it is slow. Flitting from pillar to pillar to chair to pillar, she steps over the human debris of the fight, counting off almost equal numbers of Algerians and Bressards until she reaches the transepts where she finds a huddle of four Algerians, all dead, lured into one place and ambushed. So perhaps Landis does know Algerian, or one of his men does.

'Fuck.'

Picaut crabs sideways into shadow. Lise could be anywhere and she can't risk calling out. She could be dead, leaching hot blood on to the tiles. Please, not that.

Arms extended, safety off, finger on the trigger – how light is the touch? – she edges forwards, towards the Maid's chapel, where someone is breathing, in pain, and it sounds like a woman.

The fire begins when she is perhaps ten metres away. Every breath she takes is saturated with the bitter smell of gunfire, the scent of blood, of fear, of fury. But the last few weeks have rendered her inordinately sensitive to the many and varied scents of smoke and she catches the first sharp-hot-sweetness of it before she sees any flame.

'Lise?'

She hears a scuffle, an oath. 'Inès! Go back!' Lise's whisper, raw with pain.

She is not alone here. Cheb Yasine hisses at her from somewhere more distant in front and to her left. 'The Bressards are lighting their pyre. They will have their martyr, even if it is not you. You should leave now, Capitaine. We are here who choose to be. This is not your fight.'

But it is, and not only for Lise. This is her duty. Put it down to the gun in her hand, or the proximity of death, or the weight of understanding of all that the Family plans, but she knows now the depth of the error she made in supporting Luc, and now that she knows it, she has to stop him.

She pushes on. Three metres . . . two, and she has a view

into the Maid's chapel, peering in past a line of chairs. Luc's fire is not a good one: a circle of flamelets dance on the pyre, gathering, growing, but not yet blazing. Smoke weaves up; pale patterns spin in the dark.

Lise Bressard is propped nearby in a patch of blue-shaded starlight. Blood blooms on her left arm, from shoulder to elbow. Her face is a mask of pain. The cable ties have been replaced. Silk ropes bind her at wrist and ankle, their ends left untidy, ravelled like old spaghetti across the skull that Iain Holloway photographed.

And, because the ropes have been moved, Picaut can see the rest of the skeleton: a haphazard collection of leg and arm bones, spinal vertebrae and disarticulated ribs.

And, because she is her father's daughter, because his obsessions were the backbone of her life and he did not let her grow to adulthood in ignorance, the remains of Marguerite de Valois, shown by DNA evidence to be a close relative of Louis XI, are an open book.

In one glance Picaut estimates gender and age, details the old injuries and marks of wear: arthritis at a hip joint, a break in a collarbone, an old injury to a femur. But it is the density of the bones that is striking. She has seen weight-lifters with slimmer bones than these.

A woman, then. Sturdy. By the angles of her hips, and the arthritis there, a lifelong rider. A woman who has borne much weight from a young age. A woman with broken ribs and injuries to thigh and collarbone, all of which healed long before a good and timely death.

A woman . . . *that* woman?

How?

CHAPTER SIXTY-TWO

CHÂTEAU DE BOUVREUIL, ROUEN,
29 May 1431

'**M**Y LADY?'
'Tomas?'

They have unchained her legs; Cauchon has found within himself a shred of mercy. She rises smoothly, in the way she used to by the fireside, say, at Jargeau; by the guns at Troyes. She is holding her strength for the morning and he does not know how deep or shallow are the reserves she has left.

She has been allowed to hear Mass, to take the Eucharist, to make confession although not to Tomas, nor to Huguet. They have not been banned, though; the guards have let them through, and the swarthy, grey-haired barber they have brought with the shears to cut her hair, and the nun, for propriety.

She comes to the door, steps back as they push it open. 'Why are you here?'

'To make you ready. If you will let us all in?'

Tomas is in. They all are. The door shuts and is locked. The guards leave them; they have been well paid for that, in silver that they think comes from Bedford. In truth it is

Bedford's coin, only he has not sanctioned this, the entry into the Maid's cell of one nun, two priests and a barber. What harm can they do?

'I bring you someone.' Tomas steps aside to let the nun be seen. This was the hardest part, persuading a girl who lives for God that she must wear a habit to which she is not entitled.

It is Hanne's plan, though, and he has only modified it. She steps past him now, as if she owns this place, and it a palace.

'Sister. We have come to do our father's bidding.'

'Hanne!' That voice, that name. As he heard it in Rouen, he hears it now, but with a raw pain that is entirely new.

She sways.

Tomas steps forward to catch her, but she rights herself, reaches out her hand, lays it on Hanne's cheek. The tenderness.

He will weep, who has fought two days against it.

'My dear, you are so thin!'

'She will not eat,' Tomas says. He has not slept in the past two days, has paced, has argued, has turned words inside out, has lifted the bible and set it down again, as if other answers might be discovered beneath it, squirrelled away, where only those on the edge of madness might find them. And he has come to this; they all have.

De Belleville says, 'Your sister is killing herself, after the manner of Catherine of Siena.' His voice is rough with pain and his own lack of sleep. 'She will be made a saint if it slays her.'

Huguet carries their only candle. He lifts it and the light tints de Belleville's face, his powder-grey hair, his coarse cloth.

'Oh, Jean . . . !'

Duc Jean de Belleville, a man for whom women are as sisters, friends, perhaps even great, heart-felt friends, holds the Maid to his chest, in a grip strong enough to stop a horse. Love is there, a deep longstanding love, but even so, her gaze grates past him.

To Hanne, gently, she says, 'Ma chérie, you must eat.'

Tomas says, 'She blames herself for all that has befallen you. She threatened to go to Bedford and Cauchon, and tell them they had the wrong woman.'

The Maid is smiling, as if this is part of a game played since childhood. She is still gentle, still relishing their presence. 'I have made this bed, I must lie in it. I did know. From the start, we did speak of this.'

Hanne won't have it. 'Not really. Not like this.'

'Yes, like this. How else? Come to me . . .' They embrace, woman to woman. They are so very much alike, except that the Maid is smiling, strong, kind. Who can find kindness for others, who faces death in a fire? He should have killed her when she was on the field at Compiègne. He could do it now, still, and then himself . . .

She strokes Hanne's head, over the drab linen veil. 'None of this is your fault. I should not have been taken at Compiègne. And I could have recanted long ago; that I have not is for my own honour, and for France. I will not have them say that the king was crowned without the sight of God.'

Hanne is angry. She grips the Maid's hands in her own. 'You have not given yourself to God as I have. You have not promised Him your body, your soul, your mind.'

'I had not before I came here. Now . . . our father speaks to me, and he is with God. So now I have promised Him these things.'

'Not as I have. Our father speaks to you of war, of France, of the ways the kingdom may be made whole under one

552

king. But did he not also promise you deliverance? I heard you in the court, day after day, "My counsel tells me that before sentence, I shall be freed." Did you not say that? Was it not true?'

'I believed it to be true when I said it. Maybe I misheard. Or perhaps there are different kinds of freedom. Just to see you is to be free. I shall die in happiness, for this.'

'Then I shall follow you to heaven. All my life, I have prayed to God that He might take me, and now He will. You don't understand. God calls me, not you, to be at His side; for France, and for our souls. You must be here, to help the armies. Who else knows the ways of war that Papa taught you?'

'Chérie, it cannot be.' The Maid sweeps up her hands, and – afterwards Tomas thinks there must have been divine action in this – the veil on Hanne's head slips off. In shock, the Maid's hands fall away. 'Hanne . . . You've shaved your head—'

Tomas takes the Maid's arm, the first time he has touched her without express permission. He feels her stiffen, but not greatly; she does not hate him yet. That will come later.

Now, using words they agreed, he says, 'We are sent to shave your head for execution. If she is to take your place, she must be like you. They will not see beyond a face that matches yours, a thinness of body, and a woman who goes to her death praising God and France. She even shares the mark on your neck, and they must have seen it, some of them.'

'What if they have? It makes no difference. You must know it cannot happen.'

'It can. It has to. She will starve herself to death if you die; she has almost done it already. She has the poppy and the henbane, the belladonna, to take if she needs it, though I think she won't. And France does need you: d'Alençon, La

Hire, Arthur de Richmond; they will all still listen to you, and with that we may win. My lady, I'm sorry. One day, you may forgive me.'

He is serious.

So is she. 'No! You cannot do this!' She throws back her head. 'Help! Gua—'

He has brought a maul, a small one, wrapped with felt. With it he delivers the crack on her skull, short, sharp, hard. He is a past master of swift suppression.

She falls.

He catches her, so thin, so very strong.

Hanne is already doffing the nun's habit. Her hands are steady, her gaze is a caress. Over and over, she speaks her thanks, and when the change is done – the nun, overcome by grief, must be helped out, but what surprise, when women are so feeble? – she embraces them, one by one.

'Tomas, Jean, Huguet . . . I shall take your names to heaven with me. I shall tell God of this and it will weigh against all else you have done, and prove the stronger.'

'Guerite . . .' It *is* her name, now; she is a warrior, as much as the Maid, only she fights differently. He cannot speak. He weeps as he has never wept, so that the world blurs and his words will not stick together. 'Take the poppy. It is enough, I swear it. You shall feel nothing.'

'And go to heaven with my eyes closed? I don't think so. They would know, anyway, and I will not have it said of her that she was not strong. She would hate me for that, even more than she will already.'

'She will hate all of us.'

'And as your penance, you will live with that, and in time you too will know God's grace.'

When they leave, with the Maid insensate between them, Hanne is kneeling in prayer. He has never seen her so radiant.

CHAPTER SIXTY-THREE

ORLÉANS,
Friday, 28 February 2014
00.45

THERE IS A MOMENT of perfect crystalline stillness as Picaut holds everything separate in her mind: the forensic detail of the skeleton, Iain Holloway's ciphers, the DNA results, Luc's elliptical references to truth – and adds to them all that her father taught, all that he believed.

Then it all snaps together and he was right. Her father was right. Every part of everything he said was correct. He was *right*.

I am so sorry. I should have had more faith.

The fire is taking hold, the heat a wall. She knows the pattern of it. She looks up. Lise Bressard lies in the Maid's chapel, tied hand and foot; a woman, left in a fire to die.

Lise found it very touching, didn't you, cousin? The love that gives itself in sacrifice.

Their eyes lock. Lise's mouth forms a single word. 'Leave.'

'No.' Picaut is armed. And here, tonight, now, she is not afraid of fire.

She rises up, slides forward into the chapel, gun out. 'You are not going to die. I won't allow it. We're going to get you out of here.'

The fire encircles them. Smoke curls about her throat. The ropes tying Lise Bressard's feet are tied with professional security and Picaut has no knife. By the fire's light, she is untying, pulling, stretching. She bends to use her teeth, gains traction, wrenches her neck left and right.

'Inès, you have to leave. Get out now, while you still can.'

That's not worth an answer, and anyway she can't speak with a mouth full of rope. She feels the knot give and slides her thumb into it, frees her mouth. 'Where's Landis?'

'Here.'

She whips round. He's at the entrance to the chapel, cold-eyed; ever in control. He is armed, but he hasn't had the practice she's had; his gun is still rising when hers is already in the aim.

She says, 'Forget it. I was never going to be Luc's king-maker, and I'm not going to be his martyr now.'

He's beyond listening. He fires. She slews, rolls, fires back. She was right, the Beretta's trigger is very light indeed. It may be that she fired first. She thinks this is possible. She is supposed to shout a warning, but there isn't time. She sees Landis's head snap to the left. His throat bursts open. He falls back, hard.

From beyond the smoke, Cheb Yasine shouts, 'Nicely done, Capitaine! My cousin will piss on him from heaven. Now we must all get out!'

She had forgotten he was there. He shouts again in Algerian and she hears three more spit-silenced shots and then the sound of men running.

'Go!' Lise again. 'Please, Inès. There's no point in us both dying.'

'No.'

She spends precious seconds teasing the silk apart and then Lise's legs are free. 'Your hands. Quickly. You'll run better with your hands free.'

'You can't. They're too tight.'

She's right. It will take more time than they have.

She has no intention of letting the fire devour them. She wants to take the bones but cannot. The living matter more than the dead. More, even, than proof that her father was right.

'We need to get your jacket over your head so you can run through the fire. Bend your elbows in . . .'

The leather is thicker than it looks. It takes two tries to flip it inside out.

'Go straight for the door. Don't stop.' A push between the shoulder blades. '*Go!*'

Lise goes.

Head down, half blinded by her own jacket, Picaut follows.

The fire is a living beast, hunting her. She takes a breath, holds it, takes a leap and rolls into smoke and fire and heat and no clean air. She dare not breathe in. Her face is scorched, her eyes hurt. Flames reach for her, batting at her back, her arms, her legs.

'Lise?' She looks left, right, sees a shape moving too slowly, and not, she thinks, in the right direction. She trips over a chair, pulls herself up. They have barely gone five feet; not nearly enough. She hasn't breathed yet. She's going to have to breathe. Ahead, a scream, cut off.

'Lise!' She has to breathe to shout; a mistake. She blunders forward with lungs full of smoke. Tears stream down her face.

She cannons into Lise's hunched form, grabs her arm, pulls her up, but she's not moving anywhere fast. She swings round, and Lise is not who she sees.

Luc.

He has Lise, holding her with his other arm. He's stretched between them now, gripping Lise with his left hand, pulled by Picaut on his right. Which is his gun hand. She wrenches it aside, feels the burn of the shot past her arm. She thinks it goes past her arm, but she might be hit. She brings up her own gun, pulls the trigger twice . . . three times . . . and hears no sound. The gun has not fired. She has run out of rounds.

She still has hold of Luc's arm, and leans all her weight into pulling him round, towards her, away from Lise. She remembers what Patrice did, and slings out a high kick, not a full capoeira roundhouse, but enough to make him flinch back, draw his hand up to his face, let go of his cousin, who is still alive enough to cough. And if she can cough she can fucking run.

'Lise, go!'

She doesn't stop to see what happens. She has Luc off balance and she cannot let him regain his feet, or bring up his gun. Digging in her heels, she leans back, dragging him round, twisting, wrenching at his elbow, both hands on his wrist, his forearm across her body, a particular twisting pull that Garonne showed her, an age ago, when she was young and new and he was not—

She feels the crack of breaking bone. Luc lets go, howling, and she falls away, but she has his gun now, and, choking, flailing, eyes streaming, struggles to bring it round, to point it at the mass of where he was before the smoke took over, to fire and fire until this gun, too, is empty.

And then to stop.

Her mind is achingly, brilliantly clear. Somewhere ahead is the door, lost in a tunnel of smoke. Somewhere nearby, burning, are the bones that prove her father right, the remains of a woman trained for war who did not burn but lived to a good age, carrying the marks of her youthful injuries.

Marguerite de Valois: I did not burn her bones. Keep her safe, please.

They are not out of reach. Possibly not out of reach. It's worth a try. Here, she suspects, is proof that whoever stood on the scaffold in Rouen was someone who cared enough to want the Maid to live. Do we speak of love? We must, I think.

She turns back into the smoke. By feel, she strives towards the place where Lise was tied. She doesn't need much: a femur, a pelvis, a humerus, the skull. If she can bring two or three of these, enough to match with Iain Holloway's samples, it will be proof enough.

Her fingers close on bone. She is breathing smoke. And Éric is right: in the smoke, there is little pain. She is here, dying in a fire, holding the woman who did not. And with her other hand, she grasps at Luc, who planned to destroy them both.

Flame blooms around her. She thinks of Patrice. It may be she speaks his name. Certainly, she can hear him saying hers.

'Inès! Inès! Let them go. They're dead. Don't you die on me now. Don't even think about it. *Inès . . . !*'

CHAPTER SIXTY-FOUR

ROUEN MARKET PLACE,
30 May 1431

S HE IS SO SMALL, the pyre so great.
They will not let him near her. Bedford has secured
for him a place on the wooden viewing platform, along with
Cauchon and Warwick, Talbot and Jean de la Fontaine,
Nicolas Midi . . . all the men of France and England who
have caused this to happen. They are upwind, and a
hundred paces away; they plan for the hottest of fires, which
no man may safely come near.

She is shriven, blessed. They have dressed her in sack-
cloth and she could not look more effortlessly pure. The
crowd should jeer, women should throw their clogs, or old
food; men should show in graphic mime how they would
desecrate her still-warm body. Nobody speaks; since she
came out of the castle, her shaved head pale under the
thickening sky, the crowd has held silence.

The sun stabs through a weakness in the cloud. She looks
up, bathes in the pale gold light: a friendly fire that carries
her the last two strides to the stake.

The pyre is bigger than any Tomas has seen. Walking

past, the air was sweet with the scents of resin and sawn wood. They have set it on a plinth, so she may be raised up, and seen.

Thirage himself is half naked. He has oiled his flesh for this, his moment of fame. Never will he burn anyone, man or woman, as well known as this; never will there be a greater crowd. The market place at Rouen is full, all the overlooking windows are full; boys and young men line the rooftops.

There is a moment's conference, maid to man. He steps back. She is left alone. Jump. Hanne, my dear, just jump. You might die; is it not at least worth a try?

But no, she looks round the crowd, finds him, or so he fancies: he promised he would be here, bearing witness. Jean and Huguet have the other part and he tells himself it is no easier; they will be with the Maid when she wakes, and they will bear the brunt of her fury. He thinks he has dosed her enough to get them to Belleville. He is not sure.

So he thinks she is watching him when she begins to speak, but it may be Cauchon, who is close, and at this distance all she is really looking at is a mass of black-robed men and one white friar.

'*Mesdames et messieurs*, bishops and priests, lords and ladies of France, let the one who is about to die say this to you: nothing happens beneath the blue sky but God wills it. No battle is won or lost, no life begun or ended, but at heaven's decree. If I have erred at all, it is in listening to the voice of God, who has said always that France shall be whole and . . .

'. . . and to the end. This night, I will rest with our holy father in heaven. You must live on until He calls you to Him. And you have this choice. Will you live in a France that is free? Or will you take the yoke of servitude under a foreign king? I, who go now to eternal freedom under God, instruct you to ask this of yourselves each night. I ask only this, and that you pray for me.'

He cannot breathe. Almost, he cannot see.

Beside him, men wring their noses into their sleeves, heel dry their eyes, wrap their faces in their hands. He cannot see Cauchon, but Nicolas Midi is here on his left, stricken, and Jean de la Fontaine on his right, shuddering, and all about, men are crossing themselves.

Thirage no longer looks like a man whose vocation is pain. As a gentleman with his newly-wed, he ushers her on to the pyre, a step at a time, settles her amongst the faggots, moves aside a sawn plank and sets it at an angle away from her, to make her comfortable.

Chains are already stapled to the post to hold her arms. He fastens them now, speaking to her all the while. Nobody can hear what he says. The wind is freshening from behind, not enough to blow the flames away, but enough to raise them up.

Let it be swift. Dear God in heaven, let it be swift.

'A torch!' He hears that; everyone does. A thousand inbreaths suck all the air from the market place. A white-faced boy tosses up a torch. Thirage catches it, hesitates, turns to her, speaks again. She shakes her head, emphatic.

Is he offering her poppy? Still she will not take it.

Oh, my dear . . .

It should be now: a thrust, a plume of smoke, a crack and flash of flame, but there is some more fiddling with wood, and a sack of straw called up and opened and great creaming fistfuls stuffed in amongst the wood at her feet, and on either side, where the wood rises to waist height. A boy cries something from a rooftop; an exhortation for speed, or a cry to desist; either is possible; neither is heeded. Time stretches, every heartbeat counted.

And now, dear God, at last, the torch, blazing, thrust into

the pyre's heart, in a place beneath her feet, where has been left a gap. The straw is about it; a fast catch, tongues of flame a-leaping, a surge of smoke, white as snow.

Because he is who he is and is what he is, Tomas watches the sack that flaps in Thirage's left hand. He sees – he thinks – the flicker of the fine rope, almost a wire, that comes out of it, the loop that snakes out towards the stake.

Certainly – almost certainly – he sees her head snap back, her eyes flare before the smoke hugs her close, and then the flames. He sees Thirage's shoulders rip out taut, as the smoke claims him, too. For a big man, he is putting a lot of effort into holding that sack. And then he releases it, throws it into the hissing, roaring, ravening blaze, staggers back beyond reach of the heat. His chest is blistered where the oil has caught.

She does not scream.

For the rest of his life, Tomas Rustbeard knows that she made no sound as the fire claimed her.

In his nightmares, weeping, he watches her gown catch light and flare, sees the flesh char and burn, peel away from her bones. He sees Thirage take a long-handled hook and strip her gown away to prove she is woman, but she is dead by then, and dead still when the fire burns down to ash, and is built again, at Bedford's order, to reduce that ash to dust.

But she makes no sound. Not here, not now, not in his nightmares.

Nothing.

My dear, oh, my dear.

Let it have been merciful.

EPILOGUE

Reuters; Tuesday 4 March: French local election results

The results of the mayoral election in Orléans show a record turnout and a landslide of unprecedented proportions. Eighty per cent of those eligible voted for Luc Bressard, deceased. By agreement with all the relevant parties, his cousin, Annelise Bressard, will take his position on her release from hospital. A memorial service will be held on Sunday for all those killed in the recent fires. A minute's silence was observed throughout France at eleven o'clock this morning in remembrance of the dead.

Captain Inès Picaut has been moved from the intensive care ward and is recovering from smoke inhalation and burns. Her condition is said to be stable.

AFTERWORD

While many of the foremost authorities have come close to suggesting that the woman we came to know as the Maid of Orléans cannot have been an untrained peasant girl, most stop short of saying it explicitly, largely, I think, because there has been no obvious candidate for the post.

This novel grew out of an article about a Ukrainian orthopaedic surgeon who found a set of bones of a woman in her late middle age in the basilica at Cléry-Saint-André. That woman had, in his opinion, been trained to wear armour and ride a warhorse from an early age.

The article is here: http://www.misterdann.com/euraratstake.htm and I record my debt to Serguei Gorbenko below. If the bones are genuinely those of a woman who had been trained to ride a warhorse in full armour from her youth, and if she was Marguerite de Valois, we have to question the identity of the woman who died at the stake.

She must have looked broadly similar, although when someone has had their head shaved for execution that similarity doesn't have to be exact. She must have cared very deeply indeed for the woman whose place she took. A martyr complex would help make sense of it, and isn't unheard of – we are in an era where young women were reared on stories of worthy saints guaranteeing their route into heaven by earthly suffering. Thus we have the Maid's half-sister, who is as close as I could imagine, and has all the necessary prerequisites.

I cannot, of course, prove any of this. For those who wish to continue with the magical thinking of the accepted mythology: good luck. For the rest, I am sure this isn't the only interpretation of the events of the past, but it's the one I prefer.

For those who need to separate fact from fiction: I have endeavoured where possible to include those words and letters that are recorded in history. Her letters to the citizens of Troyes and of Riom both still exist. We should remember that her letters were written by a clerk, and at her trial she denied having spoken some of the words that were written in a letter to the king of England – with the implication that the clerk miscopied. This may or may not be true; we have no way of knowing.

Her words were recorded daily at her trial by a number of notaries who then combined their notes to produce a fair copy, which was then copied out again in French and Latin and distributed to every court in Europe at the trial's conclusion.

Two things need to be taken into account.

The first is that eye witnesses who spoke at her rehabilitation trial say that the words recorded were, in certain key respects, not the words she spoke. This must be the case, because eye witnesses say that she was interrogated by as many as six men speaking at once, who interrupted each other and herself in their answers, and that the interrogations lasted from three to four hours in the morning and two to three hours in the afternoon, and the trial transcripts do not contain enough recorded dialogue for even one morning session at this rate. We do not have a record of which areas were false and what she truly said.

The second is that she was a girl of around nineteen years old, being questioned by massed numbers of men of ultimate authority. They asked questions that were designed to elicit specific answers, by which they could reasonably charge her with heresy. They were not seeking after truth. They never asked how she was able to do the things she did, how she gained her strategic and tactical skills, how she learned to ride, to wield weapons, to couch a lance. Simply to acknowledge she had done these things was unthinkable, and even after the trial, she was referred to as 'the girl known as Jehanne, who consorted with the "fiende" known as the Maid'. There was a degree of denial which separated the girl in front of them from the one who had faced down Bedford and the massed knights of England at Montépilloy. That was another agency, it couldn't have been a living girl. The question, then, was whether that agency came from good sources or bad, and they had to prove the latter in order to taint the anointing of the French king, and so make way for a fresh anointing of their juvenile monarch, Henry VI.

All this notwithstanding, I have used the words recorded in her trial. Whoever and whatever she was, throughout her time in the public eye, the Maid demonstrated astonishing fortitude, intelligence and courage and I honour these above all else.

One final historical note: the plaque in Orléans celebrating the names of my countrymen who fought for the city does exist, and therefore they existed. My apologies to Patrick Ogilvy who was (almost) certainly not as I have made him.

To find out more about the history and the writing, join the conversation at http://www.mandascott.co.uk and #IntoTheWoods

Manda Scott
Shropshire, 21 June 2014

ADDITIONAL READING

Amongst the enormous wealth of material, the following bear further reading:

Castor, Helen: *Joan of Arc*

DeVries, Kelly: *Joan of Arc: A Military Leader*

Hobbins, Daniel (trans.): *The Trial of Joan of Arc*

Pernoud, Régine and Clin, Marie-Véronique: *Joan of Arc: Her Story*

Sackville-West, Vita: *Saint Joan of Arc*

Sullivan, Karen: *The Interrogation of Joan of Arc*

Trask, Willard (trans.): *Joan of Arc: In Her Own Words*

Wheeler, Bonnie and Wood, Charles (ed.): *Fresh Verdicts on Joan of Arc*

ACKNOWLEDGEMENTS

As ever, the list of those who have given of their time, expertise, good humour and assistance is virtually endless, but there are some names without whom, genuinely, this novel would not exist.

First, heartfelt thanks to Serguei Gorbenko. I have put a link to his website in the Afterword, but want here to acknowledge my debt to him, and my thanks. Serguei and I corresponded by email during the early stages of writing and I was able to confirm the initial reports of his discovery. We continued to exchange pleasantries until the outbreak of unrest in the Crimea at the start of 2014. Despite many emails sent into the heart of the Ukraine, I have not heard from him since. It is my hope that he remains alive and that he approves of the layers I have added to his initial concept.

Thereafter, wholehearted thanks to:

—my agent Mark Lucas, who has been instigator, encourager and midwife of this project, and without whom there would be no book. We share a love of all things Gallic, which helps. Mark: I am endlessly grateful.

—Patsy Irwin, publicity director at Transworld Publishers, who went far and away above and beyond the call of duty to bring this book to fruition: Patsy, without you it would not have happened. I am forever grateful.

—Vivien Thompson, production editor at Transworld, who rescued me on the most important day of my life, who merged versions, corralled proofs and made life so very much easier – heartfelt thanks.

—Stephanie Cabot, my US agent, whose fresh insight and incisive reading helped to polish the text. Stephanie, thank you for believing in us.

—Ellen Goodson, also of the Gernert Company, who honed the text, and caught the loose threads. Ellen, your perspicacity, clarity and good humour have transformed the editing process.

—John Barratt, historian, author, mine of historical information and outstanding organizer. John, you have made life so much simpler in so many ways. I am in awe of the breadth and depth of your knowledge, particularly when it comes to medieval Europe. My pavants shall ever be pavisses in your honour.

—Rob Low, a highly accomplished historical author and fellow member of the HWA committee, who read an early draft. You are one of the treasures of my writing life.

—Mike Jecks, accomplished fellow author and medievalist, who read the later drafts for accuracy, and who offered tea and sympathy in Devon, for which I am ever grateful.

—Tony Gallucci, medievalist and friend, for words of encouragement and checking of drafts.

—Amy Weatherup, friend, core-reader and spotter-of-anachronisms, for reading one of the later drafts, thank you hugely.

—Sally Ford, Francophile and linguist, for her outstanding help in ensuring that the contemporary story was accurate, and for reading the final draft so swiftly and with such integrity.

—Mary Hannigan, who posted textbooks from

Cambridge when I needed them. As ever, any errors in interpretation or fact are mine alone: nobody else bears any responsibility.

There's a slight gap here where I thank those academics who wish to remain anonymous because putting their name to a project which flies in the face of 'accepted history' is academic suicide, even when that accepted history belongs in the realms of piskies and flying pigs. Thank you for being so gracious.

Finally, and for ever, thanks to my editor. Bill Scott-Kerr is one of those fonts of serenity in an increasingly manic world. Thank you for wisdom, patience and insight. Thanks also to the stellar team at Transworld, particularly to Gavin and Suzanne for getting the website going, to Lyndsey, Polly and Lucy for making the world of publicity turn smoothly, and to Alun Owen who weaves connections amongst the bookshops in the West Midlands. Especial thanks to Nancy Webber, copy editor without equal. And a thousand thanks to Phil, for maps, design and clarity.

Thanks to the dreamers, especially those who came to the Valley at midsummer, and to Shivam for letting us use his tipis. The soul recharging of that time and place were exceptional.

Thanks to Sue and to Tilly for keeping me sane and sorted.

And last, but never least, heartfelt thanks and love to Faith, for equanimity, love and balance, and for taking over dog walks when I needed more time in the days – and for letting me have another cat.

ROME

THE EMPEROR'S SPY

Manda Scott

'Stop this fire, whatever it takes. I, your Emperor, order it'

THE EMPEROR Nero, Emperor of Rome and all her provinces, feared by his subjects for his temper and cruelty, is in possession of an ancient document predicting that Rome will burn.

THE SPY Sebastos Pantera, assassin and spy for the Roman Legions, is ordered to stop the impending cataclysm. He knows that if he does not, his life – and those of thousands of others – is in terrible danger.

THE CHARIOT BOY Math, a young charioteer, is a pawn drawn into the deadly game between the Emperor and the Spy, where death stalks the drivers – on the track and off it.

From the author of the bestselling *Boudica* series, *The Emperor's Spy* begins a compelling new series of novels featuring **Sebastos Pantera**. Rich characterization and spine-tingling adventure combine in a vividly realized novel set amid the bloodshed and the chaos, the heroism and murderous betrayal of ancient Rome.

'As exciting as Ben Hur, *and far more accurate'*
Independent

'A gripping tale, with more to come'
Daily Mail

ROME

THE ART OF WAR

Manda Scott

Rome: AD69, the Year of the Four Emperors. Three Emperors have ruled in Rome this year and a fourth, Vespasian, has been named in the East.

As the legions march toward civil war, Sebastos Pantera, the spy whose name means leopard, returns to Rome intent on bribery, blackmail and persuasion: whatever it takes to bring the commanders and their men to Vespasian's side.

But in Rome, as he uses every skill he has ever learned of subterfuge, codes and camouflage, it becomes clear that one of those closest to him is a traitor, who will let Rome fall to destroy him.

Together the two spies spin a web of deceit with Rome as the prize and death the only escape.

'A memorable tale of treachery, espionage and violence . . . Ancient Rome is brought vividly and vibrantly to life'
BBC History Magazine

'Superior in almost every way . . . One of the most entertaining "Roman" novels I have read . . . Head and shoulders above the crowd'
Simon Scarrow

BOUDICA

DREAMING THE EAGLE
DREAMING THE BULL
DREAMING THE HOUND
DREAMING THE SERPENT SPEAR

——— Manda Scott ———

Boudica: at twelve, she killed her first warrior. At twenty-one, she defended her land against an invasion by the most powerful empire the world had ever seen. At forty, she led her people in a bloody revolt – and became a legend.

Set in a Britain before the Romans came, Manda Scott's thrillingly imagined novels bring the brutal world of druids, dreamers, warriors and their gods to vivid life in a story of passion, courage and spectacular heroism pitched against overwhelming odds . . .

'Alive with the love, deceit, wisdom and the heroics of humanity'
Jean M. Auel

'Manda Scott has created a fictional universe all her own, but close enough to our reality for it both to warm and break our hearts. Breathtakingly good, it reveals the best and worst in all of us'
Val McDermid

'Utterly convincing and compelling . . . A stunning feat of the imagination and an absolute must-read'
Steven Pressfield